"A daring, brilliant thriller, full of characters you both love and hate and more unexpected turns than a mountain road at night without your headlights. Tremendous fun!"

—Scott Turow, bestselling author of
*Presumed Innocent* and *The Last Trial*

"Absolutely dazzling! David Ellis is a master storyteller who keeps us riveted to the pages. A whip-smart and diabolically plotted thriller, with crackling dialogue, nonstop pacing, and tour de force structure. A profoundly insightful study of greed, obsession, revenge, and justice. Riveting, compelling, and completely entertaining!"

—Hank Phillippi Ryan, bestselling author of
*Her Perfect Life*

# LOOK CLOSER

## David Ellis

G. P. PUTNAM'S SONS
*New York*

**PUTNAM**
— EST. 1838 —

G. P. PUTNAM'S SONS
*Publishers Since 1838*
An imprint of Penguin Random House LLC
penguinrandomhouse.com

The Library of Congress has catalogued the
G. P. Putnam's Sons hardcover edition as follows:

Names: Ellis, David, 1967– author.
Title: Look closer / David Ellis.
Description: New York: G. P. Putnam's Sons, [2022]
Identifiers: LCCN 2022011441 (print) | LCCN 2022011442 (ebook) |
ISBN 9780399170928 (hardcover) | ISBN 9780698161993 (ebook)
Subjects: LCGFT: Novels.
Classification: LCC PS3555.L59485 L66 2022 (print) |
LCC PS3555.L59485 (ebook) | DDC 813/.54—dc23
LC record available at https://lccn.loc.gov/2022011441
LC ebook record available at https://lccn.loc.gov/2022011442

First G. P. Putnam's Sons hardcover edition / July 2022
First G. P. Putnam's Sons trade paperback edition / June 2023
G. P. Putnam's Sons trade paperback ISBN: 9780425280867

Printed in the United States of America
4th printing

This is a work of fiction. Names, characters, places, and incidents either are the product
of the author's imagination or are used fictitiously, and any resemblance to actual
persons, living or dead, businesses, companies, events, or locales is entirely coinci-
dental.

*To my beautiful Susan*

# LOOK CLOSER

LOOK CLOSER

# 1

## Simon

I check my green burner phone for the time. It's now 8:51 p.m., nine minutes to nine. Nearly two hours since trick-or-treating ended and Grace Village plunged into darkness, the residents of this bedroom community hunkering down for the night.

Police cruisers will be out tonight, but there are none currently on Lathrow Avenue, at least as best I can tell standing in Lauren's foyer, looking through the peephole of her front door with emotion clouding my eyes. Not tears. I am not crying. I thought it possible that tears would come, even likely, but they have not. Now I'm sure they won't. Tears are for sadness, regret, remorse.

I am not calm exactly, certainly not what I would describe as normal; far from that. A dull ringing fills my ears and the *THUMP-THUMP, THUMP-THUMP* of my pulse echoes through me, a bellowing bass drum no symphony orchestra could match. Still, my hand does not shake as I reach for the inside door handle, an ornate gold latch you'd expect to open a vault of princely treasures. But no jewels or riches beyond this door, only danger. I am not supposed to be here, inside Lauren's house.

I turn one last time and look behind me in the foyer.

Lauren's body dangles from the second-floor landing, her toes no more than a few feet above the marble foyer floor. She is motionless, coming to rest facing me, her head lolled unnaturally to the right, resting on the knotted rope wrapped around her neck, her head so askew it looks as if it might detach and fall to the marbled floor. She is wearing a skintight cat costume, complete with makeup, painted whiskers, and button nose; even the nails on her fingers and toes are painted black. Halloween Barbie, if there is such a thing, and I'm sure there is. Rising from the noose, the rope strains taut against the ornate wrought iron railing on the second story, overlooking the open foyer. Watching her, no matter how glamorous her looks, how sexy her outfit, conjures the image of a butcher's freezer, the slabs of beef hanging from large hooks in the ceiling.

Happy Halloween, Lauren.

I take a step forward, but my boot crunches on a shard of broken glass from the bowl of Halloween candy shattered in the foyer. Whatever the reason I had for stepping toward her—one last goodbye? Replacing the heel that fell off her left foot?—I think better of it and turn to the door.

I pull down the latch and open the front door, the cool October air rushing into the space inside the hood over my head, which covers my face completely and blocks my peripheral vision. I forgot to check through the peephole again before opening the door. That was sloppy. This is not a night to be sloppy.

I walk through the empty streets of the Village in my Grim Reaper costume, pillowcase clutched in my left hand, passing skeletons hanging from trees, tombstones planted in front yards, orange lights illuminating shrubbery, ghosts frowning at me through windows.

My head buried inside this elongated hood, my height at five feet eleven, I could pass as a teenager trick-or-treating late (which wouldn't fly, given the Village's strict curfew) or an adult leaving some kind of party (for which I can name no host or address). I should walk with a natural stride, like I haven't a care in the world, an anonymous man covered head to toe in a black robe and hood on the one night of the year that it wouldn't seem odd. Still, I should have an answer at the ready should a police cruiser stop by.

As a wise woman once told me: The best lies are the ones closest to the truth.

*Walking home,* I will say if asked. *Too much to drink.*

That will have to do. The drinking part isn't true but hard to disprove. The walking home part is close enough. I'm walking in that direction, at least.

So on I walk through the square grid of the small village, reaching the park on the southeast end of town, crossing the diagonal path, passing some homeless people, swing sets, and jungle gyms, a pack of teenagers huddled on the hill with beers they try to conceal. I put one foot in front of the other and try to act normal and think about normal things. It's been a long time since I've thought about normal things.

I haven't felt normal since May 13.

I play the game of what-if. What if I hadn't gone to get my haircut on May 13? What if the dean hadn't called me to his office, delaying me? Ten, fifteen seconds' difference, and I might never have seen her. I wouldn't have known she'd come back.

But that doesn't calm me, so I think about what happens next. My journal. My journal with the green cover, to match my green phone. I got rid of that journal, right? Burned it to a crisp, to a heap of ash in my fireplace. Right? I didn't just dream that, did I? If the police ever got their hands on that green journal, it would be game, set, match.

That's not helping stress levels, either, so I try the language games I used as a kid to calm my nerves, to slow me down when I was freaking out, like how the word "fridge" has a "d" but "refrigerator" does not; how "tomb" is pronounced *toom* and "womb" is pronounced *woom*, but "bomb" is not pronounced *boom*; how "rough" and "dough" and "cough" and "through" should rhyme but don't. I don't know why oddness and contradiction calm me, but they always have, maybe because of their familiarity, because I see so much of those traits in myself.

Then I stop. My legs suddenly, inexplicably no sturdier than rubber, exhaustion sweeping over me, my pulse ratcheting up again, vibrating in my throat. Only steps away from Harlem Avenue, only moments from crossing the town border, only a matter of feet from leaving Grace Village and crossing into its sister town Grace Park, where I live, a far bigger town.

I manage to duck behind the equipment shed owned by the park district. I plop down on the ground, pull off my hood, remove the head mask I'm wearing, and rest my sweaty head against the brick wall. I fish around in the pillowcase for the knife. It's a large knife that we used to slice the Thanksgiving turkey when I was a kid. I thought I might need it tonight.

I pull out my green phone and start typing:

> I'm sorry, Lauren. I'm sorry for what I did and I'm sorry you didn't love me. But I'm not sorry for loving you like nobody else

could. I'm coming to you now. I hope you'll accept me and let
me love you in a way you wouldn't in this world.

When I'm done, I put the phone in my lap, next to the knife. I hold out
my hand, palm down, and stare at it. It remains utterly still and steady.
I take a breath and nod my head. I can do this. I'm ready.

# BEFORE HALLOWEEN

## May 13

# 2

## Simon

"You know what your problem is?" Anshu says to me, though I didn't ask him. If we're going through a list of my problems, we'll be here all afternoon. "You don't look the part," he says without waiting for a prompt from me.

"I don't . . ." I give myself a once-over, my button-down oxford and blue jeans. "What's wrong with how I look?"

"You dress like one of the students. You're supposed to be the professor."

"What do you want, a tweed coat with patches? Should I carry a pipe, too?"

I'm sitting in my office on the third floor of the law school with Professor Anshuman Bindra, who looks the part naturally, with his owlish face and trim beard, hair the consistency of a scrub brush, which manages to not move but look unkempt regardless. Anshu leans back in his chair. "Simon, my friend, you just got quoted in a U.S. Supreme Court opinion. It's like the Supremes collectively leaned over from Washington to Chicago and whispered to the committee, 'Make this guy a full professor.' You should be walking tall today. You should be the new King of the Fourth Amendment. But instead, you show up looking like you're going to a frat party."

"It shouldn't matter how I dress. It's what I say, what I teach, what I write, that—"

But he's already making a mouth out of his hand, *yada yada yada*.

"Now Reid, he looks the part. He wears a sport coat and dress pants every day."

Reid Southern? That guy is to academia what Pauly Shore is to dramatic acting. He has parents with pull, and that's it.

"He wears a sport coat because his stomach hangs over his belt," I say. "And he probably can't fit into jeans."

Anshu drops his head, pinches the bridge of his nose. "Yeah, and you run marathons, and half your students probably want to bone you, but Reid looks like a law professor. He *acts* like one. The guy listens to Mozart in his office. You listen to REM and Panic! at the Disco and N.W.A."

"Okay, first of all," I say, leaning forward, "I do not and would not listen to Panic! at the Disco. And now it matters what music I listen to?"

"It's not one thing. It's the whole package. The ... grungy look, the music, the whole attitude. You don't think appearances matter? I know they shouldn't, but you know—"

"No, they do, I know." But I'm not going to change for them. Why should I? There's no dress code here. I'm twice the teacher Reid Southern is. His students hate him. I've read the reviews. And his scholarship is pedantic at best. He's writing about a different way to understand mutual consent in contract law. I'm writing about the government violating the constitutional rights of its citizens on a daily basis.

"You're too self-deprecating, while we're at it," says Anshu.

Sure, why not, let's keep going.

"You'd rather I was pompous and self-congratulatory? Anshu, jeez, you're undoing everything my mother taught me."

He flips his hand at me. "What did you just say to Loomis in the hallway? The vice-chair of the damn tenure committee compliments you on your article getting cited by the Supreme Court and what did you say?"

"I don't know, what did I say?"

"You said, 'Must have been a slow day at the Court.'"

Oh, yeah, that's right, I did.

"I mean, how about thank you?" he says. "The highest court in the land just cited one of your articles. Can't you bask in the glow just a little? But no, you can't take the compliment. You have to tear yourself down. And Reid doesn't have a blog," he adds.

I open my hands. "What's wrong with my blog?"

"You make jokes," he says. "You crack wise."

"And I talk about judicial decisions and whether they're right or wrong."

"You wrote a limerick about the chief justice of the United States."

"Yeah, but it was funny."

"I know, but you're so . . . so casual and irreverent."

"You mean I'm not stuffy? I don't use footnotes or Latin words? You know how I feel about footnotes and—"

"Yes, I know how you feel about footnotes." He reaches out with his hands, as if beseeching me. "But law professors use footnotes! Law professors use Latin!"

I'm not doing it. I'm not changing how I dress and I'm not sucking up to the faculty at poker games and cocktail parties and I'm not using Latin words and I sure as shit am not using footnotes.

Okay, it's not quite Roosevelt charging up San Juan Hill, but I'm taking a stand.

"Get the spot first," he says. "Once you're a tenured full professor, challenge every convention of academia. But this whole laid-back thing . . ."

I'm not laid-back. I'm anything but laid-back. I'm stubborn. There's a difference.

"Here's some Latin for you," I say. "*Ego facturus est via mea.*"

Anshu sighs. "Now I suppose you're going to tell me what that means."

"It means, I'm going to do it my way."

"Of course you are." He flips a hand. "Of course you are."

"Now if you'll excuse me, Professor, I need a haircut."

"That was on my list, too. Your hair's too long. You look—"

"Like one of the students, I know."

And then my phone rings.


Not five minutes later, I'm entering the office of one of the associate deans, Martin Comstock, who also happens to be the chair of the tenure committee. Silver-haired and dapper, going all-in on the stereotype with the bright red bow tie.

Actually, he wears bow ties so people will ask him about them, and he can *reluctantly* reveal that he clerked for U.S. Supreme Court Justice John Paul Stevens, who wore bow ties, and then served as an aide to U.S. Senator

Paul Simon, who also wore them. *Oh, this? Well, I suppose it's kind of an homage, if you must know . . .*

Our dean is retiring next year, and everyone says Comstock will take the reins. Not everybody's happy about that. I might be one of those people. He's a politician, not an academic. A blue blood, not a scholar. He's everything I hate about academia.

Other than that, I'm sure he's a great guy.

"Ah, Simon, good," he says when I knock on his opened door.

"Hi, Dean." He likes being called by his title. He pretends he doesn't, but he does.

He manages a quick, disapproving appraisal of my outfit. For the record, my button-down shirt is tucked in, and my jeans are clean and not torn. I look just fine.

"Thanks for stopping by," he says. "I'll get to the point."

His office, all leather and walnut, is a monument to his greatness, with all his diplomas and awards, photographs with presidents and high-court judges. He sits in a high-back leather chair behind a magnificent desk.

"Simon, you applied for full professor," he says, his hands forming a temple in his lap.

"I did, yes."

"Yes, good stuff, good for you," he says. "You've done fine work, I'll say it to anyone."

It's time for the *but . . .*

"Now, I don't want you to take this the wrong way, Simon."

In the history of mankind, nobody has followed *I don't want you to take this the wrong way* with something that could be taken any other way.

"I wonder," he begins. "Well, here. You may be aware that Reid Southern has applied for the position as well."

I sure am! I'm also aware that his daddy has given more than five million dollars to the school over the last decade, which just happened to coincide with when his son started working here.

"Yeah," I say.

"And Reid, I'm sure you're aware, has been here a year longer than you."

"I'm aware of that. And I'm aware that you're only granting one position."

"Just so, just so," he says, so eager and condescending that it feels like he might toss a dog treat into my mouth. "And, well, this is delicate, but you can probably imagine that Reid has a fair level of support. You know how these things go—it's his turn."

Plenty of associate professors have been denied a full professorship. We don't tell people it's *their turn*. Not unless their father is a walking ATM.

"I would just hate . . ." His fingers work the air, like he's trying to capture just the way to put it, like he doesn't have this speech prepared. "I think it might be preferable for you if you waited until the next opening. Then you'd be applying without the mark of having applied once and been denied."

"You think I'll be denied." I don't say it as a question. But it *is* a question, I think. There are some old-school, clubby types who probably don't take to me, but there are plenty of good, nonpolitical people here, like Anshu, who think that quality teaching and standout scholarship are what matter, not how you dress or who you know.

"Well, obviously, it's nothing that committal. But as I say, Reid does enjoy substantial support. Not that anyone remotely questions your scholarship, Simon. You've done fine work."

Right, you'll say it to anyone.

"You've given me a lot to think about, Dean," I say.

I leave the office so he can pick up the phone and call Reid's dad and tell him that he had *the talk* with me, and things are going swimmingly.


Now I'm late for the haircut. I usually walk, as it's only a few blocks away. Instead I head out the Superior Street side and into the outdoor faculty parking lot. I usually get here earlier than others and park in one of the front rows.

I find the silver Mercedes coupe and pull out my key. After a glance around, I run the key along the side of the car, a hideous scrape across the driver's-side panel.

Sorry about that, Dean.

Now for that haircut.


And thus I go, a dressed-down associate professor off to have the old Russian guy named Ygor (seriously) cut my hair, lest the faculty at my law school think I'm less than tenure quality because my hair is too long. Not that it matters—apparently, I'm withdrawing my application.

The afternoon is steamy hot as I work through the crowd on Michigan Avenue, tourists and rich people and street performers and the homeless, the Magnificent Mile. Though they should really rethink that name these days. But I have more important issues on my mind.

Why do privileged old white men in black robes get to decide what it's like to be an African American kid stopped on the street by a cop? Why do lawyers think that saying "*inter alia*" instead of "among other things" makes them sound smarter? Why does the word "queue" have not only four consecutive silent letters, which is bad enough, but also the same ones repeated? What, they weren't silent enough the first time through?

Deep thoughts, all of them, as I cross Chicago Avenue, just a block south of the barbershop.

And then I stop moving, my feet planting in the crosswalk, someone bumping into me from behind and forcing me to stumble forward a step.

Because I feel it. I feel *you*, I swear I do, before I actually see you, walking out of the Bloomingdale's building. The shape of your head, maybe. The curve of your chin. The way you purse your lips in concentration. Something that defines you as you, even nineteen years later. Something that screams *Lauren*—

Lauren.

Lauren.

Hey, Simon, how are you?

Great, Lauren. How are you?

—before you fully turn in my direction, wearing those oversize sunglasses like Audrey Hepburn.

It's you. Your hair is longer and a shade blonder, but it's you.

You step into the crosswalk, a bounce in your stride, confident like someone accustomed to moving through a crowd without making eye contact with the numerous pairs of eyes on her. Your lips are moving. I don't see a phone, but when the wind carries your hair, I see an AirPod tucked in your ear.

My usual move when I want to avoid someone—the phone. Plant it against your ear, duck your head like reception is bad and you're trying to hear. I've avoided hundreds of conversations that way in the hallways of my law school.

But I don't reach for my phone.

I should move, not just stand there in the middle of the crosswalk like a small inlet amid a sea of pedestrians passing me on both sides. I should walk toward you as confidently as you walk toward me, but I can't. I'm on system shutdown. My feet not moving. My pulse pounding between my ears. My insides stripped raw.

I think I catch a whiff of your perfume as you pass me. You changed it.

You don't notice me. Probably the swarm of people conceals me, or you're concentrating on your phone conversation. Or maybe you wouldn't have noticed me even if you saw me. I'm a distant memory to you. Am I?

I turn and follow you.

"Um, no thanks. It's called having some dignity?" you say as a question that isn't really a question. Then you laugh.

The laugh hasn't changed. It's you.

You're wearing a pink dress that complements your figure. You're carrying two shopping bags. You have money. That's no surprise. You have a big rock on your finger. That's no surprise, either. You never had trouble drawing the attention of wealthy men.

Tap you on the shoulder, Hey, stranger, remember me?

Grab you by the arm, HEY, LAUREN, REMEMBER ME?

I'm too close, so I drop back.

People look at you. Of course they do. Men and women. You're a work of art. You must know that. You don't break stride.

My legs like foam. Bile in the back of my throat.

You cross Chicago Avenue and turn into a building.

If I walk into that building, into what I assume is the lobby of a condo building, I can't be anonymous. People don't casually walk into lobbies of private residential buildings.

But I don't care. I push through the revolving door about five seconds after you do, just enough time so you won't see me. I walk into comforting air-conditioning, a sleek, polished, ornate lobby of a fancy downtown condo building.

"Mrs. Betancourt!" says the man standing behind the desk. "Are you here for the weekend?"

"Just dropping some things off, Charlie," you say. "How are the kids?"

*Betancourt. Betancourt.*

You got married, Lauren.

I head back outside into the searing heat, people crossing my path from both sides, jostling me, my foot dropping down off the sidewalk into the street, a car horn blaring at me—

I step back, narrowly missing the taxi heading southbound on Michigan Avenue.

I put my hand on a parked car for balance, the engine hot.

"Dude, what the fuck?" Another cabbie, idling at the curb, sticks his head out the window.

I raise my hand in apology, stumble back to the sidewalk, not sure which way to turn.

I shake my head and whisper, "Betancourt. Betancourt."

Betancourt Betancourt Betancourt Betancourt.

Dozens of people with that last name in the greater Chicago area. But only one named Lauren. And it's you. Your Facebook profile, in a tight white dress with an oversize fancy hat, like from the Kentucky Derby, raising a glass of sparkly and pursing your lips. Were you really that happy when you took that picture, Lauren? Or were you thinking all along, This would be an awesome profile pic for Facebook? Was it fake like it's fake when people tell stories about something they did and make it sound a lot more fun than it really was? Do you worry more about how others see you than how you see yourself?

Thousands of friends, thousands of "likes" on your hundreds of photos, those tiny windows into your life over the last decade. The top of the Eiffel Tower, a safari in South Africa, drinks in Times Square, the polar ice plunge in Lake Michigan, a triathlon, some race that you did in mud, always surrounded by friends and handsome men, sun-drenched and happy, glamorous and sexy, fun and energetic and free-spirited.

You're married to someone named Conrad Betancourt. But no kids.

And you don't live in Chicago *per se*. You live in Grace Village, just west of the city. In the next town over from where I live, Grace Park.

You've come home, Lauren.


Deep breath. Calm, Simon. Use language games. Something. Deep breath.

Why don't "monkey" and "donkey" rhyme?

Deep breath.

Why is it an unwritten but ironclad rule that we put opinion adjectives before size adjectives? Why must it always be "dirty little secret" and never "little dirty secret"?

And why size adjectives always before age? Why not "old little lady"?

Why can't I say "an old little lovely lady"?

Deep breath.


It's all coming back, washing over me again. It's growing like a tumor inside me, poison flowing through my veins. I should stop right now. I should forget I saw you. I've put you behind me. You need to stay right where you've been, in my rearview mirror. I'm better now. I know I'm better. Vicky says I'm better. I can't go back there. Everything's fine.

Yes, that's what I'll do. I'll put you behind me. I've put you behind me, Lauren. You are officially yesterday's news, or nineteen years ago's news.

Okay, that's that. I'm going to forget I ever saw you today.

# SEVEN WEEKS LATER

## July

# 3

**Monday, July 4, 2022**

*"Oh . . . my . . . God," I whispered. Even though the whole reason I came to the club today, my first time in several years, was that I thought you might be at the Fourth of July festivities. Even though I'd been thinking about you since that day in May—who am I kidding with "that day in May," it was Friday, May 13, at 2:04 p.m.—when I saw you on Michigan Avenue. Even though I'd tried to conjure up ways to "accidentally" run into you. Even though I'd literally rehearsed lines in a mirror like a nervous schoolboy.*

*Still, seeing you, Lauren, standing on the club's outdoor patio, a view of the golf course behind you. It felt like something fresh and clean and right, as if I were seeing you for the first time.*

*I opened my hands, palms up, like I'd conjured something from magic. Because magic was a good word to describe it. "It's . . . you."*

*You were wearing a white sundress. Your skin was tanned. You were once again wearing those Audrey Hepburn sunglasses. Your hair was pulled up in back. You'd been laughing with friends, but I must have caught your peripheral vision and you turned, for some reason. I'd like to think it was the gods smiling down on us, some mystical inspiration that made you turn your head.*

*"It's <u>you</u>," you replied, removing your shades, squinting into the sun. You seemed less surprised than me. "Simon," you said, like you enjoyed saying my name.*

*You broke away from your group, which did not appear to include your husband, Conrad. I appreciated that you thought our first meeting (our first one in nineteen years, at least) deserved some privacy, even if we were surrounded by a couple hundred people at the club's Fourth of July BBQ and fireworks.*

*"What are . . . what are you . . ." I didn't finish the sentence.*

*"Oh, I—I moved back into town," you said. "Well, the Village."*

*"You live in Grace Village?" I asked.*

*"Yeah, I'm married. I've been here a few years. You're still in Grace Park?"*

*"Same house," I said.*

*You nodded. "I thought you might be. I thought I might run into you here at the club. I remember your family were members here. I . . . thought about calling, just to maybe break the ice—"*

*I waved a hand. "Oh, no worries. That was . . . a long time ago."*

*You seemed relieved, a real weight lifted, at those words. You smiled at me as if grateful.*

*I was supposed to be so nervous. I'd built this hypothetical reunion up in my head so much that I figured I'd be sweaty and jumpy, stuttering and stammering. But my nerves instantly fluttered away when I saw you, whatever lines I'd rehearsed vanished. It was just you and me again.*

*"You're married?" you asked me, seeing the ring on my finger.*

*"Almost ten years," I said. "Her name is Vicky."*

*"Is Vicky here?"*

*No. Vicky wasn't at the club. Vicky wouldn't be caught dead at a country club.*

*"She couldn't make it," I said. I think my face showed something, because yours did in reaction, like you realized you'd touched a nerve.*

*You weren't as beautiful as you were nineteen years ago, Lauren; you were more beautiful. You looked experienced, tested, wiser. You weren't the hot, blond twenty-year-old paralegal burning a path through my father's law firm but someone who had ripened into a poised, confident woman, who had lived and learned, who knew where she was and who she was.*

*It bothered me that I didn't tell you that I'd seen you back in May on Michigan Avenue, that the only reason I'd come to this stupid event at the Grace Country Club was that I'd looked up the membership roster and saw that you and your husband, Conrad, were members, and I thought I might* run into you at this Fourth of July party. That my "surprise" at seeing you was not completely sincere. It bothered me that something that could be so real between us was starting under false pretenses.

So I told myself, *Okay, one white lie, but that's it. I will never lie to you again, Lauren.*

On my way home from the club, I stopped and bought this spiral notebook, just some ordinary notebook with a green cover. (Green for fresh and new, I suppose.) It's been years, Lauren, years since I kept a journal. I'd given up writing my daily thoughts. Maybe because I no longer had anything interesting to say. I have a blog and law review articles and class to talk about the law, and the law has basically become my blood and oxygen and nourishment. What else is there to talk about? ~~A wife who doesn't love me~~ A marriage that's grown loveless and stale? My personal best time in some 10K?

So it's back to a journal—hello, Green Journal—because now I have something to write about, Lauren. Or some<u>one</u>, that is.

Someone who agreed to meet me next week for coffee!

No harm in having some coffee, is there?

# 4
## Simon

This is risky. Just parking here, up the street from Lauren's house, a bit before eight in the morning, could bring trouble. These are the homes we used to call the "Lathrow mansions," running through the middle of Grace Village like a tourist attraction. Some of the pearl-clutching neighbors on Lathrow Avenue tend to call the police whenever they see someone who is "not from the neighborhood." Usually that code stands for something very different than me, a middle-aged white guy in a respectable-looking SUV, but still . . . If I idle here for too long, I'm bound to draw someone's attention, followed not long thereafter by a police cruiser swinging by for a quick inquiry. *How's your day going, sir? Can I ask what you're doing? See some ID?*

And it's not as if I'd have a great answer. Making the most of my time in early July, when classes are out and my schedule is flexible, to spy on an old girlfriend and her husband, trying to learn more about her and him and them, trying to glean whatever morsels of information I can? That doesn't sound so good.

That's all I need—the cops show up and make a scene. Maybe even give me a ticket for some residential parking violation. Meanwhile, Lauren walks out of her house or looks out her window and sees ol' Simon Dobias parked nearby for no apparent reason. Creepy!

I'm from around here, but not really from around *here.* I'm from Grace Park, mostly middle-class and proudly progressive—just ask us. But when Mortimer Grace founded the Park in the 1800s, he broke off a three-square-mile chunk and incorporated it separately as Grace Village. Mortimer's views on class and race and religion would not be considered enlightened by today's standards. He wanted the Village to be a gated community of wealthy, white, Anglo-Saxon Protestants like him.

The gates are gone, and the charter was amended to remove insensitive comments back in the 1940s, but some would argue that the Village hasn't really changed all that much. More than anything, the wealth. Most of the kids don't attend Grace Consolidated High School like I did; they go to private prep schools. And when they grow up, most return to the Village to raise families of their own. There are sixth-generation Villagers there.

Lauren's not from here, either. She's from Old Irving Park on the north side of Chicago and still lived there when I first met her (Lauren as a paralegal at my dad's law firm, me as a college kid doing gofer work). But here she is now, living in a palatial home, married to Conrad Betancourt, a twice-divorced guy fifteen years her senior, who runs one of the most successful hedge funds in the world.

I've probably exhausted my luck with my recon missions this week. And I've compiled enough information for now. I rip out the page from my green journal and review.

A town car picks up Conrad Betancourt every morning at six sharp and heads for the expressway downtown. He works out at the East Bank Club and then drives to his offices in the Civic Opera Building on Wacker Drive. He doesn't return home at any predictable time—at least he hasn't this week.

Lauren, from what I can tell, has no job. Every day this week, she has played tennis in the morning at the Grace Country Club. A round of golf afterward. Twice this week, she had dinner downtown, neither time with Conrad, always with a group of women. Each of those times, she spent the night in her condo on Michigan Avenue, not returning to the Village.

Every morning that she has awakened here in Grace Village, she has gone for a run. She runs through the town, usually about three or four miles in total, back by 8:30 a.m.

Run, tennis, golf. No wonder you're so fit, Lauren.

Two teenage girls come walking by on the sidewalk, gabbing and looking at their phones while the Pomeranian on a leash sniffs a fire hydrant.

One of the teens glances at me and does a double take. I have my earbuds tucked into my ears, so I start talking, as if in a phone conversation, which for some reason makes me seem less weird sitting in a parked car.

God, what am I doing? I should stop this. Forget the whole thing. Forget I ever saw you, Lauren. Move on, like I told myself I'd done. But it's an argument I keep losing.

I don't think I can let go again.

# 5

## Vicky

The administrator in the emergency department sees my credentials, hanging from a lanyard around my neck, and nods at me. We've never met. Some of them have gotten to know me. "Social services?"

"Right. I'm Vicky from Safe Haven. I'm here for a Brandi Stratton."

Near eight o'clock, the emergency department is in a lull. A woman sits with her arm around a boy sniffling while he plays a game on a tablet. A man is holding his hand, wrapped in a towel, with a woman sitting next to him.

"Curtain six," says the administrator, "but they're still stitching her up. Sit tight."

"Sure."

My phone rings, a FaceTime call from the M&Ms—Mariah and Macy, my sister's girls. I step through the automated doors and narrowly avoid a gurney on its way in, a woman grimacing but stoically silent as paramedics wheel her by.

I throw in my AirPods and answer the call. Both girls are on—Macy, age ten, and Mariah, age thirteen-going-on-nineteen. They both take after their mother, my sister, Monica, beautiful just like she was, those almond-shaped eyes and the lustrous hair, traits that somehow avoided me. I used to joke that Monica and I must have had different fathers, which in hindsight might not have been a joke.

"Hi, monkeys!" I try to be cheerful. I don't do cheerful well.

"Hey, Vicky," they say in unison, the faces huddled together to see me.

"Calling you back," says Mariah. "We were at the pool when you called. Dad said we had to finish piano before we could call."

Makes sense because we sometimes spend a long time together on the phone. That won't happen now, with the call I must make on Brandi Stratton, curtain six.

I called the girls earlier today just to check on them. I wasn't sure if they realized what today was, the anniversary of their mother's death. Everyone remembers birthdays. People don't focus as much on days of death. I do. I will sometimes forget my sister's birthday. I will never forget the day she died.

But it seems to have escaped my nieces' notice. To them, today was just another July day at the pool with their nanny and their friends. So I'm sure as hell not going to remind them. They seem to be doing better now. Macy, the younger one, not as well as her older sister, but they both seem to be living pretty normal and happy lives. At least that's how it seems, with most of my contact recently by FaceTime. And even in person, you can only penetrate the adolescent psyche so far.

"I'm working," I say, "so I'll probably have to call you tomorrow. Macy, you should be in bed anyway, shouldn't you?"

"Um, it's summer?"

I walk back into the emergency area. The administrator nods to me. "Gotta run, princesses. Talk tomorrow? I love you, monkeys!"

"Curtain six," the administrator reminds me. "You know the way?"

I definitely know the way.

The administrator pops the doors, and I wind my way through to curtain six, with the familiar cocktail of smells—disinfectant, body odor, alcohol. A man moaning in one curtain, another shouting out, belligerent and drunk.

A police officer, a young woman, stands outside the curtain. "Social services?"

"Right. Safe Haven. Officer Gilford?"

"That's me." The officer nods toward a quieter spot, a nook around the bend of the corner, and I follow. "Her husband did a pretty good number on her. Beat her with a frying pan. Apparently, he wasn't impressed with the dinner she made. He didn't even wait for the pan to cool down. Then he went old-school and just used his fists."

I break eye contact. "But she's not pressing charges."

"Nope, she sure isn't." The officer tries to remain clinical, but there's only so much disgust and disappointment you can hide, no matter how much you see this stuff.

"And there's a daughter?"

"Yeah, cute little girl named Ashley. Age four."

That's what my intake record says, too. "And the asshole's name is . . . Steven?"

"Steven Stratton, yep."

I push through the curtain. The mother, Brandi, age twenty-two, sits on the hospital bed, her little girl, Ashley, asleep in her lap. The little one, thank God, appears untouched. Brandi's right eye is swollen shut. The left side of her face is heavily bandaged. Her right forearm is wrapped—a burn, according to the intake sheet, when she tried to deflect the frying pan.

Brandi looks me over, fixes on my credentials.

"Hi, Brandi," I say quietly, though I doubt the girl will awaken. "I'm Vicky, with Safe Haven. You want a place to stay tonight?"

"I can't . . ." She looks away, tucks a strand of hair behind her ear with her free hand.

She can't go back there. She can't go back tonight. She can't go back ever.

But almost all of them do. He'll apologize. He'll shower her with affection. He'll make her laugh and feel loved. She'll blame herself. And she'll consider her lack of other options. Rinse and repeat.

"It's your decision, Brandi. Our facility isn't much. You'd have to share a room, and our A/C sucks, so it's just fans. But it's quiet and it's safe. We have locks and a security guard. Maybe . . . maybe you and Ashley deserve a quiet, peaceful night's sleep?"

Maybe you'll come to our facility and let me convince you to leave that abusive creep you call a husband? We can do so much for them if they let us. They can stay with us for up to two weeks. We can get them counseling. We can find them a pro bono lawyer to get restraining orders and file divorce papers. We can find them alternative housing.

But they have to say yes. They have to learn to fight for themselves.

# 6

*Well, once again, I built up all these terrible outcomes in my mind, and it turned out so much better than I expected.*

*I wasn't even sure this would happen. Telling someone, Sure, let's meet for coffee, is easy enough to do and then cancel later. Promise to follow up, sure, but then it doesn't happen, or you don't return a text. And it's too amorphous to know whether it was an intentional blow-off or just one of those many things in life that ends up not happening, nobody's fault, "no worries," etc.*

*I'd basically convinced myself that when we saw each other at the club last week, you only agreed to meet for coffee to be nice, because what else were you going to say? Say yes now, blow me off later.*

*But there you were, Lauren, at Max's Café, just as promised, in a white tennis outfit, ponytail tucked through the back of your hat.*

*And you spent so much time asking me about me, which is good manners and very thoughtful, though for some reason not what I expected. And I didn't lie or sugarcoat anything when I talked, Lauren. I made a vow that I would never lie to you again, and I didn't.*

*I didn't lie to you about Vicky, either. It started as small talk, what she does for a living, how long we've been married, and pretty soon I was opening up about Vicky's childhood, growing up in poverty in West Virginia, running away from home at age seventeen, getting hooked on drugs and doing degrading things to support herself. How she was a mess when I met her, but so was I in different ways, both of us adrift and helping each other get back to the shoreline. How proud I am of her, how much we mean to each other, and before I knew it, Lauren, I was so comfortable that I was unloading, telling you everything, and I mean EVERYTHING. How I love Vicky and always will, but that we're different, we started in very different places and never really met in the middle. How we care about each other, we'd do anything for each other, but however our relationship had evolved, the spark is gone. We're more like roommates than spouses, more like pals than lovers.*

*I laughed a nervous chuckle when I was finished. "Gee, aren't you glad you asked?" I said. "Sorry about that brutal-honesty thing."*

*But you didn't smile, you didn't wave it off. No, what you said in response changed my life.*

*"Would it make you feel any better," you said, "if I told you my marriage was a train wreck?"*

*It did make me feel better, actually, and here's an example of why you will never read this journal, Lauren. I wouldn't want you to know how much I wanted to hear those words. I know how that sounds, but it's true. I was hoping you'd tell me you were unhappily married, too.*

*We spent the next hour going back and forth on our marriages. Sometimes it's easier with a stranger, not someone close to you. And maybe it's even easier to do it with someone who's been a recent stranger, but ~~whom you once loved more than any~~ with whom you once were intimate.*

*Or maybe it's none of that, and we just connect.*

*I would never have imagined having so much fun telling someone that my wife doesn't love me anymore. But those two hours outside at Max's Café felt like a life in itself, the birth of something, the promise of forever.*

*Corny, I know. But fuck it. Nobody else will read this journal. If I want to be corny, I will. Aren't we all corny in our thoughts? Aren't we corny with the ones we love? We're just too afraid to say it to others for fear of embarrassment.*

*And then the kiss. Had it been up to me to initiate it, I'm not sure it ever would have happened. It was our goodbye after coffee (which turned into a piece of carrot cake, too), two friends catching up and bidding adieu by your car.*

*You leaned up and kissed me softly. I wasn't ready for it. I almost didn't close my lips before you did it, which would have been awkward. Your lips lingered on mine just long enough to make sure there was no misunderstanding, this wasn't a friendly peck, it wasn't a platonic gesture, it wasn't a "this was so much fun!" goodbye.*

*No. It wasn't. My heart was hammering against my chest.*

*You looked up at me and said—and look, some of this dialogue I've had to paraphrase from memory, but this line I will never forget.*

*You said, "Would you like to see me again?"*

*You already knew the answer.*

# 7
## Vicky

I meet Rambo in the parking lot of the Home Depot off U.S. 30 in Merrill-ville, Indiana. I didn't want to talk over the phone or use email. This has to be in person. And I don't have much time, because I'm meeting Simon for lunch, so I need to head back to Chicago soon.

When he gets out of his beater Chevy, manila file in hand, he says, "Miss Vicky," as he's always called me, dating back to when he was a cop and one of my clients in the "entertainment" business, back before I moved to Chicago and met Simon and got straight. Rambo was okay. Never got rough with me. And he paid me, even though as a cop, he probably could have gotten freebies. I always figured one of the reasons I never got busted for solicitation was a cop like him having my back, though he never actually said that to me.

Roger Rampkin is his full name, but everyone calls him Rambo. Not just a play off his name but his army background before joining the force in Indianapolis, and he's got some size on him, too. The kind of cop who would scare the shit out of you in an interrogation room.

He retired from the force four years ago, now working as a private detective and doing some "security" work as well. He's done some work for me in the last few years and proven his worth.

"You clean up nice," he says.

Not sure I'd say the same for Rambo. The years have not been so kind to him. He has at least twenty more pounds in his midsection, his eyes heavily bagged, his beard more salt than pepper. Less badass-cop now, more mountain-man-crazy.

I take the file from him and hand him an envelope of cash. "Thank you very much, sir."

He tosses the envelope through the open window of his car onto the front seat and lights a cigarette, offers me one. I decline. I quit smoking when I quit everything else. Smoking was harder to kick than cocaine.

"Tell me why," he says.

"You've never asked why before," I say.

He blows out smoke. "I've always *known* why before. But I take your point."

Mind your own business, is the point. "That's a good boy, Rambo." I wag the folder, noting how light it is. "Not much in there."

"Not much in there," he agrees.

"Give me the highlights."

"The highlights are . . . there's not much in there. I did a full workup, all over again, like you asked. Every source I could tap. Vicky Lanier was born in Fairmont, West Virginia, went to Fairmont Senior High School, disappeared in 2003 at the age of seventeen and was never heard from again. Declared a missing person, but it was never known if she was a runaway or abducted or murdered. Never showed up on the grid. Never filed a tax return, never got arrested or fingerprinted, never enrolled for school, never opened a bank account, never took out a credit card, never got a W-2 or 1099, never opened a social media account, never did a single thing after age seventeen." He looks at me, squinting into the sun.

"Okay, so no irregularities? No red flags?"

"No irregularities. No red flags."

"Bottom line," I say. "I'm still safe using Vicky Lanier's identity."

"You are safe. Though I never understood why you picked an alias with the same first name as you."

How quickly he forgets. I slip my foot out of my shoe, bend my leg, and hold my foot up for him to see the tattoo above my right ankle, a small red heart with the name Vicky wrapped around the top half. A bad idea when I was sixteen years old. And pretty hard to explain if I used an alias with the name Jane or Molly or Gina.

"Oh, yeah, I guess I forgot about that. It's been a while since I've . . ."

Since you've seen me naked. Yeah, Rambo. I'd just as soon put that behind me. I *have* put it behind me, as much as you can ever put something like that behind you.

"So, Rambo, nobody could say I'm *not* Vicky Lanier, right?"

"Nobody could say that. As long as your story is that you ran away from home at age seventeen from Fairmont, West Virginia, and kicked around doing things that kept you off the grid. Paid in cash, that kind of thing."

The sad part is that my real bio isn't far off from that. And that's no accident; that's why I picked Vicky Lanier for my identity. Rambo himself was the one who said it to me—back in the day when he was a cop hearing bullshit from suspects, sorting out the truth from the crap—*the best lies are the ones closest to the truth*. I didn't live in West Virginia, and nobody abducted me, but I did leave home at age seventeen in 2003. So when I had Rambo create me an identity, I had him find a girl named Vicky who went missing in 2003 at age seventeen. I wasn't sure there would be a match with criteria that specific. Turns out, there were three girls who fit that description, which is disturbing in itself. Vicky Lanier from Fairmont, West Virginia, looked the most like me, so I chose her.

"Just make sure nobody does a fingerprint-based background check on you," Rambo says. "Then your prints would come up with your real name."

Right. But I can't do anything about that.

He cocks his head. "You realize you just paid me to do the same thing I did when I created this identity for you. I wouldn't have given you 'Vicky Lanier' in the first place if it wasn't clean."

"Always good to update," I say.

"Nah," he says out of the side of his mouth. "You're expecting someone to inquire. To look into your background. You're expecting trouble."

I stare at him with a perfunctory smile.

"Never mind," he says. "I don't want to know."

He's right on both counts. There's going to be trouble. And he doesn't want to know.

# 8

## Simon

I'm meeting Vicky for lunch at the Chinese restaurant by the law school. She often works days, so when she doesn't, we try to hook up for lunch, especially in the summer, when my schedule is so light.

She kisses me on the cheek. "Hey, handsome." She wets her finger, wipes the lipstick off my cheek, and takes her seat across from me in the booth. "How's your buddy, the dean?"

"Not this again," I say. "What am I supposed to do, defy him? Spit in the face of the most powerful guy at the school?"

"He spit in your face first."

Vicky, bless her heart, fights for me. She doesn't like the idea of Dean Comstock forcing me out of consideration for the full professor slot. She can get pretty worked up when people disrespect me. I find that incredibly sexy about her, for some reason.

"Simon, all you're doing is applying for full professor. You have just as much a right to do that as that schmuck with the rich daddy, Reid whatever. Who cares what Dean what's-his-name, Dean Cumstain, thinks?"

"Comstock." I laugh. "The guy who could single-handedly derail my career? I think I do care what he thinks."

She shakes her head, disappointed and angry. I meant what I wrote in my journal. I love this woman and I always will. But she doesn't love me back. She likes me and cares about me, but I don't do it for her in that way. And that, for me, takes the air out of the balloon. Maybe Freud would have something to say here about the id or superego, but I'm not one of those guys who likes challenges. I'm not attracted to someone who's not attracted to me.

When I first met Vicky, just six weeks after her sister's suicide, she was so angry. Sad, too, but mostly angry. I was able to help her. Maybe that's the only reason she was drawn to me. Maybe that's why *I* was drawn to *her*. Your heart doesn't come with explanatory notes.

"You already put your name in, right?" she asks. "All that's left is submitting all the materials. And you have until sometime in September?"

"Yes, yes, and yes," I say. "But I'm going to withdraw my name."

She reaches across the table and takes my hand. It still stirs something inside me when she touches me like that, no matter what else I may tell myself.

"You deserve this promotion, Simon. You're one of the best minds at that school. You love it. It's what you were meant to do. I hate seeing some pompous jerk stick a finger in your eye, and you're supposed to say, 'Thank you, sir, may I have another?'"

"I know that. I don't like it, either."

"Then do something about it. At least make him promise he'll back you the next time."

"It doesn't . . . work that way."

"Why doesn't it work that way?" She falls back against the booth cushion. "Sure it works that way. You said this guy's more a politician than anything else. So make a deal with him. You'll walk away this time if he promises to support you next time."

I swipe up my menu, not because there's any mystery about what I order but because she's right, I should do something, but I probably won't, and I don't want to look her in the eye.

"You have options, you know," she says, a hint of mischief to her voice.

I peek over the menu. "No, Vick."

"You don't even know what I was—"

"I have a pretty good idea," I say, "and my answer is no."

The waiter arrives with our drinks—water for me, pinot grigio for Vicky—and pretends he's not eavesdropping on our conversation.

She picks up her glass and sips her wine.

"Tell me you heard me say no, Vick."

Her eyes bulge. "I heard you, I heard you," she says.

# 9

*Friday, July 29, 2022*

*Maybe it's best you went on vacation with your girlfriends to Paris for two weeks, Lauren, after we met for coffee. It gave me time to cool off, to think.*

*And here's what I'm thinking: I don't do things like this. I'm an ordinary guy with an ordinary marriage, working an ordinary job, living in an ordinary suburb, doing ordinary things. I don't have affairs. I don't have mistresses!*

*And it's not too late to hit the brakes. Nothing's happened yet. And who knows, maybe you'll stop it—maybe you'll be the one who gets cold feet.*

*But I know my reason. Vicky. Vicky Lanier Dobias, my bride of almost ten years. I know that, deep down, Vicky isn't happy in our marriage, and she'd want me to be happy. She would. But she trusts me, and that trust means everything to her. I think I was the first man she ever trusted after that wreck of a childhood she had, and it helped her build a foundation of a life. If I tear that down, I'm not sure what will happen to her. I can't do that to her.*

*No, I can't do this. I have to stop this before it starts.*

*I'll tell you in person, Lauren, when you return. And that will be that.*

# THE DAY AFTER
# HALLOWEEN

# 10

## Jane

"Mary, Mother of God," Sergeant Jane Burke whispers to herself as she stares at the body of Lauren Betancourt, dangling from a rope attached to the second-floor bannister. Her first homicide. The first homicide, as far as she knows, in the history of Grace Village.

Her partner, Sergeant Andy Tate, comes down the stairs carefully, avoiding the railing and boot and scuff marks on the individual stairs. "Chief call yet?"

"Any second."

She's been on the phone with the chief three times already over the last hour, since the cleaning lady entered the Betancourt house this morning and found Mrs. Betancourt dangling here. Jane was still at home, getting ready for work, when she got the call.

"Mr. Betancourt is on his way back now," says Andy. "We'll have an officer meet him at O'Hare."

"Where was he again?" Jane asks.

"Naples. Golf trip with his sons." Andy walks around the dead body like it's a chandelier to avoid. "Not a bad alibi."

Yeah, but if the husband's involved, and if he has as much money as Jane is hearing he has, he wouldn't do the dirty work himself.

"She was something," Andy mumbles, looking her over. Even with the onset of rigor mortis, Jane agrees, Lauren Betancourt is gorgeous, slim and shapely with a delicate, sculpted face and silky blond hair. Her outfit, however garish it seems now in death, leaves little to the imagination: a form-fitting leopard-print bodysuit—a cat costume for Halloween. Her eyes, wide open, look down on Jane, lips parted as if in mid-thought. Her lips are painted black, matching the whiskers painted on her face. She has an expensive manicure, black polish.

From the back side, nothing obvious to see, other than a dark stain between her legs. The loss of sphincter control is one of the many ugly accoutrements of death.

Jane's phone buzzes in her AirPods. She whacks Andy and nods her head. "Chief."

*"Okay, Janey, I'm in the car. I should be there in about three hours. First, is there press yet?"*

"Not that I know of." She looks out a window. No reporters yet, but the neighbors are out in full force, spilled onto their lawns or the street, in housecoats and slippers, some dressed for work; children with their backpacks headed off to school on a Tuesday morning, the first bell in ten minutes. The half dozen police cruisers would be enough on their own, but Jane imagines that word has filtered back to the neighbors now.

*"Christ,"* says the chief. *"The first damn homicide ever, and I'm at a seminar in Indiana."*

Jane walks to the south door of the house, the kitchen door, because from everything they can tell thus far, it was not the point of entry or the site of the struggle. She wants to keep the crime scene as pristine as possible until Major Crimes brings its forensics unit.

She removes her shoe covers and walks outside, appreciating the fresh air. Andy follows her around the side of the house to the front, where the action occurred.

Grace Village, the day after Halloween. Remnants of smashed pumpkins, candy wrappers scattered in yards or stuck in the curb drains, plastic bags blowing about or clinging to the branches of naked trees.

The Village does a mean Halloween business, a mecca for kids from the west side of Chicago, from the other side of the Des Plaines River, even from Grace Park. Sometimes they take buses over here to the mansions, with the huge candy bars and elaborate decorations. The older teenagers come at the end of the four-hour window for trick-or-treating, hoping to clean up the remaining candy in the bowls, usually prompting calls from one of the more uptight residents.

Hundreds and hundreds of strangers roamed these streets last night, many in face paint or masks or disguises, on the one night of the year that it wouldn't stand out. It's going to make this investigation twice as hard.

You want to kill someone, Halloween's not a bad night.

"I'll walk you through what we know so far, Chief. It's early."

*"I'm listening."*

"First, the window on the front of the house."

Manicured shrubs along the façade of the house. A large window behind them. She walks along the grass and peeks over the shrubs.

Boot impressions in front of one of the windows. Good and deep, cemented in the dirt.

"We have deep boot impressions," she says. "Looks like an adult boot. Our guess is adult size, maybe twelve, thirteen. We'll have forensics do impressions and run 'em through the database."

*"Good."*

"It rained just a little yesterday afternoon, right before trick-or-treating started. That was a gift to us. The ground behind the shrubs was just soft enough to allow for impressions. Looks like he was standing there for a while."

*"Looking through her window?"*

"Exactly. Nothing else he could do, standing in that direction, but look through this window."

*"We have a time frame?"*

"Well, that's the thing, boss. Last night was Halloween. So you know how that goes."

*"Three-to-seven, then lights out."*

Per tradition, the residents of Grace Village turn off their lights at seven o'clock, to tell everyone that trick-or-treating is over. At seven bells sharp, all the parents shout, "Happy Halloween!"—probably mumbling under their breath, *Now get out of my neighborhood*—then kill their outside lights.

"No way our creeper peeper was lurking outside her window before seven," says Jane. "Trick-or-treaters would walk right past him. Everyone would see him."

*"But once seven o'clock hit . . ."*

"Once seven o'clock hits, it's the darkest night of the year in the Village. He could've stood there without notice for as long as he wanted."

*"Okay, what's next?"*

"Our creeper peeper goes to the front door," she says. "We don't see his boot prints on the walkway or the driveway. He goes from the window to the front door."

The front door is enclosed within a small A-frame brick canopy with stone trim. The welcome mat bears the family name, Betancourt. The outside light is turned off. The front door frame is intact. The floor on this porch is stone. And quite dirty, from the activity last night, all the shoes, dirty or otherwise, of trick-or-treaters.

"We see his boot impressions on the front porch," she says. "They're far more prominent than the other scuff marks and prints from the trick-or-treaters. The most recent, I'd guess. And we see them on the door, Chief."

*"The door. Meaning he was kicking the front door."*

"Right. The impressions are at a slight angle. We're thinking he reared back and kicked hard."

*"Is that how he got in? He kicked in the door?"*

"No. There's no forced entry, no splintering, no damage to the door whatsoever."

*"So she let him in."*

"She let him in."

*"She let in someone who was kicking at her front door?"*

"I know, right? So we're thinking they must have known each other."

*"Huh. All right, all right, I hear you, you piece of shit!"*

That sounds like the chief, the way he drives, drawing angry horns from fellow drivers. Cops think they can drive like cops even when they aren't being cops.

*"Sorry. Anyway, yeah, seems pretty obvious that she knew the guy and let him in."*

"Maybe he was making a scene outside," says Jane, "and she didn't want that."

*"That's a theory. That's a very specific theory. Don't get locked in too quickly, Janey."*

"I'm not locked in on anything, Chief. But there's almost no doubt that the guy standing by the bushes, peeping through her window, went to her front door and started kicking it, and she let him in voluntarily."

*"Okay, then what?"*

Jane and Andy put back on their shoe covers. Jane opens the front door carefully, ushers Andy in, and closes it quickly behind her. The last thing she needs is for the neighbors to see a body hanging from the second-floor railing.

"Inside," she says. "A glass bowl of Halloween candy, shattered in the foyer. Maybe he knocks it out of her hand, maybe she throws it at him. Hard to say."

*"Okay."*

"She runs for the stairs."

*"The stairs. Not the kitchen, for a knife?"*

"Nope. There's no sign they were in the kitchen, and every sign he chased her up the stairs." She follows the same boot impressions along the marble floor, then onto the wooden staircase. "Lauren was running in heels, which couldn't have been easy, although on stairs, it's easier than on flat ground."

*"Is that true?"*

"Stairs, you run on the balls of your feet, even in heels. Flat ground, you can't."

She follows the boot impressions, and a few scuff marks where the heels did manage to strike down, all the way up the wraparound staircase.

"They reach the top of the stairs. This, we think, is where he subdues her." She stops before walking any farther on the landing. "There's blood up here, right on the landing, the second-floor hallway. Forensics hasn't been through yet, so we're just eyeballing. But he hits her up here on the second floor, on the back of the head."

Jane looks down on Lauren's dead body, in particular her scalp, bearing a bloody gash.

*"Hits her with what?"*

"We don't know yet. But he hits her hard enough to draw blood. We figure it stuns her enough, at least momentarily, so he can get the noose around her neck."

*"How'd he tie off the rope?"*

"Well, it was kind of clever," she says, squatting down. "This is a thick, knotted rope, knotted every foot or so. The wrought iron bannister—well, you saw the photos."

*"I saw them but didn't focus on the bannister."*

"Sure. It's one of these ornate spiral patterns, right? It looks like some Gothic design, like some old family coat of arms."

"Or a series of Rorschach tests," says Andy.

"Right, or like Rorschach tests. A bunch of intricate spirals and whirls and shapes."

*"Okay, so . . ."*

"He shoved one end of the rope into the curves of the pattern and wrapped it around once or twice. It held firm."

*"And then what?"*

Jane shrugs. "Then he chucked her over the railing."

*"Ugh."*

Yeah, ugh. But the most likely way this happened.

*"Why not just strangle her?"*

"He probably couldn't," says Jane. "Or not easily, at least. She put up a struggle. He's behind her, with the slipknot around her neck and tugging, but she doesn't go down easily. We have some broken painted fingernails up here. She was struggling against the noose around her throat. And if she were able to kick with those heels—well, they'd be sharp as knives. It might have been easier to keep the noose taut around her neck with one hand, stuff one end of the rope into the bannister curves with the other, then pick her up and throw her over."

*"Jesus. Okay. I got it. So, Jane, listen. Major Crimes can bring forensics, but otherwise this stays in-house, understand?"*

"Yes." Jane feels butterflies through her chest, not for the first time today.

*"No statements to the press until I get there. Understand?"*

"Yes."

He goes silent. He's thinking.

Outside, Jane hears heavy car doors closing. Probably the medical examiner or forensics arriving.

*"You think this was a lover's quarrel, something like that?"*

"No robbery," she says. "No sexual assault or, from what we see preliminarily, even an attempt at sexual assault. It sure seems like this guy came here to do one thing and one thing only, and that's kill Lauren Betancourt."

"*Personal,*" says the chief. "*Someone who really wanted her dead.*"

Jane looks down at the body and shudders.

"Or really wanted *her*, period," she says, "but couldn't have her."

# BEFORE HALLOWEEN

## August

# 11

*I tried. I swear I did! I showed up at your door today, seeing you for the first time since you got back from Paris, and I was all ready to do the right thing. When you opened the door, tanned and elegant and, well, just gorgeous, I said, Go ahead, Simon, do it. Tell Lauren, say it, do it, and I did, I told you, I told you I couldn't betray Vicky like that, we had to stop this thing before it started.*

*And you, Lauren, bless your heart, you said you understood. "The fact that you'd say something like that is why you're such a great guy," you said. My stomach twisted in knots and my chest was about to explode, but we stood there a moment and I said to myself, You're going to be glad later that you did this even though it sucks right now.*

*Then I hugged you and you hugged me back and we held each other and the feel of you was too much and then your hands started moving and then mine did, too, and it felt like my insides caught fire and then our lips were pressed together and you moaned and, Lauren, I can't tell you what that did to me, hearing you respond to me, feeling like I had that effect on you. Do you know how long it's been since I felt a woman respond to me that way?*

*So all that time over the last several weeks ruminating and deciding that this can't happen and within ten minutes, it's happening. We can't keep our hands off each other, we're naked on your couch, going at it like animals, raw and sweaty and ravenous.*

*And there was nothing in the world that has ever felt as satisfying as hearing you climax, Lauren, that tiny hitch in your voice, that harsh gasp in my ear, the spasm of your hips. I felt like the greatest man alive! Is that what love feels like? Feeling like when you're with the one you love, you're on top of the world? It's been so long I've forgotten.*

*I feel like I've just taken my hands off the wheel, closed my eyes, and floored the accelerator.*

# 12

## Simon

In the morning, I start with my Five at Five—a five-mile run at five in the morning. My mother used to do that. Four days a week, at five bells, she'd strap on her shoes and "eat some pavement," as she put it. She had eighteen marathons to her credit, qualifying for Boston repeatedly. "It's time all your own," she used to say. "No stress, no phone calls, no arguments, just you. It's like a million dollars' worth of therapy."

I head east, crossing over Austin into the west side of Chicago. You wouldn't call the most crime-ridden and violent part of the city scenic, but there is something about its dilapidated humility and gritty determination that moves me.

Everyone thinks about the shootings and carnage, but I see the teenage girl playing violin by her second-story bedroom window near Augusta and Waller every morning at the crack of dawn; the old man in a beige uniform sitting on his stoop, getting ready for a red-eye shift, drinking coffee out of a thermos and calling me "a damn fool!" as I run past Long Avenue; the grandmother doing Bible study with several teens on the front porch, weather permitting, otherwise by the front living-room window; the woman in the apartment on Leclaire, coming home in a green waitress uniform with a backpack full of books after her overnight shift ended.

Running through this neighborhood reminds me that some people have bigger things to worry about than whether they get promoted to a stupid full professorship at their school. Some people are fighting for a decent life.

Everyone thinks I'm crazy for jogging through here, and maybe Vicky's right that I'm just too stubborn *not* to run here, like I'm trying to prove something. I've lost count of the number of times I've been followed by a police cruiser, the officers slowing next to me and asking me what the hell I'm thinking. Maybe I am a damn fool. But hey, I've been called worse.

Like "Mini-Me," for example. That's what Mitchell Kitchens, a massive senior, an all-state varsity wrestler, used to call me, back when I was a diminutive freshman at Grace Consolidated, barely over five feet tall and maybe a hundred pounds. Mitchell was built like a brick house, with a neck like a tree stump, so thick it was hard to see where it ended and his head began. He had these nasty teeth and bad breath and a nose that had been broken several times. His eyes were narrow and spread wide apart, giving him a prehistoric look.

That *Austin Powers* sequel had come out that summer. Apparently, Mitchell had seen it over Thanksgiving break my freshman year. I remember, after that break, Mitchell spotting me in the hallway and pointing and shouting, "Hey, it's Mini-Me!" And it stuck, right? Of course it stuck. Only the nicknames you hate stick.

When I'd get off the bus every day, there he'd be, just outside the fence, calling out to me, *"C'mere, Mini-Me!"* He'd shout it in the hallways. He'd call it out when I walked into math class (yes, a senior was taking the same math class as a freshman, to give you an idea of his scholastic advancement). Initially, I tried ignoring him, not responding, but that only made him shout it over and over again and that only made things worse, so eventually I started responding the first time.

Yeah, I didn't like Mitchell. I don't obsess over him or anything. But if I'm ever tempted to forget him, I just have to look in the mirror and see the scar on my left cheek, that day he lost his temper.

"A good lawyer knows the answer to every question before she asks it," my mother used to say. "A good lawyer knows what she wants to say in closing argument before the trial has even begun. You work backward from how you want it to end, and you plan out the trial so that, by the end, you can support everything you wanted to tell them with evidence."

By quarter after six, I'm shaving after my shower, rubbing a circle out of the steam on the mirror so I can get a fuzzy reflection.

Vicky pushes through the bathroom door with a moan, her eyes all but shut, her hair all over her face. She leans against my back and says, "How do you get up this early?"

"My favorite time of day," I say.

"That bed . . . is *so* comfortable."

"Glad you like it."

She drops onto the toilet to pee while I finish up shaving and tap my razor in the sink.

"Late night?" I ask.

Her head drops. "We got a call five minutes before midnight."

"Ugh. Five minutes before your shift ended? You could've pawned it off."

"Well, I didn't. Her husband was at the ER, too, trying to get her to come home and drop the charges. It was a real scene. Took three cops to restrain the guy. He even swung at me."

"Yeah? Did he connect?"

"No."

That's probably lucky for the guy.

"And the woman?" I ask. "Did she go with you?"

"Yeah, eventually. I didn't leave until about two in the morning."

She flushes and drags herself to the sink to wash her hands.

"Go back to sleep," I say.

"Don't worry, I will." She shuffles back to bed, the Bataan Death March, then drops face-first onto the pillow and moans with satisfaction.

I get dressed and put on some coffee. I take a cup for the road. I have a decent drive ahead. I walk back up to the bedroom to say goodbye. "Hey, gorgeous, Daddy's leaving."

She opens one eye. "Creepy."

I watch her for a while. She looks sexy just lying there in that oversize Cubs shirt, this hard, tough woman so innocent and vulnerable in sleep.

I have to protect her. I have to make sure she comes out of this okay.

_____

Before I head up to Wisconsin, I drive by Lauren's house. I don't stay long. By now, her husband, Conrad, is long gone, chauffeured downtown for his workout at the swanky East Bank Club before lording over his millions of dollars of investments. Is he checking out all the hard-bodied women in their spandex workout gear? Does he have one eye out for wife number four, should the mood strike him? Is that what he did with Lauren—got bored with his aging second wife and traded her in for a younger model?

Well, you better start looking again, Conrad, old boy. Three years with Lauren wasn't a bad run. You're not getting a fourth.

I look across the street at her place. The master bedroom takes up the entire north side of the house, with a terrace behind it where Lauren likes to sunbathe in privacy. Or so she thinks. I'd bet green money the men who live nearby have managed to find their binoculars.

Or maybe she knows that. Do you, Lauren? Do you like to tease other men, make them want you? Do you still need that validation? Have you figured out that none of that matters?

Or will you always want more?

"The pink one," I say. "No, the hot pink."

The chubby clerk with the pockmarked face in the "superstore" in Racine, Wisconsin—about eighty miles north of Chicago—lifts the phone case off the rack and runs it over the scanner.

"So this is a thousand minutes?" I confirm.

"Yeah, a thousand minutes. And with our plan, you can get monthly—"

"Nope, no plan."

"You don't want a plan?"

"No. Just this phone, a thousand minutes, and that hot-pink case. Don't worry," I add with a chuckle, "I'm not a criminal. This is for my daughter. It's a trial run. I want to see how quickly she burns through these minutes before I decide whether a ten-year-old needs a phone."

I wish I did have kids. Vicky said no way. She thinks the taint of her rotten childhood would somehow seep into any children she had.

The clerk glances at me briefly before nodding and taking my wad of cash and giving me another look. A no-plan, prepaid phone, paid for in cash.

"The green one," I tell the elderly saleswoman in the "superstore" in Valparaiso, Indiana, which is 130 miles southwest of Racine, Wisconsin, and about 60 miles from Chicago. Green again, like my green journal, for fresh and new and blossoming and, you know, all that shit.

"And you say you want a thousand minutes?" she asks.

"Yes." I pull out cash and drop it on the counter.

"And . . . would you be interested in one of our monthly plans—"

"No, ma'am, no thank you. Just the phone and the minutes and the green case."

She looks down at the cash.

"I'm a drug dealer," I say. "I sell heroin to children."

She looks up at me.

"Just kidding. It's for my ten-year-old son. It's a trial run. I don't want him getting more minutes each month until I see how fast he burns through these minutes."

"Oh, I have a granddaughter who's ten years old," she says, brightening. "Is your son going into the fifth grade?"

"He sure is!"

"Where does he go?"

Uh, boy. "We homeschool," I say, and pull my phone out of my pocket as if I'm answering it, before this woman gets any nosier.

This sneaking-around stuff is harder than it looks.

# 13

## Vicky

I get out of bed a few hours after Simon leaves and search through his chest of drawers. Simon is organized enough to keep a backup list of all his important passwords but is far too paranoid to put them on a computer or phone. Electronic surveillance is the bread-and-butter of Simon's scholarship; he is convinced the government looks at a lot more of our information than it lets on, and the Fourth Amendment is being shredded in the process. He says "old-school," good old pen and paper, is the smarter way. He writes his passwords on a piece of notebook paper he keeps in his sock drawer, or maybe he said underwear drawer, I don't remember.

On top of the chest of drawers are photographs of Simon's mother, Glory. Some are from before she married Ted Dobias, Simon's father, but most are after. I see a lot of Simon in her, the chestnut hair and warm eyes and radiant smile, which is how I describe Simon's smile when he chooses to flash it, which isn't often enough.

The early pictures: a high school yearbook photo of Glory looking over her shoulder in that awkward school-picture pose. A picture of her with her parents at Wrigley Field when she was a toddler, her face smeared with mustard. One of her standing on Navy Pier in her cap and gown, holding her diploma from the University of Chicago Law School.

The later ones, after she married Ted Dobias, do not feature Ted at all, just Glory and Simon. Glory holding her swaddled newborn in the hospital bed, a beaming but exhausted mother. A photo of them laughing at each other, noses almost touching, when Simon was five or six. The two of them outside Orchestra Hall. Eating pizza at Gino's East, the cheese stretched like rubber. Little Simon in his mother's arms after she just completed the Chicago Marathon, her hair matted with sweat, a silver runner's poncho over her shoulders, Simon holding the runner's medal and staring at it with that inquisitive look he never lost.

That's the Glory I always hear about, vibrant and active and silly and whimsical, always ready with a corny joke or a smile.

Then there's Glory the lawyer, the laser-focused attorney. The photo of mother and son on the steps of the United States Supreme Court the day that Glory argued a case before them. The sharpest of legal minds, Simon always says, "and the sharpest of tongues. Fearlessly blunt."

On the wall in a frame, a page of a transcript from a court hearing when Glory was a new lawyer working at some fancy, highbrow law firm, one of only a handful of women back then:

THE COURT: The objection is sustained, Mrs. Dobias.

COUNSEL: Your Honor, we weren't offering the testimony for the truth of the matter asserted, but merely to show the fact that the statement was made.

THE COURT: I understand, hon, but when a judge sustains an objection, the attorney moves on to the next question, I don't care how pretty she is.

COUNSEL: I think I understand. And—what does the lawyer do when the judge is acting like a horse's ass?

THE COURT: I'm sorry? What did you say to me?

COUNSEL: I was just speaking hypothetically, Your Honor. Please understand, all these rules and formalities are enough to overwhelm a girl.

THE COURT: Did you just call me a horse's ass?

COUNSEL: Did you just call me hon? Did you just call me pretty? Maybe we both misheard.

Apparently, at that point, the judge ordered the lawyers into chambers and shooed away the court reporter. Simon said the judge asked Glory for one reason why he shouldn't hold her in contempt. She replied that she was concerned about how the Judicial Inquiry Board might feel about a sitting judge making on-the-record demeaning comments toward a female lawyer. The judge announced a recess for the rest of the day.

Word got back to the law firm, and the firm's executive committee demanded she apologize to the judge. She refused. She left the firm that day and never went back.

But one of the women in the courtroom gallery that day obtained a copy of the transcript, framed this page, and gave it to Glory as a present.

It sounds like I would've liked Simon's mom.

The last two photos were near the end, when Glory was bound to a wheelchair and had lost a good amount of her functioning. The animation in her face was replaced by a more deadened stare, her beaming smile now a crooked turn of her lip. I don't know why Simon keeps these around. The last two years of her life were difficult for everyone and not the way to remember her, not the way she'd want to be remembered, if everything I've heard about her is true.

I think Simon keeps those photos to remember how everything fell apart.

Here it is, the password list, in his sock drawer. The password to his trust account is Glory010455, his mother's name and date of birth.

I head downstairs. Simon put on coffee before he left, still hot in the thermos mug. It's delicious. He uses good beans. And he sprinkled on some pumpkin spice before he brewed it. It's not quite September, but it reminds me of autumn, my favorite season, which I'm sure is why he did it. He does little things like that for me all the time.

I wish it could be different with Simon and me. I wish he'd come out of that bubble more often. I don't know if the law became his refuge after everything that happened with his parents or whether he's just hardwired that way, but teaching and talking and writing about the law is everything to him, his passion, his life. The way he lights up when he breaks down a legal issue into simple parts and then reconstructs it, the way he brings it to life like a breathing organism. Even I, knowing only as much about the law as I've seen on television, can get sucked in listening to him.

They say the law is a jealous mistress. But that's not true. The law has an ironclad grip on Simon's heart. I'm the jealous mistress.

That's what I tell myself, at least, the problem I focus on, probably so I can pin the blame on him. The bigger problem, why we will never work, is children. Simon wants them. He wants it all, marriage and kids, a nuclear family. The family I had growing up was nuclear, all right, but not in a good way. I'm not doing it.

Simon says I'm just scared, like any future parent would be. Yes, I'm scared. I'm scared I'll wreck them. I'm scared they'll turn out like me. What could I teach them? What kind of role model would I be? What if I had them and realized I couldn't handle it after it's too late?

I love my nieces, the M&Ms. I like being the aunt. Isn't that enough? Not for Simon, it isn't.

Oh, he'd compromise, I know. He'd live without children. But I don't want to be the reason he settles.

We just don't work.

I sit down at the kitchen table and open my laptop. I pull up the website and type in the password to access his trust account.

Simon inherited money from his father after his father died twelve years ago. As far as I know, he hasn't touched a penny. It was substantial to begin with, but it's built up with interest and some conservative but decent investment decisions made by the trustee, who is *not* Simon. Which is good because Simon is terrible with money.

As of today, the balance in Simon's trust is $21,106,432.

Twenty-one million and change.

Talk about delicious.

I continue the Google search that I started previously, looking for investment advisers. I've narrowed it down to four. A guy by the name of Broderick, middle-aged and bald, who talks about his personal relationship with his clients. I'm guessing he has halitosis and high blood pressure.

A man named Lombardi, in high-end "wealth management," a phrase I see repeatedly. He has a full-wattage smile and kind of a waxy look to him, like he should be selling carpet shampoo on an infomercial.

A guy named Bowers, with tons of initials after his name, offers "full-service wealth management and security," which I think means he's going to want to sell me insurance as well as being my investment adviser. Kind of a bookish guy, with small eyes and a pencil neck.

The last one is Christian Newsome, who doesn't look like any investment adviser that I've ever seen. He looks like a Calvin Klein model, at least from the chest up in his photo.

Younger, mid-thirties, two different photos of him on the site with a nice suit but no tie, just an open collar of a crisply starched white shirt. Wide shoulders, thick neck. Maybe that's why he doesn't wear the tie, to give his neck room to show off. Athletic, back in his day, I'd venture, but probably nothing too violent; he wouldn't want to mess up that pretty face of his, the strong, rough-shaven jaw, large blue eyes, the sweep of hair with the bangs falling forward—the carefully practiced messy look. He knows he's handsome, which is annoying.

But he looks like a winner, I'll give him that.

I probe further. The bio stuff is impressive: Harvard undergrad and MBA, made a killing in the market before he was out of school.

There's an article on his website from *Fortune* magazine from thirteen years ago—March of 2009—about how young Christian Newsome, at the ripe age of twenty-one, was one of the first to invest in "credit default swaps" before the mortgage crisis hit in 2008, correctly predicting what others did not—that the market for "mortgage-backed securities" would crash.

Another article featured on his website, from *Newsweek*, from three years ago, was about how Christian Newsome's new venture features a small group of investors in a fund worth more than five hundred million dollars. "Newsome, notoriously tight-lipped about his next moves in the market and the investors he represents, would only say his next idea 'will make credit default swaps look like penny stocks.'"

I sip my coffee. Reread the articles. Look at his photo for a while.

Then I pick up my cell phone and start making appointments.

# 14

**Tuesday, August 16, 2022**

*I met you at your condo on Michigan Avenue this afternoon. Having that condo makes everything so much easier. I can pop over from the law school, you can use whatever excuse you need to be downtown.*

*I'm doing this. We. We are doing this! Everything I said about Vicky, I know, but we're doing this and I can't stop myself.*

*And I couldn't wait to show you the phones! I hadn't told you about it. I wanted to surprise you.*

*First things first, when I got inside your condo—we stripped and did it against the window overlooking Michigan Avenue, fourteen stories up, you planted against the windowpane. It's a lot harder than it looks in the movies, and I thought my back might give out, so we finished up on your bed.*

*Then we drank some wine, and I was bursting to show you. So I did. The hot-pink phone for you, the green phone for me.*

*You didn't speak at first. My heart started doing calisthenics, not the good kind, the burn kind.*

*"Am I your mistress now?" you said, looking up at me.*

*"I just . . . I thought it would be good if we could communicate—"*

*"You want to be able to call me whenever you want to fuck me."*

*"No, it's . . . not like that," I said.*

*"I'm your call girl, is that it?" you said. "Like your wife was before you met her. You want me to be like your wife? You want another Vicky?"*

"No, listen, it's not like that at all." I said something like that, I think. I'm not really sure what stammering protest was coming out of my mouth.

But this part I remember clear as day. You walked over to me. You have a way of sauntering over to me that makes my legs weak. I think the word "saunter" was invented for you, Lauren. There should have been a saxophone playing in the background.

You leaned up and whispered in my ear, "Do you want me to be your whore, Professor Dobias? Tell me. Tell me what you want."

I don't want you to be anything but you, Lauren. I don't need role plays or dirty talk. That's never been my thing. I just want you, exactly as you are.

But it seemed like the right thing to say at the time, so I went with it.

I gripped your hair and made you look at me. "That's what I want," I said.

Your eyes lit up. The corners of your mouth only curved up slightly.

"Then fuck me that way," you said.

# 15
## Vicky

The lobby register says that Newsome Capital Growth is in suite 1320. I thought most buildings didn't have a thirteenth floor out of superstition. An omen?

I push through the glass doors, greeted by a young woman seated behind a thin desk, wearing a headset, the sleek professional look of today's corporate America, I guess. Where I work, at the shelter, we can hardly afford a single landline. We use fans instead of air-conditioning. We use milk past the expiration date, as long as it doesn't smell.

"Vicky Lanier for Christian Newsome," I say.

"Yes, Mrs. Lanier, one moment." She pushes a button on a large phone. "Your four o'clock, Mrs. Lanier, is here? Sure." She looks at me. "He'll be just a minute. Can I get you anything?"

"I'm fine."

Voices from one of the offices behind reception. A strong, throaty laugh. A confident man. Or a man trying to project confidence, at least.

"Mrs. Lanier? Christian Newsome." He sweeps out of his office and takes my hand, a firm shake. He's the fourth financial adviser to greet me today but the first to really shake my hand. The other men just gave a gentle squeeze, as if my hand would crumble to dust under the strength of their powerful grip.

He looks like he did in his photos. You never know, but he's true to it. Mid-thirties, the obligatory well-tailored suit but still no tie, because no, he won't be tied down by convention, he thinks outside the box, and besides, it shows off his thick neck.

Still rough-shaven, just like his beauty pics on the website, which is interesting because it means he takes the time to shave it just so, not too hairy, but sexy stubble. Still that sweep of the hair made to look messy. This one goes to a lot of trouble to look like he didn't go to a lot of trouble.

His office doesn't present like the other sedate ones I saw. He has a leather couch on one side with some fancy lamp hanging over it. A bar with premium liquor. An ego wall, framed articles written about him, some photographs of him with famous people. Three flat-screen TVs on another wall—CNBC, Fox Business, and Bloomberg—plus rolling indices from Nasdaq and Nikkei and the Dow Jones. None of it means anything to me. I understand the financial world like I understand nuclear physics.

"Closest thing in life to a contact sport," he says to me. "Everyone out there competing. I like to keep an eye on the playing field at all times."

He sits behind a steel desk and looks me over. He checks me out without trying to be too obvious about it, but men are usually obvious. I have a pretty good idea of what he's seeing. He wouldn't mind going a round or two with me, but not marriage material.

My sister, Monica, she was marriage material. Monica was the prom queen, the cheerleader, the A-student, the girl with the radiant smile and infectious laugh every boy chased. Me, I was the trashy younger sister, not nearly as pretty but with bigger boobs and a come-hither smile, who smoked cigarettes off campus with the burnouts and got kicked out of school for having sex in a library carrel.

When I couldn't be my sister, I was determined to be everything she wasn't. And at that, I wildly succeeded.

"The great thing is, it's not a zero-sum game," he says. "Everyone can win. You just have to play it right." He drops his hand down on his thin steel desk, which contains nothing but an autographed baseball and two fancy computers. "So, Mrs. Vicky Lanier, how can I help you?"

"I'm interviewing financial advisers. People you probably know." I lay out the business cards of the other three advisers I met today. "I'm about to come into some money."

He glances at the cards. "I've just relocated to Chicago," he says. "So I don't know them personally. But I *know* them, if you know what I mean. I know thousands of them. And I'm sure any of them could adequately 'manage' your money. But that's not what you want."

"It's not?"

"No, you want to grow it. You don't want to fly first-class. You want to own your own jet."

I sit back in my chair, cross my legs. Definitely a more aggressive approach. Those other men, with their smooth small talk, their bullshit about forging relationships and getting to know the individual needs and wants of each investor, risk-mitigation, and asset-preservation strategies. Trying to make me feel secure and safe. This one, he's saying, buckle up and prepare for blastoff.

"You said you're about to come into some money," he says. "An inheritance? Not a death in the family, I hope?"

"No. My husband Simon's money, actually."

"Ah, Mr. Lanier."

"Dobias," I say. "Simon Dobias. I kept my maiden name."

"Very good."

"But I'll be making the decisions about money," I say. "In twelve weeks, at least, I will. I want to be ready when that happens."

He pauses on that. He doesn't understand. "What happens in twelve weeks?"

"We celebrate our tenth wedding anniversary. November the third. Then I get the money."

"Ah," he says. "Sounds like there's a trust involved."

Very good, Christian Newsome. Indeed, there is.

"Simon's father left money in a trust for him, yes," I say. "You've dealt with trusts before?"

He waves a hand. "All the time. You'd be amazed at what people do with their money. That's their business, not mine."

"Right now, the money is held in Simon's name only. According to the trust, once we're married for ten years, it becomes joint property."

"Those were his father's terms? You had to be married for ten years before you could access the money?"

"Before I could access it . . . or before Simon could even spend it on me."

Christian sits back in his chair. "Really."

"Oh, yeah," I say, an edge to my voice. "There's a trustee who has to approve every expenditure from the trust. Simon could buy a car, but it has to be in the trust's name only, meaning Simon's name only. He could buy a second house in Florida or something, but in the trust's name only—Simon's name only. Simon tried to buy me a diamond necklace for our fifth anniversary and the trustee said no, not with trust money, he couldn't."

"That *is* restrictive."

I smile. "Simon's father didn't trust me."

That seems to spark Christian's interest, his eyes lighting up. Am I a naughty girl?

I don't know, am I?

"He figured that if I really loved Simon, I wouldn't mind waiting ten years for the money. And if I *was* in it for the money, as he suspected, I wouldn't be willing to wait ten years."

He doesn't answer, but he sees the logic. And he's thinking there must be a healthy amount of money in that trust. But he hasn't asked. Not yet. His website, the small print, says that the minimum investment for his services is ten million dollars. On the phone, the receptionist said the same thing but added that Christian was sometimes willing to make exceptions. I told her that ten million wouldn't be a problem.

"And you haven't grown on Simon's father over the years?" he asks me, smiling.

"Oh, Simon's father passed away before we were even married."

"Ah, sorry to hear that. And now you've been married ten years," he says. "Or you will be, come November third."

"Come November third," I say, "I can spend that money however I want, whenever I want, on whatever I want. And I want to get it as far away from that stupid bank and that condescending trustee with his bullshit about asset protection and conservative—"

I catch myself getting carried away.

"Sorry," I say. "I might be . . . a little bitter."

"I don't blame you," he says. "You've been a second-class citizen in your own marriage."

I nod. "Not that Simon wants it that way. He doesn't have a choice. He can't change the terms of the trust. But yeah, a second-class citizen, that's a really good way of putting it."

He raises a hand. "I should keep my opinions to myself."

"No, really, that sums up how I've felt."

I lean forward. It's probably time to cut to the chase.

"Let me ask you something, Mr. Newsome. When that trust becomes community property on November third, does that mean I can spend the money without Simon's approval? Or even without his knowledge?"

I asked that question three times previously today and got the same answer each time. First, they'd have to see the language of the trust. Second, generally, if someone is listed on an account, they can spend that money without the approval of the other account holder. But third, it's probably best to include the other account holder in the conversation to avoid disputes on the back end, including potential litigation—litigation that could include the investment adviser.

Christian Newsome doesn't immediately answer. He presumably has the same response, more or less, at the ready. But he's not thinking about the legal niceties. He's thinking about what kind of person I am to be asking that question. And he doesn't seem particularly bothered. A tiny smirk plays on his face for one beat.

"There are ways to make that happen, yes," he says. "And call me Christian."

I look around the office, the rolling indices from the various stock exchanges, the diplomas from Harvard, the certifications from the state agencies. All these guys are alike in so many ways.

But not in every way.

"Christian, that's the best answer I've heard all day."

I take the three business cards I put on his desk and make a show of ripping each of them in half.

"And you should probably call me Vicky," I say.

# 16
## Simon

I walk a mile and a half from the law school down to the Chicago Title & Trust Building on Clark and Randolph in the Loop. I take a longer route so I can travel along one of my favorite spots, the concrete promenade on the lakefront, the turbulent water to my left, the cars flying past me on Lake Shore Drive to my right. Poisonous clouds cover the sky, but that hasn't stopped the cyclists and Rollerbladers and joggers shooting past each other north and south just below me. I do love this city.

The building has a different name now, but a lot of people still call it the Chicago Title & Trust Building. That's what it was called when my father had a law firm here in the nineties. It was the firm he opened on his own, after splitting off from his partners over some dispute. Back then, a bunch of law firms had offices in this building. Maybe they still do.

I remember coming here with him on a Saturday once. We took the Green Line downtown—itself an adventure, especially on weekends—and rode the elevator up to the seventeenth floor. He had a suite in the middle of that floor. I remember the frosted glass door and how cool it seemed with LAW OFFICES OF THEODORE DOBIAS stenciled in a fancy font.

That was back when Dad was "scrapping," as he'd call it. Personal injury and workers comp, mostly. Car crashes and slip-and-falls and stuff like that. He even did some criminal, mostly DUIs and possession cases. He had to bone up on the Fourth Amendment, but fortunately he had my mother for that. Mostly he was an ambulance chaser.

*Were you injured at work? Then you need someone on your side!*

Luckily, he never ran any schlocky commercials. I never saw his face on the side of a bus.

Then he hit the motherlode, a massive electrical-injury case that made him millions. He changed office space. He changed a lot of things.

Inside the Chicago Title & Trust Building, I grab a Starbucks in the lobby and plop down on one of their leather couches.

I pull out the green phone I just bought in Indiana and slide in the SIM card. For the first time ever, I turn on the green phone, waiting for it to pop to life, the first few seconds of my thousand minutes. I take a deep breath and type:

> Testing . . . Testing . . . 1, 2, 3. Testing . . . testing . . . 1, 2, 3. Is this thing on?

I hit "send" and let out my breath.

She's expecting my text—our first text—at ten this morning. At least I hope she is. I hope she's sitting there with that hot-pink phone just waiting to hear from me.

My green phone vibrates with her reply. I almost spill my coffee.

> *Well, hello, stranger*

Her replies are in a different font than my texts. Mine are boxy and plain, hers have curves, daintier and more sensual. That seems appropriate. I respond:

> Reception ok?

Not the sexiest of responses. Not at all. But Lauren has an old house with thick walls, like a lot of houses in Grace Village. Some people I've known in the Village have trouble with cell reception.

She texts back:

> *On the balcony*

Right, the balcony off the master bedroom.

I text:

> **We have to be careful.**

But I don't send it. My first texts were lame. This whole new exciting way to communicate secretly with your mistress, and I start by asking about her cellular reception? And now I say we have to be careful? Talk about unsexy.

I should have thought this out more. But I didn't. I erase and type this instead:

> **We have to be careful. I don't want to screw anything up**
> **for you.**

Better, because it shows caring. But still comfortably occupying wet-blanket territory. Up your game, Simon.

> **I've never done anything like this before.**

No. It's true, I haven't done anything like this before, but no.
Pop quiz: What would someone *not* feeling insecure say to her right now?

    (a)  Do you really like me? Are you sure? Cuz I like you tons!
    (b)  Are you tired? Because you've been running through my
          mind all night.
    (c)  I've never met anyone like you.
    (d)  I think I love you.
    (e)  None of the above.

I'm going with (e). I'm not going to use the "L" word. How about this:

> **I can't stop thinking about you.**

That's better. Yeah. I send it before I can talk myself out of it. Take another sip of my Starbucks. Her text box starts bubbling. She's typing a response:

*C u later*

Wow. Phew. That went well.

I close out the phone, power it off, and remove the SIM card.

Wicker Park. Back when I was in college, this was the cutting edge of hip, the place to live, the place to hang. It still is to a lot of people, but it's become a bit too yuppie now for the younger crowd, and some of the cool dives and concert rooms and coffee bars have been replaced with AT&T and Lululemon stores and Fifth Third Bank branches.

I work late at the law school. At about seven-fifteen, I start out from the school on a ten-mile round-tripper to Wicker Park and back. At the halfway point, I stop outside a bar called Viva Mediterránea, on Damen north of North Avenue in the city. Never been here. The back patio, adjacent to the alley, is full of revelers tonight, people in work clothes enjoying an extended happy hour, college kids and grad students just getting started.

I stand in the alley, sweaty and the good kind of tired, and look around. To my right, Viva's back patio. To my left, the rear side of a condominium building on the next street over, a few of the condo owners out on their back patios grilling meat and enjoying a cocktail of their own.

I'm near people having fun without being elbowed and jostled. Not especially well lit, either.

Yes, this is going to be my spot. The alley behind Viva Mediterránea.

Our plan is to text twice a day, ten in the morning and eight at night, times that fit with our schedules. We will leave our phones off the rest of the time. We have to be careful. Anyone could understand why. You can't just leave your burner phone lying around to beep or ring when the wrong person—say, your spouse—happens to be near it.

It means I will have to adjust my running schedule, which is disappointing, because I love my morning runs, but there's something to be said for running in the evening, too, and this route from the law school to Viva wasn't bad at all.

I pull out my green phone, as it's 8:00 p.m., insert the SIM card, and send this:

Testing, testing . . . oh never mind. Good evening my fair lady.

She replies promptly:

> Hello stranger danger

Emphasis on the danger. I try not to think about it. But it's always going to be there. She replies again quickly:

> Just a *fair* lady?

Fair as in blond, but she's playing with me.

You are a little more than fair, I'd say. You are sexy and funny and surprising and you make my heart race a mile a minute. How's that?

She responds:

> That's more like it.

A chant goes up on the patio, the patrons at Viva. There's a TV out there, and Contreras just hit a homer for the Cubs. It's good to be young. I return my attention to the phone:

I want to do things to you.

Her reply:

> To me or with me?

That's a softball:

To you.

Bubbles, as she plays with a response. Then:

*Oh, my. For someone with such a religious name to*
*have such a naughty side . . .*

Nice. I like that. For the record, my mother didn't name me Simon Peter as a nod to a biblical character. She always wanted Simon for my first name, and Peter was her father's name. But the religious ed teachers at Saint Augustine loved to use my full name.

I reply:

**You haven't seen naughty yet.**

I smile to myself and power off the phone. I remove the SIM card and stuff them both into the pocket of my running shorts.

This way of communication will serve our purposes perfectly. As long as we're careful.

As long as we're very, very careful.

# THE DAY AFTER
# HALLOWEEN

# 17
## Jane

Sergeant Jane Burke bends down and looks carefully at Lauren Betancourt's face.

All photographs have been taken, from every conceivable angle, of Lauren dangling from the bannister, including the close-ups of where the knotty rope wound in and through the bannister's wrought iron design. It was finally time to remove the body. The lowering of her body took place under the supervision of the Cook County medical examiner, who issued instructions to the Village officers, some on ladders, some on the floor of the foyer, as the rope was untied from the bannister and the body surrendered to gravity, into a body bag placed on a gurney.

Lauren's face has scratches around her jawline, which Jane is certain will match the broken nails on her fingers, where she desperately attacked the rope wrapped around her throat. The rope abrasions make it clear that the slipknot was forced against her throat in more than one direction. There's the obvious abrasion pattern from the rope when it ultimately cut off her oxygen and snapped her neck in the hanging position. But there is another abrasion pattern running more horizontally across her throat, as if the assailant was directly behind her and yanking hard on her windpipe, just as Jane suspected, as Lauren tried to free the noose from her neck.

She knows that it may be impossible to perfectly reconstruct the events. And that may be doubly true if the assailant tried to mess with the scene, though it doesn't appear that he did. Even a pristine crime scene, her mother always explained, never tells the story precisely how it happened.

———

"Jane." Jane's partner, Sergeant Andy Tate, who is heading the neighborhood canvass, comes in through the south entry, the kitchen door.

"What's up?"

He wiggles his fingers. She follows him outside. Andy points across the street and to the north. "That white Victorian," he says. "Northwest corner of Thomas and Lathrow."

"Yeah?"

"The Dunleavy family," he says. "Including six-year-old Mary Dunleavy."

"Okay."

"Mary goes to bed last night about seven-thirty p.m. A little early for her, but she has a tummy ache. Too much Halloween candy, right?"

"Right."

"Somewhere around eight or eight-thirty, she looks out her bedroom window, which looks south."

Jane can see the window from here.

"She sees a man standing behind a tree, looking in the direction of the Betancourts' house. She said she watched him for a long time. She couldn't be more specific than a 'long time.' But she said he was staring, watching for a long time, looking in the direction of the Betancourt house. She finally got spooked enough that she went downstairs and told her mother she was scared. But she didn't say why. Not 'til today, just now."

Jane points. "That huge tree right there, on the southeast corner?"

"That one, yes."

"Tell me about the man," she says.

"He was wearing a costume. A black costume with a big, long hood. Head to toe, covered in a hood and long black robe. She never saw his face."

"Could she be more specific about the costume?"

"As a matter of fact, she could," he says, showing Jane his phone. "We went through a catalog of Halloween costumes online."

Jane looks at the image on Andy's phone and shudders. A long black robe with an elongated hood.

"All it's missing is that sickle or whatever he carries," says Andy.

Jane looks at her partner. "This is . . . the Grim Reaper?"

———

"Jane, they want you back inside."

Jane heads back in. Ria Peraino, a forensics technician with the West Suburban Major Crimes Task Force, is standing on the landing halfway up the staircase to the second floor. Jane worked with Ria on a sexual assault a couple of years ago and took a shine to her.

"We found something you'll want to see," she sings.

Jane takes the stairs carefully, Andy Tate following her. When they reach the second floor, Ria stops them. "Nobody moves except me," she says. "We have blood spatter all over this landing."

"Roger that," says Jane.

Ria carefully steps over to the far wall, stepping around evidence markers. Flush against the wall, below colorful impressionist artwork left undisturbed, is a small antique wood table, a warm brown color, probably with a fancy name like cappuccino, with scalloped legs and a storage shelf below that is empty. The table appears to have served as the base for a vase of fresh flowers (lying in pieces on the floor) and a framed photograph of Conrad and Lauren Betancourt (knocked flat on its face).

Ria looks at them with a sheepish grin, like a game-show hostess about to unveil the grand prize. With a flourish, she lifts the wood table straight up, revealing what was lying below it, nearly flush against the wall.

"A phone," Jane mumbles.

A hot-pink phone.

"Andy, call the number for Lauren's cell phone again," Jane says. "The one registered with the Village."

They hear a buzzing coming from the evidence bag holding the cell phone registered to Lauren Betancourt, one they found on the kitchen counter.

"So what is *this* phone?" Jane mumbles.

"That's a burner if I've ever seen one," says Andy. "That's no fancy iPhone or Samsung that a rich woman like Lauren Betancourt would carry around. That, my friend, is a love phone."

# BEFORE HALLOWEEN

## August

# 18
## Simon

"You wanted to see me, Dean?" I say.

"Oh, Simon, good. Come, sit." Today, Dean Comstock is wearing a purple bow tie, matching the law school's color. I've never worn a bow tie in my life. I hate bow ties.

He could come to my office. It wouldn't kill him. But it would alter the dynamic. As if he doesn't already hold enough power over me.

"I hope you've had a chance to think about what we discussed."

Yeah, we *discussed* that you wanted me to go away quietly and let your benefactor's son, Reid Southern, waltz into the full professor slot without opposition.

"I promised you I'd consider it carefully," I say. "I am."

And yet, I still haven't withdrawn my name for full professor. I haven't completed my application, haven't submitted my materials, but I still could. I still have a few weeks left before the deadline.

Why, exactly, I have not officially pulled the plug is anyone's guess. Maybe it's my passive-aggressive protest against the dean strong-arming me, making him wait to wonder whether I will submit my materials at the last minute and defy him.

Or maybe I really am going to submit my materials. Vicky has made her opinion clear, and she has a way of moving the needle with me.

The dean apparently had something different in mind. He figured I would formally withdraw my name immediately after our talk before summer break. Who knows, maybe he promised as much to Reid Southern's daddy, Mr. Big Bucks. Which means I am making him look bad. Can't have that, can we?

"I hope you understand that I had your best interests in mind, truly," says he.

I nod my head, because if I tried to give a socially acceptable response, I'd probably vomit.

"Simon." With that, he leans back in his big leather chair. "I'm sure you can understand that these days, the law school has to be exceptionally careful about questions of character among its faculty."

Then why are *you* here, Dean?

"Of course," I say.

"These days, as you know, we have to be exceptionally careful not only about a candidate's character but about his . . . his past."

I blink.

Then I do a slow burn, as he watches me.

"Why, we've all seen examples of people losing their positions of prominence these days for things that happened as long as . . . twelve, even fifteen years ago."

Twelve years ago. Fifteen years ago. He didn't pick those numbers at random.

You've been busy, Dean.

"Particularly when the choice of candidates is so close, such as between you and Reid," he says. "The smallest thing could make the difference."

He's smiling. He's actually enjoying himself.

"Of course, if the choice were obvious, as it might be if you were to apply next time," he says with that condescending ponderous look, "it might not be necessary to dig so deeply. Why, I doubt anyone would so much as *inquire* what a young fellow was doing with himself some twelve years ago."

Some twelve years ago. Some twelve years ago.

"But in a close competition like this one . . ." I say, trying to keep my voice steady.

He opens his hand. "People naturally look for tiebreakers, for a slight edge to one side. They dig more deeply. They look into the candidate's entire history. Even things that the candidate forgot to mention back when he first applied to the school."

My jaw clenching so tight it hurts. My teeth grinding together. Black spots clouding my vision.

"I was under no obligation to disclose that," I whisper.

"Understood, Simon, understood," he says. "And the presumption of innocence, as well. Nothing was ever proven, obviously. I just wonder . . . how things will go for you if that were to be publicly disclosed? The whole court fight and everything."

Yes, the whole court fight and everything.

"Which is why I say again, I have only your best interests in mind when I suggest that now might not be the best time to apply for the position."

My eyes slowly rise to his. To his credit, he doesn't look away. He holds that smarmy smirk, but he doesn't look away.

"And if I withdraw my application?" I say.

"Well, then, there's no need for anyone to be concerned with ancient history," he says. "Which, as far as I'm concerned, is exactly what it is."

# 19

## Vicky

I get back from the day shift at the shelter—buying groceries, a group counseling session, trying to fix the broken A/C window unit in the dorm upstairs—near six o'clock. I pull into the alley behind the house and park in the alley garage. I walk through the backyard, the tall shrubbery and its privacy, and through the rear door of the house to the alarm's *ding-dong* and sultry electronic female voice, *Back door*.

I don't hear Simon banging around. Not downstairs in the den or upstairs.

"Hello?" I call out.

I put down my bag and wander toward the stairs. "Simon?"

Nothing. The shower isn't running. I'd hear the water.

"Simon Peter Dobias!"

Maybe he's not home. He said he would be. Maybe he decided to go for a run. That boy and his running.

I walk up the stairs. "Hello-o," I sing.

I hear something. Something above. I go into the hallway. The stairs have been pulled down from the ceiling. He's on the rooftop deck.

I take the stairs up, open the storm door, and step onto the wooden deck. Simon is sitting on one of the lawn chairs he's put up here, gripping a bottle of Jack Daniel's.

"Hey," I call out.

He turns, waves me over. "Didn't hear you," he says, but he's slurring his words.

"You okay?"

I sit in the other lawn chair but turn to face him. Yep, glassy eyes. He's thrown a few back, all right.

I take the bottle from his hand. "What happened?"

"'What happened?'" He pushes himself out of the chair, opens his arms as if preaching to the masses. "What happened? What happened is he knows, that's what happened."

"Who knows what?"

"Dean Cumstain, as you call him." He raises his chin and nods. "Come to think of it, I'm gonna call him that, too."

"Knows *what*, Simon? What does the dean know?"

"He *knows*." He turns and stumbles. He's not close to the edge of the roof, but he's starting to make me nervous.

"Simon—"

"Twelve years ago, I believe it was!" he calls out like a circus announcer, whirling around to his audience in all directions.

Twelve year—

Oh, no. Oh, shit.

"The year of 2010! I believe it involved a grand jury looking into the murder of a prominent—"

"Hey." I grab him by both arms, put my forehead against his. "Keep your voice down. Someone might hear you."

"I don't care—"

"Yes, you *do*," I hiss, holding his arms as he tries to break free. "Quit acting like an idiot and talk to me. Let me help."

"I am so fucked," Simon says, slumped over the wooden railing of the roof deck, head in his hands. "The dean owns me now."

I run my hand up and down his back. "You aren't fucked. We're gonna figure this out."

"There's nothing to figure out. He's got me by the short hairs."

"What does he have? That court opinion didn't name you—"

"Oh, come on, Vick." He turns to me, ashen, shaken. "It might as well have. It would take anyone with a brain about five seconds to figure out that the court of appeals was talking about me in that opinion. 'A male family member,' they wrote. Another place, they said the 'family member' was twenty-four years old. How many family members did my father have, period, much less a man who was twenty-four in May of 2010? Mom was dead, I'm an only child, and so was my dad. He didn't have a wife, any other children, any brothers or sisters, nieces or neph—"

"Okay, okay." I take his hand. "I get it. If anyone read the opinion and knew the context, they'd know it was you."

"And they'd ask me, anyway," he says. "If this came to the attention of the faculty and the tenure committee, they'd just come out and ask me to confirm that the subject of that judicial opinion was me. I'd have to say yes."

"You wouldn't *have* to."

He shoots me a look. "Even if I were willing to lie about it, which I'm not—nobody would believe me. Then I'd be a liar, too, if being a murder suspect weren't enough."

"Oh, stop with this 'murder suspect' crap," I say. "He's been dead twelve years, Simon. I don't see anyone putting you in handcuffs."

"Yeah, and guess why? Read the opinion. I got off on a technicality—that's what everyone will think."

"You're overreacting. You think a bunch of law professors, of all people, wouldn't appreciate the importance of a therapist/patient privilege?"

"Sure, they would. They'd probably agree with the court's decision, too. But that doesn't mean I didn't murder my father."

I have no answer for that. He's right. I'm trying to rally him, but he's right. This judicial opinion has been lurking out there all along, for the last twelve years, talking about a subpoena issued by a grand jury investigating the murder of Theodore Dobias at his home in St. Louis, Missouri, where he moved after Glory died and Simon disowned him. It didn't name Simon specifically, but it described a twenty-four-year-old male who was a member of Ted's family—and Simon's right, only he could possibly qualify.

The St. Louis County district attorney was interested in a phone call Simon made to his psychotherapist in the early morning after the night Ted was found dead in his pool, stabbed to death. The grand jury subpoenaed his therapist to testify, but she refused to answer on the grounds of privilege. Simon hired a lawyer and fought the case up to the court of appeals, which ruled in Simon's favor. Nobody got to ask the shrink what Simon said to her that morning.

The police probably still think Simon killed his father, but realized, at some point, they couldn't prove it. And Simon's right. It will look like he was never charged because of a legal technicality. If the tenure committee hears about this, Simon is finished.

Simon has wandered into the middle of the massive rooftop deck, hands on his hips, looking around. "My mom and dad would dance up here," he says. "I ever tell you that?"

I walk up to him. "No."

"Oh, yeah, they'd come up with a bottle of wine and a little boom box and play music and dance. Sometimes Mom would sing. She was an awful singer, but boy, she didn't care." He gestures to the chairs. "Sometimes we'd have a little picnic up here, and I'd sit over in the chair with my juice box and sandwich while they danced. You should've . . ."

His head drops. He rubs his neck.

"You should've seen how she looked at my dad. I remember thinking how great it must be to have someone look at you like that."

I touch his arm.

"I'm sorry," he says. "I'm . . . I've had too much to drink."

I put my arms around him, put my face against his chest. "Dance with *me*," I whisper.

We rock back and forth. I'm no singer, probably no better than his mother, so we sway to the street sounds below, kids playing and shouting, music from passing vehicles, some help from birds chirping nearby. He presses me tightly against him. I can feel his heart pounding.

Simon deserves someone who will look at him the way his mother looked at his father. He deserves more than I can give him.

"I don't know what it was, why she was so taken with him," he says. "When you're a kid, you don't realize—I mean, they're just your parents. In hindsight, I mean, she was twenty times the person he was in every way, but God, she just swooned over him. He was everything to her. And then when he—when he—"

"I know," I whisper. "I know."

"It just broke her. Y'know? It just . . . *broke* her."

It broke Simon, too, as it does now, as he chokes back tears.

I rub his back. "It's all gonna be okay," I tell him. "Everything will turn out fine."

"I wish I was so confident."

"Let me help you with this problem," I say. "Let me help you with the dean."

"No." Simon breaks away from me and wags his finger. "No. Thank you, but no."

"Why not? You said it yourself. The dean owns you. If you buckle the moment he raises your past, he'll know he always has this over you. You'll never get out from under his thumb."

"I don't care. I'll . . . go to another school or something."

"But you'll obsess about this the rest of your life, Simon. I know you. You'll obsess about Dean Cumstain and Reid Southern like you obsess over that high school jock Mitchell Kitchens."

He picks up the bottle of Jack and takes another pull, the wind carrying his bangs. "I don't obsess about him."

"Ha!"

He looks at me and starts to reply but thinks better of it. Simon has often joked that he has Irish Alzheimer's—he only remembers the slights, the grudges.

"This is different," he says. "This is my career. This is what I've chosen to do with my life. I don't want this to be . . . I don't know . . . tainted, I guess. I don't want to get this position because I turned the tables on the dean and blackmailed him or something."

"You won't get the position unless the faculty votes you in, unless you get it on merit," I say. "All you're doing is making sure the dean doesn't sabotage you."

He shakes his head, long and slowly. "No, Vicky. I'm not doing it."

Simon heads off to bed drunk and depressed, and past his bedtime, given how early he gets up in the morning. I tuck him in and head down the hall to the office.

I told Christian Newsome I'd show him the trust language that restricts how Simon spends his trust—how it cuts his wife off from any access to the money until ten years of marriage.

I pull up the PDF of the amendment to the Theodore Dobias Trust that gave Simon his money, but with the string attached. I fix on that language, that wonderful little surprise that Ted left Simon on his death:

> (a) In the event SIMON gets married to an individual ("SPOUSE"), the proceeds of this trust may not be spent in any way by or for the benefit of SPOUSE for a period of ten (10) years following the first day of SIMON's marriage to SPOUSE. This restriction includes, but is not limited to, the following: (1) expenditures on anything that would jointly benefit both SIMON and SPOUSE, including but not limited to . . .

What an asshole, to do that to Simon against his wishes. Give him the money or don't. But to do what he did, to hog-tie Simon like that, to put his foot on the chest of Simon's marriage before it even starts? Talk about emasculating.

And, of course, there's this:

> In and only in the event that SIMON and SPOUSE remain married for the period of ten (10) years, and no petition for dissolution of marriage has been filed by either SIMON or SPOUSE within that time, the restriction on the expenditure of proceeds in paragraph (a) above shall cease to operate.

If you stay married to Simon for ten years like a good girl, "spouse," and if nobody's even filed for divorce within those ten years, "spouse," then you can put your greedy, grimy hands on the money. Because then you'll have earned it, "spouse."

Why so cynical, Teddy? Not every woman marries for money.

Only some do.

In the corner of the room, the printer starts grinding and spitting out the pages of the trust. My phone rings, a FaceTime call from my nieces, the M&Ms, Mariah and Macy. I throw in my AirPods so the noise won't awaken Simon.

When I answer, it's only Mariah, the thirteen-year-old, on the call. As best as I can make out through the grainy image, she doesn't look happy. No one can perfect a frown better than a thirteen-year-old girl.

"Hi, pumpkin!" I say, trying to keep my voice down, closing the office door.

"It happened," she says.

It— Oh, right.

"Okay. Well, okay. We knew this would be coming, right?"

She nods, but her face wrinkles into a grimace.

"It's okay, Mariah, it's normal, perfectly normal. You put a pad on?"

She nods her head, tears falling. It's emotional enough, getting your period the first time; not having your mother around, and having all that come back, too, doubles the fun.

"Great! So listen, did you talk to your dad?"

"No!" she spits out.

"Well, honey, you can't keep this from your father. He knows it's coming, too."

Yes, her father, my ex-brother-in-law, Adam, knows that adolescent girls get their period. And without a wife, without a woman in the home, he's been terrified of this moment. Men have no clue about the female anatomy.

"When are you . . . when are you coming?" she manages.

"I'll come this weekend, honey, okay? I'll come Friday night and stay the weekend."

"Okay," she whines, "but when are you coming for good?"

Oh, that. "November," I say. "Remember, I told you—"

"But November's over two months away!"

I take a breath. November's more than two months away, yes, but it feels like it's coming quickly.

"Mariah, honey, I will be here anytime you want to call me between now and November. I'll come see you this weekend. I'll spend the whole weekend. We'll get milkshakes at that place you like."

"Barton's."

"Barton's. It'll be fun. Really," I say, "November will be here before you know it."

---

When I'm done with Mariah, I walk down the hallway to check on Simon. He's peacefully asleep, having drunken dreams about grand juries and law school deans.

I'm leaving in November, no doubt. It's best for everyone, Simon and me both, and those girls need me closer. But I can't leave Simon like this. Not with his future at the law school twisting in the wind.

Because that's exactly where things stand. If Simon lets the dean hold his past over him, he might as well pack up now and leave. And that would kill him. He could teach elsewhere, sure, but he loves Chicago, and he loves his law school.

He'll always have that look he had on his face tonight. The look of defeat, resignation.

No. I won't let that happen. I'm done asking for Simon's permission. This dean is mine.

I pick up my phone and dial Rambo's number.

*"Miss Vicky!"* he calls out from his speakerphone. *"Isn't this past your bedtime?"*

"I need your services again," I say. "When can we meet?"

# 20
## Simon

I don't "obsess" about Mitchell Kitchens. I just think about him sometimes.

There was the "Mini-Me" nickname, of course. He'd pick the most embarrassing times to use it. Coming off the bus every morning in front of the others. In front of a hallway full of students. Sometimes he'd find me in the crowd at a school assembly. He even said it once in front of my mother, on a day she had to pick me up from the principal's office because I was sick, and we passed through the gym while Mitchell was working out with the other wrestlers on a mat. (The gym teacher was the wrestling coach, so while everyone else had a regular phys-ed curriculum, the wrestlers all had the same gym class and they just used it as a regular wrestling practice in addition to the one after school.)

Anyway, my mother and I were passing through the gym, and there's Mitchell calling out, "It's Mini-Me! Hey, Mini-Me!" I didn't respond. I knew what that usually meant—he'd yell louder and keep at it until I acknowledged him, until he'd thoroughly humiliated me. But I figured that with my mother standing there, he'd back down. He didn't.

My mother stopped on a dime and turned in his direction. She didn't speak. I didn't even see the look on her face, but I could imagine it. Knowing my mother and her wicked intellect and verbal skills, she probably had a dozen comments at the ready that would have left a Neanderthal like Mitchell mute. But she just stared him down, and then we kept walking.

She never brought it up. She must have known how humiliating it was, and she probably decided that she would leave it to me to raise it. I never did.

I wish it had stopped at the nickname. That was bad enough. But it didn't stop there.

Not pleasant memories. So it's a good thing I don't obsess about him.


Anshu is just arriving at his office down the hall from mine, just fitting his key into the door, when I'm heading to my eight o'clock class.

"Professor Bindra," I say. "You're in early."

"Meetings, meetings, and more meetings," he says. "The perks of being a full professor. Hey, you should apply to be one! It's not too late!"

"Don't start."

Anshu doesn't know the full story. He knows the dean asked me to hold off and let Reid Southern apply without opposition. He doesn't know about my second visit with the dean and the not-so-veiled threats. And he never will. That's the beauty of what the dean did to me—he knows I can't reveal it without revealing the story behind it.

I'm lucky the story didn't come out at the time up here in Chicago. It was the locale, I think, that kept it out of the Chicago media. By the time he was murdered, my father hadn't been a lawyer in Chicago for several years; he was then practicing in downstate Madison County, where asbestos litigation made a lot of lawyers rich and a lot of companies bankrupt, and living across the border in St. Louis. So the murder, investigation, and court fight happened in a different state altogether.

When the police up here searched my house, I was sure everything would spill out to the newspapers. But it didn't. What spared me, oddly enough, was road construction on my block. The two squad cars and the forensics team truck had to park in the alley behind my house instead of out front. Other than my neighbors the Dearborns, who weren't in town at the time, nobody could see the cops coming and going into the back entrance of my house. The Grace Park Police assisted on the search, but they didn't leak to the press. A few of my neighbors probably wondered what the hell was going on, but if they did, nobody said anything to me. I was hardly around, anyway, commuting every day to school.

I kept waiting for some headline. POLICE RAID HOME OF MURDER VICTIM'S SON. GRACE PARK MAN PROBED IN ST. LOUIS MURDER. Something like that. But it never happened. For months, years, I held my breath, waiting for the other shoe to drop and all of this to be exposed. When they tried to talk to Dr. McMorrow about our conversation the morning after my father's murder, and I had to fight up to the Missouri Court of Appeals to keep that conversation confidential, I was certain this would all become news. But it never did. It did in St. Louis, but never up in Chicago.

I never disclosed it when I applied to be a professor. Why should I? What was there to disclose? I was kinda, sorta a suspect in a murder, but nothing came of it?

Well, I was more than kinda, sorta a suspect. But nothing ever came of it.

I'm not sure what the police expected to find in the search of my home. Did they think that a murderer would be dumb enough to leave a bunch of evidence lying around his house?

It was almost insulting.

"Do you really think, if I was going to kill my father," I said to them, the cops, back then, when they hauled me down to St. Louis for questioning, "that I would pick the night before my last final exam in college to do it? What, I'd drive all the way from Grace Park down to St. Louis, stab him in the stomach, then drive another six hours back up, basically get no sleep, then take my last final exam at eight in the morning? What kind of sense would that make?"

"It wouldn't," said the cop taking the lead on the case, a detective named Rick Gully. "Which is why it's the perfect alibi."

It was hard not to smile.

I got an A on that final, by the way.

"Thank you, Maria," I say, clapping my hands once. "So the majority held that the police can root through your garbage and obtain evidence of a crime against you without first obtaining a warrant. What did Justice Brennan have to say about that? Anyone besides Maria, who has admirably shouldered the burden so far?"

I dislike the Socratic method, calling on students and grilling them mercilessly. I hated the stress in law school, the anticipation, the dread as you sat in the class and the law professor looked up and down the roll call for the student who'd be put under the laser heat that hour.

Make no mistake, once they volunteer, I'll work them over. They know that. But there are ways to do it that promote critical examination and debate, that hone and sharpen their focus, and ways that do not. Fear, in my mind, does not.

"Brad," I say, when he raises his hand.

"Justice Brennan disagreed," he says.

"Yes, Brad, that would be the very definition of a dissent, I believe, but thank you for that reminder. Could I trouble you to elaborate, kind sir?" I bow.

"He said that when people seal up their garbage, they expect it to remain private. We throw things out because we have to throw things out, but we don't expect that someone will open it up and go through it."

"But we expect garbage collectors to take it," I say. "Do we not?"

"We expect them to take our trash and toss it in some landfill," he says. "Not take it and open it and look through it."

"But isn't putting your trash out on the curb the very definition of abandoning your possessory interest in it? Aren't you saying to the world, I don't want this stuff anymore?"

"I mean, I guess so."

"So once you've abandoned your property, why do you have the right to expect anything whatsoever from it? Why do you have the right to object to what happens to it?"

There are many answers to that question, many distinctions and subtleties—the lifeblood of the law, what makes it so glorious. The most important part of law school isn't the ABCs but learning how to think, how to find those distinctions, how to advocate for your position, how to highlight your strengths and minimize your weaknesses. How to fight with passion and reason.

After my early class, I walk down from the law school to the Chicago Title & Trust Building and make it there by ten. Once in the lobby with my Starbucks, I insert the SIM card and power on my green phone. I text:

And how are we this morning?

She replies quickly:

> *Well, hello, stranger*

It's become her standard start. My response:

Stranger? I don't think I can be any stranger than I already am.

She replies:

> *Then how about: hello tall, dark and handsome*

That brings a smile to my face. I'm not that tall, my hair is not all that dark, and "handsome" is overstated, but that's good. I'm even willing to overlook that she didn't use the Oxford comma. My phone vibrates again:

> *You're not strange you're enigmatic*

Nice of her to say so. But no, I'm strange. My phone vibrates again:

> *I like your darkness. I like being your light.*

I breathe out a sigh. At least one thing's going right in my life.

# 21

***Tuesday, August 30, 2022***

*This is a joyous, thrilling ride, but the end is a cliff. Is this what it feels like to be addicted to a drug, to ingest something because nothing in the present is so important as the feeling that pill or powder gives you, even while you know that the course you're on will lead to destruction? You do it anyway, ~~because you~~ No, it's not enough to say that "you do it anyway"—you not only do it, but you want nothing more than to do it, you embrace self-demolition over all else. Does that mean, perhaps, that was the point of it all along, the self-destruction, but you can't be honest enough with yourself to admit it, so you wrap it up in something superficially and temporarily pleasurable like the high from a pill?*

*I mean, if the point really is self-destruction, why not save everyone the time and just find a knife or a gun and end it all? You don't do that, do you? No, because it's not the end you want but the suffering, the pain, the decline, the growing ruin as your body breaks down or your bank account empties or you fail those you love, you want to see yourself slowly degrade. You want to punish yourself.*

*Is that what I'm doing with you? Are you my addiction, Lauren? Am I punishing myself, allowing myself to get wrapped up in you again and knowing that you'll just leave me again? Am I barreling toward a cliff?*

*Sometimes I feel that way, when I'm lying in bed at night, thinking about what we're doing and where we're headed, plagued with this sense of disbelief that anything like this could be real. I question your love. I question your commitment. I convince myself that you will wake up one day, ask yourself what is so great about me, and not like the answer.*

*If that happens, I don't know what I'll do. Nothing else in my life makes sense right now but you.*

# THE DAY AFTER HALLOWEEN

# 22

## Jane

"Okay, let's hear it," says Chief Ray Carlyle, popping into the conference room they've commandeered at the station. He's been back in town for ninety minutes, stopping first at the Betancourt house, where Jane took him around and updated him.

Sergeant Jane Burke looks up, blinks, adjusts her eyes. Age thirty-seven, she's always had excellent vision and only recently flirted with the idea of getting cheaters for close-up reading. After spending the last forty-five minutes going over transcripts of text messages from the pink phone found in Lauren Betancourt's house, she's wishing she had some right now.

Outside the conference room, the house is buzzing. All hands on deck. All twelve patrol officers currently on duty are coordinating with the Major Crimes forensics team, four of the six sergeants in-house, the chief and deputy chief giving this their undivided attention as well. Most of Jane's job now, she realizes, will simply consist of managing all these people.

"Lauren's burner phone only texted with one other phone," she says. "No calls. Just texts. Well, a few missed calls just before Halloween, but otherwise—just texts."

"So the phones had a specific purpose."

"Very," says Sergeant Andy Tate. "Like we thought. These two were having an affair."

"No names, I take it?"

"That would be too easy." Jane flips a stack of the printouts to him. "They were very careful. Careful in all ways. They texted each other twice a day, at ten in the morning and eight at night. Occasionally, they'd miss a text session, but when they did text, it was only at those designated times."

Chief Carlyle nods. "It worked for them, those times. They had to be free of their spouses. Or at least Lauren did. Who knows if her special guy was married?"

"On our first run through these messages, it wasn't clear to us whether he was or wasn't," says Andy Tate. "But we're going to pore over every detail. Careful or not, there must be something here."

"Let's start with the punch line, Chief," says Jane. "The last text the offender ever sent. It's alone on the last page."

Chief Carlyle picks up the stack of printouts and flips to the final page. Jane reads along herself:

*Mon, Oct 31, 10:47 PM*

I'm sorry, Lauren. I'm sorry for what
I did and I'm sorry you didn't love
me. But I'm not sorry for loving you
like nobody else could. I'm coming
to you now. I hope you'll accept me
and let me love you in a way you
wouldn't in this world.

"Huh. 'I'm sorry for what I did.' So we have a confession. 'I'm coming to you now . . . Let me love you in a way you wouldn't in this world.' So our offender decided to do everyone a favor and take his own life?" The chief looks at Jane. "Any chance he was good enough to let us know where he was going to commit that selfless act?"

"We have an area-wide bulletin out for suspicious deaths last night," says Jane. "We'll know soon enough."

The chief smirks. "Any indication how it came to this point?"

"The last night in particular," says Jane. "Halloween night. Flip two pages forward."

Chief Carlyle flips there. Jane reads along with the chief, the communications on October 31, after trick-or-treating ended:

**UNKNOWN CALLER**                    **VICTIM'S PHONE (EVIDENCE #1)**

*Mon, Oct 31, 8:09 PM*

Trick or treat?

*Mon, Oct 31, 8:12 PM*

Hello? Are you home? I need to talk
to you.

*Mon, Oct 31, 8:14 PM*

Testing . . . testing . . . 1, 2, 3 . . .
testing, testing . . . 1, 2, 3

                                      *Mon, Oct 31, 8:15 PM*

                                      Not home, told you out of town

*Mon, Oct 31, 8:16 PM*

That's strange coulda sworn I just
saw you walking through the
family room I must be seeing
ghosts!

                                      *Mon, Oct 31, 8:16 PM*

                                      You're outside my house????

*Mon, Oct 31, 8:17 PM*

Just want to talk that's all

                                      *Mon, Oct 31, 8:18 PM*

                                      Nothing to talk about please go
                                      home please!

*Mon, Oct 31, 8:18 PM*

Let me in treat me like an adult. I
know you still love me. Why
pretend you don't?

*Mon, Oct 31, 8:19 PM*

Go home ACT like an adult I'm sorry you know I am but it's over

*Mon, Oct 31, 8:21 PM*

What are you doing have you lost your mind??

*Mon, Oct 31, 8:22 PM*

Stop kicking my door I'm going to call the police

*Mon, Oct 31, 8:23 PM*

Go ahead call them I dare you

*Mon, Oct 31, 8:25 PM*

I will let you in if you promise to be calm

*Mon, Oct 31, 8:26 PM*

I promise I swear

The chief whistles. "Fuck if *that's* not a theory of the case. She soured on him and dumped him. He couldn't handle it. He stands outside the house, lurking around. He texts her, she lies about not being home, he calls her on it because he sees her through the window. He makes a scene outside, kicking the door. So she lets him inside the house. And he kills her."

"While wearing a Grim Reaper costume," Andy adds. "On a dark, dark night."

"Well, he can wear whatever costume he wants," says the chief. "He won't get far now."

# BEFORE HALLOWEEN

September

# 23

## Vicky

After Labor Day, I return to Christian's office, a four o'clock appointment again. When I'm done reading his proposal, I look up at him. Still rough-shaven and handsome, same basic kind of expensive dark suit with the open collar, still that cocky look about him like someone who knows to-day's going to be another "win" for him.

"Water?" I say.

"It's the next big thing," says Christian. "Water is becoming a scarcity. That will become truer and truer as the population growth continues to spike. Less than one-tenth of one percent of the world's water can be used to feed and nourish seven, eight billion people."

"Wow."

"Exactly," he says, pointing his pen at me. "So how do we tap into that possibility? We could invest in water-rich areas and transport the water, but that's a nonstarter. The barriers to entry are too high."

"The barriers . . . ?"

"It's hard to transport water. You need pipelines, which raises all kinds of issues. They're expensive, they're politically unpopular, they raise property-rights issues. They disturb ecosystems. And think about it—we're moving water away from its original source. The ripple effect on the environment—water life, plant life, coastlines—could be cata-strophic."

"So what do you do instead?"

"The way to invest in water is through food. It's the least contentious, least controversial way to redistribute water. You don't transport the water. You *grow food* in water-rich areas and transport it for sale in water-poor areas. You have any idea how much water it takes to produce even small quantities of food? It takes nearly two thousand gallons of water to ultimately produce one pound of beef off a cow. And selling food is profitable, right? So that guarantees sustainable redistribution. Meaning, industry won't stop doing it."

"So you're buying up farmland."

"Right. You see the returns we've already gotten. I've already given my investors over a three hundred percent ROI. The next five years are going to be even better. You give me twenty-one million dollars, I'll give you a hundred million in five years. I promise you, Vicky, I will take you for the ride of your life."

I take a breath. The ride of my life, indeed. When I was six, I had to tie a shoelace around my left shoe because the sole had come off completely and we couldn't afford new ones. I walked with a limp that entire year, just to keep my shoe on. When I was eighteen and on my own, I started donating my plasma once a week for the money. When I was twenty, I fucked my landlord to pay the rent.

When I don't answer, Christian says, "Or, if you're risk averse, give me ten million and I'll turn it into fifty. We'll put your other ten in Asian equities. That's going to blow sky-high, too, though not as much as water. But the diversification might give you comfort."

By the time I was twenty-four, sex was the only way I knew how to survive. It was transactional. I was an escort living in Indianapolis. I met a woman early on who taught me that the best way to survive as a prostitute was to have some cops for clients. They'd make sure you never got arrested; they'd stand up for you if someone got rough with you. My clients were mostly married men with money who were looking for a thrill on the side. And cops. And when it wasn't a direct trade, it was an indirect one. I learned how to make men do things for me. Expensive dinners that ended up in my bedroom or his, but for me it was about having two days of leftovers in the fridge.

The sums of money Christian is talking about, they're as real to me as flying to Mars.

"Or," he says, "we don't do any of that."

I snap out of my fog and focus on him.

"Listen, Vicky, this isn't for everybody," he says. "My investors, they love the upside of my investments and aren't that concerned with the downside. They can risk twenty million in the market because they have plenty more. You don't. I get that. And look, twenty million dollars is a lot of money. You could sit on it, invest in low-risk bond funds and some index funds, live mostly off the interest, and cut into the principal slowly. You can be comfortable. Your whole life, you'll be very, very comfortable. If that's where your head is—then you should do that. I could put that together for you. Or you could use one of those other financial advisers you interviewed. No hard feelings. This isn't a hard sell."

I look up from the proposal. "You'd put together a low-risk portfolio for me?"

"If that's what you prefer."

"But you don't do that. I mean, everything I've read about you—that's not your game."

"No, it isn't. Actually, I've never done it before."

"But you'd do it for me."

He lifts a shoulder. "I would."

"Why?" I prod.

"I . . . like you," he says. "I like your style."

That's what I thought.

I slowly nod my head. He keeps my eye contact. Finally, I break it, looking over at the leather couch in the corner. Then back at him. He's still looking at me.

"You have any other appointments today?"

He pauses a beat. "I do not," he says.

"When does your receptionist leave?"

He looks over toward the door, more confident now that he's reading this correctly. "Five o'clock," he says.

"Maybe give her a break today, let her off early," I suggest.

Now he's sure, and he knows how to handle it. "I could do that."

I smirk. "Then do it."

He pushes a button on his phone. "Emily, I don't have anything else today. Why don't you take off a little early?"

I stand up and unbutton my dress, taking my time with each button, watching him watch me. My dress drops to the floor. I step my heels out of it and lean over the table.

"I'm going with option one, Mr. Newsome," I say. "Take me for the ride of my life."

# 24

## Vicky

"Maybe you had a point about water," I say. "Because I need some right now." I untangle my sweaty body from Christian's and get off the couch.

"In the fridge by the bar," he says. "Where are my manners?" He has that smug, self-satisfied look that men have after they think they've rocked my world.

He was fine. Not as good as he thought he was, but fine. He knew what he was doing. It's just that I've never gotten to the point that I find intimacy in sex. Brief, raw pleasure is the most I can get from it, on a good day.

I grab a bottle for each of us and return to the couch. He does a sit-up to get to the seated position, allowing him one more opportunity to show me his ripped abdominal muscles. He's got a great body, I'll give him that. The guy must spend hours a day in the gym honing it. Whoever compared bodybuilding to masturbation had a point.

Christian takes a drink from the bottle and lets out a satisfied sigh. "Well, Mrs. Dobias, that was . . ."

Don't say amazing. Please don't.

". . . fun."

"You have a lot of energy," I say.

"You bring it out in me."

"I'll bet you say that to all the girls." I take a drink of water and find my phone. It's a quarter to seven. We've been going at it for over two hours. I'm going to be sore tomorrow. I'm out of practice. I haven't had sex for months.

"Can I ask you a question?" he says.

"Shoot."

"Have you ever done this before?"

I pull on my underwear, hook up my bra. "Do you want me to answer that?"

"I do."

"Are you sure? You wouldn't prefer to remain in your male-fantasy bubble, that you're the only one who can unleash the tigress inside me?"

"Wow," he says, though he chuckles.

I lean over him, face-to-face. "No, Christian, I have never done anything like this before. I've been a very good girl for the last ten years."

I put my dress back on, a little wrinkled now. As he's pulling on his trousers, Christian says, "By the way, we never circled back on that trust language."

"What about it?"

"I've never seen language quite like that, but your take on it is accurate. It's valid and enforceable. You must stay married for ten years before you can touch that money."

"Tell me about it. But what about my question?"

"Whether you can spend it, without his approval, once you have it."

I turn and look at him. "That was my question, yes."

He gives me a poker face for a moment, then winks. "Yes, you can. My lawyer will draw up something just to lock that down and if Simon will sign it, you have no worries. You spend that money however you want. You're probably okay either way, but best if he signs it."

"He'll sign it," I say. "He trusts me."

We both pause on the irony of that statement.

"I care about him," I say. "I don't want him to get hurt. That's not my intention."

"Of course not." He waves a hand. "With the money I'll make you, whatever else happens, he'll be rich beyond his wildest dreams."

I nod, look away, start gathering my things.

"What happens next?" he says to me.

"Meaning what? I'll get him to sign whatever form you give me."

"No," he says. "I meant . . . this. Us."

I look at him.

"Whatever you decide is fine," he says. "No pressure."

"Doesn't the girl usually ask that question?"

He laughs. "Maybe so."

"Well, now the girl's asking," I say. "You tell me. Where is this going?"

"I'm . . ." He flips his hand. "I already told you, I like you. I'm bullish if you are."

This time it's my turn to wink.

"I'll be in touch," I say. Always keep 'em wanting more.

# 25

## Christian

After jackhammering Vicky on my office couch for the last two hours, I make it home near eight o'clock. Sex with a married woman is the best, because you're their outlet, their Discovery Channel, not their dumpy old husbands they bang out of obligation or gratitude. You should see some of the things I've gotten married women to do.

Speaking of couches—Gavin's already on mine in my apartment, a beer in his hand, tooling around on his laptop. "The fuck?" he says. "You're late. Hope you at least got laid." He looks up at me as I walk in. "Oh, you *did* get laid. Who's the lucky mental patient?"

I make a motion, a jump shot. "He shoots . . . he scores! The crowd can't believe it!"

"No shit? Number 7? The one with the twenty mil and the huge rack?"

We don't use names. He's never heard Vicky's name and he never will. Vicky, to Gavin, is just "Number 7." My seventh target.

That anonymity, that Chinese wall, keeps our friendship out of trouble. I don't want to know what Gavin's doing with his financial scams, and he doesn't want to know what I'm doing with mine. No matter how much I trust Gavin, my friend since childhood, if he ever gets caught in his own scams, he might be tempted to lighten his load by flipping on me. And he has the same thing to fear from me, vice versa. I don't think he'd ever give me up, and I don't think I'd ever do that to him if the feds ever nabbed me, but it keeps things light and clean by removing the potential.

No, in this apartment, Vicky Lanier Dobias is just "Number 7." When

Gavin put together the financial plan for her, he left the name blank. I just typed it in and hit "print."

"I fucking got her, G. Reeled her in like a largemouth bass."

He puts down his laptop. "Well, Nicky Bag-o-Donuts, good for you."

I take a grand bow.

"Do tell," he says. "I need some deets."

I grab a bottle of Scotch from the bar in my condo. I moved back to Chicago this summer, after finishing my last job. Number 6 lived in Lexington, Kentucky, a fifty-three-year-old woman who left her husband for me and took a million in a lump-sum divorce settlement that she gave to me to invest. I skedaddled, of course, and laid low for a few months before returning for the summer to Chicago, where Gavin lives and not far from where we grew up.

"A gentleman never kisses and tells," I say.

"Okay, well, let me know if a *gentleman* shows up. In the meantime, throw me a bone here. You get laid twenty times more than me."

"Twenty times zero?" I pour a couple fingers of Scotch, raise it in salute, and swallow it, followed by a satisfying smack.

"C'mon, Nick."

I wag my finger. "Don't call me that."

"Oh, sorry. *Christian.* Why the fuck would you pick a name like that for a cover?"

I swallow another pour of the Scotch. I prefer hard alcohol—no carbs. "Because nobody would pick a name like 'Christian' for a cover."

If I had my druthers, Gavin wouldn't know my alias. It's the one flaw in my plan to segregate our friendship from our professional relationship. But he creates my fake identity and everything that comes with it—fake credit and employment history, fake driver's license and credit cards, fake diplomas and certifications, even those fake news articles from *Fortune* and *Newsweek*. He couldn't do that without knowing the name Christian Newsome.

I drop down in a chair. "I'm telling you, G, this is it. I thought Number 5 was big."

"Number 5 was the one in Milwaukee? She *was* big. She was good for a couple mil, right?"

"Yeah. I mean, it was a gold mine at the time. But this one? Number 7? Twenty million dollars? I get this, I'm done. I retire at age thirty-fucking-four. I hit the lottery."

"She liked the proposal? The water stuff? The Asian equities?"

"Ate it up. It's real, right? You said it was real."

"I mean, basically, yeah," he says. "People are speculating in water right now. But a return like you promised in five years? No freakin' way. But what does she know?"

"I don't know," I say. "I don't care."

He shakes his head. "Why do you get all the good luck? Me, I'm busting my ass for fifty, maybe a hundred K a pop. You, you're stealing this sexy broad's twenty million and you get to bang her on top of that?"

"I'm banging her *so* I can steal it, G. She initiated it. What am I supposed to do? She unzips her dress, wiggles out of it in the middle of my office, strips down to her bra and panties, and I tell her I'm not interested? She'd be out the door in a heartbeat. I'd never see her again."

"She unzipped her dress? Like, in the middle of the meeting? Why doesn't that shit happen to me?"

Because your diet choices have remained stagnant since the fourth grade. Because you don't do five hundred ab crunches a day and spend two hours daily on free weights and climbs. Because you're a big, scary motherfucker, even if you're my best friend.

"Number 7 is different, though," I say.

"What, you care about her?"

"God, no. I mean, I don't need her to fall for me, to leave her husband."

That's usually how it works. That's the one unifying theme of every scam I've pulled. I need them to divorce their husbands, who don't even know I exist, much less that I'm banging their wives. Then I can get control of the money and run off with it. It's the perfect scam, because they keep my existence hush-hush for obvious reasons, and they're often so ashamed and humiliated afterward that they don't want to report it. I convince the women to keep their divorce demand low so they can get their husbands to agree to a quick exit. Something in a lump-sum amount that their wealthy husbands are happy to give to be done with the matter in one fell swoop with a discount. The discount is the

downside, sure, but it allows me to stay anonymous and allows for an easy
*adios*.

How I do it varies, and that's purposeful, too. I can't run the same scam
every time or I'll develop a signature. A couple times, I've played the big-
shot investor like I'm doing with Vicky, but the last time I did that was
years ago with Number 4 in Santa Fe. I can be anything I need to be. A
fitness instructor with Number 3 in Naples. A wannabe actor who waits
tables with Number 2 in Sacramento. A grad student with Number 6 in
Lexington. I find the woman I want—or sometimes she finds me—and I
make her want me, I steal her from her husband, I get my hands on the
money.

"Number 7 is different," I say, "because I don't *need* her to leave her
husband. She's got her husband wrapped around her finger. She can do
whatever she wants with the money. And it sure sounds like she plans to
do just that."

Gavin gets it now, leaning forward, pointing at me. "So you don't get
half, or some fraction in a lump-sum divorce settlement? You get it *all*?"

"I get all twenty million," I say. "Twenty-one million, actually."

"Unbelievable. You are unbelievably lucky."

"You're getting your ten percent, pal. You'll make out okay, too."

Ten percent to Gavin, because I couldn't pull off this shit without the
identities he creates for me and, in this case, his financial knowledge.

"But the problem is, I have to straddle a line," I say. "I have to keep
things kosher until November, when that money is hers."

"Oh, that trust language, right." Gavin went through the trust for
me, too—though I blacked out Simon's name, to keep our firewall of
anonymity up, and Vicky's name never actually appears, only the word
"SPOUSE."

"If she wants to keep screwing you, you do it," says Gavin. "And if she
doesn't, if you were just a fling and she doesn't want it to go any further,
you have to be okay with that, too. But not just okay with it—you have to
make sure she's comfortable with the whole thing. If she starts feeling
guilty about cheating on her husband, and you're a reminder of that guilt,
she might just decide to take her money elsewhere."

That sums it up perfectly. Between now and November 3, I have to handle this thing perfectly. I have to keep everything smooth and comfortable with Vicky.

"But my money says she doesn't feel one bit guilty," I say. "She did exactly what she wanted to do. She wasn't conflicted. No, Number 7 has paid her dues for the last ten years. Now her payoff is finally coming. She's not gonna let a little thing like guilt get in the way."

# 26

## Simon

"My name is Simon Dobias," I say to the room. Thirteen people. Two of them new—a man with hair sprouting from beneath a baseball cap, and a middle-aged woman dressed in black—and eleven returners, all seated in cheap folding chairs in the church's dim basement.

"For those who are new, for those who are not—welcome to SOS. The main thing I want to tell you is there are no rules here. You can come and go as you please, obviously. No one's going to make you feel guilty if you stop coming and then return. No one's going to assign you a sponsor who hectors you to do things. We don't have twelve steps or any steps. No one's going to make you speak. If you're just here to listen, then just listen. And if you ever want to call me, my number's up there on the chalkboard.

"I know it's the 'in' thing now to talk about 'safe spaces.' I think a lot of that is BS, to be honest, but this really is a safe place. We just want to help. I think we can. We've all been through similar experiences."

I clear my throat and take a breath.

"My mother committed suicide eighteen years ago," I say. "They called it an accidental overdose. I think my father actually believed that. I can tell you, I wish I did, too. I really do. Because an accident—well, it's a tragedy, it stinks, it's awful, but you don't blame yourself. An accident is just, well, one of those random things. But I know better. Her overdose was deliberate.

"My mother was a brilliant law professor and a marathon runner. She loved life. She loved everything about life. She had a terrible singing voice, but it never stopped her from belting out songs. She had a corny joke or play on words for every situation. She had this laugh like a hyena that was so infectious. And she was the smartest person I've ever known.

"But then she had a stroke, a severe one, and she lost so much of what she had. She couldn't teach any longer. She couldn't run or even walk. She was confined to a wheelchair. She was on heavy medication for all kinds of things, including drugs for pain. My father—well, my father wasn't exactly the Florence Nightingale type. He wasn't a caregiver. He hired someone to take care of Mom, and I tried to help, too, while I was starting college in Chicago.

"Then our financial situation cratered. We had some money, actually a good amount, but my father made some bad financial decisions and we lost it all. We were broke. He was a lawyer, and he could scrap for money, but not enough to afford a full-time caregiver. It was just too expensive. So we had to let the caregiver go.

"My father, well, he said the only realistic thing to do was to put Mom in some facility or nursing home. I didn't want that. I said I'd stay home from college. Skip a year or two and take care of her until we figured something out."

I sigh. "My mother overdosed on pain meds. It was probably a combination of reasons. Losing her functionality, losing her ability to do all the things she loved, the thought of not being in our house with us, and it's probably fair to say that the stroke robbed her of some of her cognitive reasoning. I can't put a finger on exactly what put her over the edge."

Actually, I can. But I'm going to leave that part out.

The secrets, the lies. I don't tell people that part.

I don't tell them that my father broke my mother's heart. That he cheated on her. That in her final days, my mother knew that her husband no longer wanted her, that she not only had lost the functionality of her body and part of her brain, but she also had lost the love and loyalty of the man who had promised to devote himself to her through thick and thin, for better or worse, 'til death.

I don't tell them that I *knew* my father was cheating, that I caught him, that I didn't tell my mother because I knew it would crush her, that I was complicit in his betrayal, that I could have tried harder to stop him, that if I had, everything might have turned out differently.

I don't mention that part because it sounds an awful lot, *ahem*, like a motive to kill my father. And that investigation in St. Louis remains un-solved. Ain't no statute of limitations on murder.

"I didn't know how to handle her death," I say. "I did some dumb things, got into some trouble. I spent some time in an institution. I'm lucky it wasn't worse. It wasn't until I stopped lashing out and started listening that I was able to get my head above water again. I talked to all kinds of therapists, who explained to me that we look at suicide through this prism of control. We think we can control other things and other people. So when someone we love takes their own life, we think we could have stopped it. We think we had control, and we blew it. We are so unwilling to give up this notion that we control things and people around us that we'd rather feel guilt over the suicide than admit that we didn't have that control in the first place."

This advice, in my experience working with other survivors, is spot-on. It helps most people. Not me, but most people.

No, the person who healed me was Vicky. And I healed her. This is where we met, here at Survivors of Suicide. Her loss of her sister, Monica, had been much more recent than mine, but when we talked, just the two of us, we helped each other. We got through it. We made a pact.

A plan of attack, Vicky called it, declaring war on our grief.

It happened on a Thursday night. The next day would be my last day work-ing at my dad's law firm that summer, before I started at U of C as an in-coming college freshman. I'd saved up some money I made that summer and bought him a present. It was a little thing, nothing bigger than a small trophy, the scales of justice in gold, the words LAW OFFICES OF THEODORE DOBIAS engraved in the wooden base.

I waited until the end of the day to pick it up. He thought I'd left for the day and gone home. Instead, I'd stopped at the jewelry store to pick up the order, killed some time downtown waiting for everyone to leave the office, then snuck back up to the office after seven.

It was rare for anyone to be in the office that late. Personal-injury law-yers don't get paid by the hour, so unlike defense firms that value their associates by the number of billable hours they generate—by how long it takes them to complete a task—P.I. lawyers are more efficient with their

written work product and don't burn the midnight oil unless they're preparing for trial. Trials aren't that common anymore, so the odds of anyone
being in the office were small.

I used my key card and swiped through. The reception lights were off,
and usually the last person to leave turned those off. But then I swiped
through the second glass door and could see, instantly, that his office light
was on, peeking out from under the closed door. I stopped and thought a
moment. My plan had been to put the gift on his desk so he'd find it Friday
morning when we arrived at work together. That wasn't going to happen
with him still here, but at least I could sneak into my cubicle and hide it
and give it to him in the morning.

I heard a sound. My first reaction, he was in pain. My first mental image, he was moving something heavy. He was moving furniture and hurt
himself, something like that. A heart attack, maybe.

Sometimes I chide myself in hindsight for my naivete. But then—
maybe it was okay that a teenage boy didn't immediately leap to the worst
conclusions about his father.

I moved slowly toward the door, carefully along the carpet, as the
moaning and the grunting continued, then a thumping noise, and a woman's breathless voice.

We didn't have locks on the office doors. I remember my father saying
that was a kind of statement, some bullshit about an open-door, egalitar-
ian philosophy around the office.

I wish the door had been locked. I wish I hadn't opened it.

I wish I didn't have to listen to him grovel and apologize and try to
justify to me why he was fucking around on my mother, who was probably
being fed her dinner, spoon to mouth, at that moment by our in-home
nurse, Edie.

That was the moment. It got worse, after the money was gone, and we
could no longer afford Edie, and Mom was headed for a nursing home at
the age of forty-nine. But right there in the law firm, on the seventeenth
floor of the Chicago Title & Trust Building, with my father chasing after
me down the hall as he pulled up his trousers, trying to block me from the
elevator while shoving his shirt inside his pants, begging me to listen to
reason, not to go home and do something everyone would regret—that
was the moment, for me, when everything changed.

I wish I didn't let him convince me not to say anything to my mother.

I wish I didn't let him make me a coconspirator in his crime.

Because he didn't stop. Oh, no, even after I found out, he kept on. He didn't tell me, but I caught him again. A few months later, just before Thanksgiving, stepping onto the back patio for some fresh air, I found an empty bottle of champagne and two glasses tucked in the corner of the porch.

Two glasses, not one, even though my mother could no longer drink alcohol. He wasn't just cheating on my mother; his lady friend was sneaking over to the house at night after my mother was asleep and I was working late at the school.

A stupid bottle of champagne, two red-tinted plastic champagne flutes you'd buy at a convenience store. Those things told me that my father wasn't just a weak man who succumbed to a moment of temptation—he was a liar. He was a cheat. His carnal needs were more important than his commitment to my mother, to our family.

I didn't throw them away. I started to. I tossed the bottle of champagne and glasses into an empty garbage bag but, instead of heading to the garbage bin, I took it to my room and placed it inside my closet. I didn't want to forget. I wanted to look at it every day to remind myself what and who my father was.

The day I found that bottle, the day I realized my father was never going to stop cheating—*that* was the day that Ted Dobias died.

The night he was found with a knife in his stomach, floating in his pool, was just the moment he stopped breathing.

# 27

*Monday, September 12, 2022*

*You knew something was wrong tonight. I'd tried to play it off. I greeted you the same way I always did, clutching you in my arms, kissing you in that way we kiss, lifting you off your feet.*

*But afterward, you could tell. You prodded me. And I've made this vow, Lauren, as I've said before on these pages, that I will not lie to you, I will not hide from you. So I told you.*

*"My father cheated on my mother," I told you. "It destroyed her."*

*That surprised you. You knew my father for a short time as your boss, not your immediate supervisor but the big boss, the name on the door, and you probably thought he was a nice enough guy. Or maybe you didn't. Maybe you thought he was an asshole. Either way, you didn't know him know him.*

*Apparently, I didn't, either. I thought I did. I wasn't as close to him as I was to Mom. But I thought I knew him. I didn't see until later how insecure he was, because he was in the same profession, generally speaking, as my mother, but she was smarter, she was better at it, she was more successful.*

*She taught constitutional law at one of the most prestigious law schools in the country, the University of Chicago. And Dad was a scrapping, lowbrow attorney taking slip-and-falls and DUIs, whatever he could grab.*

*What he didn't understand was that Mom didn't care about that. She didn't measure people that way. But Dad did. Probably a male thing.*

*Then Dad hit it big. When that kid he grew up with in Edison Park was working on a construction site, and the boom of a rig he was operating contacted a live overhead electrical power line, sending deadly streaks of electricity through his body and leaving him horribly scarred and disfigured, Dad got the case. A thirty-million-dollar settlement, a third for the Law Offices of Theodore Dobias, meaning nearly ten million in Dad's pocket.*

*I thought that would validate him, make him feel like he was in the big leagues now, the equal or roughly the equal to Mom.*

*But apparently, he needed more. Now he was Mr. Big-Time, a big-shot lawyer with expensive suits and steak dinners and a Porsche, and he had to have a piece of arm candy on his side, too.*

*I confronted him, more than once, but Dad didn't stop. He was in love, he said. And there were things that a young man like me might not be able to appreciate, which was code for, he still wanted to get his rocks off and it was hard with a woman bound to a wheelchair. Yeah, I was eighteen, not eight. I knew what he meant. But there were some other things that a boy like me could appreciate, like committing yourself to someone forever, even through something as tragic as her stroke, ESPECIALLY through something as tragic as her stroke.*

*Dad blew all the money on his newfound swanky lifestyle, making ridiculously bad investments that bombed, spending lavishly on his mistress. And then the money was gone.*

*Mom was home, requiring extensive care, and Dad was without money to pay for a caregiver.*

*After the money was gone, Mom learned the truth. Dad confessed to her. She wasn't the same after her stroke, but there was enough of her left for me to see how much it crushed her to know that her husband had strayed from her.*

*And I'll never know this for certain, because my mother was far too proud a woman to ever say it, but I think she knew that I knew, too, and never told her. I can't even fathom the humiliation she must have felt, the utter devastation.*

*My mother killed herself because she had nothing left of the life she thought she'd had. She was married to a man she no longer recognized, who no longer loved her.*

*And now . . . what am I doing?*

*I'm cheating on my wife.*

*I have become the man I despise.*

# 28

## Christian

I don't need to know much about Vicky's husband, Simon. I probably don't need to know anything other than he's loaded, and his wife is going to take his money and give it to me. But a little due diligence never hurts.

I didn't expect this.

Born and raised in Grace Park. Check. Childhood, nothing of interest. Went to Hilltop Elementary, Grace Park Middle School, Grace Consolidated High School. Valedictorian, okay, and apparently quite the cross-country and track star. He finished second in state his junior year in cross-country and broke the school's record for the two-mile in track. Good for Simon.

But this is more interesting. Simon graduated Grace Consolidated High School in May of 2003. But he didn't graduate from the University of Chicago undergrad until May of 2010.

Seven years to graduate college, Simon, Mr. Valedictorian? Did you take some time off? What were you doing during that time?

Flag that and move on.

His father, Theodore Dobias, hits it big twenty years ago, in 2002, a thirty-million-dollar verdict in an electrical-injury case, which I assume means someone got electrocuted. Theodore was the guy's lawyer, and they got a big pot of cash. Hooray for them.

In 2004, Glory Dobias—Simon's mom, Theodore's wife—a law professor at the University of Chicago, dies of a painkiller overdose. Suicide? The news reports and the U of C's press release are vague. Seems she'd had health problems, a stroke, but nothing concrete.

Then Theodore leaves town. He leaves Grace Park and the Chicago area and moves to St. Louis. He works in a law firm in Alton, Illinois, near the Illinois-Missouri border, where he ends up banking serious dough doing asbestos-exposure cases. The bio from his law firm that I was able to drag up from a long time ago said he netted over two hundred million dollars in recoveries for his clients. That's a lot of money for the lawyer, who gets a third of the recovery usually.

And that explains where Simon's big-dollar trust fund comes from.

But the *really* interesting part is twelve years ago, in May 2010. Theodore Dobias, by now a mega-wealthy, well-established attorney in Alton and the St. Louis area, a leading advocate in asbestos litigation, ends up dead. Murdered, found dead in his swimming pool with a stab wound to the stomach. And guess who the police suspected?

They never arrested him, from what I can tell. They brought him in for questioning multiple times and confirmed to the press that a "person of interest" was being interviewed, which the media had no trouble figuring out meant his only child.

"Simon Peter Dobias," I whisper to myself. "Did you murder your father?"

I remember what Vicky said to me. That insane trust language that kept Simon's wife away from the trust money until ten years of marriage.

*Simon's father didn't trust me,* she said.

Ol' Theodore thought you were a moneygrubbing whore, Vicky. And it seems like he was right. How'd that make you feel?

What were *you* doing, Mrs. Vicky Lanier Dobias, on the night Simon's dad was murdered?

# 29

## Simon

I leave the law school at a quarter after seven for my ten-mile round-trip run to Wicker Park—to the alley outside Viva Mediterránea—and back. I reach the alley in plenty of time, well before the appointed time of 8:00 p.m. for our text messages. I'm not near the times I used to post when I was younger, but I can run a six-minute mile in my sleep.

I stretch and listen to the partiers out on Viva's patio. Look at the people in the condos across the alley, grilling out on their back porches or just having cocktails.

I never lived around here or in a neighborhood like this one. I never lived in the city. I never left Grace Park. My father took off not long after my mother died, when I made it clear that I no longer had a father. He moved down to St. Louis and joined up with a firm that handled asbestos litigation—suing any company that had any product that remotely used asbestos, representing people with alleged exposure to that asbestos who later developed mesothelioma. Madison County, Illinois, was a beacon for those "meso" cases, and it made the lawyers rich.

So Dad finally hit it big and had the validation he so dearly craved.

And I stayed in the house in Grace Park and commuted downtown to college. I guess I was unwilling to let the house go, its connection with Mom. So I never did what most young college or law students did, much less postgrad students, and live in the city.

In a neighborhood just like this one, in one of these condos.

Instead, I lived in a suburb, in a big house all by myself.

Not to mention those eighteen months at New Horizons. The nuthouse, if you want to be politically incorrect, a *facility for struggling individuals*, if you're speaking in polite company.

It helped. Dr. McMorrow was a good therapist who listened more than she spoke. I was a basket case after my mother's death, and I tried to continue my sophomore year of college but knew I couldn't and checked myself in voluntarily. Dr. McMorrow—Anne; she wanted me to call her by her first name—challenged the guilt I felt, preached all those things that I now preach at Survivors of Suicide, about how we can't control everything or everybody, and we have to acknowledge that fact.

But what really turned me around were these words, so simple and obvious: "Your mother wouldn't want you to feel this way. She'd want you to go to college and have a good life. So what the hell are you waiting for?"

That's when I realized it was time to go back to college. And then get a law degree. Anne was right. I was able to move on.

Not heal. But move on.

Move on but remember.

At eight, I put the SIM card into my green phone and power it up. I send this:

How is golf looking tomorrow?

Kind of an inside joke, pretending to be talking in code, when anyone who read through all our text messages would obviously see through the ruse. She replies promptly:

*Anxious for it*

Right, good. She replies again quickly:

*Anxious to talk to you*

That could mean a lot of things. It's deliberately vague.

Everything ok?

She responds:

*Thinking a lot about us. Better to talk in person*

I respond quickly:

Good or bad?
Should I be worried?

# 30

*Tuesday, September 13, 2022*

*So what the hell was that text message tonight? You've been thinking a lot about us, and better we talk in person? Are you going to break up with me, Lauren? Are we done?*

*I don't know what I'll do. The times we see each other each week, the twice a day we text, are the only things that matter in my life now.*

*Was it because of what I said last night about my father cheating on my mother? How I'd grown up hating infidelity more than just about anything in the world, and now I was doing it, too?*

*Oh, why did I have to open my mouth? This isn't the same thing, Lauren. Vicky doesn't love me anymore. I'm not proud of cheating, but this is different than what my father did to my mother! And your marriage isn't real, either.*

*We aren't cheating, not in that way. We aren't!*

*This, this, THIS is what I hate, this weakness, this feeling of vulnerability. I swore I'd never let this happen again, but I did. I kept my guard up for nearly two decades after you laid waste to me, but the moment I saw you on Michigan Avenue, I tore down that wall and exposed myself all over again.*

*Maybe I'm making too much of this. Maybe all the other crap going on—my job prospects suddenly in the dumpster and my marriage just a friendship—is clouding my brain. Maybe I'm not thinking clearly and everything is fine.*

*Don't you realize getting texts like those—we have to talk, better in person—is pure torture? Now I have to wait until tomorrow morning before you even turn on your damn cell phone again. And it's not like I can just run over there, is it? Thanks, Lauren. Thanks so much for turning me inside out yet again.*

*I knew this would happen. I knew it.*

# 31
## Simon

I met Lauren Lemoyne on my first day working at my father's law firm.

I'd graduated high school and was getting ready for college. High school had been easy for me academically but difficult socially. I'd had a late growth spurt, shooting up to five feet eleven my senior year, which I realize is not much more than average male height, but when you start as a freshman at five feet two, and people call you "Mini-Me" and things like that, five feet eleven feels like Paul Bunyan.

I spent most of high school a bookish, small, not very confident boy. I ended a bookish, taller, but only slightly confident boy.

I needed some money before college, so Dad said I could be a gofer at his law firm. Times were good financially because Dad had just rung the bell (as he liked to say) with that enormous verdict in the electrical-injury case. The Law Offices of Theodore Dobias had three partners, five associates, ten assistants, and four paralegals.

One of those paralegals was Lauren Lemoyne. I was introduced to everyone by one of the partners (my father didn't want to do it himself, wanted me to learn my own way), and I first saw Lauren bent over a banker's box of files, wearing a tight miniskirt and showing a lot of leg. It felt like my own personal porn movie, though she quickly righted herself and pulled down her skirt and greeted me in a friendly but perfunctory fashion.

It wasn't perfunctory to me, though. I was immediately taken but intimidated. She would be my pinup girl, gorgeous and exotic, whom I could admire from afar, but well beyond my reach, way out of my league. I stammered a return hello, trying to sound easy and cool and pretty sure I had failed miserably.

It wasn't until the second week of work that our paths crossed again. I was in the firm's kitchen, or at least that's what we called it, where there was a sink and fridge and coffee maker. I was washing my hands because I'd just brought back some filings from the courthouse and the box was dirty.

"So you're Ted's boy."

I saw her and tried to act nonchalant but, again, failed miserably. I turned away from the sink, my hands dripping, and straightened my posture.

"I'm Lauren," she said. "You've probably learned a lot of names all at once."

She was right, I'd had to learn a lot of names right away, which wasn't my strong suit. But Lauren's, I hadn't forgotten.

"Nice to meet you," I said, even though we'd already met. I'd even managed to steal a few nuggets of information from the office manager—Lauren was from the north side of Chicago, age twenty, still lived at home, saving up money for college, huge Cubs fan. I didn't want to ask the office manager too many questions and be too obvious, as if he didn't already know why I was asking. It didn't need to be spoken. Lauren was that kind of untouchable gorgeous.

"So I hear you're starting at U of C this fall," she said. "I also heard you were valedictorian of your high school class. *And* an all-state cross-country runner." Her smile lit up my soul. "Your dad likes to brag about you."

"It was all luck, I swear."

She laughed, and I felt like I'd won the lottery or something. I'd heard my mother use that line years ago, after she won her land-use case before the United States Supreme Court. It sounded like a deft way to handle a compliment, and I stored it away for future use. And thank God. I'd just made this beautiful creature laugh!

She narrowed her eyes in playful skepticism. "Mmm, smart, handsome, and modest on top of all that," she said. "Simon Dobias, you are going to break some hearts."

# 32

**Wednesday, September 14, 2022**

*I couldn't wait any longer. I had to see you. I went to your house, instead of texting you, at ten this morning. You were surprised, alarmed even, to see me at your front door. But you had to know, Lauren, you HAD to know that the text you sent me, that we had to talk, but only in person, would keep me in suspense, would be worse than torture banned by the Geneva Convention.*

*I didn't sleep one wink last night. I must have looked awful this morning. I didn't care. Whatever it was, and I'd braced myself for anything, I had to hear it, and I had to hear it now.*

*"I thought a lot about what you said," you told me. "How your father cheated on your mother, and you didn't want to become your father. I don't want that, either. I don't want you to be a cheater. I don't want to be a cheater, either."*

*I braced myself, having prepared for this. I knew it might end this morning, and I told myself, Simon, you're an adult, just handle it, handle it right, no matter how painful. Be proud of how you react.*

*But I wasn't prepared, it turns out. I wasn't prepared for this at all.*

*"I want us to get married," you said.*

# THE DAY AFTER
# HALLOWEEN

# 33
## Jane

"Ohhh, yes, I've met Lauren."

Cassandra Barclay crosses her legs and sits back in her chair in the interview room down the hall from the squad room.

Cassandra was married to Conrad Betancourt for twenty-six years. They had two children, boys, now ages twenty-four and twenty-two. Their divorce was completed only months before Conrad married Lauren, three years ago.

"Quite the little Kewpie doll, isn't she? She's a golfer, you know. That's how they met. Connie can't play to save his life, but he likes getting out there with his buddies and having a cigar and talking money. He likes the *idea* of playing golf more than he likes golf itself."

"And you met her," says Jane.

"Lauren? Many times now. I still go to the club sometimes."

"The Grace Country Club."

"That's the one. I don't go as much anymore; the kids have lost interest, so I have for the most part, too. But if I want to go, I go. I'm not giving her the satisfaction of driving me away from my club."

Jane nods. Better to let her elaborate.

"She's just what you'd think," she says. "It's not complicated. She stole him from me. Connie has money and she wanted it. She was fifteen years younger than me and prettier than I ever was, even at her age. I was boring and she was exciting. She was new and I was old."

Cassandra Barclay doesn't look boring, and the passage of time has been kind to her, at least how Jane sees it. Fit, thin, nice skin, stylishly dressed. Jane hopes she looks that good at age fifty-five.

"For the record," says Cassandra, her hand out, "I didn't steal Connie from anyone. I met him after he was divorced the first time, and he hadn't built his fortune yet. We were young and truly in love."

Funny how people care so much what you think of them, even if you've never met before and probably won't ever cross paths again.

"When was the last time you two talked?" Jane asks.

"Well, this morning. When I heard about Lauren, I called him. I told him I was sorry to hear the news, which might have been a little generous."

"What did Conrad say to you?"

"He was still processing it, I think." She thinks about it. "I'd imagine his feelings about Lauren had become quite complicated."

Jane stays quiet, hoping for more. When there isn't more, when Cassandra stares back at her, Jane says, "Complicated how?"

"Well, it's never nice to hear something bad happening to someone, even if you're estranged."

"Estranged. Conrad and Lauren were estranged?"

Cassandra cocks her head at Jane. "Conrad and Lauren were getting divorced. You didn't know?"

"I did not. My phone conversation with Mr. Betancourt was short. He should be here soon, though."

"Very well. But yes, Conrad had already filed."

"Do you know when?"

"Oh, not offhand. He called me to let me know, but I couldn't put a specific time on it. September, maybe early October. Within the last month, maybe six weeks."

"He called to tell you he and Lauren were splitting up?"

"Yes. And to thank me." She tries to hide any semblance of satisfaction, curling her lip.

"Thank you for what?"

"For suggesting he get a prenup. At the time, I didn't mean it as advice. I meant it for what it was, an insult. But a truthful one."

Jane waits for more. Once again, more isn't forthcoming. Cassandra likes an audience. "Can you elaborate on that, Ms. Barclay?"

"Well, obviously, I was trying to make a point that she was marrying him for his money, not love. It didn't stop Connie from marrying her, but apparently he was smart enough to heed my warning and lock her down on that prenup."

"How much?" Jane asks. "The prenup."

"I believe it was a million dollars."

Not exactly chump change, but a small fraction of Conrad's net worth.

"May I ask you something, Sergeant?"

"Sure," Jane says.

"Was Lauren involved with another man?"

Jane tries hard not to jump at that question. "Why . . . would you ask that?"

Cassandra lets out a small chuckle. "Well, because *someone* must have killed her. And because it's Lauren Lemoyne we're talking about."

"You'd expect that from her. To cheat."

She tries to smile, but the set of her jaw is too firm to allow it. "I'd all but *guarantee* it from her, Sergeant. Lauren? Lauren always looked out for number one. I could see that from a mile away. If Conrad could have gotten past her beauty, he would've seen it, too."

"We're still looking at a number of things, Ms. Barclay. Do you have any information about Lauren seeing another man?"

"I wouldn't have the slightest idea about Lauren's life. Conrad would never discuss her with me, nor would I want him to. I base my question on just knowing the kind of person she is."

Interesting. But is this just the opinion of a bitter ex-wife? Or is Cassandra getting Lauren right?

"I have no doubt that Lauren would be moving on to her next man," says Cassandra. "And a man with money, of course. A million dollars was not gonna cut it for her. You mark my words: Lauren Lemoyne was looking for her next sugar daddy."

# BEFORE HALLOWEEN

## September

# 34
## Christian

With a flourish—her jaw clenched, a small expulsion of air, a shiver—Vicky collapses on me. I wrap my arms around her sweaty body, propping her on my lap. She prefers being on top, I've noticed, and likes to keep her heels on, though that's probably for me. And yeah, the heels are a thing for me. I'm not that original in my kinks. The biggest turn-on for me, by far, is that ring on her finger.

After a moment of catching our breath, she climbs off me and heads for the bathroom, leaving me tired and satisfied on the couch in my apartment.

This is the fourth time we've hooked up. After the first time at my office, we've come here to my apartment. I've come to learn this much about Vicky, my Number 7: She isn't quiet during sex, far from it, but she's quiet at the end, when she gets off. She retreats to another place, focuses, concentrates. A lesser man would think she's thinking of someone else. But I doubt that. I'm what Vicky wants. I can tell.

Which is good, because otherwise, I'd wonder. Vicky doesn't hand out compliments. She doesn't moan with satisfaction afterward and tell me how wonderful I was, or how much better it is with me than with her husband.

"What is *this*?" she calls out from the bathroom.

Uh-oh. What did I do? Did I leave something out for her to see that she shouldn't—

I rush into the bathroom without acting like I was rushing. She's holding my toothbrush.

"Oh," I say.

"What is this? This is, like, some fancy metal—"

"Titanium," I say.

"You have a titanium toothbrush? And . . ." She looks through my medicine cabinet. "And nail clippers and . . . some trimmer and . . . What is this?"

"It holds dental floss," I say sheepishly, as if I'm a little bit embarrassed to have a toothbrush made of pure titanium, matte black with a protective, antibacterial coating in the socket, and matching titanium nail clippers, electric razor, nose-hair trimmer, and dental-floss holder.

"How much did this *cost*, Christian?"

Market value was more than $8,500, or so I discovered after looking it up. It was a gift, actually, from one of my targets—Number 4, in Santa Fe—before she knew she was a target.

At first, I was going to hide it, but Vicky needs to see a thing or two, small things, to show that some massively expensive, over-the-top item is merely chump change to me.

"Seriously," she says. "This must have cost thousands."

"Good return on investment," I say. "They're built well and last a long time. Amortize it over their life and the per-unit price—well, it's expensive but much more reasonable."

"I didn't know people amortized toothbrushes." She puts down the toothbrush and puts her hands on my bare chest. "Must be nice to be so rich and smart."

She puts her lips against mine. I can feel her smile.

She wants more of me. This time, we'll use the bed.


Afterward, Vicky looks over my apartment, lost in thought.

I don't own this place. I'm renting, though I'd never tell Vicky that. When I moved back to Chicago last summer, I didn't see the wisdom in buying. I knew I wouldn't be staying too long, and besides, I only have about a million dollars saved up, and I want to keep as much of that liquid as possible. Rent a really nice place in an expensive neighborhood, I decided, and even though the rent will be exorbitant, it will be short-term.

Still, as nice as this place is, it doesn't scream mega-wealthy. My bio suggests that I've made hundreds of millions of dollars in my bold investments, so this condo might not seem nice enough. My go-to line is that I tie up most of my money in my investments, so *I'm putting my money where my mouth is, I'm in the same investments that I'm putting you in,* which is a pretty nice sell job in itself.

On those occasions that my cover story is a man with money, like here, I try to make clear to the target that I grew up humbly (true), learned to be frugal (sometimes true), and those habits have remained. Yeah, I have all this dough, but I'm not going to plate everything in gold or buy more space than I need.

It's a balance. Wealth is attractive to women. Uber-wealth, in my experience, can be intimidating. So I try to straddle the line, show her an occasional glimpse of my obnoxious wealth—see the titanium toothbrush—but otherwise try to keep a humble, low profile that downplays materialism.

"The condo's temporary," I say. "I like the neighborhood, and the property values are still rising around here. It's a solid investment."

"Everything's an investment with you." She puts on her bra and panties, then her skirt, then her top, in that order. "You think you're going to settle here in Chicago?"

There it is. I knew she'd ask eventually. She's wondering about my intentions. I think I know hers: She's going to leave. I'd bet anything. When she takes that money from Simon after serving her ten-year marital sentence, she won't want to stick around and see Simon's sad face. She's getting the hell out. But where, I don't know.

New York? No, I don't see it. I don't see her as a Manhattan girl. I mean, she'd enjoy the buzz and nightlife, she'd fit right in there, but she doesn't really strike me as big-city. She doesn't seem to give one shit about the difference between a four-hundred-dollar bottle of Carruades de Lafite and some bottle of red I'd pick up for twenty bucks in a grocery store. When I've brought up theater and music, she doesn't bite, hardly adds anything to the conversation. But then again, it's hard to see her settling in some small town and having my babies and baking cookies, either.

Vicky has done an admirable job thus far of keeping her own counsel.

And even to me, someone who has staked his life's work on reading women, the opposite sex remains somewhat of a mystery.

What I know about Vicky Lanier is this: almost nothing. Every time I ask her about herself, she deflects. She mentioned something about an unhappy childhood. She's made one offhand comment about "West Virginia," and I did what I could with that last week, some unsophisticated googling. Research is not my strong suit and not something I really need for my purposes, and I can't bring in Gavin because then he'd know her name; she would be Vicky Lanier Dobias and not "Number 7." But I did enough on my own to know that a teenager named Vicky Lanier went missing in 2003 from Fairmont, West Virginia.

That must be her. So she didn't get off to a good start in life. She's a scrapper, a survivor. She's had to go it alone. My guess? Simon Dobias gave her stability and comfort more than love and passion. And she saw a meal ticket. She saw all those dollar signs and made a decision based on need. These almost-ten years married to Simon have been an investment.

But now, asking me about my intentions? That's Vicky's way of feeling me out about next steps. She's thinking about a life with me. She's too cautious to say that outright, but she's thinking about it. And it scares her. I have to make sure she trusts me.

"The great thing about my job," I say, "is I can do it anywhere. Here or Manhattan or with my toes in the sand in Monterey. I've thought about Paris, I've thought about the Tuscany region. I'll probably stick to the States, so I can keep my eye on trends, which is harder to do remotely. But who knows?"

She's watching me as I say this, matter-of-factly, while I pull on my pants. I usually leave off my shirt for as long as possible because women love my abs.

"So it wouldn't have to be in a big city?" she asks.

Yep, she wants to know. She's fantasizing about places—though which ones, I don't know—and me with her.

"Not necessarily," I say. "What about you? Do you always want to stay in Chicago?"

Volleying that serve back in her court, in just the same, low-key, indirect way, not confronting her with the idea of a future together but dancing near it. If she's going to move slowly, so am I. Don't rock the boat, like

Gavin and I discussed. Keep Number 7 on the steady and narrow until November 3.

When I look over at her, she's gazing out the picture window that looks onto my patio and far away to the city's magnificent skyline.

"I'm not staying in Chicago," she says. "Anywhere but Chicago."


"Let me take you to dinner," I say.

"Where?" she asks.

"Wherever. You name it. There are twenty places within walking distance. Or anywhere else."

She chews on her lip, checks her watch. It's coming up on seven in the evening. "It's getting late."

"Afraid to be seen in public with me?" I laugh.

She looks at me. "Not in the way you mean it, but actually, yes, I am very afraid of that. Wouldn't you be, if you were me? What if someone saw us?"

"Well, yeah, I suppose."

"Well, yeah, you suppose? This isn't a joke, Christian. What if Simon found out?"

"Okay, I—"

"What if Simon found out and filed for divorce?"

I put up my hands. I've struck a nerve. Her eyes are on fire.

"What if Simon found out and filed for divorce *before November third*?" she says. "Did you read that trust language?"

"I did—"

"If he even files for divorce before our ten years are up, I'm done. I don't get a penny."

"I know."

She gets off the couch, grabs her bag. "Okay, I'm glad you know. Do you also know that I don't have four hundred *million* dollars in investments or whatever you have? That this money is the only money I have?"

Whoa, whoa, whoa, this is spiraling.

"Yes, and I'm sorry," I say. "I don't mean to be so casual about that. Hey." I walk up to her, though she appears to be in no mood for comfort or intimacy right now. "Vicky, I will never do anything that jeopardizes that.

Nothing. If it's important to you, it's important to me. *You're* important to me. Haven't you figured that out yet?"

She's still fuming, still upset, her eyes turned from mine. I don't move, following her lead.

But eventually, as I knew she would, she looks into my eyes.

# 35
## Vicky

"I can do the grocery run," I say.

"Jeez, with what?" says Miriam, my boss, bent down in her office with the safe open, trying to scrounge up whatever petty cash she can. Her "office" is really a converted garage. We've tried to maximize every square inch of this property to fit as many people as we can in our shelter.

Miriam is a lifer at Safe Haven, one of the people who started it up thirty years ago after escaping an abusive relationship of her own. She has a severe look to her, rarely smiling, heavy lines on her face and silver hair pulled back tight, trim as a drill sergeant with much the same demeanor, though she has as big a heart as anyone I know.

"Low on funds already?" I ask. "It's only the middle of the month."

"We have twenty-two dollars," she says. "To buy two hundred dollars' worth of groceries." She fishes into her jeans pocket and pulls out some cash.

"That's okay, I have some money," I say. I think I have maybe forty dollars.

"Don't start spending your own money," she tells me. "I don't pay you enough as it is."

But people have to eat. These women who come to us, seeking refuge from abuse, often with their kids—we aren't providing much of a "haven" if we can't supply them with meals. As it is, we buy as cheaply as we can, cutting out coupons, looking for sales, buying generic. Good thing I have many, many years of practice doing so.

"It's fine," I say. "Just drop it. I'll get as much as I can."

—

I go to the shelter's kitchen, reviewing the stock of groceries we have remaining and putting together a list. Then I debate whether to go to the
superstore ten miles away or the local grocery store, with the four pages
of coupons. The superstore is usually cheaper; we pay a one-time annual
subscription fee—which I assume is how that chain makes its money—
and buy groceries at a lower cost. But with coupons for the local grocery
store, I might be able to stretch my dollar more. I have the twenty-two dollars that Miriam gave me and thirty-seven of my own, and I have to make
it count.

I'm midway through the comparison, clipping coupons and banging on
the calculator, when my phone buzzes. It's from Rambo, of all people, a
text message. Why is my private investigator texting me? I open the message, all of three numbers: 911.

I pop out of the chair and head outside. I'll want good reception. And
more importantly, privacy.

"You've *got* to be kidding me," I say, walking into the parking lot outside
the shelter, phone pressed against my ear, my feet crunching gravel.
"Please, just—just *tell* me this is a joke."

"Sorry, kiddo," Rambo says to me. "It's no joke."

"When?" I say. "When did this happen?"

"They found the body five weeks ago. They identified her through DNA
two days ago. The article was in the *Register-Herald* online. You can read
it yourself."

There's no way in hell I'm looking up that article. Not on any phone or
computer that can be connected to me.

"Where—where was the body found?" I ask, as if that matters.

"Bolt Mountain. You know that place?"

"Never heard of it. I've never even been to that part of the country."

"Me neither," he says. "It's about a buck fifty, two hundred miles from
where she lived."

"And you're sure it's her?" I ask, flailing.

"I can only tell you what I'm reading, kiddo. 'The skeletal remains of a woman found in August on Bolt Mountain have been identified as Vicky Lanier, who disappeared in 2003 from her home in Fairmont, West Virginia, at the age of seventeen.' So that sure sounds right to me."

God, that poor girl. Somebody killed her and buried her up in a mountain.

But also—poor me.

I look up at the sky. "So the missing person I picked as an alias is no longer a missing person. She's no longer off the grid."

"Well, she is in one sense, I suppose."

"You're not funny, Rambo. I'm totally screwed, in other words."

No. No. Not when I'm this close. Not when I'm— This—this can't be happening. Could my luck be any worse?

"Miss Vicky, Miss Vicky." Rambo sighs. "I don't know what you're up to, and I don't *wanna* know. But as of this moment, yes, if you've been telling everybody that you're Vicky Lanier from Fairmont, West Virginia, who left at age seventeen in 2003, then a quick Google search will tell them one of two things. Either you're lying, or a town of less than twenty thousand people had two girls named Vicky Lanier of the same age who went missing the same year."

"Well, c'mon, help me out here, Rambo. Is there anything I can do? What would you do?"

"There's nothing *to* do. You can't make this news disappear. You wanna know what *I'd* do?" he says. "I'd pray nobody looks me up. Or whatever it was I was doing that relied on my alias—I'd stop doing it."

No. Stopping is not an option. Not when I've gotten this far. Not when I'm so close. November is only seven weeks away.

I'll just to have to pray that I'm not exposed in the next seven weeks. If I am, all of this comes crashing down.

# 36

*Friday, September 16, 2022*

*Married. I'm getting married again! But where?!?*

*"Paris," you said. "I always dreamed of getting married in Paris."*

*Venice, maybe. Cabo. Maui. Anywhere. I would marry you anywhere, Lauren. I would marry you in a basement. I would marry you in a tub of ice water.*

*Vicky and I got married in Mexico on a whim. My parents were both gone by then, and Vicky hadn't seen her parents since she left West Virginia as a teenager, so it's not like we needed a big family wedding or anything. But still, I'm a homebody at heart, and I always wished we'd married in Chicago.*

*Vicky. Oh, Vicky. This won't be easy. I'll have to find the right way to break this to her. It will be hard, but eventually she'll see that it's for the best.*

*And I don't have to tell her immediately, do I? After all, I have to wait to file for divorce until November 3—our tenth anniversary—so she gets her share of the money. Maybe that will be the best way to break it to her.*

*Bad news, we're splitting up. Good news, here's ten million dollars.*

*Yes, it can wait. Everything will be fine. I don't know why I worry so much.*

# 37

## Simon

When I finish with my latest entry, I put the green journal into my work bag, where it always stays. Not exactly something I want other people reading, right?

Anshu pokes his head into my office. "Hey, give me five minutes."

"Fine."

Anshu's taking me out to lunch today. He'd never say so, but he's trying to cheer me up. Today is Friday, the sixteenth of September, the deadline day for submitting the application for full professorship. He knows the dean asked me not to submit my application, and he knows I didn't submit it, though he doesn't know why.

Yes, it bothers me, but what bothers me even more is that he can *tell* it bothers me. I pride myself on not showing my emotions.

"Okay, I'm good." He walks in with his coat over his arm and bag packed.

"Done for the day?" I ask. "At one o'clock?"

"Well, I figured it might turn into a liquid lunch," he says. "Hey, it's a Friday afternoon."

Yeah, he's consoling me. Anshu really is a good egg. He's one of the only people around here I can stomach, one of the only ones who doesn't take himself too seriously. He is probably one of the top ten tort law professors in the country, but you'd never know it to talk to him. He'd rather talk about his wife and kids or the Cubs, who are currently in the midst of another September nosedive.

"I'm fine," I say. "Really. I don't need cheering up."

"Well, I do," he says. "I want people who deserve the job. I don't like people clouting their way into a professorship because of their donor father. This school has enough money already. So help me drown my sorrows, okay?"

How can I say no to that?

"Only if you let me buy," I say.

"Even better."


The place is just a walk down from the law school, a block south and near Michigan Avenue, a French place that, according to Anshu, has the best monkfish in the world. I've never eaten monkfish and probably won't start today. I'm looking forward more to the well-stocked bar area after lunch.

"Bindra, party of two," says Anshu when we walk in. "Oh, you gotta be kidding me."

I glance around the room. It doesn't take me long.

Dean Comstock and his new protégé, Associate Professor Reid Southern, soon to be full professor, sitting in one of the booths, a bottle of champagne on ice by the table.

You have *seriously* got to be kidding me. They're celebrating his ascension to full professor, and I have to be in the same fucking room with them? I mean, why doesn't someone come over and waterboard me while we're at it?

"We can go somewhere else," Anshu whispers. "I really don't care where—"

"Not at all," I say, patting his arm. "I'm dying to try that monkfish."

"Simon, really."

"They already saw us," I say. "If I walk out now, I look like an asshole."

It's true. They've seen us. And now the dean and Reid are whispering something to each other and putting on their good-sportsmanship-pity faces.

"Are we all set, gentlemen?" the woman at the reception podium asks us.

All set! Just don't seat us next to them, or near them, and maybe I can get through this.

"Professors!" Dean Comstock calls out, Mr. Orange Bow Tie today, his silver cuff link gleaming as he extends a hand to us. I was kind of hoping handshakes would go the way of the dodo bird after COVID-19, but the dean's an old-school kind of guy, so I shake his hand.

"Good to see you, Reid," I say, though I'd rather have my fingernails removed with pliers.

As Anshu has pointed out several times, Reid indeed looks the part of a law professor, with his sport coat, circular eyeglasses, salt-and-pepper goatee, and general air of smugness.

"No class today?" Reid asks me, sizing up my usual attire, a button-down shirt and jeans.

Well, that was a little below the belt, wasn't it, Reid? I mean, you know how I dress, and you know that your buddy Dean Cumstain just bulldozed the field so you could glide into the full-professor spot untouched. You could at least show some semblance of grace, but you can't help yourself, you have to take me down a peg anyway?

You do know how this all played out, don't you, Reid? I'd imagine the dean didn't spell out every detail for you, but I have no doubt that he let you, and your big-bucks daddy, know that he was responsible for "talking some sense" into me or "helping" me "understand" the situation. He "took care of it," I'm sure he told you, in his faux-diplomatic way.

Yeah, you know that. You're smiling at me with that patronizing, blue-blood smirk, that aura of cutthroat privilege. You don't mind that the hierarchical levers were pulled on your behalf. Hell, you're proud of it, and you're happy to let me know it. Sure, I didn't submit my materials, so ultimately I was a good little boy, but how dare I even *think* of applying for that seat when you applied on the first day and let the world know that REID SOUTHERN wanted that position. How dare I even *consider* challenging your ascension to the throne. Really, who do I think I am, contemplating that I am even remotely on your level?

Right, Reid?

"Congratulations," Anshu says to Reid. "I look forward to your joining us."

"That's good of you to say, Professor," Reid replies. "By the way, Simon, I read your blog the other day," he adds, calling me by name after referring to Anshu by his title. Yeah, I notice things like that. "Something about the Eleventh Circuit and the third-party doctrine?"

"Right."

"It was a fun piece," he says.

A fun piece? I dissected that court opinion and exposed it for the circular reasoning that it was.

A fun piece. Our courts are lying down and allowing the government to expand its reach beyond anything anyone would ever have envisioned, and it's a fun piece?

I smile at him.

Easy now, Simon.

I pat my pocket, pull out my phone like I just got a text. "Will you guys excuse me one minute?"

I step away while they chitchat. I take a breath.

Easy now. Good, clean thoughts. Calming exercises, go.

"Tear" and "tier" are pronounced the same but "tear" and "tear" are not.

"Fat chance" and "slim chance" mean the same thing.

I dig into my email. Not the In-Box or the Sent but the Drafts folder.

"Arkansas" and "Kansas" are pronounced differently.

We drive on a parkway but park in a driveway.

If a vegetarian eats vegetables, is a humanitarian a cannibal?

Fuck it. I'm done being calm. I find the email for Joyce Radler in administration and read it over:

> Dear Joyce: Please find enclosed the full set of materials for
> my application for full professor, in PDF format as requested.
> Please let me know if I can provide you with any additional
> information.

I hit "send." With three and a half hours to spare.

With the massive attachment, it takes a good half a minute to send. When my phone belches a confirmatory *tha-woop*, I look up and smile.

So now I've applied, Reid. It's you and me, vying for the slot.

Yeah, I put all the materials together, just in case. I didn't really think I'd submit them. Especially because now the dean will go with the nuclear option and destroy me and my future with the law school, if not with academia writ large.

Or maybe he won't.

I would've let this go, Reid. I would've taken my beating and hoped for a better result the next time a slot opened. But you had to goad me, didn't you?

I mean, I try to be reasonable. But sometimes, I let things bother me more than they should.

# 38
## Christian

"Let's go out," Gavin says when he shows up at my apartment, making a beeline for my booze in the kitchen. "Let's get some tickets to the Cubs, then hit some clubs." He seems to like that idea, humming "Cubs and clubs, Cubs and clubs" as he pours himself a bourbon.

"Not sure I'm up for it," I say.

"Not up for the Cubbies? Okay, just the clubs, then. We'll grab a steak and then hit the West Loop."

I moan.

"The Triangle, then," he says. "Maybe Tavern."

"I don't know."

"What don't you know? It's Friday night. What, you wanna stay home?"

"Maybe. I'm tired."

He shakes his head. "No, no, no. Nicky isn't tired on Friday night. Nicky gets loaded with his buddy Gavin, then he takes his pick of fillies home—"

"I just don't feel good, G. Sue me."

Gavin takes a long sip of the bourbon and eyeballs me. With a wag of a finger, he says, "How's it going with Number 7?"

"Good. All good. Got her right where I want her."

"Yeah?"

"Yeah."

"Okay, we can have a drink or two here before we go," he says. "Tell me about her."

"That's not the deal."

"Well, not her *name*, but I mean, y'know, generally. I mean, what's her story?"

I shrug. "Not much of a story. She was a runaway, best I can tell."

That surprises him. It surprised me, too, when I looked her up, but then it didn't. The more time I spend with Vicky, the more I see that she's a loner, a fighter. Most of the women I target—all six of the previous targets, in fact—had pretty normal, privileged lives. None of them had lives that remotely resembled mine.

"Like she ran away from home when she was a kid?" Gavin says. "What'd she do?"

"I don't know. She won't talk about her past. Nothing online I can find."

"You know what she did," says Gavin, pouring himself a second bourbon.

"I don't."

"What else *would* she do? She runs away from home, has to fend for herself?"

"Shut up, G."

"She was a hooker, Nicky. Or a porn actress. Something in the sex trade. She had to be."

I grab a bottle of water from the fridge.

"Does she fuck like a hooker?"

"I said *shut up*!" I throw down the bottle of water, the top coming off, the water splashing everywhere.

"Jesus." Gavin steps back. "What the fuck, pal?"

I grab a towel and mop up the water on the floor. Meanwhile, Gavin goes into the living room and flips on the flat-screen TV.

I toss the wet rag in the sink, pour myself a bourbon, and walk out onto the patio. The nightlife around here is as full throttle as the city gets. I love it here. I always figured I'd end up in Chicago after I'd collected enough from my scams, if things worked out that way. But I've always been prepared to leave the country, if that's what it takes to stay safe. I think I've done everything I need to do to stay ahead of the law. Most of these women don't even bother to chase me after I take them for everything, the sheer embarrassment of what they'd have to admit, and their ex-husbands couldn't give one shit about them, after they cheated and left them for another man and took lump-sum divorce settlements.

And what could they do, even if they tracked me down? I was their paramour, their dirty hidden secret, so it's not like their friends met me or anything. And I used a different alias every time—Collin Daniels, Richard Nantz, David Jenner—so all I have to do is deny, deny, deny. Nope, that's not me. What money? They can't trace anything. They can't prove anything.

Vicky? I'm not sure what she'll do after I take her money. She's basically going to take her husband for everything, and I'm going to take *her* for everything. How far can she complain? Can a thief complain about another thief? Oh, probably so. She might try. Vicky seems like the type who doesn't let go of a grudge. But as I keep telling myself, I don't really know her.

No, she'll come after me. That's what I'd do. And she's like me.

I make my way into the living room, where Gavin is slouched on the sofa, watching a movie and drinking my bourbon. He points at the screen.

"*Spy Game*," he says. "You seen this movie?"

"No."

"Old movie. Redford, Pitt. Redford, he's the old-school CIA agent, right? He's teaching Pitt the ropes. He's like, don't ever get attached to anything or anybody, stash away money for retirement and don't ever spend it, look out for yourself first, right? Then it turns out, for all his tough talk, he has a heart of gold. You know what you and Redford have in common?"

I sit down on the couch. "No, what do we have in common?"

He kills the TV, leaving us in silence.

"Nothing," he says. "Because that's a fucking movie, a work of fiction, a fairy tale. And you, Nicky, this is your real life. So do yourself and, more importantly, *me* a favor, all right?"

"What's that?"

"Don't grow a conscience," he says. "And do not, absolutely *do* not fall for this woman. Take her fucking money and be done with it. Then go find your princess."

"All right, one more," says Gavin, "then we're getting a steak."

"I don't feel like it."

We're out on my patio now, the second story, overlooking an alley and nightlife.

"What about there, at least?" Gavin says.

"Where?"

"Right across the alley, Einstein. That patio down there where everyone's drinking and enjoying themselves, unlike us? The patio with about twenty different hotties that would probably have their legs in the air for you if you so much as winked at them. I mean, if you weren't in love with Number 7 already."

"Would you shut up with that?"

"I'll shut up after November third, when Number 7 takes that money from her husband and you take it from her. Then, I'll take my cut and shut up. Until then, you're worrying me."

"I'm not falling for her, and I won't fall for her."

"Good, now how about we have dinner at that place down there? They got any steak?"

"I don't think so. I've got a menu somewhere."

"We're not ordering, sunshine, we're going there. Tell me what they have, if they don't have steak, for Christ's sake."

"The chicken shawarma's pretty good—"

"Chicken *what*?"

"—and the kofta kebabs aren't bad."

"Kaf-what? Kafka? Jesus, Nicky, what is happening to you?"

I lean forward and lower my voice. "Would you stop fucking calling me Nick? For a guy who's so worried about me pulling this off without a hitch, you're shouting 'Nick' from this balcony? How about you take out an ad in the *Chicago* fucking *Tribune* and announce to the world that my name isn't Christian Newsome?"

He nods, takes a drink. "Fair point, *Christian*. I humbly apologize. And I realize that you have to eat frou-frou food to keep that attractive figure of yours. So I will withdraw my previous objection and humbly request that you join me at . . ." He looks down at the patio across the alley. "What's the name of that place?"

"Viva," I say. "Viva Mediterránea."

# 39

## Simon

Monday morning. I wake up alone. Vicky went to Elm Grove for the weekend again to see her nieces. The older one, Mariah, got her first period a few weeks ago and freaked about it, probably more than anything because her mother isn't there for her, so it was sort of a one-two punch of emotions. Vicky, who clings to the idea that she could have prevented her sister's suicide had she been more proactive, has been spending a lot of weekends with them lately.

Hey, that's one of the reasons I love her.

My mother would have liked her. She wouldn't have minded Vicky's rough edges. She would have admired her bluntness. Mom always said what she thought, sometimes to a fault, often to her disadvantage. My dad told the story of my mother at the law firm she joined out of law school in 1980, some silk-stocking firm of nine hundred lawyers, only six of whom were women. Mom would organize events for the women—lunches, drinks after work, an unofficial support group. One time early on, the firm's senior partner held up one of the flyers she had printed out and mused aloud, "'Women's Night Out'? Why no men's night out?" (At this point in the telling, my mother would interject that it was no accident that this comment was made while she was standing nearby in the hallway.) To the surprise of no one who knew my mother, she replied that "*Every* night is men's night out."

"Don't speak unless you have something to say," she used to say to me during our talks when she tucked me in. "But when you do choose to speak, say what you mean, mean what you say, and be ready to support your points. If you can't support your point of view, then it wasn't much of a point of view to begin with."

It's early, just a little past five. I'm not running in the morning these days, no Five at Five for now, as I am now doing nightly runs to Wicker Park. So I go for a long walk, come home, shower, post an essay on my blog, *Simon Says*, about a new case from the Wisconsin Supreme Court on the good-faith exception to the warrant requirement, and make it into my office at eight.

My mother would have loved having a blog that allowed her to sound off on all matters legal for anyone interested. She had her specialties in the law like any professor, but she would read decisions on any subject matter. She'd devour every opinion from the U.S. Supreme Court on any topic and discuss it over dinner. She'd summarize the facts, argue both sides, the pros and the cons, and then announce to us the correct outcome—which, as the law proceeded through the eighties, usually differed from the one reached by the Rehnquist Court.

Around nine-thirty, I start my walk along the promenade toward the Chicago Title & Trust Building. Yes, every morning when I come here, it makes me think of my father and the law firm he had here. And yes, that brings back many an unpleasant memory. And yes, a shrink might say it's unhealthy for me to be coming here every day. Then again, the day the St. Louis police tried to ask Dr. McMorrow about a conversation we had the morning after my father's murder was the day that I stopped talking to shrinks. It tends to chill the candor needed for a good therapist-patient conversation.

I grab a Starbucks and take a seat in the lobby of the building. I power up my phone and text her:

Top of the mornin' to yah, lassie.

She doesn't respond. I try again:

Good morning, my queen.

Still nothing. Not even bubbles. No indication she even received it.

Sounds like you're otherwise occupied. Will try you tonight
my love.

I kill the phone and remove the SIM card. That was a waste. At least it was a nice morning for a walk.

I don't obsess about Mitchell Kitchens. I just think about him sometimes.

Mitchell could pick up a hundred pounds in his hands and toss it fifteen feet. I know that because I weighed a hundred pounds my freshman year, and he used to toss me fifteen feet. His record was eighteen feet, three inches.

The gym where the wrestlers worked out was right by the front entrance of the school, where the bus dropped us off. Mitchell would call out to me—"Mini-Me," that is—and I quickly learned that if I didn't respond, he'd walk over and grab me anyway.

Into the wrestlers' gym, where the mats were laid out, red tape laid down for the starting point and blue tape to mark Mitchell's personal best. One hand on my belt and one gripping my shirt, Mitchell would toss me through the air, and I would land hard on the mats. His buddies would laugh and cheer and measure the distance. Sometimes, if he was unhappy with his first toss, he'd make me come back so he could toss me again.

"You don't mind, do you, Mini-Me?" he used to say, patting me so hard on the back that I almost fell over. I remember that part, though; the guy had the IQ of a fire hydrant, but he always made sure I told him it was okay, so he could use that as a defense, if need be. *He said he didn't mind. He liked it. We were just having fun.*

I did mind, of course. It was humiliating. And sometimes it hurt. But I got pretty good at breaking my landing, protecting my face when I hit the mat, fingers balled into fists so I didn't break any of them.

I always wondered, Why me? What did I ever do to the guy? Sure, I was a diminutive, nerdy freshman. I was a walking cliché for a bully's target. But I wasn't the only one.

Looking back, it's not hard to see. We had math together. I was in geometry, which was basically an honors class for a freshman, and he was taking it as a senior. I was getting A's and he could barely pass.

If our before-school time together wasn't fun enough, he'd find me at lunch, too. He'd walk over to my table in the lunchroom and pat me on the head. I had a bottle of Gatorade in my lunch every day. My mother was trying to put weight on me. "You don't mind, do you, Mini-Me?" he'd say to me and swipe the Gatorade off the table. One day, to compensate for this daily interaction, I brought a second bottle to keep for myself, but he swiped up that one, too. "Must be my birthday," he said. The other kids at my table, mostly freshmen like me, just looked away. Nobody ever said anything to me. They knew that they'd do the same thing in my shoes—nothing.

Mitchell was one of the kings of the school. He had colleges coming from near and far to watch him wrestle and recruit him. In the end, it didn't work out for him. He screwed up at some big meet and later ended up running crosswise of the law, nearly went to prison.

So maybe there's karma in the world, after all. Maybe I should let it lie there. But every time I trace that scar on my left cheek, he re-enters my mind.


A little after seven at night, I leave the law school and run my five miles to Wicker Park. I stop in the alley between the back patio of Viva Mediterránea and the row of condos on the next street over. There's been a bit of rain this evening, and the autumn weather is flirting with us, enough to dampen enthusiasm for Viva's outdoor patio, but a few people are outside in light jackets and sweaters enjoying cocktails and clinging to the vestiges of summer.

At eight sharp, I pull out my green burner phone, insert the SIM card, and type a message:

Top of the evenin' to yah, lassie.

She replies:

*Um, Lassie was a dog but ok*

Ah, testy. I text:

Cranky are we?

She replies:

> *Didn't sleep well last night Con snores so loudly*
> *<yawns>*

That's vivid. Even mentions *the husband* by name. Oh, well. My response:

So that's why I missed you this morning?

She replies:

> *Once he left I slept half the morning*

Ah, that works. I type:

Can't say I enjoy image of you sleeping with him.

She replies:

> *Well it's his house don't be healing*

Bubbles, and she replies again:

> *LOL don't be JEALOUS damn autocorrect bye for now*

Fair enough. I power down the phone, remove the SIM card, and stuff both into the pocket of my running shorts.

I look up at the row of condos, the rear balconies overlooking this alley. The third one down is empty, but the lights are on inside the apartment.

The third condo down belongs to Christian Newsome, who has been screwing Vicky for the last couple of weeks.

Yeah, I know about that. I've even seen Christian out on his patio a couple of times when I've come here for my nightly runs. Sometimes Christian sits out there alone. Sometimes he's out there with his friend Gavin.

Never Vicky, though. No, Vicky would be far, far too cautious to allow herself to be seen in public with Christian.

Am I upset about Vicky having sex with another man? Of course. I'm only human. But one could argue that I lack standing to complain under the circumstances.

I'm trying to be reasonable about this. Sometimes I am a perfectly reasonable man.

Other times, I let things bother me more than they should.

# THE DAY AFTER
# HALLOWEEN

# 40
## Jane

Conrad Betancourt sits slumped against the couch in his living room. His eyes are glassy, with thick, dark pouches beneath. His only saving grace is a decent suntan.

An officer met him at O'Hare, where he landed about two hours ago. He was driven to the Cook County morgue, where he identified the body of his wife, Lauren. The report from the officer was sparse: Other than uttering the words "Sweet Jesus" and confirming the deceased was, indeed, his wife of three years, he asked for a few private moments. If he cried softly or bawled like a devastated husband or remained steely and steadfast, Jane wouldn't know, because her officer didn't know. When he emerged from the exam room, he said nothing on the way to his house.

"Who did this to my wife and why?" Conrad asks.

*My wife.* Not *Lauren.* Since he arrived at the house, he hasn't uttered her name, just referred to her as a possession. How very male. Jane has wondered how she would feel if she were married and her husband referred to her that way, instead of by name. It would be nice to find out, someday.

"Help us figure this out," Jane says.

"Well, she didn't commit suicide."

"No? Why not?"

"She wouldn't do that." He doesn't elaborate. He seems like a boss, a leader, issuing authoritative statements without the need to explain. She's reasonably sure she would not enjoy working for him.

"Was she depressed?" Jane asks.

"Not in the way you mean. We—we were getting divorced," he says. "So I suppose that's not a *happy* time."

"One of you had already filed?" she asks, though she already knows from his ex-wife Cassandra.

"I did."

"May I ask why?" She questions herself, whether she phrased that question properly, as if she needs permission. She's a cop investigating a murder. She's entitled to that answer, however personal it may be. She makes a mental note.

Betancourt sizes her up, eyes squinted in disapproval. "Irreconcilable differences."

"Can you elaborate?"

He seems to find that amusing at first—pushy, he'd probably say to her if she weren't a cop, *a pushy broad*—but then breaks eye contact and fixes his stare on the wall. "The marriage wasn't working out."

"Did your wife agree with that assessment?"

That question, he finds even more amusing. "I am sure she did."

"When did you file?"

"Couple weeks ago."

"So in October, mid-October."

He shrugs. "Look it up. It's public information."

She lets that go, because he's right.

"Was there infidelity?"

He works his jaw, an unreadable expression. "Was she having an affair? I don't know. I was basically staying downtown by that point, in our condo on Michigan Avenue. We have a condo at Superior and Michigan downtown. I've been staying there exclusively since, oh, sometime in August or September. It wouldn't have been hard for her to carry on with somebody. And it wouldn't surprise me. But if you're asking me if I know for fact, no, I don't know for fact."

"What about you?" Jane asks.

"Oh, here." He snaps his fingers. "I moved out on September eleventh. I remember that because it was 9/11. I remember thinking to myself, my marriage had crashed like the Twin Towers."

Jane catches something in the expression on her partner Andy Tate's face but lets it go. She asks her question again. "What about you, Mr. Betancourt? Have you been faithful?"

He knew that was coming. His face shows a hint of disappointment that his attempt to focus on Lauren, and being far more elaborate in his answer than he'd been with any previous question, would have taken Jane in a different direction. Now he focuses on his fingernails, his meaty, rough hand cupped. "Next question," he says.

So that would be a no, he hasn't been faithful. Jane stays silent and stares at him. It's worth a shot. The old adage is that if you sit silently, the nervous witness will keep talking to fill in the space. She doubts that will work with Conrad Betancourt.

It doesn't. Finally, he looks at her and repeats his answer. "Next question."

It's a delicate dance, all of this. She wants to push but not too hard. Because the witness has an Ace card that, frankly, she's surprised he hasn't played yet—he can refuse to answer and demand an attorney.

But that will tell her something, too. A man doesn't have to be physically present to have his wife murdered, not if he has all the money in the world. What better way, in fact, than spending a long weekend with your sons in Florida while it's happening?

"Okay, Mr. Betancourt," she says. "My next question is: How much money are you worth?"

"Ah, there it is." He angles his large head, a bitter smile. "Am I really a suspect? You think I had my wife killed so I wouldn't have to fork over a bunch of money to her? Did you learn being a cop by watching made-for-TV movies or something?"

Jane sits back in her chair, opens her hands. "I have to rule you out, Mr. Betancourt. You know I do. So help me do that."

"We had a prenuptial agreement," says Conrad. "She was entitled to one million dollars in a divorce. That was something I could comfortably afford. And I offered to pay her attorney fees on top of that."

"Maybe she wanted to contest that prenup," says Jane.

"Maybe she did, but she'd fail. Besides, the rest of my money was placed in a trust before we married. She didn't have access to it. It's impenetrable. So whether she was or was not going to contest it, I would not have been the least bit worried."

"Mr. Betancourt," says Andy, "you're sure you moved out on 9/11?"

Conrad takes his time before looking over at Andy. "I already told you that. I thought of the Twin Towers. Yes, I am sure I moved out and into the condo downtown."

"But you're certain about the date," Andy presses.

Conrad blinks. A natural reaction to being pinned down. His eyes rise to the ceiling, then back down to Andy. "Yes, I'm certain about that date."

"And you never came back to this house, maybe spent the night?"

"No. Never. I never returned to this house after September eleventh."

"Did Lauren ever spend the night at the condo downtown after September eleventh?"

Conrad leans forward, putting out his hands. "Let me make this simple. I have not laid eyes on Lauren since September eleventh. Is that clear enough? Feel free to ask the staff at the condo building. The doormen will tell you."

Andy sits back in his chair.

"Let me show you something." Jane lifts the pink phone out of the evidence bag. "Ever seen this phone?"

"Not— No," he says. "What is that? I mean, it's a phone, but—whose?"

"You don't know?"

"I have no idea." His expression hardens. The same notion, no doubt, is springing to his mind that came to Jane and Andy when they saw it. A burner phone she used for an extramarital affair.

He looks around like he wants to hit something. "So there *was* someone else," he says. Now that he's beyond speculation, he seems to care more than he let on a moment earlier. The anger shows in his coloring, the tightness of the jaw. "Who? Who's the other man?"

"We don't know if there *was* another man," Jane says. "And if there was, we don't know who."

"What's the . . ." He gestures to the phone. "Are there text messages? There must be."

"It's not something we can get into right now," she says.

"Answer me that, though. Are there messages? Love notes?"

"There are text messages, yes. I promise that when I can give you—"

"When did they start? How long has this . . ." He looks away with a bitter smirk.

"I can't, sir."

"Just tell me that much. Give me a date."

"Mr. Betancourt, please. Soon, I promise, but not now."

Conrad stews on that, trying to deal with his anger in a composed manner and only barely succeeding. But slowly he decelerates and seems to realize that his reaction to the prospect of his wife's extramarital affair could only deepen any suspicions the officers might have of him.

"Great," he mumbles. "That's just . . . great."

"Mr. Betancourt, can you excuse us a second?" Andy says.

Jane follows Andy into the Betancourts' kitchen, where Andy removes from a folder a copy of the transcript of text messages.

"Here," Andy whispers. "Here, read these messages from September nineteenth."

Jane reads over his shoulder:

**UNKNOWN CALLER**                    **VICTIM'S PHONE (EVIDENCE #1)**

*Mon, Sept 19, 10:01 AM*

Top of the mornin' to yah, lassie.

*Mon, Sept 19, 10:04 AM*

Good morning, my queen.

*Mon, Sept 19, 10:06 AM*

Sounds like you're otherwise
occupied. Will try you tonight my
love.

*Mon, Sept 19, 8:00 PM*

Top of the evenin' to yah, lassie.

                                      *Mon, Sept 19, 8:01 PM*

                                      Um, Lassie was a dog but ok

*Mon, Sept 19, 8:01 PM*

Cranky are we?

*Mon, Sept 19, 8:02 PM*

Didn't sleep well last night Con
snores so loudly <yawns>

*Mon, Sept 19, 8:02 PM*

So that's why I missed you this
morning?

*Mon, Sept 19, 8:04 PM*

Once he left I slept half the morning

*Mon, Sept 19, 8:05 PM*

Can't say I enjoy image of you
sleeping with him.

*Mon, Sept 19, 8:05 PM*

Well it's his house don't be healing

*Mon, Sept 19, 8:06 PM*

LOL don't be JEALOUS damn
autocorrect bye for now

That . . . doesn't make sense.

"Doesn't make sense," says Andy. "On September nineteenth, Lauren's complaining that the night before, Conrad was snoring so loud she couldn't sleep. Conrad swears to us he wasn't anywhere near Lauren after September eleventh. And I can't see him lying about that. I mean, we can check that very easily. Conrad would have to be an idiot to lie about that so specifically."

"Agreed," Jane whispers. "Conrad's not lying. *Lauren* is, to her secret boyfriend."

"But why?" Andy asks. "Why would Lauren be lying to her guy on the side?"

"And if she lied to him about that," says Jane, "what else did she lie about?"

# BEFORE HALLOWEEN

## October

# 41

*Tuesday, October 18, 2022*

*This could be trouble, this problem. What am I going to do?*

*It matters a lot to me, Lauren. I can't do that to Vicky. I can tell her, yes. I can tell her tonight, when she gets home, that I've met you, that I'm going to get a divorce and marry you. But I can't file for divorce before November 3. I can't file before our tenth anniversary. If I do, she'll be cut off from the trust money.*

*I told you that, all of that. "I'll tell Vicky tonight," I said. "I'll move out of the house and get another place. We can move in together right now. I just can't file for divorce yet. It's less than a month away. What difference does a month make?"*

*"She has no right to that money," you said. "You inherited it from your father. It's your money. She doesn't deserve it."*

*"'Deserve it'? We've been married for almost ten years."*

*"And why do you think that is?" you said. "Do you not see it, Simon?"*

*I didn't catch your meaning. Or maybe I didn't want to.*

*You paused, like you were searching for words. Then you breathed out like you were done sugarcoating it.*

*"You two aren't in love and you never were," you said.*

*I felt like the wind had been knocked out of me. "That's not true."*

*"She never loved you, Simon. She needed someone to take care of her. And you did. And now she's eyeballing that trust money that's so close she can taste it. She's put in nine years and eleven months."*

*I stepped back, almost falling over the bed. "You make it sound like a prison sentence."*

*You walked over and took my hands. "You deserve so much better," you said. "You want to do right by Vicky, then fine. Pay her alimony off your professor's salary. But don't give her millions of dollars. That's your money."*

*You kissed me, first softly then deeply, my internal thermometer ratcheting up. "You mean our money," I said.*

*"You know I don't care about the money," you whispered, reaching for my belt buckle.*

*"I know."*

*You dropped to your knees and worked the zipper on my pants.*

*"Promise me you'll file now," you said.*

# 42
## Simon

I decide to go for a run in the morning, a version of my Five at Five that I've abandoned since I started running at nights from the law school to Wicker Park. I miss jogging on the west side of Chicago, but today is not the day to make up for that. This morning, I run instead the other direction, west from my house, toward Grace Village. Toward Lauren's house.

I've driven my car over there in the mornings enough. If I am too regular in doing so, one of those nosy neighbors might start to notice. That's the last thing I need.

I drove over here yesterday morning and parked down the street from Lauren's house, arriving at 5:30 a.m. It was the first time in a few weeks.

I was waiting for Conrad's town car to pick him up at six sharp and drive down to the East Bank Club for his morning workout. But no town car ever came.

Now here I am, jogging up, down, and near Lathrow Avenue, crossing streets, switching directions, trying not to stand out as the sun begins to show its face on a Friday morning, as five-thirty becomes five-forty-five, as five-fifty becomes six o'clock, as six o'clock becomes ten after six.

Once again, no town car arrives to pick up Conrad Betancourt.

Maybe he's out of town on business or took a long weekend with some buddies. Maybe that's it.

Where'd you go, Conrad?

———

I stop a half block down from Lauren's house and look back at it. It's not too late, I tell myself yet again. It's not too late to put the brakes on everything and just forget that I ever saw Lauren on Michigan Avenue last May. God, it feels like so much more than five months ago that she re-entered my life. Maybe that's because, to me, she never really left.


"I hear someone has a big birthday coming up," Lauren whispered in my ear, the smell of beer on her breath, more than nineteen years ago. Times were good that summer at my dad's law firm, after Teddy had scored that enormous settlement in the electrical-injury case and the place was flush with cash. Happy hours every Friday night. I never stayed long; I usually went straight home after work and spent the evenings with my mother, who by then was in a wheelchair and spent her days at home with her caregiver, Edie.

But my father always let me have one beer, despite my being seventeen, his way of showing me the cool-parent thing, and the happy hours always started at four o'clock, so I usually hung around for the first hour before taking the Green Line home.

Lauren had been nice to me that first month of the summer, joking and complimentary and maybe, in hindsight, even flirtatious. But I hadn't thought much of it, as I was the boss's son, and pretty much everyone treated me with kid gloves—a lot more pleases and thank-yous when I dropped off a package or delivered a message than the other staffers presumably received.

But that night, that last Friday in June, Lauren looked at me differently. A couple of beers down and the atmosphere loose, she smiled at me in a way that made me feel like an adult for the first time in my life.

"I have a present for you," she whispered.

I'd never been with a woman. My experience to date had been a few awkward kisses my junior and senior years of high school, a couple of painful dates that left me feeling inadequate and anxious.

I met her that Sunday, at her house in Old Irving Park, at 3:00 p.m. I got there early, parking my mother's Honda along Kedvale, nervous and tense.

The truth was, I was dreading it. I was scared, not aroused. Queasy, not excited. I wanted to turn the car around and drive back to Grace Park before I had the chance to disappoint her.

Lauren, who was twenty at the time, still lived with her parents in a humble, brick A-frame house north of Waveland. The parents were gone, or so I assumed. She never mentioned them one way or the other. She answered the door in a button-down shirt and bare legs.

"Hello, birthday boy," she said to me.

In any other context, I would've been so aroused. This was the stuff of my fantasies, a woman who could be pinned up on my bedroom wall seducing me—me!—but I was feeling limp in every sense of the word, wilting under the pressure.

"Don't be nervous," she said, making a stark appraisal of my reaction. She took me by the hand and led me through her house, a small kitchen with dishes in the sink, a radiator with peeling paint, a bowl of kibble, and cat litter. It calmed me. Seeing the mundane in her life brought her back to earth, or at least that's where I tried to maintain my focus.

Once inside her bedroom, she made it so easy. I had no context, other than the occasional foray into internet porn or sex scenes from movies, where everyone is so smooth and confident.

She took it slow, drawing close to me, letting me smell her perfume, gently brushing her lips against my neck, running her hands up the sides of my legs. She started swaying, though there was no music, humming something I didn't recognize.

She turned around, pressing her buttocks against my crotch, her head against my shoulder, as I silently begged for an erection, to get past the nerves and get into the moment. She took my hands and cupped them around her breasts and moaned.

"You feel good," she whispered.

Then my hands took on a life of their own, squeezing her breasts, cupping her neck, running through her hair, pressing against her silk panties.

And then, batter up, I was in the moment. She had helped me get there, had guided me through the first curves and turns, and now I was ready to take the wheel.

I wish I could say that Lauren enjoyed hours of ecstasy. My best estimate is that it was four minutes—and that was with me trying hard to hold it in—and I'm not sure any particular moment would have qualified to her as ecstatic. I didn't have any idea how long I was supposed to hold out, not the slightest concept of how to bring a member of the female species to orgasm.

But she made me feel like she'd had the time of her life. She wrapped her legs around my back and held me there, afterward, for a long time.

"I like feeling you inside me," she whispered.

The truth, I was more relieved than anything.

She brought in a couple of beers and we drank them and talked on her bed. I was a few months away from college, and she told me she was saving up so she could afford college, too. We talked about music, about baseball, and one beer became another. That was one more beer than I'd ever drunk, but the buzz from my first sexual encounter was far more intoxication than any alcohol could provide.

We were standing by her dresser, looking at pictures of her from high school, when she looked at the clock on the wall. "My parents will be home in about an hour," she said. "Sometimes they come home a little early."

"So the birthday boy should probably get going," I said.

"Mmm." She put her hands on my chest. "You're not a boy, you're a man," she said. "So how 'bout you fuck me one more time before you leave?"

She sure knew how to punch my buttons.


And now, here we are, nineteen years later. I am rapidly approaching that cliff. It's not too late to turn back. That's the beauty of it; until I jump, I can always change my mind.

My life has been okay. I put myself together and moved on. I can keep that life, nice and safe, more or less, boring and uneventful, maybe, but meaningful to me. As long as I can still teach, even if I'm run out of my law school by Dean Comstock—I can find some school, prestigious or not, it won't matter as long as I can still teach and talk and write about the law.

If I take the plunge, I don't know where I will land. It might be the biggest mistake of my life. It could well be the end of me.

# 43

## Vicky

I sit in a high-back chair outside the ballroom at the Peninsula Hotel, where inside, eight hundred of the wealthiest people in Chicago mingle and play casino games to raise money for autism awareness. I am not dressed for a night like this and have no invitation, but I wore a dress, anyway, to generally fit in.

In my lap is my phone, in my ears, AirPods. I look like I'm watching something on my phone. I am not. The screen is blank. But the words from inside the Gold Coast Room come through the AirPods with decent clarity:

> HE: *"So are you staying here tonight?"*
> SHE: *"No. Are you?"*
> HE: *"I have a suite."*
> SHE: *"I see. And why are you telling me that?"*
> HE: *"Uh-oh. Am I being inappropriate?"*
> SHE: *"You tell me. Tell me what you're thinking right now."*
> HE: *"I'm not sure that's wise."*
> SHE: *"Why not?"*
> HE: *"I might get my face slapped."*

A pause.

> SHE: *"You think I'd slap you in the face."*
> HE: *"Or maybe my wife would, if she heard me."*

Well done. A test. He's cautious. He dips his toe in and gives her open-ings but allows himself an easy retreat.

SHE: *"Well, then, I guess it's a good thing your wife's not here to-night."*

Seventy-five minutes later. Quicker than I expected. The sound is better inside the hotel room than in the ballroom, far less noise and interference. His moaning is annoying but helpful.

HE: *"You are just . . . full of surprises."*
SHE: *"Do you like that?"*
HE: *"I like that . . . I like that a lot."*
SHE: *"Does your wife do this for you, Paul?"*
HE: *"My wife? Give me a break. She just lies there like a sack of potatoes. I have to check her for a pulse."*

They laugh.

Melanie comes down the stairs over an hour later, past midnight, wearing her dress from the night, a small jacket over her shoulders. I know Mel from our days in the "entertainment" business, which she has yet to leave, though she's going to school for a degree in sociology. I hope she completes it and gets out of this business. You can tell yourself whatever you need to tell yourself to get through the nights, but you can't survive this work for very long.

I hand her an envelope. She opens it and counts the money. "This is more than we discussed," she says. "This is too much."

"Consider it a bonus. You got some good stuff in there."

"Yeah, well, he doesn't like his wife, does he?"

She unpins the crystal brooch from her dress and hands it to me. "Pretty sure we captured the whole thing on here," she says. "If you use it, you'll black out my face?"

"Of course, Mel. And I don't think it will ever come to that, anyway."

I give her a hug and we say our goodbyes. "Get that degree," I say to her. "Promise."

"I promise. I'm about two semesters away." She looks around and leans in to whisper in my ear. "So what did this guy do, anyway, to piss you off?"

# 44
## Christian

Vicky lies on me, twisting her finger in and out of my chest hair, thinking about something, though I don't know what. She keeps her thoughts to herself, and I'm too cautious to push too hard lest I push her away.

I guess I don't need to know if I'm anything more to Vicky than a financial whiz who also happens to be easy on the eyes and terrific in bed. Gavin is right. All that matters is that money. I need to keep my eye on the prize, a prize that is less than a month away now.

But the closer November 3 gets, the more I worry, like a pitcher throwing a no-hitter who's just rolling along doing his thing, but now it's the ninth inning, and the prize is in sight, and you feel yourself tightening up.

"What was it with you and Simon's father?" I ask, because the whole thing with Theodore Dobias is something I should understand better. If Simon Dobias can be pushed as far as murder, I should probably know that before I help Vicky steal all his money, yes?

"Well, he obviously thought I wanted Simon for his money. Maybe it was personal to me, or maybe that's just how he felt, generally, about women."

"Maybe he didn't trust Simon."

"Oh, that's definitely part of it. Simon..." She puts her chin on my chest and looks at me. "You look at Simon, he's a nice-looking man, he can be charming and funny, but he never really had many good relationships with women before he met me. As far as I know, he only had one real girlfriend, back when he was like eighteen, this woman named Lauren who broke his heart. That was right around the time his mother died, and his world kind of crashed after that."

"Oh, when did his mother die?" I ask, playing dumb.

"Well, it's a whole story," says Vicky. "Simon's mother—Glory was her name—Glory was a law professor like Simon ended up. Anyway, she had a stroke that put her in a wheelchair and took away a lot of her mental capabilities and basically ended her career. Simon's dad, Teddy—Teddy was making good money then and he started living this sort of swinger-bachelor lifestyle. He cheated on his wife. Simon caught him."

"He *caught* him?"

"Yeah. Walked in on him. Teddy was having sex with this woman in his office, and Simon walked right in and saw it."

"Harsh."

"Yeah, harsh. And doubly harsh because Simon *idolized* his mother. He couldn't bear to tell her what Teddy was doing. So he kept it quiet. And pretty soon, Teddy ended up blowing all his money and didn't have the finances to take care of Glory, to pay for in-home care. Long story short, he wanted to put Glory in a nursing home, Simon freaked out, and right around then, Glory swallowed a bottleful of pain meds." She looks at me. "Glad you asked?"

"So after blowing all his money on women, Teddy didn't want Simon doing the same thing? And that's why he put that language in the trust?"

"I guess so."

"So what happened to Teddy?"

She looks at me for a long time.

I didn't phrase that question well. What *happened* to Teddy? I should have been more generic, like *What happened after Glory died? Did Simon ever make peace with his father?* Something that doesn't hint that I know that someone stuck a knife in Teddy.

Do better, Nicky. Stay on your game.

But then I realize that Vicky isn't wondering why I would ask that question, or if I already knew something. She's deciding how much to tell me. She's deciding how much to let me into her life.

"Teddy, believe it or not, was murdered," Vicky says. "He was living in St. Louis by then, and someone stabbed him and pushed him into his pool."

"Whoa," I say. "Who stabbed him?"

Her eyes trail off. "They never found out. They looked at Simon as a suspect, but Simon was up in Chicago taking final exams at U of C. It would have been very hard for him to have pulled that off."

Very hard but not impossible. In fact, that would kinda be the beauty of it.

"What are you thinking?" she asks me.

I snap out of my trance. "Nothing."

"You're wondering whether Simon killed Teddy."

"No, I mean—"

"You're wondering whether I did."

"God, no," I say. "Of course not."

But of course, I am.

"I'm just worried about you," I say. "If you and Simon get into a fight over this trust money, and he's capable of something like violence—"

"So you do think he did it."

"Hey." I pull her up to me so we're face-to-face. "I've never met the guy. I have no idea what he's capable of. You tell me he didn't do it, then he didn't do it. I just want you to be careful. *You* are what matters to me. You're my long-term investment."

"Ahh . . ." Vicky reaches down between my legs. "All this talk of violence and murder got you worked up."

God, this woman knows me well, which is pretty impressive, considering my entire identity is a lie.

She straddles me, and I slide into her, thrusting upward. Vicky moans in response. It's been an hour since our last time, so I have some staying power. I'll take her for a good long ride.

She goes off into that faraway place of hers, then leans forward, her arms taut on each side of me. Her face close to mine. Her jaw clenched.

She opens her eyes and slows things down to a gentle rhythm. She leans forward, nose to nose, and whispers to me.

"Simon did it. He killed his father. I didn't try to stop him. And I married him anyway. I married him for his money. So now you know. Now's your chance to run as far away as you can."

I thrust upward, Vicky bobbing, closing her eyes in response.

"I'm not . . . running away," I say.

"You don't know me," she says, eyes still closed, her head turned away. "You can't trust me."

"I know you. I trust you." Running my hands over her body, picking up speed, the heat rising within me.

"Nobody's . . . ever . . . trusted me," she says, breathing hard, head leaned back.

I've never come so hard in my life.

# 45

*Wednesday, October 19, 2022*

*"You didn't tell her," you said, reading my face when you opened the door.*

*"It's . . . not an easy conversation to have."*

*"Have you made an appointment with that divorce lawyer?"*

*"I called him," I said, but that was a lie, and I made that vow, I'd never lie to you, Lauren, so with my tail between my legs, I corrected the record. "I started to call but hung up. This isn't easy, Lauren. C'mon."*

*"You want me to 'c'mon,' like this is some casual thing? Are you committed to us or not?"*

*I am madly, desperately in love with you, Lauren. That is one thing that is not in doubt. But you have to know how hard this will be for Vicky. Why can't you understand that? Why can't you let me make this decision?*

*"I'm not going to be that woman," you said. "I'm not going to nag at you and beg and plead and demand. If you don't want to commit to me—"*

*"I'll tell her tonight," I promised.*

*And I will. Vicky will be home soon, and I'm going to tell her. God, this is going to be brutal. Oh, she's home, she's coming up the stairs right*

# 46
## Simon

I drop my green journal into my work bag as Vicky comes into my home office upstairs. "I thought I might find you here," she says.

"You found me."

She's holding a laptop, carrying it like a book in school.

"I want you to look at something," she says. "Don't say a word until you're finished."

*"Does your wife do this for you, Paul?"* the woman on the video screen asks.

*"My wife? Give me a break. She just lies there like a sack of potatoes. I have to check her for a pulse."*

"Okay, enough," I say, hitting the "pause" button on the video, handing the laptop back to Vicky. "You promised me you wouldn't do anything."

"And I've *kept* my promise," she says. "I haven't done anything with it. He has no idea he was recorded. I leave that up to you."

I run my fingers through my hair. "This is Paul Southern? Reid's father?"

"The very one," she says. "The man who's bankrolling his idiot son all the way into a full professorship."

"I wish you'd told me," I say.

"You would've told me not to do it."

"Exactly."

"Well, so far, I haven't done anything. All I did was load the gun. It's up to you whether you pull the trigger."

I drop my head into my hands. I should've figured she'd do something like this. "I take it you couldn't find anything on Dean Comstock?"

"Nothing all that good." She closes the laptop. "But I was thinking. If you go straight at Dean Cumstain, you have an archenemy on your hands. That's not in your best interest. Why not go to the source, the one the dean is trying to please?"

"So, what—we show this to Paul and tell him to back me instead of his own son?"

She shrugs. "That's exactly what we do."

"Won't that seem odd to the dean? Suddenly, Reid's father says, Give the promotion to the other guy?"

"Who cares what seems odd?" she says. "You know all this money Paul Southern has—it didn't come from his own blood, sweat, and tears. Did you know that?"

"I did not."

"He married into it. His wife inherited a fortune, and the company. Paul's the CEO, but he's beholden to her." She pats the laptop. "How do you think wifey's gonna feel about what her husband said about her, much less what he was doing?"

"She wouldn't like it. If she ever saw this video, which she won't."

"Of course she won't. Paul would never let that happen. He'd be out on his ass."

"*Paul* is never going to see this video, either, Vicky. I'm not going to use this."

I look up at her. She looks down on me like a disapproving parent. Which is kind of ironic, because I'm the one trying to take the high road here.

"This isn't Paul Southern's fault," I say. "He's just trying to help his son. I don't like it, but he's not malicious. He doesn't deserve this."

"Yeah, I feel *real* sorry for Paul. He seems like a great guy!" That sarcastic look, that faux cheerfulness.

This is one of the ways where Vicky and I differ. I may push back when people do things to me, but I don't generally distrust people. Vicky, she made her way through life being used by other people, mostly men, so she basically starts with the opposite presumption, that everyone deserves a good kick in the shin until proven otherwise. She would look at Paul as someone who had it coming, even if he never personally did anything to us.

"You're letting them push you around," she says.

"Hey, I applied, didn't I? You have to give me that much."

"I do, yes. But now the dean's going to steamroll you if you don't protect yourself. Why won't you let me help you do that?"

Because I don't want anything else in my life to taint my job.

Because I've let my life be controlled by what others have done, and my inexplicable need to settle the score, and okay, inside my own internal courtroom, I make the rules, I am judge, jury, and prosecutor, fine, but that's my fucked-up internal world, not my job.

Because what I love about the law is its purity, its honesty, its search for justice and fairness.

Because I love teaching the tools of that craft, honing minds, showing them the majesty of the law at its zenith.

Because I won't let anything contaminate that.

That's why.

Most people would laugh at me if I said these things aloud. Vicky would not. She would appreciate them. But I don't need to speak those words. She already knows. She understands me.

I come out of my fog and look up at her. She has her hand out, like she's raising it for attention but isn't into the whole arm-raising thing.

The first time I met Vicky, she raised her hand just like that. We were in SOS, her first time, a girl in a tank top and shorts and baseball cap sitting in the back row, and after several other people had spoken, as the session seemed to be dying down, she raised her hand just like that, not even shoulder level, showing me her palm, a look on her face like she didn't really like having to be called on.

"My sister committed suicide six weeks ago," she said. "I've been listening to everyone talk about how guilty they feel. Am I the only one who's fucking pissed off?"

Everyone laughed and started clapping, appreciating the release in the tension, her blunt acknowledgment of an emotion most of us survivors experience. That was the moment I fell in love with her. That's the moment I realized I'd do anything for her.

"Never mind," she says to me now. "It was a bad idea. I won't mention it again."

The reason I still love Vicky, oddly enough, is that what I have to offer her is not enough. After the life she led, having to do unspeakable things to survive, you'd think it would be enough to have a man who loves you, who thinks the world of you, who will treat you with respect, who will care for you, who will give you anything you want. I check every one of those boxes.

But through all of that, she has demanded more. She wants to be in love. She wants the fairy tale. And no matter what other feelings she may have toward me, I can't give her that.

That's why she'll leave me. She's never said so explicitly, but I know it. She'll leave in November.

# 47

*When I walked through the door this afternoon, you stood there, a distance apart, waiting for what I had to say.*

*"I saw the divorce lawyer today," I told you.*

*You nodded. "Did you tell Vicky?"*

*"I did not. But I will."*

*"When?"*

*"Before I file," I said. "Which will be after November 3. I can't cut Vicky out of the money, Lauren. I can't do that to her. I won't."*

*Your face went cold. "I see," you whispered. You didn't seem all that surprised.*

*"What you have to decide," I said, "is whether you can respect my decision. I hope you can. But that's my decision, and it's final."*

*We can get past this, right? You'll come to understand. This is where you're supposed to say, That's one of the reasons I love you, Simon, that you'd want to make sure you take care of Vicky before saying goodbye to her.*

*But all you said was "I need time to think. I need the weekend."*

*That didn't sound like a good sign.*

# 48

## Simon

Friday night. Most people would be spending time with their family or blowing off steam over a couple drinks with friends. Me, I'm in my office at the law school, finishing up a blog post on a case involving a Title III intercept from the Ninth Circuit that is before the U.S. Supreme Court this session.

I have the house to myself this weekend, as Vicky is off to Elm Grove again to spend time with her nieces. So I work later than usual, until after eight o'clock, before starting my routine run from the law school to Wicker Park. To the alley outside Viva Mediterránea. To the alley behind Christian Newsome's condo.

I suit up, leaving my blue jeans and button-down hanging on the back of my office door, throwing on running pants and shoes, a high-neck top with ski cap. The temps are in the mid-forties with no precipitation, perfect running conditions, if you discount the occasional difficulties navigating these populated city streets in the dark.

Viva's patio is almost vacant, despite the heat lamps blowing and the city allowing restaurants to keep their outside areas open late into the year. Only a handful of people are braving the elements, drinking cocktails in their heavy coats.

Usually, I make sure I reach the alley in Wicker Park by 8:00 p.m. for the nightly text messages. But we don't text on Friday nights or the weekends. The phones stay off from Friday morning to Monday morning. I'm not here for texting.

No, I just wanted to get a good look at Christian's place.

The front of his building on Winchester is fenced, but it's not a security gate, just something to keep the dogs away from the small garden out front. Up the stairs is the front door, a secured door with a buzzer. In the alley are the garages. Christian's garage is third from the end, directly beneath his condo. The garage is controlled by an automatic door, like most are, which is surprisingly secure.

Still, that's the better point of entry. Certainly the less visible one, given the poorly lit alley. And unless you're going in and out of that garage while patrons are out on Viva's back patio, there aren't likely to be too many people hanging around back there.

That's how Vicky comes in when she visits. She doesn't walk up to the front door, stand under a light, buzz, and take the stairs up. No, she enters in the shadows, through the garage, without having to ever see a neighbor.

What are you doing tonight, Christian, with Vicky away? Are you and your buddy Gavin out drinking and carousing?

Mind if I take a look around your condo?

Nah. Not tonight, at least. Maybe later.

# 49

## Vicky

"It's good you're here. They like it when you're here." Adam hands me a glass of pinot as we watch his daughters, my nieces, Mariah and Macy, the M&Ms, finish up a game of one-on-one basketball in the driveway.

"I like it, too." I zip up my coat to my chin. I just wish it wasn't so cold.

"Still okay with moving in with us?"

"Still okay if you're okay," I say. "November. Maybe Thanksgiving-ish." I look at Adam. He's just hitting forty, with a hint of gray creeping in at the temples. Adam Tremont is the all-American boy, the thick head of hair and big smile, full of good cheer, someone who grew up with money and basically seemed to have life right where he wanted it. He and my sister, Monica, were the Perfect Couple, Barbie and Ken, handsome and charismatic, bubbling with energy and positive vibes. It was enough to make me puke most of the time, when I wasn't busy resenting Monica for her good fortune.

Adam met Monica in college, at Madison, and swept her off her feet. In a good way. Adam is the real deal.

"Last night," he says, "Macy asked me if she looked like Mommy."

"She does," I say. "Mariah more so. When Mariah was younger, she looked like you. But now that she's growing up, that face? That's Monica."

"I know. It kinda freaks me out."

Me, too. It can be shocking sometimes, to see the face of my sister again in her daughters, to be reminded of the woman I didn't do enough to help.

I elbow him. "You getting out there at all?"

"Hm." He finishes a sip of his wine and shakes his head. "You mean like dating?"

"I mean 'like dating.'"

"Oh . . . a grand total of two dates. Nothing serious."

Mariah, the elder at age thirteen, swats away a shot from Macy, three years younger. Macy claims that's "no fair" because Mariah is older and taller.

"They'll understand, y'know," I tell him. "It might be a little weird or awkward, but they can handle it."

"I'm not sure *I* can," he says. "This online dating stuff? It's freakin' nuts. It's not for me. If I ever do it, it's gonna be the old-fashioned way."

"A handsome, successful guy like you? I think you'll be fine."

"Not so sure about either of those things."

I catch on that, take a swallow of wine. The Tremont family started a chain of microbreweries that did quite well. Adam, the only child, took over the business, more or less, about a decade ago, and things ran smoothly until the last few years, when COVID-19 hit and struck a massive blow to the business.

"The restaurant side is just now coming back," he says. "Good thing for us we had the retail sales. One thing people didn't stop doing during the pandemic was drink alcohol."

"Money's still tight?" I ask, as if I'm only moving along the conversation and not probing.

"Pretty tight, yeah. We closed another brewery last week."

"I didn't know that. I'm sorry."

He lets out a bitter chuckle. "If Monica were here, she'd be telling me to look forward, not back."

Yep, that sounds like her. I'm glad he remembers her that way, because that was the Monica he met in college, the Monica with whom he fell in love, the Monica who was the mother to his children. Not the Monica who injured her back and started on OxyContin, who didn't realize when she crossed that line from needing oxy for the pain to just needing oxy, period, who eventually did the unthinkable—unthinkable for Monica, at least—and walked away from her family for a man who was more than happy to keep supplying her with pain-killing opioids.

I, of all people, was Monica's confidante, to the extent she let any of us know that she was falling into the grips of that poison, that it was slowly predominating over everything else in her life. Maybe it was because I'd been such a fuckup myself, the black sheep of the family, that she felt more comfortable sharing with me than Adam. I was three hundred miles away, so it was mostly by phone. I didn't realize how warped her reality had become because I wasn't there in person.

Or that's what I try to tell myself, at least. I was the younger, screwup sister, talking and texting with her from a distance. She was the belle of our high school, the prom queen who went to college and married a handsome, wealthy guy and had two beautiful children. How seriously could she take advice from the high school dropout who'd never made a good decision in her life?

But I knew she was faltering. I could tell those drugs were messing with her judgment. I knew she needed someone to shake some sense into her.

Did I *really* help as much as I could have? Or was there a part of me that drew some satisfaction from seeing Ms. Perfect stumble from her perch?

"Do you need money, Adam?" I ask, point-blank.

"Why, you offering?" That's just like him to deflect, to joke. "We'll get through this," he says. "It'll be tight for a while. Might have to whittle down the number of breweries some more. Girls, it's getting cold! Let's wrap up the game!"

Macy howls in protest, as her older sister seems to be getting the better of her, and she doesn't want to be on the losing end of the final score. She says, "Just a little longer," which Adam probably already factored in. With these girls, everything is a negotiation, every command merely an opening bid.

And he changed the subject, I note.

He exhales a heavy sigh. "Amazing how life can turn," he says. "One minute, you think you've got it all figured out, all planned and secure, and then . . ." He snaps his fingers. "And then everything you believed in, every assumption you had made—poof."

"Yeah."

"And we—we were just getting over Monica," he says. "That year of torture when she left, when I tried to explain to the girls that Mommy left because of the drugs, not because of them, and then she OD'd, and any hope we had that she might come back . . ."

"I know."

"And we're finally crawling out from under that—y'know, two of the most brutal years of our lives—and COVID hits. My breweries tank, I have half of what I used to have and will probably lose more . . ."

I grab his arm. "They might hear you."

He looks at the girls, who aren't paying attention, scrambling for a loose basketball on the driveway court.

"Jesus, I'm sorry." He chuckles. "I promise, most of the time, I'm okay. Just sometimes, especially if I've had a couple of these," he says, raising his glass of wine. "Sometimes it all comes tidal-waving back."

"You have every right to all of those feelings. You'll be okay."

He smiles at me. "Look forward, right?"

Exactly. Just like Monica used to say. Look forward, not back.

Well, maybe you can look back a *little*.

# THE DAY AFTER
# HALLOWEEN

# 50

## Jane

"I don't know if I'm supposed to talk about this, but ... Lauren and Conrad were getting a divorce." Shari Rowe sits back in the chair in the interview room and awaits a reaction. She is the last of a circle of Lauren's friends, most of whom live downtown, that Jane Burke and Andy Tate have interviewed tonight.

"We're aware," Jane tells her. "How did Lauren feel about that?"

"I mean, it's not happy times, but . . ." Shari is thirty-six, divorced, a schoolteacher downtown. Glamorous and confident, one of those women with whom Jane never really felt a kinship, but traits that generally matched all five of Lauren's band of friends. Lauren's Facebook page is full of photos of these women out at clubs, brunching on weekends, in yoga class, chill moments on "movie nights."

"But what?"

"Lauren was ready to move on, I'd say. It had been bad with Conrad for a while. It's not like any of us were surprised. But an affair? She never said anything about that."

"Would you expect that she would? That she'd tell you?"

Shari thinks about that. "People have their secrets, right? But we were pretty open with each other. We talked about every other damn thing. We had each other's backs. I'll say this much, if she wanted to have an affair, she'd have plenty of takers."

"Men were drawn to her?"

"Oh, yeah, when we'd go out, sure. She started going out with us again over the last year, when things got bad with Conrad. Men would swarm around her. I mean, just look at her." She freezes on that comment, her eyes misting, realizing that nobody will be looking at Lauren again. "You think she was having an affair, and the guy . . . killed her?"

"We're just checking every option," says Andy, who has clearly enjoyed these interviews with Lauren Betancourt's attractive friends.

"I think . . ." Shari inclines her head. "I think she was looking forward to getting out there again. She said she 'missed sex.' I know from firsthand experience that when a marriage is breaking down, sex is the first thing to go."

"Yeah?" Jane tries to sound disinterested. "When did Lauren say she missed sex?"

"Oh, that was the last time we were out."

"Last Thursday, October twenty-seventh?" Apparently all six of the women made it out to a dance bar in River North last Thursday.

"Right. God, just a week ago. I still can't . . . can't believe she's gone." She shakes her head, blinking away tears.

Jane sneaks a look at Andy, whose eyebrows dance.


"Give me the latest," says the chief, arching his back. It's past nine o'clock, and it seems like nobody wants to be the first one to leave tonight, after the discovery of Lauren Betancourt's body this morning.

"Okay, first, the phones," says Jane.

"We tracked down the telecom provider for both Lauren's burner and the burner she was texting," says Andy Tate. "Same carrier, as we figured. We tried real-time CSLI for the other burner, but we couldn't locate the phone."

"His phone's turned off," the chief says.

"His phone's off, yes. So no signal."

"Maybe it's with him in the bottom of a river."

Jane lifts a shoulder. She's not so sure about the suicide angle. Yes, no question, the last text message Lauren's boyfriend sent more than suggested he was going to take his own life—*I'm coming to you now, let me love you in a way you wouldn't in this world*—but talking about suicide is one thing. Actually going through with it is another.

"We should have historical data in a day or two," says Jane.

"Good. What else?"

"Lauren's friends," says Jane. "We managed to get all five of them in tonight. They all say the same thing. Lauren was splitting up with Conrad, so there was that sort of uncertainty about what happens next in your life. But she was anxious to move on. And get this, she told one of her friends last Thursday, when they all went out downtown, that she 'missed sex.'"

"She missed sex?"

"Right, I know," says Andy Tate. "You read those text messages—she and her secret guy were screwing their eyeballs out. But she didn't mention a boyfriend, an affair, a special someone—she didn't mention anything like that to her friends. For all they knew, she'd been faithful to Conrad."

"So put that together with other stuff we've found," says Jane. "She's keeping her affair secret from her closest friends. And we know she wasn't honest on those text messages with her boyfriend, at least in that one text where she talks about Conrad still sleeping at home and snoring, when we know he'd moved out by then."

"She kept her cards close to the vest." The chief screws up his face. "Sounds like a woman with a plan."

Jane nods. "Right. The secret life of Lauren Betancourt keeps getting odder and odder."

As Jane and Andy leave the chief's office, Sergeant Matthew Mooney is walking up with a purpose, holding a paper in his hand.

"Hey, Matt."

"You wanted any records on our victim."

"Yeah. Lauren had a sheet?"

"Well, sort of. Take a look at this."

Jane takes the paper, a PDF copy of an old police report, with Andy Tate reading over her shoulder.

"Holy shit," Jane mumbles.

"This could have legs," says Andy. "But this is from so long ago. Who knows if this guy even still lives around here?"

"He does," says Jane. "Last I saw him, at least."

"Last you— You know this guy, Janey?"

Jane looks up at the ceiling. "Personally, not that well. Class of '03, Grace Consolidated. He was the valedictorian of our class. Quiet, shy, kept to himself. I do remember he was a really good runner, too—really good. I saw him at the fifteenth reunion a few years back, but I don't think we said more than two words to each other."

Andy takes the report from Jane and reads it again. "Well, Sergeant Burke, looks like you might be having another 'reunion' with Simon Dobias very soon."

# BEFORE HALLOWEEN

## October

# 51

*Saturday, October 22, 2022*

*You wanted the weekend to think, Lauren, and I've been doing some think-*
*ing, too. I've decided to show you how important you are to me. I'm going*
*to do as you ask. I'm going to file for divorce now, before November 3. It will*
*cut off Vicky's marital right to the money.*

*I can't wait to tell you. I wish I could do it now. But I know you went up*
*to Wisconsin this weekend, and I know you wouldn't have brought your*
*pink phone. So I'll have to wait until Monday. I can't wait to start a life*
*with you!*

*Sunday, October 23, 2022*

*I can't do it. Whatever I tell myself, I picture telling Vicky, and I picture the*
*look on her face, and I can't betray her like that. The symbolism alone,*
*that I made a point of getting that divorce petition filed just under the*
*deadline. It sounds so diabolical and spiteful. I can't do it. I can't crush*
*Vicky like that.*

*I know you'll understand. I hope you'll understand. You'll understand.*
*Or you're not the person I thought you were.*

### Monday, October 24, 2022

*You wanted to meet on neutral ground, the south end of the parking lot at the Grace Country Club, which I took as a bad sign.*

*I arrived first, early, sweating despite the cool morning air, my heart drumming. But I was hopeful. Deep down, I felt sure you'd understand, even if you didn't like it. And I know you don't care about the money itself, but even if I give Vicky half, that's still ten million dollars! That's more money than anyone needs.*

*Your car pulled up and parked next to mine. When you got out, you looked tired. You looked . . . different, couldn't really put my finger on it.*

*I had nothing to say. The ball was in your court. You looked like you were about to cry.*

*"Whatever you have to say, it's okay," I said, touching your arm.*

*You let out a humorless laugh and wiped a tear from your cheek. "Sure about that?" you said.*

*"I'm sure." I was sure. Or at least I thought I was.*

*"I'm pregnant," you said.*

# 52
## Simon

Dawn. I couldn't sleep, with everything coming to a head now, with the cliff fast approaching. I'm drawing up the document myself. It's not rocket science, after all. I'm a lawyer, and I know all the information, and it's not that difficult to figure out the elements of a cause of action to terminate a marriage. You're married, you don't want to be anymore, you tried to make it work, and it's not going to work.

I slurp some coffee and review what I have so far:

### IN THE CIRCUIT COURT OF COOK COUNTY, ILLINOIS
### COUNTY DEPARTMENT, DOMESTIC RELATIONS DIVISION

*In re the Marriage of:*
SIMON PETER DOBIAS,
Petitioner,

v.                                                                    No.

VICTORIA LANIER DOBIAS,
Respondent.

### PETITION FOR DISSOLUTION OF MARRIAGE

Now comes the Petitioner, Simon P. Dobias, and for his Petition for Dissolution of Marriage against the Respondent, Victoria Lanier Dobias, states as follows:

1. The Petitioner, Simon Peter Dobias, is 37 years old and a resident of the Village of Grace Park, County of Cook, State of Illinois.

2. The Respondent, Victoria Lanier Dobias, is 36 years old and a resident of the Village of Grace Park, County of Cook, State of Illinois.

3. The parties were married on the 3rd day of November, 2012, in Playa del Carmen, Mexico.

4. Irreconcilable differences have arisen between the parties that have caused the irretrievable breakdown of the marriage. Past efforts at reconciliation have failed, and future attempts at reconciliation would be impracticable.

"Irreconcilable differences," the phrase that launched a thousand ships, the legal term that describes in bland terms the countless different complexities that compel a couple once in love to go their separate ways.

"I'm not right for you," Vicky said, the first time I proposed to her, though in hindsight, I think she meant that *I* wasn't right for *her*. "Our differences would be irreconcilable," she might as well have said. And she would have been right.

I walk down the hallway from my home office to the bedroom. Vicky is asleep, her face buried in the pillow.

"The best part of my life is you," my mother said to me on what ended up being the last day I saw her alive, sitting in our kitchen, her wheelchair parked next to the dinner table. It was difficult for her to speak. It came out like her tongue was heavy, like she was intoxicated, which might not have been far from the truth if you consider the painkillers she was taking.

I took her hands and kissed them. "The best part of *my* life is you."

She made a disapproving sound, closed her eyes, and shook her head. "I hope one day . . . that isn't true. Prom—promise me . . . you'll have children. You'll never know . . . such love."

"Sure, Mom, I'm sure I will," I said, having no idea she was giving me parting advice. Looking back, it should have been more obvious to me.

At that point, at age nineteen, the concept of having a serious relationship, much less children, was not on my immediate horizon. My one and only attempt at romance, with Lauren, had failed in spectacular fashion. I hadn't just gotten my hand too close to the stove. I'd dropped my hand flat on the burner and watched it sizzle. So I gave my mother those reassurances without much feeling. Sure, I'd have kids. Yeah, sure, someday...

She was no longer herself, no longer that boisterous, energetic soul with the wide smile and singsong voice and infectious laugh. But the stroke hadn't robbed her of all her mental faculties. She knew when she was being coddled, dismissed with empty words.

Her weak right hand gripped mine with force. "Promise . . . me."

"Okay, I promise, Mom. I promise I'll have kids."

I do want children. I told Vicky that the first time I proposed to her. I gave her a little speech, how I wanted to marry her and have babies, to be a family that was honest and open and took care of each other. Us against the world—a team, a mighty, happy team.

And her words: "I'm not right for you." It took me too long to realize she was right.

I wish it could have been different for us, Vicky. I really do.

I return to the office and open my green journal.

### *Tuesday, October 25, 2022*

*I was beginning to think it would never happen, that the promise I made to my mother would never come true. I'd become okay with it, actually. Time had passed, I wasn't getting any younger, as they say, and I came to think that my life was fine just the way it was.*

*You have redefined everything for me, Lauren. You have shown me what is possible. You've made me realize how much more I wanted from life.*

*I promise you this: I will do everything I can to make sure our child feels loved and protected. I will give you and our child everything I'm capable of giving.*

*You didn't even have to say it, Lauren. Everything is different now. I'm editing the divorce petition right now. My lawyer needs me to fill in some personal information and details, but I'll be sure to get it ready and filed before—yes, before—November 3.*

*Wednesday, November 2, to be precise, the day before, just one day before D-Day, Anniversary 10. I already have the date locked in with my lawyer. He couldn't do it earlier, but that's okay, one day before is just as good as one week before. We will finalize the divorce petition and file it.*

*It feels good, locking that in, cementing the plan.*

*You're right, Lauren, about everything. I shouldn't have to settle. I shouldn't have to settle for someone who doesn't love me. I shouldn't have to settle for someone who refuses to have children.*

*And I shouldn't have to give Vicky half the money. It's not her money. It's our money. Yours, mine, and the baby's.*

*And you're right about when I should break this to Vicky.*

*"Tell her after you've filed," you said to me.*

*That hadn't been my plan. "I shouldn't tell her beforehand?"*

*"File it first," you said. "Then tell her. Trust me."*

*I guess that's the old adage, right? Better to seek forgiveness than permission.*

As I finish the entry in my green journal, I tap my phone to see the time.

"Oh, shit."

It's after seven. I'm late, very late for my eight a.m. class. I guess I got caught up in what I was doing.

I hurry out of the office, pass the bedroom, and peek in. Vicky is still asleep, a slight whistle in her breathing.

I do wish things had been different.

# 53

## Vicky

I wake from a nightmare, the sound of an anguished cry fading away as I open my eyes. I pop up in bed and grab my phone. It's nearly nine in the morning.

I stretch, use the bathroom, and walk out of the bedroom. Down the hall, the light is still on in Simon's office. I can't help but smile. He knows how much I hate wasting electricity, how much I pinch pennies, a vestige of years of living payday to payday. Sometimes, I think he leaves on lights just to needle me, a little joke.

I go downstairs to the kitchen. There is coffee, the remnants of a pot that Simon made when he first got up at the crack of dawn. Usually, he makes a fresh thermos that awaits me when I get up. And usually, his travel mug is gone.

This morning, no fresh coffee. And his travel mug is resting on the kitchen island, top off, empty. He must have lost track of time and hurried out the door. I thought I heard him bounding down the stairs in a rush. Simon hates, hates, hates being late.

I make my own coffee and carry a cup upstairs. Glance at that light on in Simon's office.

When I enter his office, his personal laptop is open on the desk, a green notebook sitting next to it.

The screensaver is on, a cartoon of Uncle Sam as Pac-Man, Pac-Sam, gobbling up constitutional rights as he moves about the screen.

I sit down at the desk and tap the keyboard. The password box appears.

I don't need to rummage through his sock drawer to find his list of passwords. I already know the password to his laptop.

It's I_Love_Vicky.

# 54
## Simon

After class, I walk to the Chicago Title & Trust Building. The usual routine, the Starbucks, sitting down in the lobby, powering on the phone, inserting the SIM card. At ten, I send a text:

Hello, princess.

She replies quickly:

*Hello, Prince Charming. How r u?*

The word "charming" is not a word usually associated with me. I reply:

I can't concentrate on anything but you. I forgot what case I was teaching this morning. You have me floating, lady.

She responds:

*Can't really talk right now. Tonight no good either. But tomorrow?*

I text:

> Tomorrow it is, my queen. Pretty soon, we'll have all the time
> we need.

I shut off the phone, remove the SIM card, and close my eyes. We're really doing this.

On my way back to my office at the law school, I see my favorite person coming from the other direction. On any given day, I'd rather eat bark off a tree than force myself to have a conversation with Dean Comstock.

But I'm not in the mood to run or hide. Not now.

His expression changes when he sees me.

"Hello there, Simon," he says, stuffing his hands in his pockets, lest I be under the impression that a handshake is in our future. "Aren't you full of surprises."

We haven't talked since I submitted all my materials in the closing hours of the application period. I would've loved to see the look on his face when he heard.

"I thought we had an understanding," he says.

"I don't remember ever agreeing to anything, Dean."

"No, that's right. But I thought you understood that I was looking out for your best interests. What with your . . ."

"My what? My sordid history?"

"Since you put it that way, yes."

I glance around, as did he, making sure we are alone in the hallway. I lean in slightly and lower my voice. "You're going to trash me to the faculty, Dean? That your plan?"

"Well, as I said before, Simon, in any kind of a close contest between applicants, people will naturally look for—"

"Tiebreakers, yes, I remember," I say. "You and I both know I'm the better professor. I'm the better scholar. I'm the one who deserves the job."

"You're certainly entitled to your opinion."

"So is everyone else. On the merits. On the merits, Dean. Not rumor or gossip or innuendo."

"Well, Simon, I don't dictate to the faculty what it should or should not deem relevant—"

"You don't have the balls," I say.

The dean draws back. "Say again?"

"Sure, I'll say it again. You, Dean, do not have the balls."

I'll say this for the old chap, he has a good poker face. His eyes glisten and his jaw steels, but otherwise he keeps up a good front. He even lets out a small chuckle.

"My friend, do not make the mistake of underestimating me," he says.

I pat him on the shoulder. "Funny," I say. "I was just about to say the same thing to you."

# 55
## Christian

I come into work like every morning. A quick hello to my receptionist, Emily, and then I go into my office. As I am not actually a financial guy, I don't really need this office, but appearances are appearances. Besides, I'll go crazy spending the entire day at home every day. A change of scenery is nice.

Sometimes I do actually work. Though "work" isn't checking the markets and forecasting investments; it's scouting for targets and considering other cities for the next venture. But now that I've found Vicky and her twenty-one million dollars, I won't need any other targets. I'm going to be done soon.

For Emily, a nineteen-year-old I found from a temp agency who is going to college part-time, I play the same role I play for Vicky, a rich, genius money guy who only has a few hugely wealthy clients. Most of these clients have been with me for years, I've explained, they live all around the world, and they have my personal cell number, so this office of mine downtown doesn't really function as much of an office.

I imagine Emily thinks I'm one of those uber-rich, uber-brainy eccentrics for whom the expense of an office and receptionist is just pocket money, who just wants a place to call an office. But she doesn't complain. Why would she? It's a perfect fit for her. She has morning and night classes at DePaul and only works afternoons for me. She spends almost all her time doing homework at her desk. To keep up appearances, I let her pay the company's few bills and give her research assignments now and then. But this job is a walk in the park for her.

Just after eleven, my phone rings. Not my regular cell phone. My burner, the one I use for Vicky. She doesn't know that I have a special phone for her, but it's necessary. Once I take her money, I need to cut off all connections between us, remove any trace of myself from her life, and hers from mine.

"I need to talk to you," Vicky says, breathless.

"What's up? You okay?"

"No, I am definitely not okay. Where are you?"

"At the office."

"I don't want to come to your office. Can we meet somewhere else?"

Vicky is standing in the alley by my garage when I pull my car in. She is dressed in a sweatshirt and blue jeans, no makeup, her hair a mess. I've never seen her like this. I don't mind it—I actually dig the look—but the tight expression on her face is making me nervous.

She hikes a blue bag over her shoulder and says, "Upstairs," when I get out of the car.

I follow her up the stairs to my apartment. She pulls a laptop and a green notebook out of her bag, places them on the kitchen table, and points at them like they're kryptonite.

"He's going . . . to leave me," she says, her voice shaking. "He's going to file for divorce before November . . . November third."

"Wait, what?" I say. "Just . . . hold on a second."

"'Hold on a second'? Okay, I'll hold on a second while that *tramp* steals Simon and his money. *My* money. *My* fucking money."

"Who—who's a tramp? Will you just—"

"Lauren," she spits out. "Lauren Lemoyne. That skank he dated when he was a teenager. Remember?"

"Um, yeah, you said somebody broke his heart—"

"Well, apparently, she won it back. She's back in town and they're together and they're going to get married!"

"I'm sure you're overreacting."

"I'm overreacting?" She opens the laptop, the screen dark, and types in a password. The screen comes alive.

It's a court document. I'm not an attorney, but I've seen my share of divorce filings in my day, among the many women I've targeted. It says "Petition for Dissolution of Marriage," the official phrasing. Simon Peter Dobias, petitioner, v. Victoria Lanier Dobias, respondent, in the Circuit Court of Cook County. "Irreconcilable differences have arisen between the parties that have caused the irretrievable breakdown of the marriage. Past efforts at reconciliation have failed, and future attempts at reconciliation would be impracticable."

Fuck me. Simon's divorcing Vicky.

"Still think I'm overreacting?"

"Hang on, hang on."

I open the notebook with a green cover. Some kind of a diary, handwritten in pen. With dated entries. The first one, the Fourth of July.

"God, I can't *believe* this," Vicky says. "I am *nine days* away from our tenth anniversary. Nine days!"

I clear my throat and read from the first entry. "'The whole reason I came to the club today, my first time in several years, was that I thought you might be at the Fourth of July festivities,'" I read. "'I'd been thinking about you since that day in May—'"

"Oh, yeah, apparently he spots her on Michigan Avenue last May, and his pathetic little heart goes pitter-patter. And then he's rehearsing lines in the mirror for when he sees her again."

The next entry, July 15. Simon and Lauren are meeting at some café. "'And then the kiss,'" I read aloud. "'Had it been up to me to initiate it, I'm not sure it ever would have—'"

"Had it been up to him." Vicky snorts. "It *never* would've been up to him. She set her sights on him. She gamed out this whole thing. She's playing him like a fiddle. She wants his money!"

"You don't know that," I say. "Let's—"

"Um, I think I *do* know that. Keep reading. Cut to the end if you like, so I don't have to listen to more descriptions of that little *slut* spreading her legs for him and talking dirty to him and manipulating the shit out of him. She has him wrapped around her skanky little finger."

I read the last few entries, sitting down now, the initial shock ending and a growing ache forming in the pit of my stomach.

"She's pregnant?"

"That's what she told Simon," she says. "My ass, she's pregnant."

"You think she's making that—"

"Anyone could say they're pregnant. You read those last few diary entries? She's trying to convince him to file for divorce before our tenth anniversary. And he keeps resisting. She keeps pushing, he keeps saying no. Then suddenly she's pregnant? No way. No fucking way." She shakes her head, a bitter smile on her face. "She knows that's what's splitting up Simon and me. I don't want kids. He does. So when all else fails, she pulls the pregnant card, that conniving little—"

"Just let me read this, Vicky. Let me read all of it."

"Read fast," she says. "I don't have much time."

I read fast, trying to digest the highlights. The start of the romance, where Simon's sounding like a lovestruck puppy. Lauren was his first love, apparently, as Vicky told me before. He's acting like it on these pages. She broke his heart but came back to Chicago, nearly two decades later. Back to Chicago, to Grace Village, where she feels like she's in a doomed marriage and so, apparently, does Simon.

I wonder how long it took her to get the goods on Simon's trust money? Couldn't have taken long. Says here she used to work at Simon's dad's law firm, so she must have known ol' Teddy was loaded. And no doubt she learned at some point that Teddy was dead. She must have known early on that Simon had inherited a lot of money.

Oh, and then she turned on the charm.

By the sixteenth of August: "Do you want me to be your whore, Professor Dobias?"

The thirtieth of August, even Simon knows he's hooked, he's struggling with it: "Are you my addiction, Lauren?"

But still, Simon's conscience is getting the better of him. Recounting, in the September 12 entry, how Teddy cheated on Simon's mother, and how Simon was repeating the cycle. "I have become the man I despise." Looks like he spilled all that to Lauren, and she must have sent him some cryptic text message on that pink phone he bought her, one of those we-have-to-talk messages that left Simon in agony until they met. And then, yep, Lauren is good—she said we won't be cheating if we're married!

Well done, Lauren. She let him dangle for a night about the prospect of losing her, wondering what he'd do without her, and then she springs the idea of marriage on him, making it seem like the idea actually came from him.

So then she had her hooks in him. Simon was on cloud nine. He was fantasizing about it. He was dreading telling Vicky, yes, but otherwise happier than he'd ever been.

Lauren was smart. She wasn't too obvious about it. She waited until mid-October, just last week, to start talking about the trust money.

And then, these last entries, the end of last week and this week. Vicky's read on this is right. Simon was agonizing over when to file the divorce petition. Lauren was giving it the old college try, coming on pretty strong at times. "You two aren't in love and you never were," Lauren said. "She never loved you, Simon. She needed someone to take care of her. And you did. And now she's eyeballing that trust money that's so close she can taste it."

Well, Lauren wasn't wrong about that. Vicky can taste that money.

So can I.

But yeah, Lauren gamed this whole thing out. Manipulated Simon every step of the way. Dropping that pregnancy bomb was a thing of beauty. A Hail Mary if all else failed, and all else had failed. Simon's loyalty to Vicky was too deep, so Lauren pulled out the nuclear option—the one thing Vicky wouldn't give him.

I could learn to like this Lauren. Checking her out on Facebook, I could definitely learn to like her. She is Grade A, no question.

But she's in my way. She may have gotten to Simon before I got to Vicky, but I don't play fair. That money's mine, and I'm not letting her beat me to it.

Vicky's been pacing around, cursing under her breath, sometimes not under her breath, nearly punching a hole in my living-room wall at one point. When she sees me close the notebook, she walks into the kitchen, anxiously nodding her head.

"I'm screwed, right?"

I'm surprisingly calm, staring at the loss of all my hard work, the loss of my retirement money. But panicking isn't going to help me get that money. I have a competitor, and she appears to be formidable, but this isn't my first time in competition.

And I've never lost.

"He's not filing until the day before your anniversary," I say. "November the second. That's, what, a week from tomorrow?"

Vicky nods, chewing on a nail.

"So the question is: What we do now?"

"I'll tell you what I'd like to do," she says. "I'd like to break his neck."

"And what if that happened?" I ask.

Vicky blinks, her expression changing.

"You said you care about him," I say. "How much do you care about him?"

Vicky walks to the window, looks out over the alley. My guess is she's spent the last forty-five minutes asking herself that very question.

"If he dies before our tenth anniversary," she says, "the money stays in the trust. I don't get a cent. It won't be marital property."

Interesting answer. Interesting because she didn't say, *I could never do something like that, I could never hurt Simon.* She's just saying that it wouldn't work. That means she's keeping an open mind.

"Lauren's married," I say. "Someone named Conrad?"

She flips a hand. "Apparently."

"How about we tell him about the affair?"

"He probably already knows," says Vicky, turning to me. "And if he doesn't, so what? Sounds like their marriage is in the dumper, too."

I sit down at the table. I'm not coming up with many answers here.

"He's been different," she says.

"Simon has?"

She nods. "He's been more distant the last few days. I didn't—didn't think much of it. He gets that way a lot, lost in his thoughts. I didn't think anything of it."

I blow out a breath. "What if— What if Simon were injured but not killed?"

"C'mon."

"What do you mean, 'c'mon'? I'm serious."

Vicky takes a moment with that. "Like, injure him enough that he's out of commission but not kill him, just to buy us a week until November third comes and goes?"

"Exactly," I say.

"Exactly? And how *exactly* does that happen? Hit him with a car hard enough to hospitalize him but not enough to kill him? Shoot him but miss all vital organs? Hit him over the head hard enough to put him into a coma but not enough to end all brain activity?"

"Okay, okay."

She touches my arm. "Believe me, if I could pull that off— But it's not feasible."

"Well. Then maybe, Vicky Lanier, maybe it's time you started being really, really nice to your husband?"

She takes a moment to catch my meaning, then rolls her eyes. "That won't work."

"You can be charming."

"Not that charming. Not with Simon."

"No? Says in those pages that he loves you, but you don't love him back. Maybe you show him you do?"

She thinks about it but shakes her head. "It's too late. If I'd had any idea this was happening, that's exactly what I would've done." She thumps her forehead with the butt of her hand. "How did I miss this?"

You missed it, Vicky, because you were counting dollar signs in your head, and you were falling for me.

We go silent, thinking. Dead air filled with desperation, bordering on outright panic. I'm watching everything I've worked for circle down the drain.

"What if I confront him?" she says. "Be direct? I could beg him. I'd do that. I'd beg. For ten million dollars, I'd beg."

Yeah, but that's only half. You want it all, Vicky. So do I.

Anyway, I've already considered her idea and rejected it in my own mind. "The one thing you have going for you," I say, "is that he's dreading the thought of doing this to you. That tension, that pressure, works for us. If you tell him you know, then the ice is broken, the tension is broken. He might as well just file for divorce at that point."

"But you read what that bitch said to him. File first, tell me later."

"I know, I know—but you'll make it worse if you confront him. It'll open the floodgates. He can't know that you know."

She grips her hair, letting out a low moan.

"I have to go," she says. "If he comes home, and the laptop and notebook are missing, he'll know I've seen it."

"When does he come home?"

"Probably not until later."

"Probably? 'Probably' isn't much to bank on."

She agrees, nods her head. "He has a lot of flexibility with his job. He had a class this morning, early. Nothing in the afternoon. He usually works into the late evening, writing his law review articles and blog posts. But yeah, he could come home in the afternoon if he wanted."

"Especially if he realizes he left his laptop and diary at home."

"Shit." She touches her forehead. "You're right. I'm gonna go. I can come back around six."

I follow her down the stairs and let her out through the garage.

"Hey, Vicky," I say as the door grinds open, Vicky with one foot in the alley. She raises her eyebrows at me.

"They're using burner phones, the diary said?" I say. "His is green—"

"Hers is pink, yeah. Ain't it cute."

"See if you can get a look at his phone. It's probably hidden somewhere."

Vicky thinks about that. Slowly nods. "His phone," she says. "That's a good idea."

"And remember, above all," I say. "He can't know that you know."

Vicky will be back in about five hours. I need to figure out a plan between now and then.

I dial my phone. Gavin answers on the second ring.

"I'm coming to you," I say. "I need your brain."

# 56
## Christian

Gavin is quiet, eyes closed, sitting on the bench in Wrightwood Park, his hands together as if in prayer.

We've gone over this for the last three hours, starting with lunch, then beers, now walking around the park near his condo in Lincoln Park. I had to violate our vow not to share names, that wall we put up to keep our scams from each other. He's only known Vicky as "Number 7" and Simon as "Number 7's husband," but running through all my options now with this new development, it was just too hard to keep using titles, especially with a third person—"Number 7's husband's mistress"—entering the equation.

So now Gavin knows the names Vicky Lanier, Simon Dobias, and Lauren Betancourt.

Finally, Gavin opens his eyes, spreads his hands, and says, "I can't think of another option."

"Jesus, really?" But I can't think of another one, either.

"You tell me, Nick," says Gavin. "You're the one in the middle of it. I hardly know a thing about any of these people."

Truth is, I don't, either. "I know Vicky," I say. "Vicky, I get. No problem."

"And what about this Lauren?"

I shrug. "I barely knew she existed until today. Vicky mentioned once or twice that Simon had a serious girlfriend who broke his heart or whatever when he was young. But reading that diary of Simon's, I mean—Lauren's me. She's a female version of me. She has her eye on that pot of money and she's not gonna let anybody get in the way. She's doing to Simon what I'm doing to Vicky."

"Okay. Fine. What about Simon?"

"Yeah, that's trickier," I say. "Most of what I know about Simon, I got from Vicky. But now I've read his diary, too, and it pretty much confirms what she says about him."

"Which is?"

"Brainy in that useless, academic way," I say. "Kinda guy who could recite the freakin' quadratic equation or something from memory but wouldn't know how to operate a can opener."

Gavin likes that one, nods along.

"He lets himself get led around by women, that's for sure," I say. "Falls head over heels in love, that kind of thing. He recognizes he's in a bad marriage, but never did anything about it until Lauren started batting her eyes at him."

"But it sounds like he can go pretty dark," says Gavin. "Like the St. Louis thing."

"That's the thing. That's the X factor. The guy holds a grudge, that's for sure. I mean, he's all pissed off at his father for years and years and plans out this whole thing to kill him. He drives down to St. Louis during his college finals week, stabs him in the gut, pushes him into a swimming pool, then drives back here and takes his final exam the next morning."

"That's pretty cold," Gavin agrees. "But you know something, that works both ways."

"How's that?"

"Well, on the one hand, you have to be very careful with him. You don't want to get on his wrong side."

"That's an understatement." I stretch my arms, releasing nervous tension.

"But on the other hand, you said the St. Louis cops still think he did it. They couldn't prove it, but they think he was the guy?"

"That's what Vicky said. And that's what I've read about the case."

Gavin cocks his head, a gleam in his eye. "So that could be helpful. That could be very helpful."


"Let's go over the ideas again," I say. We are back at Gavin's townhouse, a one-bedroom with a nice view west, a bachelor's pad if you ever saw one.

"Option one," Gavin says, ticking off a thumb. "You sideline Simon for a while. You can't kill him, because then Vicky gets cut out and so do you, but you hurt him just enough that he's hospitalized or unconscious or something past November third."

"If we could somehow pull that off, it would be perfect," I say. "But it's way too hard."

"Agreed. A firm 'no' on option one."

Gavin is good with this kind of stuff, the plotting and planning. He organizes his thoughts well. I'm a pretty damn good player, but he's a better coach.

"Option two, you do what you do best and try to get between Simon and Lauren," he says. "You use that pretty face of yours and play that role of the multi-multimillionaire superstar investor, and you sweep Lauren off her feet and away from Simon. She dumps Simon, he crawls back to Vicky. And that might be doable," he adds, "but there's no time. This all has to happen in a week."

"Very doable," I say. "But yeah, no time."

"Third option," says Gavin. "You threaten Lauren. You scare her off. But that's dicey. I'm not even sure how you'd do it. Put a gun to her head and tell her to break up with Simon? Then what? I'm not at all sure how that would play out."

"Right, it doesn't work." I sit down next to him on the couch. "He'd assume Vicky sent me. Who else would've sent me? And then he'd file for divorce *immediately*."

"So that only leaves one option, my friend." Gavin pats my back. "And the question is: How bad do you want that twenty-one million dollars?"

# 57

## Vicky

"So that leaves only one option," says Christian, standing in the living room of his condo.

"What's that?" I say, seated on the couch, having listened to him discount other options that were never really options at all.

It's half past six. I'm back at Christian's for the second time today, after going back to Grace Park, returning Simon's laptop and green journal to their spots on the desk in his home office, then doing some work on the shelter's website from home, or at least trying to do some work, wondering what Christian will come up with.

"And I'm not saying we'd do it," says Christian. "But I can't think of any other way—"

"Spit it out," I say.

"Okay." He puts out a hand, as if to calm me. "I took all afternoon going through every possible plan, and this is the only one, in my opinion, that could accomplish our objective."

"Speak," I say.

"Well, we . . . y'know." He makes a gun with his hand, points it at his head. "Y'know."

I stare at him.

"We . . . make her go away," he whispers.

"You mean *kill* Lauren?"

"I . . . yes. Yes," he says.

It took him all afternoon to come up with that?

It took me ten seconds.

"I was afraid you might say that," I say.

Actually, I was afraid he might *not* say that and I'd have to raise the idea. But it's much better that it came from him.

"I know it's extreme." He opens his hands. "I don't think there's any way of just scaring her off. The only viable option is to take her out of the equation entirely. I'm not saying we'd do it, just that . . ."

"It would be the only way to stop this."

"Yeah," he says.

"Uh-huh." I nod. "And . . . hypothetically—"

"Right, just hypothetically."

"—how would that happen?" I peek up at him. "If Simon's been having an affair with her, he's probably left a trail all over the place. If she dies, if she gets shot or stabbed or strangled or whatever—the first person they look at is the man who was having an affair with her. The second person they look at is that man's *wife*."

"Yeah, I figure Simon, you, and Conrad would be suspects," says Christian. "You'd be right in there. And if you're a suspect in any way, or even if Simon is—you wouldn't be in a position to take Simon's money. There'd be too much scrutiny on you."

"You're right," I say. "You're absolutely right."

"Which is why I think . . . I have to be the one who does it," he says.

"*You* . . . ?" I look at him. "But . . ."

"But what?" he says. "You said yourself, you can't be anywhere near this. They'll look hard at everything about you."

"I know, but—Christian, you're like this successful— You have all this money and you're so successful. You don't have to get mixed up with something like this."

He moves over to me, kneels down, takes my hand. "This money means everything to you. It's a chance for a new life."

"For me, yes. But you? You have more money than God."

"I wouldn't be doing it for me," he says. "I'll do it for you."

"I can't . . . I can't ask you to do that."

"You didn't ask." He touches my face. "You still don't get how I feel about you, do you?"

I look down and shake my head. "I've never been in . . . I've never—"

"Me neither," he says. "Until I met you. I didn't think I was capable."

I laugh. "I didn't think *I* was capable."

He reaches for my shirt, starts to unbutton it. "I'll do this for you," he says. "If you're okay with it. You have to be okay with it."

If I'm *okay* with it?

I am one hundred percent, absolutely, totally, completely okay with it.

Why do you think I'm with you, Christian? Because I care about you? Because you're hot? Because I'm a "lonely wife" who can't get enough of your giant, throbbing manhood?

Please. I picked you for this very task. I've known about Lauren since before I first met you. Today was just the day I decided to tell you. I've been planning this since the first time I walked into your office.

You're not a successful investor. You're Nick Caracci, a two-bit swindler, a con man, a grifter, who thinks he's hit the jackpot with me.

You were never going to invest that money. I was never going to let you *near* that money.

I just need you to help me kill Lauren Betancourt.

# 58

## Christian

Good. So far, so good with Vicky. I have buy-in. She's willing to go along with this.

I let it simmer for a while. I don't want to hit her with the entire plan all at once and overwhelm her. But Gavin and I have put together an initial outline.

For one thing, it has to happen on Halloween. Between now and November 2, when Simon goes to his divorce lawyer, there's no other day that makes sense. Today is Tuesday the twenty-fifth. Tomorrow or the next day—Wednesday or Thursday—is too soon. I need more time than that. The weekend is not going to work. Friday, Saturday, those nights are too unpredictable, and based on Lauren's Facebook page, she seems to reserve those nights for her girlfriends, usually downtown.

And Monday the thirty-first—Halloween—is perfect, right? Most people are home so they can answer the door to trick-or-treaters. I can wear a costume that lets me waltz around in anonymity. I can hide a weapon in a costume or in some fake trick-or-treat bag. It's the only day of the year that a woman would open her door to a man wearing a disguise over his face.

But like I said, I don't want to hit Vicky with this all at once, so I give her a Nicky Special, fucking her upright, holding her up, pinned against the wall, her legs wrapped around my back, drilling her until she cries out in climax. I'll bet Simon never did *that* to her. I'll bet he couldn't hold her up. It doesn't take long to make her come. It usually doesn't. And all the talk about murder is probably an aphrodisiac on top of it. I know it is for me.

That should help remind her what a great deal she'll be getting down the road, after she's done with little Simon.

She's nice and loose afterward, wearing my shirt and nothing else while sitting on the couch with a bottle of water.

"Halloween? That's . . . that's *brilliant*," she says after I lay it out for her. "Oh, and Grace Village—you know that town goes dark at seven o'clock."

I didn't. But now I do, as she explains the ritual.

"Everyone goes lights-out at seven," she says. "So maybe you could show up right before that. She might open the door for one last person."

Maybe. I still can't believe I'm doing this. I'm going to shoot someone. Kill someone. I repeat those seven syllables in my head.

*Twenty-one million dollars.*

Okay. That part was easy. The next part might not be. Gavin and I debated it, but the more I thought about it, the more I realized he was right.

Here goes.

"Listen, one other thing," I say. "I'm thinking about the police. What they'll think when they find Lauren . . ."

"Dead. Fucking dead."

A little more zeal in her than I expected. But I like the anger. The anger is good. She's all in.

"Yeah," I say. "What you said is right, Vicky. How hard will it be for them to figure out that Simon was having an affair with her? Probably not very. He has history with her, even if it goes pretty far back. And he's going to her swanky downtown condo building for afternoon love sessions? That building has staff, they have security and doormen and—"

"I'm sure it won't be hard for the police to figure that out," she says. "That's what worries me. When they look at Simon, they'll look at me, his wife."

"So that's where this thought comes in," I say. "If they're already going to be looking at him, and therefore at you . . . maybe we could help keep the focus on Simon?"

She sits up, snapping to attention. "What are you saying?"

"I'm saying . . . Maybe there's a way we can help nudge the police in Simon's—"

"Are you saying we *frame* Simon?"

I raise my hands. "I'm just trying to protect you, Vicky," I say. "That's all—"

"Hm." Vicky gets up and starts pacing.

That isn't a no. Seems like she's thinking about it, strolling slowly, looking far off, picturing it.

"I know you care about him, but—"

"That was before I knew he was fucking Lauren," she snaps. "And fucking *me* out of my money."

I'll have to keep that reaction in mind when I steal all of Vicky's money. I better fly somewhere far away.

I let the idea marinate with her. I put on some coffee and drink a cup while Vicky strolls around, mumbling to herself, occasionally shaking her head, still in disbelief at this turn of events. Wavering between anger at Simon, anger at herself for letting it happen, and deciding how far she's willing to go to correct the situation.

Halfway through the living room for the twentieth time, she stops, pivots, hands on her naked hips, nodding her head. "Let's do it. Let's make sure the cops' eyes never wander past Simon to me. Let's set that cheating fucker up." She wags her finger. "And I know *exactly* how to do it."

# THE DAY AFTER
# HALLOWEEN

# 59
## Jane

Jane Burke drives back to the Betancourt house at the end of the longest day of her career on the force, memories from high school occupying her thoughts.

"Rob," she says into her cell phone, her AirPods tucked in her ear.

*"Hey, Jane,"* says Sergeant Robert Dalillo of their sister department, Grace Park Police. *"I hear you guys actually had a real crime committed over there."*

"And guess who caught it?"

*"Yeah? Good for you. What do you need?"*

"You remember Simon Dobias from high school?"

*"Um . . . no. Should I? Was he my grade or yours?"*

"Mine," says Jane. "Real smart kid. Valedictorian. Spoke at graduation."

*"Didn't know that many kids younger than me."*

"Okay, well, anyway, your records people pulled a complaint filed by Simon Dobias back in '04."

*"This is related to your homicide?"*

"Well, who knows, but I was wondering if you could give me everything you guys have on him. Simon Dobias. D-O-B-I-A-S."

*"Okay, sure, Jane. First thing in the morning. You think a kid from your class did this woman?"*

"Way too early to know," says Jane as she curbs her car on Lathrow by the Betancourt house. "Talk to you tomorrow. Gotta run."

"Tell me you haven't been here all day," Jane says to Ria Peraino from Major Crimes forensics, who greets Jane at the front door of the Betancourt home.

"No, I went home, put the kids to bed, and came back. I knew you'd be busy with other things awhile. Besides, this is easier to do at night. There's so much sunlight streaming into this house during the day, with all these windows."

Jane gloves up, slips rubbers over her shoes, and follows Ria's careful route up the winding staircase to the second floor, to the landing where the action happened, where the offender struck Lauren, subdued her, and put the noose around her neck.

Ria douses the wood floor with luminol from a spray bottle, the *whoosh-whoosh* reminding Jane of how badly her own apartment needs cleaning. "Ready?"

"Ready," says Jane.

Ria flicks off the hallway lights, plunging them in darkness. Glowing blue patterns emerge along the second-floor hallway, dots and small puddles and streaks, the chemiluminescence reaction caused by the luminol mixing with traces of iron from the blood.

As always, there is more blood than one would think. Spatter on the hallway floor, coming in a small inkblot pattern in an area roughly between the bannister and the antique table.

"The offender hit her on the right back side of the head, probably right here," says Ria, her pointed finger visible only by contrast with the blue-glowing blood. "The thickest blood droplets are usually the closest, then the droplets get smaller as the distance from the wound increases."

Jane follows the line with her eyes.

"Not a lot of blood, all in all, but the head wound wasn't that grave."

"Then there's more blood over closer to the little hallway table," says Jane. "Where we found the phone."

"Yeah, that's interesting, isn't it?"

Ria resprays the luminol solution onto the blood over by the table, lighting it up in an even brighter blue glow.

"Blood smears," Ria says. "The phone slid across the floor a few feet, short of the table. Then it slid a second time all the way under the table."

Jane sees it. The first smear stops, then starts again in a slightly different direction, maybe a ten- or fifteen-degree difference in angle, before disappearing under the table.

"So here's what's weird for me," says Ria. "The first smear of blood, okay. That's the phone sliding across the floor from where the struggle happened. The phone has a bit of blood on it, and it takes the blood for a ride."

"Right . . . ?"

"That could have happened a number of ways. Most likely, the offender subdues her, catches her up here in the hallway, hits her, causing a blood spray, then she falls to the floor and the phone goes sliding away."

"Maybe the offender threw the phone away," Jane says. "To keep it away from her."

"Maybe. Or maybe she dropped it and reached for it and knocked it away by accident, while struggling. Who knows? That's not the problem. The phone sliding across the floor the first time isn't my problem."

"What's your problem?"

"The phone sliding the *second* time. It's a slight difference in angle, right?"

"Yeah, no question."

"It's a second, independent movement of the phone."

"Agreed," Jane says. "The phone was moved a second time. It slid across the floor, probably during the struggle, then slid a second time at a slightly different angle. Maybe . . . maybe she dove for it again, desperately trying to call 911. Or maybe the offender kicked it away, to make sure it stayed away from her grasp."

"Sure, all possible in theory, but here's the thing," says Ria. "If you swat or kick or push a phone to make it move across the floor, you're probably going to come in contact with the floor itself, right?"

"I . . . I suppose it's likely, yes."

"It's *very* likely, Jane. If I dive for a phone in a desperate attempt to reach it, that first trail of blood that we see? I'd be diving right into it. I'd mess it all up. It wouldn't look like this pristine line."

"So nobody dove across the floor for it. How about kicking it?"

"Well, nobody *stepped* into the pristine line of blood, either. No shoe prints."

"Okay, then they could have stood to the side, away from the original blood line, and lightly kicked the phone under the table. That would work, wouldn't it?"

Ria turns on the lights.

"Well, yeah," Ria says. "But isn't that weird?"

Jane takes a moment to adjust her eyes.

"I mean, who are we talking about? There are only two people in this hallway, Jane. The offender and the victim. The victim isn't going to walk over and calmly stand to the side and gently kick that phone under the table like she would tap in a putt on the eighteenth hole."

"Of course not," Jane says. "The victim wouldn't be doing anything calmly. She was struggling to survive an attack. It must have been the offender."

"Agreed. But while Lauren is still alive, the offender isn't doing *anything* calmly or carefully or gently or methodically, either. Not until the victim is dead. Until the struggle is over. Agreed?"

"Agreed." Jane takes a breath and thinks about it. "The phone was moved by the offender, and it was moved after Lauren was dead."

"So picture it." Ria walks over to reconstruct the theory. "After she's dead, the offender walks over and is careful to avoid stepping in the original blood, and . . ." She kicks with her left foot toward the table. "He kicks the phone under the table, careful not to make contact with the floor."

Jane gives it some thought, nods her head. "I agree, that's probably how it happened," she says.

"But why kick it under the table?"

"To . . . to hide it. No?"

Ria doesn't think much of that theory. "Jane, by that point, Lauren is hanging from the rafters. There's blood. The offender has to know there's going to be an investigation. Cops are going to scour this scene. He thinks the police won't look under a coffee table that's five feet from where the victim was subdued?"

"Okay, but look, Ria, criminals make mistakes all the time. Especially if they aren't pros. Especially if this was heat of the moment. He's just killed Lauren, he's freaking out, he sees that phone, and he kicks it under the table. He won't win any awards for intelligence, I grant you that, but that doesn't mean it didn't happen the way I'm saying."

Ria shakes her head.

"What am I missing?" Jane asks.

Ria shrugs. "What you're saying, that may be right. He sees the phone and panics and kicks it under the coffee table."

"Right."

"But why not take it with him?"

"Why not— Huh." Jane starts to pace, as she usually does when working through something, but thinks better of it, considering the fragility of the crime scene. "Okay," she says. "I'm the offender. I'm having an affair with Lauren. We have burner phones, and we're using them for one reason and one reason only, to send each other little love notes."

"Right."

"I've just killed Lauren," Jane goes on, "maybe premeditated, maybe more of a heat-of-passion thing, and there I see her pink burner phone on the floor. I know what that phone represents. I know if the cops get inside that phone, they'll read all our text messages, they'll know all about our affair. So I walk over to that phone . . ."

"And you kick it under the table?" Ria says. "Knowing we'll find it?"

"No. I take it." Jane looks at Ria. "I take it with me. I don't leave the phone lying there for the cops to find. I take it with me, so the police have no idea it even exists. The police would *never* know it exists. That's the point of a burner. You can't trace it back to an owner."

"So why kick it under the table, knowing we'll find it?" Ria says.

Jane throws up her hands. "He *wanted* us to find it. He didn't want to be too obvious about it—he didn't want to put it in a gift box with a bow on it. He made it look like he was trying to conceal it by kicking it under the table. But like you said, he *had* to know we'd look under a damn table right next to the crime scene."

Ria nods. "He wanted us to find it."

"He wanted us to find it." Jane chews on that. "He wanted us to focus on the person on the other end of those text messages, Lauren's boyfriend." She looks at Ria. "Holy shit."

"So maybe it wasn't the boyfriend who did this," says Ria. "And maybe we should no longer be referring to the offender as a *he*."

Jane runs her fingers through her hair. "You're blowing my mind here at the end of a long day," she says. "I need to think about this."

"Didn't mean to complicate your life," says Ria.

Jane smiles at her. But the smile doesn't last long.

"So maybe Lauren wasn't the only one in this love affair who was married," she says. "Maybe Lauren's boyfriend was married, too. His wife finds out about the affair, kills Lauren, and puts the whole thing on her cheating husband."

Ria's turn to smile. "The fantasy of every woman who's ever been cheated on," she says. "Kill two birds with one stone."

# THE DAYS BEFORE HALLOWEEN

# 60

*I'm probably just being paranoid, with everything about to happen. Maybe the guilt I'm feeling over what I'm about to do to Vicky is skewing my perception.*

*But it sure feels like Vicky has been different. More solicitous. More affectionate.*

*She got into bed with me last night. Usually, I'm early to bed, early to rise, and she's the night owl, in bed well after midnight, sleeping until eight or nine.*

*But last night, she came to bed with me.*

*"Want some company?" she said.*

*I didn't know what to do. I felt so conflicted. I'm with you now, Lauren, in every way but officially, and so I felt suddenly like sleeping with my wife would be cheating on you.*

*Oh, how things turn. And how awkward and painful it was when I made up an excuse about not feeling well.*

*But I'm just being paranoid, right? It's just a coincidence that now she's suddenly taking an interest in me again.*

*It must be. Vicky couldn't possibly suspect a thing.*

# 61

## Vicky

Nobody pays attention to a woman in workout clothes, power walking through a neighborhood, headphones on, even if nobody recognizes her, even if she tends to stop on the sidewalk outside a particular house every day. For men, it's different. Strange men who linger are creepy, potential stalkers, someone to keep an eye on. A woman? A woman can walk a regular route every day and nobody will notice.

From what I can tell, nobody's noticed me all these weeks, casually passing Lauren's house, sometimes stopping briefly, but just briefly, looking down at my phone like I just got an important text that stopped me in my tracks. I'm just a harmless female, after all.

Sometimes I drive by her house instead of walking, but a car is different, more noticeable, more likely to arouse curiosity. I only use the car at night, and only for a few minutes.

During the daylight hours, though, like right now at eight-thirty on a Thursday morning, passing her house on foot is the preferred option. And, of course, I can rig my route so that I circle back and pass her house a second time if need be.

Lauren the Gold-Digging Skank, to her credit, has not altered much of her daily routine, even with the changing of the seasons. Around eight every morning, she goes for a three-mile run through Grace Village. She still keeps a regular tennis appointment at ten-thirty in the morning, every weekday, at the Grace Country Club. She still has lunch with her tennis partner and then meets a foursome for golf at one.

It's enough to exhaust me just thinking about it. But Lauren the Gold-Digging Skank has to keep that nice, tight figure of hers, doesn't she?

I wonder what the plan is once the weather *really* starts turning, the way the weather can turn in Chicago. Was she planning to bundle up and keep hitting those tennis courts and playing eighteen holes of golf? At some point, you'd think she'd have to call off those outdoor sports, if nothing else when the snow starts arriving.

But it's a moot point now. Lauren will never see another winter in Chicago or anywhere else. She has, let's see . . . today is Thursday . . . that's about 106 hours before trick-or-treating ends on Monday night.

Halloween will be perfect. She'll be home, it will be dark, and Christian can move around in a *costume*, for God's sake, without anyone thinking it odd. Two minutes before seven, already pretty dark out, trick-or-treating petering out, Christian steps into that private little brick canopy around her front door, she opens the door, he shoots her with a silencer, wham bam thank you ma'am. And he walks away as everyone shuts off their lights all at once, making an already dark night pitch-black.

I'm surprised more people don't get murdered on Halloween.

Thank God that Christian—

Oh, why do I bother thinking of him as Christian? Force of habit, I guess. I've been so afraid I might let the name "Nick" slip out that I've forced myself to think of him only by his alias—Christian Newsome, Christian Newsome, Christian Newsome!

Thank God that Christian came up with the idea for Halloween night for killing Lauren so I didn't have to do it for him. Men and their egos.

The idea of framing Simon, too—also his idea. Another thing I didn't want to have to mention. It's so, so much better when they think it was their idea. Lucky for me, Christian doesn't lack for confidence.

I wonder if he talked to his buddy Gavin about all this. Yes, I know about him, too. I never liked homework in high school, but I've warmed to it recently.

They probably came up with this stuff together. They probably ran through it for hours, considering every possibility. They probably discussed how Christian should "prepare" me for the idea of murder. And for the idea to pin it on Simon—as if that wasn't the most important part of this for me.

Speaking of . . . If I were interested in inviting myself into Lauren's house while she wasn't home, what would be the best way to do it?

The front of the house—no. The front door is covered by a brick canopy, which makes for nice privacy, but I doubt she leaves the front door unlocked as a practice. To the left of the front door is the three-car garage, so that's no help. To the right of the front door—my right, north—is a large window and shrubbery and garden. You can probably see into the house, but I doubt that window even opens, and trying to pry it open in front of everyone walking and driving up and down Lathrow Avenue would be about the dumbest thing in the world.

I'm thinking the south side, beyond the garage, along the gangway between the house and the large wooden border fence, where a window has been propped open for the past five days. Probably a kitchen window. It looks tall and wide enough for me to fit through. I may have to punch out a screen.

Oh, and here she comes right now, jogging up Lathrow Avenue, finishing up her three-mile run—the beautiful, sexy Lauren the Gold-Digging Skank, wearing those aqua running tights that probably give every man she passes a hard-on.

She *is* gorgeous, I will have to give her that. I can't fault Simon for falling for her.

Oh, sure I can.

So it's time to keep moving, just a casual, up-tempo walk in my workout clothes, headphones on, not even looking in her direction as she passes me.

Enjoy the rest of your life, Lauren. You have five days left.


I walk back to my car, parked up by the elementary school (one place where you can park by the curb and nobody thinks much of it), and drive back to Grace Park. I park in the alley garage, as always, and walk into the house through the private rear entrance.

There is a coat closet by the back door that Simon never uses. I open it and pull out the Halloween outfit I bought for Christian, an oafish robe with a long hood. I bought it at one of those seasonal Halloween stores that opens just in October, renting vacant commercial space and hanging those gaudy signs.

I paid for it in cash, of course. I put my hair up, wore a baseball cap, wore fake eyeglasses and a puffy coat. I didn't see any security cameras in there, but if they were there, they couldn't possibly make me out.

The "Grim Reaper," they call this costume, complete with a long sickle, but that part I threw away. The robe will cover up Christian's body features, and the elongated hood will entirely block any view of his face while allowing him to see out.

It will be perfect.

Below that, a new pair of Paul Roy Peak Explorer boots, size thirteen, Christian's shoe size. I bought those in cash, too, at a discount shoe store, wearing a completely different disguise.

I carry the shoes and the costume through the ground floor of the house to the front closet, near the front-entrance garage where Simon parks. I open the closet and look down. A pair of old loafers Simon hasn't worn for a while. A backup pair of running shoes.

And yes, another pair of Paul Roy Peak Explorer boots.

Same model, same color as the ones for Christian.

I head upstairs, into the master bedroom, and open Simon's closet. In the back of the closet hangs a Grim Reaper costume Simon bought for himself last year but never wore.

Also a perfect match for the one I bought Christian, like the boots.

Matching costumes, matching boots.

Simon isn't the only one who holds a grudge.

# 62

## Christian

"I got it," Vicky tells me when she gets upstairs into my condo.

She hands me the bag with the Grim Reaper costume.

"You paid cash for it?" I ask. "Avoided cameras?"

"Yes."

I remove the costume from the bag and pull it over my head with Vicky's help.

"How do I look?"

"I'll tell you how you look," she says. "You look like something out of a Stephen King movie. But more importantly? You look totally anonymous."

We head into the bathroom so I can look in the mirror.

"It's formless," says Vicky. "And your face is too far inside that long hood to see."

"Yeah, it works."

"You're totally anonymous. Anyone who saw you in that, they wouldn't know if it was you or some scrawny teenager. They wouldn't know if it was you or some dumpy, middle-aged parent."

"They wouldn't know if it was me or your husband, Simon?"

"Exactly," she says.

"I like it. Perfect. Good job. You have the boots, too?"

"Yes," she says. "Simon has the same pair."

"What size are they? Size thirteen, I hope?"

"Size thirteen," she says. "And yes, I also bought these in cash, and I wore glasses and a hat and dressed differently than when I bought the costume."

Good, this is good. We head back into the main room.

"We have to cut off all contact with each other," I tell Vicky. "There can't be any trace of our connection."

"Absolutely."

"What evidence do you have of a connection to me?" I ask. "Did Simon know you met with me?"

"Simon doesn't know you exist," she says. "I didn't tell him I was interviewing financial advisers. I'd never want him to know that."

"You have some materials, brochures, that kind of thing, from my office?"

"I think I still do."

"Find them and shred them or burn them."

"Okay," she says.

"You ever write my name down? Look me up on your computer?"

She thinks about that. "I looked you up on my computer when I was researching financial advisers."

"Then dump the computer."

"I can wipe the computer—"

"No, no, wiping the computer isn't enough. Cops can recover all that stuff. Break it into pieces and dump it in a river. I'm not kidding, Vicky. This is important."

"Okay, I will."

"That's what I did to my laptop," I tell her. "I smashed it, broke it in half, dismantled all the parts. I've scrubbed all evidence of you from this apartment."

"Do you have a copy of Simon's trust?" she asks.

I did, past tense. I shredded it this morning, then I burned the shreds in my fireplace.

"The cops could search this entire place," I tell her. "They would find no evidence of you, Vicky. No computer. No documents. Nothing."

"What about evidence of . . . y'know . . . me?"

"You mean DNA?" I say. "No. I got rid of my bedsheets. I washed them just to be sure, then threw them in the dumpster in the alley. They'll be long gone by the time this happens."

I sit down next to her.

"Now about your phone," I say. "You've called me and texted me."

She blushes. "It's a burner," she says.

"Your—your phone is a burner?"

"The one I use to call you is, yes. A prepaid phone. Are you surprised? You think I want Simon looking at the phone bill and wondering what number I keep calling?"

Ah, yes, that makes sense. Phew. That makes things easier. I've been using a burner with her all along, for a different reason, for when I made my escape with her money, but I've never told her that.

"So we're covered," I say. "You'll destroy your computer. You'll dump your burner. Okay." I rub my hands together.

"You have a gun yet?" she asks.

Not yet. I'm getting one from Gavin. With a silencer. But she doesn't know about Gavin. "Soon," I say.

I can't believe it. I can't believe I'm doing this.

*Twenty-one million dollars,* I tell myself. *Twenty-one million dollars.*

"What's up?" Emily says, peeking her head into my office on Thursday afternoon. "You need me?"

"Yeah, come in a second, Em. Sit down."

She's probably wondering what I could possibly want. I've asked so little of her. She answers a phone that hardly ever rings. She's been here for a grand total of five meetings I've had with potential investors, two of which were Vicky. I told the others, who came after Vicky, that my current fund was closed, but I'd be happy to talk with them when I open my next round of financing.

She hasn't taken dictation—if that's even still a thing. She hasn't written a letter or even made a pot of coffee. Most days, I've been paying this nineteen-year-old twenty dollars an hour, four hours a day, to do her homework.

She sits down, wondering if she should have a pad of paper with her, her dirty-blond ponytail bobbing as she searches for a pen.

"This won't take long," I say. "Listen, Em, I've decided to relocate. I think I'm going to go to Paris for a while. I'm going to fly out there today."

"Oh, okay." She takes it pretty well, though I'm sure she likes this job.

"So I'd say you can pack up now and go." I hand her cash, two thousand dollars. "Think of this as severance."

"I'm just a temp, Mr. Newsome. You don't have to pay me severance."

"Well, then a bonus," I say. "A contribution to Emily's college fund."

She counts it out, her mouth opening in a wow. This is more than a month's pay all in one shot. "Yeah?" she says.

"Yeah. Good luck to you, Emily. I hope to be reading great things about you someday."


When Emily's gone, I remove the sleek desktop computer from the reception desk and smash it into pieces. I take a hammer to the mainframe as well. The busted computers are too heavy for garbage bags, so I put them in duffel bags.

I go through Emily's drawers, including an appointment pad with carbon pages. Vicky's name is on them. I rip every page to shreds and throw them in a garbage bag.

The office looks ransacked, stripped naked. But appearances don't matter anymore. Newsome Capital Growth is looking at its final days in business.

And there is not a single trace of Vicky Lanier to be found.

# 63

## Vicky

Friday morning, a quarter past seven. Conrad Betancourt walks out of the condo building on Michigan Avenue. He is wearing an expensive, long wool coat and carrying nothing, but the bellman behind him is lugging a suitcase and a long piece of luggage that looks like golf clubs.

That confirms it—Conrad's been staying at the downtown condo, not his house in Grace Village.

Conrad gets into the back of the black town car while the bellman loads the luggage into the trunk.

When the car drives off, but just before the bellman has returned into the building, I hurry forward and call out, "Excuse me! Did I just miss Mr. Betancourt?"

The man, tall and gray with a kind face, smiles. "Afraid so, miss. Just left for O'Hare."

"Shoot. I'm with the *Tribune*, I had a couple questions for him. You said the airport?"

"Yes, ma'am. You can leave a message at the lobby desk for him."

"Oh, that's okay, I have his cell phone. I just wanted a photo to go with the article."

"Well, he'll be gone 'til Tuesday night, miss. Golf trip."

Conrad is leaving town?

So he'll be gone for Halloween this coming Monday. Perfect.

# 64
## Simon

Friday morning is dark and chilly, which feels about right. I walk down from the law school to the Chicago Title & Trust Building and arrive well before ten. My walk was faster than normal, though I didn't realize it. Must be the nerves.

I grab my coffee and power on my phone. At ten o'clock, I text:

Good morning princess

Her reply doesn't come right away. I sip the coffee while people come in and out of the building, checking with security, sliding passes over scanners as iron gates allow them through to the different elevator banks. Finally, my phone pings:

*Hey*

Not the warmest of greetings. My response:

I hate Fridays. Most people love Fridays but I hate them.
Because I can't talk to you again until Monday morning.

She doesn't respond. A reasonable person would think she's either distracted or reticent. I throw her some more:

Every day that I can't talk to you or be with you is like torture.

Her reply box bubbles. It takes more than two minutes before she responds:

> *I know it stinks*

Not exactly a font of conversation today, are we? I try to engage her more than that:

> Very soon, we can be together EVERY day, not just Mon-Tues-Weds-Thurs.

She doesn't respond. The coffee is cooling enough that I can drink it in greater gulps, and I do, because there's not much else to do. This is a one-sided conversation. I try this:

> Something wrong? You seem distracted

This time, her reply comes quickly:

> *Yes sorry*

Yes, what? You're distracted, or something's wrong? But a halfway normal person would let this go for now and not push. So that's what I do:

> Ok, well I hope you're doing ok and I can't wait to talk to you Monday. Have a great weekend! Love you! See you on Monday Halloween

This time, her reply comes quickly:

> *You too*

I stare at the phone for a while. Nothing else comes. I power it down, remove the SIM card, and shove the phone in my pocket. I leave the building just in time for the rainfall to begin.

# 65

## Vicky

Friday, noon sharp. I arrive in the alley by Christian's garage door. I type in the pass code to his garage. The door grinds open. I close my umbrella and step inside. Christian is by the interior door waiting for me. He hits a button to close the door behind me.

Christian looks the same superficially as always, the male-model, pretty-boy thing, but he is all nerves, wearing a frown on his face and some dark circles under his eyes.

I follow him up the stairs. It smells different in here. Usually, there isn't much of a scent one way or the other, maybe a hint of his cologne, maybe a trace of body odor if he's been working out recently. Now the air is pungent with disinfectant.

"You've been cleaning."

"I've wiped down every surface," he says. "I don't want your fingerprints anywhere. Vacuumed, too. Have to remove all trace of you."

That's a good boy, Christian.

"Well, I hope you don't mind if I use your bathroom."

"Go ahead," he says. "I'll wipe it down after you're gone."

Good that he's taken this seriously. There can't be any trace of me inside this apartment.

I step into the bathroom, a shrine to his vanity, with the matching set of titanium toothbrush, razor, nail clippers, nose-hair trimmer, and fucking dental-floss holder. I'm surprised the dirty-towel hamper in the corner isn't plated in titanium, too.

When I come back out, he's waiting right there for me, a nervous Nellie.

"Did you destroy your computer?" he asks.

"I broke it into several pieces and dumped each piece in a different spot."

"Good. And you got rid of your burner phone?"

"Not yet," I say. "I thought we might still need to talk. It's only Friday."

"No, I think we're done talking," he says. "Probably best we don't see each other between now and Monday. Or *after*, for that matter. Not for a while."

I frown, like I'm greatly disturbed at the thought of our separation, like I don't know what I'll do with myself if I have to spend one moment without the man of my dreams. "How *long* a while?" I ask.

"Vicky, we—we have to be prepared for an investigation." He puts his hands on my shoulders. Now he's going to lecture me on what will happen post-murder, and I will have to look like I'm paying attention, like I'm not ten steps ahead of him.

"This is a rich lady in a rich town," he says. "This will be a big deal. Unless Simon was incredibly smart about this—and we can't count on it—they're going to figure out she was having an affair with him. You have to be prepared for a search of your house."

I am.

"You have to be prepared to be interviewed by the police."

I'm not. Oh, God, that would be a disaster.

"You have to be prepared to look Simon in the eye and act surprised when he tells you that someone named Lauren Betancourt was just murdered in Grace Village."

Jesus, he's a bundle of nerves.

"If Simon has the slightest idea that you were behind this," he says, "maybe he goes ahead and files for divorce. And then all of this will be for noth—"

"I can handle Simon," I say. "I've been handling Simon for ten years."

"Yeah, well, this will be the performance of a lifetime, babe."

"You have the gun yet?"

"Not to mention— What?"

"Do you have the gun yet?" I repeat. "You said you were getting—"

"Yes, I have it."

"What kind is it?"

"I— Do you know about guns?" He seems surprised.

"I grew up in West Virginia, remember?"

I didn't grow up in West Virginia. Vicky Lanier, my alter ego, did. But my father was an avid hunter and took me with him sometimes. He'd take me to the shooting range, too, and let me fire his guns, at least his handguns.

"What kind of gun do you have?" I ask again.

"It's a Glock."

"A Glock what? A 23?"

He steps back. "You do know your guns. It's a Glock 17, apparently."

"Okay, fine. And you have a suppressor?"

"A what?"

"A silencer, Christian. You need a silencer."

"Yeah, I do."

"Is it already attached?"

"Yeah, he— It came attached."

*He*, meaning Gavin, I assume. Gavin Finley has a firearm owners identification card with the state, and he owns three handguns, at least three he has legally purchased.

Yeah, it's nice having an investigator like Rambo on my team.

Not that I would expect Gavin to give Christian one of his own guns. No, Gavin must have bought it from a fence or used a straw purchaser. That's what I'd do.

"Let me see it," I say. "I want to check it out."

"It's not here. But don't worry. The guy who got it, he knows guns."

"Does he know *you*?" I ask. "Does he know *me*?"

"No, no, no, nothing like that."

Yes, yes, yes—exactly like that. It must have been Gavin, and I'm sure Gavin knows who I am. He's Christian's—Nick's—best friend from childhood. He's a fellow scammer, only his are less profitable.

"Practice shooting," I say.

"You want me to practice?"

"You've never fired a weapon before. Even shooting from close range, you need to get used to it. You need to make sure the magazine is properly loaded and the slide is back, you need to get used to the weight of it in your hands and holding it with a suppressor—"

"You're, like, G.I. Jane over here."

I pat him on the chest. "Promise me you'll practice. Don't let Halloween night be the first time you've fired a gun."

"So no luck with Simon's green phone?" Christian asks me.

"I couldn't find it. And you remember what his diary said about the weekends. They keep their phones off. They don't communicate after Friday morning until Monday morning."

"Right, I remember. They go dark on the weekends. That's smart."

"Yeah, hooray for them, it's smart," I say. "But for me, it means that as of now, until Monday morning, wherever Simon stowed it away, it's going to stay stowed away. My guess is he left it at his office at the law school."

"I wonder where Lauren keeps her pink phone."

"Probably stowed away for the weekend, too," I say.

He shakes his head. "I guess at this point, it doesn't matter. We have the information we need. We have the plan. We don't need their phones."

Maybe you don't, Christian. But I do.

"You're right," I say.

Christian walks me down to the garage. I turn to him before he pops the door open.

"Now get rid of your burner phone," he says to me. "It's a connection to me."

"I'll keep it 'til Monday."

"Vicky—"

"Just in case," I say. "If there's an emergency. If I need to reach you. Or you, me."

"Okay, I guess that makes sense," he agrees.

"If there's an emergency, just text something innocuous. I'll have my phone off, but I'll check it periodically. Okay?"

"Okay."

"Otherwise, see you Monday?"

He sighs, thinks about that. "You think we should see each other on the big day?"

"Just in case," I say. "Just a check-in. Just to make sure nothing's come up. Just to run through everything again, one more time."

He relents. "I guess it doesn't hurt to make sure."

"I'll be here at noon," I say. "Right here by the garage at noon."

"Okay."

"Promise me you'll practice with the Glock this weekend," I say.

"I will."

We go silent. This is supposed to be a tender moment, I guess. He thinks I'm worried—about him, about our future together. This is supposed to be a tearful goodbye-for-a-while.

Okay, here goes.

"Promise me we'll be together when this is over," I say without gagging or vomiting.

He takes my hands, kisses me softly. "Of course we will," he whispers. "That's why we're doing this, right?"

I nod, look into his eyes. "I don't know what I'll do if . . ."

. . . if I have to pretend to be in love with this self-worshipping jagoff for another second. But I let the words drift off.

"It'll be fine," he assures me. "Everything's going to turn out fine."

# 66

## Christian

Saturday morning. I flip up the collar on my jacket. Out here in the heavily shaded woods, it feels like nighttime, not one hour past dawn. It can't be more than forty degrees.

Gavin comes walking down the trail a few minutes later, wearing a green hunting jacket and a cap on his head. "You sleep much?" he asks me.

"Hardly at all."

"You're nervous."

"Hell yes, I'm nervous. This would be much easier if you did this, not me. You're the hunter. You're the one who knows guns."

"I'm not doing it, Nick. We've been over this. It's your job. You're doing it."

I stretch my arms, roll my neck. I've never fired a gun in my life, and two days from now, I'm going to kill somebody at close range.

"You trust Vicky?" Gavin asks me.

Do I trust a woman who is willing to kill over money? Do I trust a woman who plans on stealing it all from her husband?

"What I trust," I say, "is that she wants the money, she wants me to invest it, and she wants me, period. *That* much, I trust. And that's all I need to trust."

"Yeah." Gavin works his jaw, which could use a razor. "Yeah. So . . . what happens afterward? After you kill Lauren?"

"Simon's going to be pretty devastated," I say. "There'll be no reason for him to go through with the divorce so urgently. He'll probably— He'll be blown apart, I assume. And Vicky will be the doting wife who plays dumb."

"What if Simon suspects Vicky was behind this? It's not exactly a giant leap. He's having an affair, planning on dumping his wife and cutting her out of the money, and suddenly the 'other woman' ends up shot dead?"

"Vicky says she can handle him. I trust that much, too."

"Vicky can handle him." Gavin thinks that over. "Vicky hasn't been handling him so far, has she? Simon's been stepping out on her and she didn't have a clue."

"That's probably my fault," I say. "I've done too good a job with her. She's fallen for me. She's so worried about *him* finding out about *me* that she didn't notice what he was doing behind her back."

Gavin starts walking down the trail to our site, the place I'm going to practice shooting.

"You don't seem convinced," I say to him.

"Okay, Nicky, let's say Vicky handles Simon, like you say she will. She plays dumb and plays the doting wife. November third comes and goes, and now she has control of the money."

"Right. That's the key. She handles him for a couple of days after the murder, and then we're home free on November third."

"What about the cops?" Gavin turns to me.

"Well, if they're halfway decent at their job, they'll figure out Simon was having an affair with Lauren. And they'll want to question him."

"And Vicky."

"Yeah, probably. Vicky can handle it. All she has to do is play dumb, right? There's no connection between her and me."

"Sounds like you're counting on Vicky a lot."

"Not as much as you think," I say. "For one thing, we're setting Simon up. I'm wearing the same exact boots he owns and the same Grim Reaper costume in his closet. If anyone sees me or the cops find my boot prints, it will lead to Simon. They're not gonna think *Vicky* dressed up in that outfit. And anyway, we just have to get past a couple of days, right? The day after Halloween, November first—Simon hears the news. That'll hit him like a freight train. Vicky plays dumb. Maybe Simon confesses his affair to her. Maybe he doesn't. But then we just need another twenty-four-hour period to pass—November second—and then we're at November third and their ten-year anniversary and we're golden."

"You mean *Vicky's* golden." Gavin stops along the trail. This must be the spot he had in mind for target practice.

"No, *we're* golden."

Gavin shows me one of his patented smirks. "How do you know that, once November third rolls around, Vicky won't forget you ever existed?"

"She won't," I say. "Believe me, she won't."

"How do you know?"

"Fuck, G, where's the trust? I know what I'm doing."

Gavin pulls out an empty soda can and places it on a tree stump.

"You, I trust," he says. "Vicky, I don't. What if she just wants you to be the triggerman who kills Simon's girlfriend? And once you've performed that task for her, thank you very much, she forgets that 'Christian Newsome' ever existed. What if the whole point of your existence is to be the guy who solves the 'Lauren problem' for her?"

I'm shaking my head midway through his speech. "That makes no sense. First of all, Vicky didn't *have* a 'Lauren problem' until a couple days ago. And second, for the last two months, Vicky has been thinking about two things and two things only—grabbing that money and grabbing my cock. I fuck her like she's never been fucked in her life, and in her mind, I'm the guy who can quadruple her money, too. This is what I do. I draw in my targets. I've never missed. I'm not missing now."

I pull the Glock with the silencer out of my gym bag. Gavin marks a spot, about ten feet away.

"Besides," I say, "I'm too close to that money now. I'm not letting some blondie shake her ass for Simon and fuck me out of it. Whatever the risk, it's worth it. It's twenty-one million dollars, G. Nothing is risk-free. If something happens down the road and we hit a bump, we'll figure it out."

I aim the gun at the empty soda can resting on top of the tree stump, and fire. A popping sound, nothing remotely approaching the sound you'd expect from firing a bullet. The silencer works just fine. The problem is the person firing the gun.

The soda can and tree stump, ten paces away, sit undisturbed.

"It's harder to aim with a suppressor," says Gavin. "You can't see the sights as clearly."

"I can't hit anything. I'm zero for five."

"Yeah, but I'm making you shoot a soda can from ten feet away," he says. "You'll be shooting at a person's body from two feet away. It's hard to miss. Just aim for center mass and shoot. You won't miss. I'd fire several times, if it were me. The mag holds seventeen rounds. Bang-bang-bang. Just keep firing."

I drop the gun to my side. "I can't believe I'm doing this."

"Hey, look at that," Gavin says. I follow his eyes to a nearby tree, a spare tire hanging from a tree branch, a makeshift swing.

"That would be a good backup," he says. "You always need a backup plan, right?"

"I'll drop an inner tube on her head?"

"No, dipshit, the rope." Gavin walks over to the tree, looks up at it. "You can tie the rope around your waist. That would look right for a Grim Reaper costume, anyway."

"A rope for a backup? How about a knife or something?"

"No, no, no." He shakes his head. "A knife is no good. You don't want to use a knife. Too much of a chance that you cut yourself and leave DNA behind, or maybe you get her blood on you. A rope is bloodless. Yeah," he says, "this rope is a good backup."

"So—if I can't shoot straight with the gun, I strangle her with a rope?"

"Well, yeah, if it comes to that." He feels the rope, knotted every foot or so, hanging about eight, ten feet down from a thick tree branch. "Yeah, I like this rope. Good traction on it with the knots. And it already has a noose."

"A *noose*? Jesus Christ, G, there's no way I can do that."

"Once you start, you have to finish, Nicky. If anything goes wrong—"

"What's gonna go wrong?"

"Well, shit, *I* don't know," he says. "All I know is it makes sense to have a backup plan. Help me take that rope down."

I can't believe this. I can't believe any of this. But there's no turning back now.

Twenty-one million dollars. It's Lauren or me.

# 67

## Vicky

Sunday morning. October 30. The day before Halloween.

Just another day, another workout, as I power walk in my workout gear, AirPods in my ears, and I just happen to stop to check my phone, to have a pretend phone conversation, outside the home of one Lauren Betancourt on Lathrow Avenue in Grace Village, Illinois.

I won't spend long here. It's way too close to D-Day. I walk in a small circle, saying, "I know, right?" and "You think you were surprised. You should have seen my face!" I'm animated, even laughing a little.

But all I need is a quick glance on the south side of Lauren's house, by the gangway and the large privacy fence.

It's still open. The window, presumably to the kitchen. It's been open, by my count, for more than eight consecutive days. Which means she just keeps it open all the time. Doesn't even think about it.

It's not at eye level. Looks like a stepladder or some lawn chair or bench or something will be necessary to reach it. That's more difficult. That's risky.

But it is, without a doubt, a way into her house.

# 68
## Simon

I lace up my running shoes at 7:30 p.m. My longer run for the weekend, saving it for tonight, Sunday night, a fourteen-miler.

Much as I love running through the west side of Chicago, I can't deny the violence that plagues these neighborhoods, that it's not the safest idea to be jogging along the street in the dark on a weekend night. The Halloween decorations don't help my nerves, the ghouls and witches and scream faces.

But I will never stop running through these streets. They inspire me, the people fighting through poverty and crummy schools, getting the short end of every stick, but fighting no less. I have lived a blessed life. I know that. I've had a few low points, to be sure, but I've never wondered whether there would be food on the table, I've never wondered whether I'd go to college, I've never had to avoid windows in my own home for fear of stray gunfire, I've never been told that there was no hope for me. I've never been ignored.

"You'll find someone you love," my mother said to me in her last week, forcing the words out. She was right. I haven't had a hard time finding someone I love. I've found two people. The problem is them loving me back. That's the hole I've felt, even before I realized it was a hole.

I end up running faster than even I expected—nervous energy, I suppose. I cover seven miles, give or take, in less than forty minutes.

I stop outside the alley behind Viva Mediterránea, cool air on my sweaty face, my stocking cap pulled low. Not that Christian would recognize me, even if he stood out on his patio on this chilly night and looked down at me. Has he seen a picture of me? Maybe. Probably. He's never met me in person.

At eight, I power up the green phone and pop in the SIM card. A message is already awaiting me:

> *I know you won't read this until tomorrow morning.*
> *I'm sorry that I'm writing you instead of saying this in*
> *person. It would be very hard for me to say this in*
> *person. So here goes. I've been doing a lot of thinking,*
> *and we can't be together. We just don't work. I think*
> *you're a VERY special person, but if I have learned*
> *anything, it's that two people have to make sense*
> *together. And we don't make sense together. I can't*
> *marry you and I can't be with you. I'm going out of*
> *town for a few days to get my head straight. I'm going*
> *to turn off my phone. I know that's harsh but I have to*
> *do what's right for me, and this is right for me. Please*
> *respect my decision and don't try to contact me. I am*
> *very, very sorry. I didn't mean to hurt you.*

I start typing so fast, I almost drop the phone:

Is this a joke? This can't be real. Everything is great between us. Please tell me it's a joke!

Her reply box bubbles. It doesn't take her long:

> *I'm sorry it's not a joke. I can't be with you. Please*
> *respect what I want. This is what I want. I won't*
> *change my mind. Believe me this is best for*
> *both of us*

I respond immediately:

Let's talk about this. In person. Don't do this by phone. If something's wrong, let's talk about it. Please at least give me that opportunity. Are you home right now?

Her reply is just as quick:

> *No I told you I'm out of town for a few days. If you love*
> *me, you'll respect my decision. I'm turning my phone*
> *off now.*

I respond immediately, violating the number one rule against using names:

Lauren, please. Talk to me in person. Or call me

She doesn't respond. No bubbles.

Lauren, please. If YOU love ME you'll at least talk to me

Again, no response. No bubbles.

Lauren, I'm begging you

I hit "send."

This is how you treat someone you LOVE??????

I hit "send."
And then, after a few moments, a response:

> *I don't love you. OK? I never did. I needed someone*
> *different after a bad marriage. You were my bridge.*
> *But that's all you were. Harsh, I know, but you*
> *made me say it. Please don't contact me*
> *again.*

I move out of texting and go to the phone. I call her number. The ro-botic voice tells me that the cellular customer I am trying to call is not available.

I don't leave a voicemail. I call her again. Same robotic voice.

I call her again. Same robotic voice.

I call her again. Same robotic voice.

I return to text messages. My pulse pounding, my hands trembling, I send one last text:

This isn't over

# 69

## Vicky

People may pay more attention at night, but it's still easier being a woman out on the streets of Grace Village. And what's the big deal if you're only stopping for a quick moment or two on the sidewalk in the middle of a somewhat busy street like Lathrow Avenue on a Sunday evening?

I can see why someone like Lauren would like living around here. Pretty trees hanging over the streets, big houses on wide lots. Peaceful and quiet. And I could also see why someone like Simon, in the next town over, resented a town like this.

Speak of the devil. The pink phone pings again, another text from the old boy:

> Lauren, please. If YOU love ME you'll at least talk to me

Hey, life's a bitch. Another text from him:

> Lauren, I'm begging you

Yeah, well, keep begging. I hold the pink phone in my hand and give him some more time. Keep begging, fella.

> This is how you treat someone you LOVE??????

Apparently so.

That's four consecutive texts from him. Time for Lauren's final knock-out punch:

> *I don't love you. OK? I never did. I needed someone*
> *different after a bad marriage. You were my bridge.*
> *But that's all you were. Harsh, I know, but you made*
> *me say it. Please don't contact me again.*

I hit "send," the phone belting out a *thwip* as the message carries forth to Simon's phone. Yep, pretty harsh. But Lauren the Gold-Digging Skank is capable of saying something like this, isn't she? Sure she is.

The phone rings. I let it ring.

It rings again. I don't answer.

Again. Let it ring, let it ring, let it ring . . .

Again. No one's going to answer, Simon. The question is, are you going to send another text? Are you going to let Lauren get the last word? C'mon, sport, you have it in you.

The pink phone pings, another text from the man of the hour:

This isn't over

I press down the "power" button and watch the pink phone's screen fade to black. I walk south, glancing at the gangway on the south side of her house. The window into the kitchen still open. Lauren really should be more careful.

I keep walking, happy to end on that last text from Simon. He's right. This isn't over.

But it will be in twenty-four hours.

# 70

## Simon

Three in the morning. Technically Halloween. Vicky's down for the count, sleeping peacefully in the bedroom. Me, I can't sleep, I'm too amped up. I need to run, but it's too early, even for me.

I stare at the green phone. No, not here, not now.

I don't want to wake Vicky, so I go downstairs and pace through a dark house. I shiver from the cold, or probably nerves, I don't know, but I'm so cold, like some invisible wind is whipping through me.

I pace, rubbing my arms, and think. Or at least I try to think. I can't keep settled.

Deep breath. Calm, Simon. Deep breath.

The phrase "It is what it is" is the only sentence we speak where we could, but don't ever, ever use contractions. Nobody says, "It's what it's."

Deep breath.

The phrase "only choice" is an oxymoron.

"Laid" is pronounced like "paid" but not "said" and "said" is pronounced like "bread" but not "bead" and "bead" is pronounced like "lead" but not "lead."

Deep breath.

No. No. The old tricks not working, not working at all. I can't make my mind do anything but remember. Remember your words, Lauren, nineteen years ago, and the look of pity on your face when you said them.

"I assume you weren't planning on us getting *married*," you said to me.

And then you laughed, a small chuckle, like even the slightest possibility of a relationship with me was humorous, obviously so. It was a joke to you. *I* was a joke to you.

You didn't care. It didn't even bother you.

Then, after swinging your wrecking ball, you left. At least you had the decency to leave.

And I was willing to let it go. It took a long time, it was hard, it was brutal, actually, but I said okay, let it go, put it behind you, and I did, Lauren. I put you behind me. I never forgot about you, not for one day, but I put you behind me.

But then you came back. And you didn't even tell me. You just came back here like it didn't matter, like nothing you did back then made one bit of difference and you could just stroll back here and, y'know, fuck it if I lived in the next town over. And that club, that country club, no I never go, I'm just a legacy member, but you *knew* my family belonged there and you *had* to think you might run into me there, but that didn't stop you from going, did it, Lauren, going every day, because you didn't care, did you, Lauren? Because it's all about you. It was never about anyone else but you.

I wish I hadn't seen you that day in May. Five seconds, Jesus, five *seconds* different that day and I probably would've missed you, I would've never known you were back.

I twist the gas starter on the fireplace in the living room, sit close to it as the fire pops on, burns the firewood with a cackle. I put out my hands. But I can't stop shaking.

I pick up the marriage certificate. *Acta de Matrimonio*, the act of marriage. *Nombre* Simon Peter Dobias. *Nombre* Victoria Lanier. *Fecha de Registro* 2012-11-3.

Vicky made me better. I would have loved her forever if she could've loved me back.

I pull open the metal curtain and toss the marriage certificate into the fire. Watch it blacken and bend and disappear into ash.

The green journal. I hate that journal. I'm so tired of that journal. I leaf through it, the heat blazing on my face now. I read through it, all those days over the spring and summer and fall.

*"Would you like to see me again?"*

I rip out the page and toss it in the fire.

*"Do you want me to be your whore, Professor Dobias?"*

Rip it out and toss it in. Watch it burn.

*Are you my addiction, Lauren? Am I barreling toward a cliff?*

Burn.

*I have become the man I despise.*

Burn!

*"I want us to get married."*

Burn, burn, fucking BURN—

Burn it all. Burn everything. Burn the cover. Burn every last scrap of its existence and scoop up the ashes and walk outside into the backyard, the shrubbery and trees blanketing me in privacy, in pitch-dark, and throw them into the wind like you discard the ashes of the dead.

Then go down to the basement, into the small room with the safe that came with the house, that was here when my father and mother bought this house thirty years ago.

I turn the combination to the right, 9, to the left, 19, to the right, 81, and pull open the safe. I almost need two hands to do it, heavy and creaky as the door is. The safe is built into the floor, one of these massive old things that looks more like a furnace than a storage unit for valuables. Drop a bomb on this house and the safe would still be intact. I've used it for tax documents and some vital records, but not anymore. Now it holds only two things.

One, stacks of money. A million dollars in cash. Money I withdrew this summer from the trust fund, filling up most of the safe.

And two, Vicky's gun.

A Glock 23, she said, whatever that means. I don't know very much about guns. But I know enough. I know they fire bullets. I know they kill people.

I put the gun against my temple and close my eyes.

Oh, the irony, right? The guy who runs Survivors of Suicide puts a bullet through his head?

It's not too late. It's not too late to turn back. It would save everyone a lot of trouble, a lot of pain. It might be best for everyone.

No.

I place the gun on top of the safe.

I'm not letting you off that easy, Lauren.

This isn't over. That's what I wrote in my last text message. And I meant it. This is not over.

# 71

## Vicky

I'm at the alley garage below Christian's condo at noon sharp, Monday. The sun is high, the air is cool. The temps today will reach the high forties, slight chance of rain in the early afternoon but not for long if at all. That's good. Perfect weather for trick-or-treating. A perfect night for murder. Somebody must have said that in a movie.

But what's *not* so good? The garage door isn't opening. Christian's been good at being timely, not wanting me standing outside in the alley, exposing myself to public view.

You picked a really shitty day to be late, Christian.

I know the pass code to get into his garage, but I don't want to use it. I don't want to startle him. He's already seemed nervous. I'd prefer he come out and get me.

I look up at his condo, but I'm looking into the sun and can't see any indication of what's going on up there.

At five after twelve, a mild case of panic starts to set in. I need to see him. What's he doing? Did he forget? But how could he forget?

He's freaking out, that's what's happening, he's freaking—

The door rises, startling me. I hike my bag over my shoulder and walk inside.

At the doorway into his condo stands Christian, wearing a dirty white T-shirt, hair fallen into his dark-ringed eyes.

"Happy Halloween," I say, but he doesn't smile. "What's wrong? You look like hell."

I follow him up the stairs. "Are you okay?" I ask.

He stops in the kitchen and looks at me. "I'm fine. Just nerves, I guess. I've never done something like this."

Don't go wussing out on me now, Christian. I need you, pal.

His eyes are glassy, almost like he's been crying. He's pale and sweaty and shaky.

Are you fucking kidding me? He's going south on me *now*? We're just hours away.

"Let me get you some water," I say.

"Gloves," he says, pointing at the kitchen counter.

A pair of rubber gloves, pulled out of their wrapping and waiting for me. Smart.

"I just spent . . . all weekend scrubbing you out of this condo," he says.

I snap on the rubber gloves, grab a glass from the cabinet, fill it with water, and hand it to him. "Drink," I say. "Do you have the flu or something?"

"I just . . . threw up," he admits. "Nervous stomach, I guess. I don't have the flu."

"Let me take your temperature. You have a thermometer?"

"Uh . . . I think so. An old one."

I head into his bathroom. It reeks of vomit. The toilet lid is still up. What a freakin' cream puff. But what did I expect, I guess, from a guy with a titanium toothbrush and matching nose-hair trimmer?

"I'll clean up in here a little," I call to him. "You should lie down. Get some rest."

Get some rest and grow a pair of testicles.

When I come out of the bathroom, Christian's lying on the couch, trying to relax but not succeeding. I drop my bag down and sit next to him, putting his feet on my lap.

"We're only getting one chance at this," I say.

"I know that. Don't worry. You can count on me."

"Did you practice with the Glock?"

He nods. "I practiced. It's fine. It's easy to handle."

"Okay. What time are you going?"

He blows out. "Probably six-thirty or so, I'll be there. I'll try to blend in with the crowd. I'll make it down to her house about five minutes 'til seven."

"Good. A couple minutes before seven, ring the doorbell. If it's after seven, she might not answer—"

"I know. I got it."

"And right *at* seven, people might be sticking their heads out to shout 'Happy Halloween'—"

"I know, Vicky. A couple minutes before seven. And what happens if other kids are there at that time? Other trick-or-treaters?"

"Not very likely," I say. "But if so, wait for them to leave."

"And you're sure Conrad is out of town?"

"I'm sure. It will be Lauren answering the door. She's there alone. Okay?" I shake his leg. "We okay? It's a good plan, Christian."

"Yeah," he says, like he's trying to convince himself as well as me. "I'm fine."

Jeez. Does he want his hands on that twenty-one million or not?

# 72

## Simon

This isn't over.

After Vicky leaves Monday morning, I try to find an outlet for my nervous energy. I clean the downstairs, spraying and wiping and vacuuming and dusting. When I'm done, I stretch my back, sore but calmed by the physical labor. The sunlight streaming into the family room helps, too. The middle of the night, dark and desolate, is never a good place for me. Daytime is much better.

And it's nice to have that green journal behind me, every last page burned to ash and scattered into the wind in my backyard. It's just about the last remaining connection to Lauren.

Other than the green phone, turned off, in my pocket.

I go to work. I'm not sure why. I don't have class today and I don't have office hours today, but I go anyway, maybe because I think I'm supposed to, because it will look right, it will look normal, but I can't think about the law. I can only think about her. I try to read from the e-bulletin I receive every Monday about new Fourth Amendment decisions handed down around the country, but all I can think about is her. I try to focus on my new law review article on the good-faith exception to the warrant requirement, but all I can think about is her. I put on my headphones and jam the loudest music I can find, Metallica and Rage Against the Machine—

*Trapped in myself, body my holding cell*
*An empty glass of himself shattered somewhere within*

—turning it up louder and louder and louder, but all I can think about is *Lauren Lauren Lauren Lauren LAUREN.*

I open my eyes. I'm home. I got home. Right, I drove home.

I'm in the basement, in the dark. I don't have to do this. I don't have to do this.

You don't have to do this.

Simon Peter Dobias: You can let this go. You can let her go.

I go to the pantry and open it up. Six hundred forty pieces of candy, four bags of a hundred sixty each. Happy Halloween.

What time is it? After three. Trick-or-treating starts at four in Grace Park, an hour later than the Village.

Waiting. The waiting is ripping a hole through my stomach. Nothing I can do but grit it out. Deep breaths now, Simon. Deep breaths.

Why always "trick or treat" and never, ever "treat or trick"? It means the same thing. So does "jelly and peanut butter" or "cream 'n' cookies" or "white and black."

Trick or treat, smell my feet, give me something good to eat.

Why do feet smell and noses run?

You're okay, Simon, you're okay.

Getting close to four. You'll need to answer the door. You'll need to smile and hand out candy. You'll need to be *seen* handing out candy, you want people to say, *Yes, yes, Simon Dobias was home. Yes, he was home handing out candy, why? Why do you ask, Officer? You think Simon Dobias went over to Lauren Betancourt's house and shot her in the head because she trampled over everything that mattered to him and laughed about it? Just walked away like he didn't matter and laughed about it? Well no, Officer, no.*

*He was home handing out candy.*

Upstairs, my legs shaking but I've made it upstairs.

It's not four yet and I'm not sure yet if I can answer the door and go through with it, not sure I can smile and hand out candy and say, "Happy

Halloween!" But I know I can. I can do this. I can do this. Of course I can do this, but I need to charge my phone, not the green phone but my normal phone, my iPhone, gotta charge it up by my nightstand. The drawer is ajar and I never leave the door ajar. I open it up and look inside the drawer—

Vicky's wedding ring. The one she was wearing this morning.

The ring I once nervously slid on her finger.

She said no the first time I asked her.


"Happy Halloween! Go ahead and take a couple!"

"Thank you!"

"You're welcome!" and wave to the parents with their umbrellas because it's sprinkling, Hey, remember me, remember me I'm Simon Dobias if anyone asks whether I (a) was home handing out candy or (b) was over at Lauren's house putting a bullet in her head because this time I couldn't let it go. It isn't over.


"Happy Halloween! Go ahead and take a bunch, here, take like five each!"

Five-thirty.


"Happy Halloween! Go ahead and take as many as you want!"

Six-fifteen.


I go upstairs and open my bedroom closet and look to the far right. Pull out the costume I bought last year but didn't wear to a party I was supposed to attend. A Grim Reaper costume. All black, long robe, elongated hood. It's never been worn. I decided not to go to the party. It was some student's Halloween bash, and you have to be careful socializing with students, so I decided against it at the last minute.

I pick up my iPhone, still charging on the nightstand.

I pull up Netflix. I turn on *House of Cards*. I scroll through the synopses of season one and remind myself of the characters' names—Frank, Claire,

Zoe, Peter, Stamper—and the general plot. Then I turn on season one, episode one.

I get dressed. Blue suit and red tie. Put the Barack Obama mask over my head. I'm roughly the same build as the former president, so other than the obvious difference in skin pigment, it's a pretty good look. I'm Barack Obama, the forty-fourth president of the United States.

I pull out a pillowcase and fill it with everything I need. The Grim Reaper costume makes it heavier and bulkier than I'd prefer. Nothing I can do about that.

I head out the back door, through the privacy of my backyard, into the alley.

I walk along Division, not wanting to arrive too soon. It's cold and damp outside. I'm underdressed and I get a few comments in that regard from people I pass—"Love the costume! Aren't you cold?"—but the cold is helping me now, not hindering.

Because now I'm doing it. The time for worrying, obsessing, debating, second-guessing, is over. It's liberating, I must say, to be done with the conflict. Now I can focus.

By 6:45 p.m., I'm at Lathrow and Division in Grace Village. The number of trick-or-treaters has frittered down to just a handful, mostly older kids.

Lauren's house is a block and a half to the south.

You shouldn't have come back, Lauren.

# THE DAYS AFTER HALLOWEEN

# 73

## Jane

Sergeants Jane Burke and Andy Tate get out of their car and head into the West Suburban Major Crimes Task Force center in Forest Park. Jane was in the station by six this morning—Day 2 of the investigation—Andy, by six-thirty.

"Harsh, yes," says Jane.

"Doesn't get any harsher," says Andy. "'I don't love you'? 'I never did'? 'I needed someone different after a bad marriage'? 'You were my bridge, that's all you were'? I mean, cruel doesn't get any crueler. Can you imagine someone saying that to you?"

She gives him a sidelong glance. "No," she says. "That's my point. It feels . . . I don't know, staged."

"Oh, c'mon, Janey. You really like a woman for this? You really think Lauren's boyfriend had a wife, and the wife did this?"

Jane stops before entering the door for the task force. Their breath hangs in the cool air. "I know that that blood trail Ria showed me doesn't lie, Andy. Somebody moved the pink phone after the murder. It had to be the offender. And if the offender was Lauren's boyfriend, he would have to be the dumbest shit on the planet to not pick it up and take it with him."

"And you've never met an offender who made a mistake."

A couple of uniforms from Forest Park, one of whom Jane recognizes but can't place the name, pass them on their way into the station. She steps back and nods to them.

"Yes, offenders make mistakes, but it's not like the offender ignored it or was so freaked out that he missed it. *That* I could understand." She steps forward, lowering her voice. "But he didn't miss it. He focused on it. He paid careful attention to it. He gently, carefully nudged that phone under the table. It took deliberation, Andy. It took care. It took conscious thought. That whole time he—or she—is carefully pushing that phone under the table, it never occurred to him—or her—that hey, this phone is really incriminating, probably better I scoop it up and take it with me? Or smash it into thirty thousand pieces at least?"

"So it was a woman, the lover's wife?" says Andy. "She kills two birds with one stone. She kills Lauren and frames her husband. All because a phone got moved not once, but twice?"

"Maybe it's not a smoking gun, I grant you," she says. "But something doesn't fit."

"A woman picked up Lauren and chucked her over the side, while she's kicking and screaming."

"Who said she was kicking and screaming? The blow to the head could have knocked her out. She's unconscious, the offender gets the noose around Lauren's neck and chucks her over the side. It might not be the easiest thing, but plenty of women could pull that off. Just—just do me a favor and keep an open mind."

"Here you go, Jane." Marta Glasgow, from Major Crimes forensics, pops up the image on her computer screen. "That's it. That's your boot."

Jane leans over Marta's shoulder, peering at the screen. "A . . . Peak Explorer."

"Right. The brand is Paul Roy. They have a Peak collection, and this is the Explorer. See the treads?"

On the right side of the split screen is the bottom of the boot, a diagonal tread with a strip down the middle, a triangular shape of a mountain peak, filled by small treads of the same shape.

"A Paul Roy Peak Explorer."

"Yup. Men's size thirteen."

"And you're sure."

"Yup. Matches the dental stone cast and the photographs from the impressions on the front door. Good thing for you it rained that afternoon. Just enough to moisten the mud behind the shrubs by the window."

"Any idea how old these shoes are?" Jane asks.

Marta laughs. "I'm not a miracle worker, Jane. But I will say this much. The treads weren't very worn. The shoes could've been new or not used very often."

"Thanks, Marta."

Jane dares to glance at Andy. "Don't even say it."

He leans into her. "A woman with a man's size thirteen foot?"

"Do you have any idea how many calls I've gotten in just twenty-four hours? People are incredibly upset. Some are scared." The Village president, Alex Galanis, hikes a knee up on a chair inside the chief's office. "I've had more than one person say to me they moved here from Chicago to get *away* from this kind of violence."

"I think they're overreacting, Alex," says Chief Carlyle. "My statement said the public was not in danger."

"That statement wasn't strong enough. Do we have a suspect or a person of interest at least?" Galanis sighs, plays with his tie. Alex Galanis is a downtown lawyer in his second term as village president. The word around town is he's being groomed for a shot at the state senate in 2024. Jane knew his younger brother, Nikos, in high school.

"Sergeant Burke has been running this investigation around the clock," says the chief. "She's our best. Jane, why don't you take that?"

Her instinct is to appreciate the chief letting her field the question, giving her the rope to do her job and take the credit. But credit can quickly turn to blame, and that rope to a noose.

"It seems clear to us that this was personal," she says. "We have text messages from a prepaid burner phone. Love notes. She was having an affair. And the text messages indicate that she'd just broken things off. So that gives us a pretty clear motive. Finding the person on the other end of those phone calls is the challenge."

Jane doesn't think it's quite that simple, but the summary is accurate enough.

"Well, that's good, at least, the personal part." Galanis throws up a hand. "We don't have some roving serial killer or something. And you think this killer . . . might have killed himself?"

"Well, sir, his last text to her, after she was dead, sure seemed like a suicide note, yes."

Galanis nods, not wanting to hope for someone's death, but it would obviously eliminate any further violence in his town. "So how long will this take?"

"I wish I could say, sir."

"Weeks? Months?"

"I hope not. It's too early."

"So it could take *months*?"

"It will take as long as it takes, sir," she says, steeling herself.

"Oh, it won't be months, Alex," the chief intervenes. "Sergeant Burke is very methodical. We're hopeful it won't take long at all. But we can't guarantee anything."

"You know what everyone's going to say," says Galanis. "They're going to say we're dealing with a small-town batch of keystone cops. We're in over our heads. Are we?" He looks around. "Are we?"

"Of course not. We're working with the FBI and with WESTAF, the West Suburban Major Crimes Task Force. And we have full manpower on this."

That doesn't seem to satisfy the Village president. "I want daily updates." He buttons his suit coat and leaves the office.

The chief looks at Jane and winks. "Another satisfied customer. Who's doing the CSLI with us? WESTAF or the FBI?"

"FBI," says Jane. "I know an agent there who can decode that stuff like the back of her hand."

"Okay. And that'll be today?"

"Yes, sir."

"Good. Oh and, Jane—what did Grace Park just send over to us? A bunch of file boxes."

"Everything they have on Simon Dobias," says Jane.

"That's the . . . guy who filed that complaint back in '04?"

"Right."

"He's still in town? Grace Park?"

"According to property tax records, he is."

"So you think there might be something to that? That was a long time ago."

"I know," says Jane. "I know this guy a little. Went to high school with him."

"And you could see him doing this?"

"Oh, well, it's been so long. I never really knew him."

"Yeah, but tell him that story you told me, Jane," says Andy Tate. "From high school. That story about Mitchell Kitchens."

# 74
## Jane

"Simon and I were freshmen together," says Jane. "I didn't know him well. We had some classes together. He was this little guy. He grew a lot by senior year, and he was a pretty good runner, one of those skinny track guys. But back when Simon was first entering high school, he was this small, skinny, shy, super-smart kid. And he got picked on."

"Sounds right," says the chief.

"When we were freshmen, there was this senior named Mitchell Kitchens," she says. "Big wrestler. Like the best in the state at his weight class. I was dating a sophomore on the wrestling team back then, and to him, to the younger kids, Mitchell Kitchens was like this god, right? This senior stud wrestler? All-state, looking at a scholarship, that whole thing?"

"Okay," says Chief Carlyle.

"So apparently, Mitchell bullied Simon pretty badly. This all came out afterward."

"After what?"

"Well, so here's the story. Apparently, Mitchell would pick on Simon. They said when Simon got off the bus every morning, Mitchell would pick him up and throw him."

"He'd— What do you mean, 'throw him'?"

"I mean, like, pick him up by the shirt collar and belt and toss him through the air."

"Like one of those dwarf-toss contests they used to do in bars?"

"I don't know. But yeah, Mitchell apparently treated it like a contest. How far could he toss the little freshman today?"

"Jesus. And nobody stopped him?"

Jane shrugs. "He didn't do it in front of the whole school or anything. The wrestlers used this small gym right by the school entrance. They'd go in there, and Mitchell would do his daily toss, and his wrestling buddies would laugh along. And I guess Simon never complained."

"Nice."

"The other thing, apparently—Simon would bring a lunch to school every day and it included a bottle of Gatorade. Well, apparently, Mitchell used to take it. He'd walk up to his lunch table and say, like, 'Did you bring my Gatorade?' At least that's how I heard it. Later. After everything."

"So maybe you should get to the good part, Jane."

"Right. It was wrestling season, the end of the season, and I guess they called it 'regionals.' Like, the playoffs for wrestling, the next stop is the state championship."

"The semifinals, regionals, whatever."

"I guess. Anyway, Mitchell Kitchens, this big-time wrestler, has made it to regionals. But he's up against another guy who's also supposed to be great. Same weight class. It's, like, the battle of the titans or something. My boyfriend at the time, he was so excited. We were hosting regionals at Grace Consolidated. It was Friday night. Apparently, there were college scouts there, too. The best wrestling colleges in the country. Like, Iowa, I remember, had someone there, and that was apparently a big deal."

"Okay."

"It was the craziest thing. The bleachers were packed, everyone was excited, all these pumped-up muscle heads running around in these ridiculous tight little costumes that looked like ballerina outfits."

"And . . ." The chief rolls his hand. "Mitchell Kitchens wrestled this other big wrestler?"

"Well, that's the thing," says Jane. "He didn't. They made this big announcement. Mitchell was disqualified after the drug test. He tested positive for a banned substance."

The chief sits back in his chair, his tongue peeking out, eyes narrowed.

"I don't remember the drug," she goes on. "Chloro-something. I remember it sounded like chloroform. It was some diuretic or a— They called it a 'masking agent.' Like, a drug you take to hide the presence of other illegal drugs—"

"A masking agent, right. I've heard of them. But what does that have to do with your guy Simon—" The chief drops his chin. "Oh. Are you about to tell me that this boy, Simon Dobias, put a banned substance into his own Gatorade, knowing that Mitchell Kitchens would steal it and drink it?"

"That's certainly what Mitchell claimed," Jane says.

"That's . . . Well, it's—"

"Diabolical," says Andy Tate. "No other word for it."

"And they could prove all this?" the chief asks.

"That Simon spiked his own Gatorade? Oh, gosh, no. How could they prove it? Those drugs stay in your system for several days. Simon could have slipped something into one of the Gatorade bottles Michell took earlier in the week. Several days before the drug test. By the time the drug test came back positive, that empty bottle of Gatorade was long gone, probably in some landfill or under heaps of garbage, even assuming you could've discovered traces of drugs in it. There was no way to prove it. Mitchell was sure of it, and a lot of people thought it could've happened, but no—there was no way to prove it."

"Right." The chief smiles begrudgingly. "Right."

"Mitchell tried. His family tried. But part of the problem was, to even tell the story, he had to explain why Simon would do something like that. Mitchell had to admit that he routinely stole from a younger kid's lunch. He said Simon voluntarily gave him his drink every day, but c'mon—nobody believed that. Simon himself said Mitchell would take it every day. Everyone who ate lunch at his table, eight or ten people, confirmed it."

"Sure, of course." The chief nods. "Wow. To point the finger at Simon, to show a motive, Mitchell has to admit he bullied the shit out of this kid."

"Exactly. So now consider Simon's version," says Jane. "All he had to do was deny it. He doesn't know anything about those drugs. He doesn't know anything about wrestling meets or anti-doping tests. He's just a nerdy bookworm. Nobody could prove otherwise."

"And the wrestler, Mitchell, got nowhere with his story."

"The only place he got was making himself look even worse. All Mitchell proved, after the school investigated, was that he was tormenting a smaller, much younger kid. It didn't exactly paint him in a sympathetic light. By the time the school was done investigating, Simon was looking like a victim, not a perp."

"Which he was, actually."

"Oh, yeah. He was the victim of severe bullying. And you should've seen what happened when Mitchell got hold of Simon after the meet. Like, the next Monday, at school. That's when everything came to a head."

"What happened?"

"Well, I wasn't there, but I heard about it. Everybody heard about it. Mitchell was standing there when Simon got off the school bus. He went for Simon right away. Threw him down and started pounding on him. This huge senior beating on a little freshman half his size. The school cop came out and tried to peel Mitchell off him. He punched the cop, too."

"Mitchell punched the *cop*?"

"Oh, yeah, by the time it was over, other squad cars had pulled up. It was a whole scene, I guess. They had to use a Taser on him. Mitchell got taken away in handcuffs."

"Was he arrested? Charged?"

"Yes and yes," says Jane. "Simon refused to pursue charges, but forget about Simon—Mitchell had punched a cop. And he was seventeen, so he could be charged as an adult. Aggravated battery and resisting. He didn't serve any time. The judge let him off with probation. But he got kicked out of school and got a felony conviction. I think he . . . I heard he works in construction now."

The chief takes this all in, shakes his head, and leans forward. "Okay, so maybe just maybe, Simon Dobias is some evil genius. Diabolical," he adds, nodding to Andy Tate, using his word. "He lulled this bully into basically injuring *himself* by stealing a spiked drink."

"And in a way that made it almost impossible to prove," says Jane. "And forced the bully to basically admit to his bullying to even tell the story."

"He got him good," says Andy Tate. "He got him every which way."

"Okay, and then there's his father's death in St. Louis in, what, 2010?" says the chief. "Why does St. Louis P.D. think Simon Dobias killed his father?"

"To understand the story of Ted Dobias's death in 2010," says Jane, "we have to go back to 2004. The complaint Simon filed with Grace Park P.D. It ties this all together."

# 75

## Jane

"Okay, I'm with you so far," says the chief. "So in 2002, Simon Dobias's mother has a stroke, a bad one, she's basically an invalid, living at home in a wheelchair, can hardly take care of herself."

"Right," says Jane.

"And the dad—Ted, is it?"

"Yes, sir. Theodore Dobias, sounds like he went by Ted."

The chief waves a hand. "Ted's hit it big on some personal-injury lawsuit, has a lot of money, and he's feeling like Mr. Big Shot now with his cash and success, so he decides having a wife who can't hardly feed herself isn't so conducive to his lifestyle of the rich and famous, and he wants some arm candy on the side. I'm right so far?"

"Yes, sir."

"And he basically blows all that money and can't afford to care for his wife the way she needs caring."

"Well, 'blowing the money' is not how Simon put it," says Jane. "Simon Dobias said the money was stolen."

"Stolen by who?"

Jane glances at Andy before she answers the chief.

"Stolen by Lauren Lemoyne," she says.

The chief stares at her. "Lauren. Our *victim* Lauren?"

"Lauren Lemoyne, now Lauren Betancourt, yes."

"She stole the Dobias family's money?" He slaps his hand on the desk. "She was the arm candy?"

"Yes and yes," says Jane. "Lauren Lemoyne was Ted's 'arm candy,' as you put it. They worked together at the same law firm. He was the senior partner, she was some young, beautiful paralegal. The cliché writes itself."

"No shit."

"No shit," says Jane. "Apparently, Simon found them together in Ted's office one night having sex. And the affair continued after that. Ted wouldn't break it off. He was in love."

"The complaint Simon Dobias filed was for theft, fraud, whatever Simon could think of," Andy Tate chimes in. "He wanted Grace Park P.D. to arrest Lauren. He claimed she seduced Ted, had a long affair with him, convinced him that she was in love with him, and convinced him of one other thing, too—to put her name on the money-market account."

"And did they?" the chief asks. "Arrest her?"

Jane shrugs. "There was no crime. Ted put her name on the account. She was made a signatory with full access. She had just as much a right to that money as Ted did, legally."

The chief runs his tongue along his cheek, thinking this over. "How much she steal?"

"Over six million dollars," says Jane. "Wiped the account clean. All of Ted's—virtually all of the family's money was consolidated into that account. She took every penny."

"Jay-sus." The chief shakes his head. "So she takes off, leaves the family in financial ruin, unable to support the mom."

"Well, they certainly didn't have the money to afford around-the-clock care anymore," says Jane. "They decided on a nursing home."

"And then she killed herself. Because of the affair?"

"Well, probably all of it," Jane says. "She could hardly take care of herself, her husband was stepping out on her, the money was all gone, and she was headed for a nursing home—and who knows her mental state after having a stroke? But yeah, the affair could've been the straw that broke the camel's back. Lauren left some real carnage behind." She opens her hands. "So now you understand why St. Louis PD is so sure he killed his father."

"Yeah, he strayed from Mom and brought a lioness into the den."

"And you can see why he had plenty of motive to kill Lauren Betancourt. She didn't just screw his father and break his mother's heart. That might be enough right there for some people."

"But she did a lot more than that," says the chief. "Simon probably blames Lauren Betancourt for the death of his mother and the destruction of his family."

*"Do I think Simon Dobias killed his dad? Yes, I do."*

Jane, Andy, and Chief Carlyle sit in front of the chief's laptop, on a Zoom conference with a lieutenant in the St. Louis P.D. named Brenda Tarkington, and with Rick Gully, now retired and living in Wyoming.

*"I'm with Brenda on that,"* says Gully. *"During final exams week his senior year in college, he drove down to St. Louis, clubbed Ted Dobias over the head with a wine bottle, then stabbed him in the stomach while he was down on the ground near his swimming pool and pushed him into the pool. Then he drove back up to Chicago and called up his shrink early that morning to confess his sins. Only, we couldn't force the shrink to talk to us because of the privilege. Courts ruled against us. Even though he hadn't talked to his shrink for a few years, the courts said he was still contacting her in a 'patient-therapist capacity.'"*

"And without that," says Jane, "you couldn't prove it?"

*"We had no physical evidence,"* says Gully. *"The knife didn't yield any prints. We pulled a print off the wine bottle and found some female DNA on a wineglass, but the print didn't get a hit in the NCIC or match Simon's prints, and the DNA database was a dead end, too. It was probably a weapon of opportunity; a bottle of wine Ted had shared with a lady friend some time earlier. And other than that ..."*

*"It's not like we had the tools we have now,"* adds Lieutenant Tarkington. *"Simon had some old model car, so there was no GPS function, no memory to prove where he'd driven that night, or even if he'd driven the car that night. The interstate didn't have POD cameras like now. If he stopped for gas, he*

didn't use a credit card. And we checked, I'd bet, damn near all the security cameras of every gas station off the interstate between St. Louis and Chicago. Some had taped over the footage that night by the time we asked for it. Some didn't really have functioning cameras, just used 'em for show. The ones that had working cameras and still had the footage—we never saw Simon Dobias in any of the footage."

"We couldn't disprove what he said, that he was home all night studying," Rick Gully adds. "There was no way to show that wasn't true. D.A. didn't have a case."

"He had a receipt, I think, for a pizza he ordered," says Tarkington. "Right?"

Yes. Jane saw that in the case file they sent over.

"Yeah, shit, I'd forgotten all about that." Gully laughs. "That's how we got our time window. He signed a credit card slip for a pizza delivery at some specific time in the evening, early evening, like around five p.m. The pizza delivery guy confirmed that Simon Dobias answered the door and paid for the pizza. Left him a really big tip, too, I remember."

Jane smirks. He left a big tip so he'd be memorable to the pizza guy.

"This guy is good," whispers Andy Tate.

"So when we took that time and compared it against the time he showed up for his final exam the following morning at eight a.m.," says Tarkington, "he barely had enough time to drive down to St. Louis, stab his father with a kitchen knife, and drive back up to Chicago and show up for that final exam. Just barely enough time."

"Just about a perfect alibi," says Gully.

"No other suspects?" Jane asks.

"None we could find. The dad had money, but there was no robbery. A lot of big companies probably hated him because he sued them and got huge awards, but big companies don't murder plaintiff's lawyers. They'd probably like to, but another one would just pop up and take his place."

"Ted Dobias didn't have a girlfriend at the time," says Tarkington. "From what we could tell, he was paranoid about women. He had some escorts he used, some working girls. But no real relationships. Probably because of Lauren Lemoyne stealing his money, as we later found out from Grace Park P.D."

"Besides," Gully chimes in, "we settled on Simon pretty quickly. First thought, of course, a rich guy's murdered, who benefits? Who's the heir? It was

*Simon. Stood to inherit, what, sixteen, seventeen million? But we came to find, Simon and his dad never talked after Ted moved to St. Louis. Not a phone call. Not a Christmas card. So Simon, as far as we could tell, probably didn't even know he was inheriting the money, or how much."*

"The money wasn't what did it," says Tarkington. *"It was him. Simon himself. When we interviewed him, the guy was cold. I remember thinking that— ice cold. Emotionless. And then we find out from Grace Park P.D. about the complaint Simon filed against Lauren Lemoyne back in 2004—how Ted cheated on Simon's mother and let Lauren waltz off with all the money, and his mother's suicide, and, you know, Simon was institutionalized for a while not long after her death—"*

"Yep, read that."

*"—and then we hear all about the shit he pulled with the wrestler and the spiked Gatorade. And then we come to find out, the morning after Ted's death, Simon's making a phone call to his therapist at the crack of dawn, the first call he's made to her in years."*

"Lots of bells and whistles, but no proof," says Jane. "The thing I don't get, though—why do it in 2010? His mother died in 2004. He goes into a mental institution for, what, eighteen, twenty months or so? That's still just 2006. Why wait four more years to do it? And why pick the week of his college final exams?"

A pause. Jane has silenced everyone on the call with that question.

Then Brenda Tarkington lets loose with a loud chuckle. Gully breaks into laughter as well.

"I say something funny?"

*"No, Sergeant, not at all. No disrespect intended,"* says Tarkington. *"It's just that we asked ourselves that same question. Why wait all that time? Time passes, he moves on, he's about to get his degree from a fancy undergrad and go on to a fancy law school. He's ready to rock and roll. Why pick then to get revenge on Daddy?"*

"And what was your answer?"

*"Those questions are the answer,"* says Gully. *"Because we'd ask those very questions and discount him as a suspect. Why wait so long before doing it? Why pick a time when he's in the heat of final exams and it would be incredibly inconvenient, borderline impossible, to pull it off? And when he's about to go on to law school and a successful life?"*

"He played a long game."

*"Oh, yeah, Sergeant,"* says Gully. *"He played a very long game."*

*"Seems like that's his MO,"* Tarkington adds. *"He waited for the right opportunity to screw over that wrestler who was bullying him, too."*

"But the thing with his father feels different," Andy Tate chimes in. "With the wrestler, man, he really stuck it to him. He used his bullying against him. He manipulated this bully into hurting himself and then having to admit to his bullying. His father—it wasn't manipulative."

*"Well, he couldn't manipulate things the same way with his father,"* says Tarkington. *"His dad was too far away. They were totally estranged. He'd have to spend too much time down in St. Louis putting together some plan, learning all about his father's new life down there, and he'd have to explain why he was spending so much time in St. Louis. No, with his dad, it was different. The best he could do there was give himself a solid alibi and pull it off himself."*

"Or maybe that one was so personal, he wanted to do it himself," says Jane.

*"Yeah, sure, that could be, too."* Gully wags a finger at them. *"But the more we interviewed him and the more Grace Park P.D. helped us learn about that wrestler—our take? He's a manipulator first and foremost. Brenda's right. He didn't have the resources to orchestrate some scheme down in St. Louis, or else he would have."*

Jane sits back and nods, looks at Andy for any other questions.

*"Listen, guys,"* says Gully. *"If you like him for Lauren's murder, and you probably should, you better be ready for him to have a solid alibi, and you better be ready to push the envelope. He plays a long game, like you said. He plans out everything. He won't leave a trace of his own fingerprints."*

Tarkington nods and smiles. *"He'll orchestrate the whole thing,"* she says, *"so that someone else is doing his dirty work without even realizing it."*

# HALLOWEEN

# 77

## Simon

Ten minutes to seven. Ten minutes before trick-or-treating ends and, save for a few streetlights kept far away from the homes, Grace Village will go dark. I bide my time as best I can, passing two older kids with shopping bags from Target, hardly even going through the motions of dressing up, wearing baseball jerseys and a cap and some dark paint under their eyes, hoping to mop up the remaining candy from homeowners who want to get rid of their excess.

"President Obama! All right!" one of the kids says to me, high-fiving me, probably finding it odd that I'm wearing gloves when I don't have a coat, only this blue suit and red tie to go with my Barack mask.

I slow my pace, approaching Thomas Street, only a half block away from Lauren's home. A group of three kids, once again older, are heading toward me, northbound, but they turn the corner and move west along Thomas.

Music plays through a window, Halloween kids' music, first "Monster Mash" and then something by Will Smith I haven't heard before, a riff on *A Nightmare on Elm Street*.

I almost jump when I see him, heading east on Thomas toward Lathrow.

The Grim Reaper, dark and ominous and, best of all, anonymous, shrouded by that hood.

Hello, Christian.

———

Friday, August 15, 2003. The morning after I caught you, Lauren.

The morning after I caught you and my father screwing each other's brains out in my father's corner office.

I stood in the doorway of the paralegals' office at our law firm, which you shared with three other people. My chest burned. My limbs shook. My stomach felt empty, hollowed out.

You were alone in the office, seated, flipping through documents. You startled when you saw me. For a moment there, you looked embarrassed, regretful.

"How . . . how . . . ?" I said, my voice shaking, my throat clogged with emotion.

But then you raised your chin, composed. "We're two consenting adults, Simon."

"But what about . . . what about . . ."

"Close the door," you said.

I did, then turned back to you.

"I hope this isn't about that one time at my house," you said. "That was fun. It was a birthday present. I assume you weren't planning on us getting *married*."

And then you laughed, a small chuckle, like it was a joke to you. I was a joke to you.

As if *I* was the one being unreasonable. I wasn't even talking about that time we were together. It didn't even *occur* to you that I meant something, some*one* else.

"What about . . . my mother?" I said, choking out the words.

"Oh." You broke eye contact. "It's a difficult situation for everyone, with your mother being so sick. I get that. I'm not trying to get in the middle of that. I'm not."

"But you . . . already are."

"Look." You got out of the chair and walked over to me. "Understand, your dad and mom's relationship is different now. You know what I mean. But he's never going to leave her. He's never going to stop taking care of her. I'm just a different part of his life."

But his life was with Mom. Mom and Dad, 'til death do they part.

You raised a hand, as if taking a vow. "I will never do anything that would make your father leave your mother. He'll always be with her. He'll always take care of her. He'll always *love* her. I would never in a million years interfere with that."

I didn't know what else to say. I couldn't believe, couldn't comprehend your reaction. People acted this way? People thought this way?

I wanted to yell, to cry, to grab you and do something violent to you. But my feet remained planted. My throat felt so thick and heavy I could hardly breathe. It felt like a nightmare, where you want to scream but can't summon your voice.

You looked at your watch. "Bill needs me for a deposition. I'm already late."

I didn't move. You grabbed your stuff and walked past me. Me, the immobile statue, the stupid kid, the impotent, useless fiddler while Rome burned around me.

It was the last time I laid eyes on you for nineteen years.


Three months later. The day before Thanksgiving, 2003. I talked to my mother until she fell asleep in her bed, gently snoring, lying on her back.

Then I put on a coat and gloves and went outside for some air, onto the back patio. The temperatures had dropped, but I didn't care. I always wanted fresh air after putting my mother to bed. I needed to smell something different, feel something different. I'd never been sick, really sick, so I couldn't imagine what that was like. But I certainly knew how it felt to watch someone you love deteriorate.

I'd had some time to get used to it. It had been more than a year since her stroke. What made it harder, these last few months, was that I was going to school every day, starting college at the U of C, experiencing all the nerves and excitement and rigors of a new academic and social environment—starting my life, in many senses—while my mother was withering away at home with a shit for a husband.

The wind whipped up outside. I put my face into it, let it carry my hair, let it sink inside my coat. I stood there, eyes closed, for some time.

It was only when I turned to go back inside that I saw it. On a table next to our gas grill.

A bottle of champagne, empty. And two glasses, tinted red—flutes, they call them, but cheap ones, plastic, the kind you'd buy at a convenience store for a picnic or outdoor concert.

Except my mother didn't drink alcohol, not since the stroke. She couldn't.

Two glasses, not one. Two plastic, red-tinted glasses.

I walked over and stared at it. A bottle of Laurent-Perrier ultra brut champagne. I had no idea about champagne, if Laurent-Perrier was some fancy brand or something cheap—but I did know that it wasn't the kind of thing you usually drank with your buddies on the back porch.

I wiped my mouth and stood and stared at the bottle, at those twin plastic glasses, for so long that my body started trembling from the cold.

Then I went inside and grabbed a plastic garbage bag. I returned outside and swept the bottle and two glasses inside the bag and tied it off, praying my mother never saw any of this.

I didn't say a word to my father that night. I just went to my room and closed the door.


The next day. Happy Thanksgiving 2003!

"It's just for one night," said my father, drying dishes while I washed, my mother having been put to bed an hour ago. "This potential client was in a pretty bad accident—"

"Who has a meeting the day after Thanksgiving?" I asked. "And who stays overnight with that client?"

"I told you," he said, opening a cabinet and putting away a serving tray. "The family lives in Kankakee, and it's a long drive—"

"Bullshit."

He turned to me. "What did you say to me, young man?"

"I said bullshit. You're still seeing her, aren't you? You promised me you wouldn't, but—you are, aren't you? You're still with . . . Lauren." Her name felt like poison on my tongue.

"Simon—"

"*Yes or no*, Dad?"

"Keep your—" He looked up at the ceiling. "Keep your voice down."

"I found the champagne bottle and the two glasses on the back patio,"

I said, spitting out the words in a hushed whisper. "I guess you forgot to toss the evidence."

He seized up, remembering, scolding himself. It wasn't hard to figure. The recycling bin's in the alley. On a cold night, sometimes we just put recycling out on the back porch and walk it to the alley the next morning. Or we forget, like apparently my father had done.

"So what, Dad—she's coming to our *house*? She's sneaking in here after Mom's asleep and I'm downtown late at school? What else are you and Lauren doing in this house, under Mom's bedroom, for Christ's sake, while she's—"

"Listen to me, son—"

"Yes or no?" My voice rising. I caught myself, even as my father shushed me with a hand motion. I didn't want Mom to hear. I couldn't let Mom hear.

Three minutes to seven. Three minutes until lights-out in Grace Village.

Christian slows as he approaches Lauren's house in his Grim Reaper costume. A rope is tied around his waist several times. A rope? That doesn't come with the costume. Why a rope?

His costume fits him better than mine fits me. Mine, currently resting inside the pillowcase I'm carrying, nearly touches the ground when I wear it. But Christian is taller. The bottom of his robe only reaches the top of his boots. His Paul Roy Peak Explorer boots.

You and Vicky came up with a nice plan to pin this on me, Christian. But here's the problem. As a wise man once said, If you're gonna set someone up, it better be a surprise.

Christian turns up the walkway and disappears into the canopied front porch, a little brick cocoon that will blanket him in privacy when he rings the doorbell, and Lauren answers.

Don't be long now, Christian.

The Thanksgiving dishes washed and dried, my father sat in our family room, elbows on his knees, staring at a glass of bourbon. Easier than making eye contact with me, standing by the fireplace.

"There are things that . . . a young man like you might not be able to appreciate," he said. "Your mother and I, our relationship—I still love your mother and I always will, Simon. I always will—"

"But Lauren fucks you."

"Hey, listen."

I raised my eyebrows. I'd never spoken to my father that way in my life, but he had surrendered the high ground. "Okay, I'm listening. But that's what this is, right? Mom's in a wheelchair, and that doesn't work for you, does it? You've got all this money now, you've dropped twenty pounds, you even have a new hairstyle. The New Slimmed-Down, Swingin' Single Ted Dobias. And Mom doesn't really fit into your plans anymore. You want some fun. And Lauren's *fun*, all right."

He raised a hand to his face. "You've always known how to paint me in the worst light."

"Oh, it's not that hard, Dad. Believe me." I stood up. "This has to end right now. You and Lauren end right now."

"That's not going to happen, son." On that point he was firmest, resolute.

I walked toward him, felt my lips quiver. "You're going to leave Mom? Now when she's unable to—"

"No, no, no." He waved at me. "I'm not going to leave your mother. I'd never do that."

"But you're not going to stop seeing Lauren."

He took a moment, then closed his eyes and nodded. "That's right. I'm not. That's my choice. It's not yours, Simon. I'm sorry, but it's not your decision."

I didn't know how to react. I could throw something, break something, but how would that help? I could punch my dad's lights out, but how would we explain that to Mom?

Mom. The woman who gave everything to me, to both of us.

"And I think we can agree," said my father, "that it's better if your mother doesn't know."

I didn't tell my mother. In the state she was in, a shell of her former self—sometimes lucid and alert, sometimes drifting and foggy—I kept her in the dark. I didn't tell her, afraid that it would be the last straw, that it would devastate her. I couldn't tell her.

I didn't let Lauren Lemoyne wedge her way into my parents' marriage. But I let her *stay* there with my silence. I became their accomplice.

We never spoke of Lauren again after that. I commuted back and forth to Hyde Park for my freshman year at U of C, leaving Mom at home during the day with our caregiver, Edie. I never said a word when Dad had unusually late "meetings" on Saturday nights or on Christmas Eve, when his "work" kept him later than normal on a Tuesday or Thursday night. I never commented. Nor did my mother.

Did she know? Did my mother, the smartest person I've ever known, the sharpest legal mind—even with her stroke-addled brain, did she know what he was doing? If she did, she didn't say. Neither did I.

And neither did my father, until that day, nearly a year later, late October of 2004, when Dad came home and burst into tears, desperate and ashamed, and admitted that he'd put Lauren's name on the account with all the money, adding her as a signatory with full rights and access, and now all the money was gone. "She said she felt like a second fiddle," he told me through sobs. "She just wanted to feel like something of mine was hers."

And that *something* had to be the account that held all our money?

But that's what you do with the people you love. You trust them. You trust them until they prove you wrong. Until they betray you.

And then, you react however you're wired to react.


"Happy Halloween!"

Well, turns out, it's an exaggeration to say *everyone* in Grace Village comes out their doors at seven, at least this year, but many people do, calling out the finale to trick-or-treating.

But they're pretty consistent with the lights. Within a second or two, virtually every light on every house goes out, the Village plunging into near complete darkness, only a few measly streetlamps at the intersections.

Not Lauren's light, though. It's still on. What happened? What's going on in there?

I walk along Lathrow, on the opposite side of the street, trying to be casual, the cool-customer Barack Obama, and look to my right. Lauren's front door is closed, the outdoor light on.

What's going on in there?

I slow my walk, as best I can. Visibility is poor, but it works for me, cloaking me in darkness with the contrast from Lauren's outdoor light.

I head down the street a bit, craning my head back, wondering how long I can just "casually" stroll up and down the same side of the same—

The porch light on Lauren's house goes out, leaving the outside of her house in darkness.

Then a broad gust of light—the front door opening?—disappearing just as quickly, as Christian emerges from the canopy and walks briskly down the walkway onto the sidewalk. He heads north, the direction opposite me. He's walking too fast. He needs to slow down, look more casual.

But that only matters if anyone notices him, and they probably won't. Anyone like him, like me, trick-or-treating in a town that has ended trick-or-treating, would probably be heading for the exits, anyway, as they say.

I turn and head north, too, just so I can pass her house again. The house light is off. That's good. The front door is closed. Also good. Is that door locked? Does it have a knob that locks? Hard to know. I've never been inside that house.

I let out a long breath as I keep walking.

Thank you for your service, Christian. Even if you didn't realize you were doing it for me.

# THE DAYS AFTER
# HALLOWEEN

# 78
## Jane

"Thanks for this, Dee. I owe you big time."

"No worries. Sounds like time is of the essence, so let's get to it." Special Agent Dee Meadows shows Jane Burke and Andy Tate into a conference room at the FBI field office. "You guys deal with CSLI much?"

"Don't have too much occasion to," says Jane. "But we get the gist. Your cell phone sends a signal, it pings off a cell tower, usually the nearest cell tower, and that cell tower keeps a record of the ping—which phone and when, down to the minute and second. So we can track a phone's movements, which means we can track its *owner's* movements. The phone company gave us the historical cell-site location information for Lauren Betancourt's pink burner phone and for the phone she was communicating with. And we gave it to you for analysis."

"Yep, that about covers it." Dee Meadows works mostly in forensics these days but, once upon a time, did a fair amount of field work with Jane's mother. "So first off," says Meadows, "let's talk about the history of their communications but leave out Halloween night, which seems different."

"Sure."

"Okay, aside from Halloween night: These two burners communicated with each other and only with each other," says Meadows. "Not a single other communication."

"Got it."

"And as you know, their communications were carefully planned. At ten a.m. Monday through Friday, they would text each other. And eight p.m. Monday through Thursday. They took Friday nights and the weekends off."

"Yes."

"And they kept their phones off at all other times."

"Interesting," says Jane. "Didn't know that."

"No way you would until you look at the historical CSLI. But you'll see that their phones aren't sending any signals except at those times. So that right there—those synced-up times, turning off the phone otherwise—these are obviously the classic signs of two married people having an affair. Who really didn't want their spouses to know."

"We know Lauren was married, Dee. But we don't know about the man."

"Fair enough," says Meadows. "Well, here's another thing. Every one of Lauren's communications took place at her home. I mean, down to the last one. And the other phone? The offender's burner? Other than Halloween night, which was different—"

"Right, Halloween is different."

"But putting aside the night of Halloween, it sure seems like the guy was texting from the same location every morning and the same location every night. Both locations were in Chicago. So let's get into that." Meadows starts to work her laptop. "You guys understand, I assume, that CSLI isn't an exact science down to the microscopic point. You get that?"

"Yeah, you get a range from the cell tower. You get an area. The more cell towers around there, the smaller the area per cell tower."

"Right, if you're out somewhere rural, historical CSLI isn't always your friend. But this guy was in the city, with a lot of towers, so it's a bit more precise. Okay, I told you all of Lauren's texts came from her home. Or from a fairly small area that includes her house, more accurately."

"Right," says Jane. "She could have been inside her house or on the back patio or the driveway—"

"Hell, she could've been half a block from her house, at least, and she'd still be pinging the same cell tower out in Grace Village. But yeah, all of Lauren's texts, every one of them, hit her local cell tower, so you don't need to see that. What you wanna see is the guy's phone. The offender's phone."

Agent Meadows kills the lights and returns to her laptop. An image pops up on the conference room's white wall, showing an aerial map with hundreds of blue dots and several thick red circles.

"This is the area by the elevated train downtown, near Clark and Lake," says Meadows. "For the ten a.m. text messages, and I mean every single one of them, the burner pinged one of two different cell sites. One is right at Clark and Lake, the other is a couple blocks south and east on Dearborn between Washington and Randolph. Now, these are high-density areas."

"Lots of large commercial buildings," says Andy Tate.

"Well, hang on," she says. "Each cell site has directional antennas that divide the area into sectors. So for the cell site at Clark and Lake, the southeast antenna was pinged. And for the one on Dearborn, the northwest antenna was pinged. So that gets us a fairly small cross-sectional area."

"An area of large commercial buildings?"

"Actually, no," says Meadows. "Look at the buildings that fall into these sectors. At the intersection here of Clark and Randolph, you have the Daley Center. County offices, right? Judges, prosecutors, law enforcement. Then you have the Thompson Center—state governmental employees. And the county building and city hall. Same idea—government employees." Meadows looks at Jane. "That fit your profile of the unknown subject? Some government employee? You said you had a working theory that this guy had money."

"Just a theory," Jane says.

That's what Conrad's ex-wife Cassandra thought—Lauren was looking for a fat wallet to replace the one who was divorcing her.

"Okay, well, we have a bunch of government buildings, and we have a massive parking garage in this sector. You think your guy was texting from a parking garage at ten in the morning?"

"Presumably not," Jane says. "The assumption is he was at work. Just an assumption."

"But a good one," says Meadows. "So if someone with a lot of dough is at work, and he's within this sector, he's probably working in this building right here." She taps a building on the corner of Randolph and Clark. "Forty, fifty floors tall. Lots of commercial companies, lenders, lawyers, the white-collar private-sector type. People with some money in their pocket."

Jane looks at the map. "The Grant Thornton Tower."

"That's what it's called now," says Meadows. "I'm old-school. I'll always think of it as the Chicago Title & Trust Building."

"So this is where the eight p.m. text messages came from," Meadows says. "This is the Bucktown/Wicker Park area. You know, by that three-way intersection of North, Damen, and Milwaukee."

"I know it better than I care to admit," says Jane. "From my younger days, of course."

Meadows winks at her. "So again, looking at the overlapping sectors from these cell towers, it looks like your offender was in this neighborhood right here." Meadows finger-draws a circle on the projection screen. "North of North Avenue, south of Wabansia, around Damen or Winchester."

"And what's there?" Jane peers at the map.

"Some condos on Winchester, which is residential," says Meadows. "Otherwise, you have some commercial establishments on Damen. An AT&T store, Nike, Lululemon, a pizzeria, and a restaurant called Viva Mediterránea, which I highly recommend, by the way. Great martinis."

Jane's been to Viva. Not for martinis but for a man. The martinis were better.

"But unlikely he was texting from Nike or Lululemon or Viva Mediterránea every single night. Most likely," says Meadows, "he lived right up here in Wicker Park. Probably the 1600 block of North Winchester."

"That's your best guess."

"By far," she says. "Especially because, that's where he went after the murder."

Jane sits forward. "The CSLI—"

"He's texting her on the night of the murder, on Halloween, right?"

"Right," says Jane.

"Right outside her house, right?"

"Right."

"Then the texts stop. That, we assume, is once he's inside the house."

"Right."

"So he's in the house, he kills her, and then he leaves. But this time, he doesn't leave his phone off."

"What does he do?"

"Well, as you know," says Meadows, "your cell phone will stay active even if you're not texting or calling from it. It will refresh, update—"

"So you're saying after the murder, he left it on, and his burner kept pinging cell towers, allowing us to track him."

"Yes, exactly. And if we isolate on October thirty-first, we have this nice trail."

Agent Meadows works her computer, popping up a new screen, concerned only with the CSLI from October 31, Halloween. Jane stands up and stares at the trail of cell tower pings and the areas swept in by those cell towers.

"It sure seems to me," says Agent Meadows, "he headed east from Lauren's house, he went through some park toward Harlem Avenue, then he got on the Eisenhower, drove to the Kennedy, took the Kennedy up to North Avenue, and then went to his home in Wicker Park."

Jane looks at Andy. "He probably caught a cab at Harlem and Lake," she says.

"He could have parked his car there," says Andy.

"Yeah, but it's pretty tough to park a car around there," Jane says. "I'll bet he took a cab or Uber."

"Meaning there will be records." Andy makes a note. "I'm on it."

"Anyway, so the offender gets home, someplace in Wicker Park near that three-way intersection. And then he sends his last text," says Jane. "The so-called suicide note." Jane looks at the transcript of the text messages, the final text Lauren received after her death:

*Mon, Oct 31, 10:47 PM*

I'm sorry, Lauren. I'm sorry for
what I did and I'm sorry you didn't
love me. But I'm not sorry for loving
you like nobody else could. I'm
coming to you now. I hope you'll
accept me and let me love you in a
way you wouldn't in this world.

"Time of ten-forty-seven p.m., Halloween night," says Jane.

"That makes sense," says Agent Meadows, who doesn't have the transcripts, only the CSLI information. "That's the last ping we get on the cell phone. After ten-forty-seven p.m., the signal dies for good."

"Meaning he turned off his cell phone." Jane looks at Andy. "And then . . . killed himself?"

Andy shrugs.

"Not sure why he'd bother turning off his cell phone before committing suicide," Jane says. "What, he's saving the battery?"

"We don't even know if he *did* kill himself," says Andy. "Let's find out."


"So what's your problem?" Andy asks as he and Jane leave the FBI field office.

Jane shakes her head. "You know what my problem is. It feels weird."

"What's so weird about how they were behaving?"

"Why does Lauren turn off her phone at home, after Conrad's already moved out? I mean, while he's living there, sure. But once he's gone in mid-September? He's not there to see her phone light up or hear it buzz."

"Maybe she's thinking ahead to the divorce," says Andy. "Conrad playing hardball. Hiring an investigator to track her cell records."

"A cell phone Conrad doesn't even know exists?"

"Shit, I don't know, Janey—it's not *that* odd, is it? People having an affair acting paranoid?"

Jane goes quiet. Of course, what Andy's saying is one way of looking at this.

"You're thinking about Simon Dobias," he says. "And everything we heard earlier today. How he manipulates people and covers his tracks."

"Well, yes." They reach their car. Andy takes the wheel. Jane prefers not to drive when she's spitballing a theory. "You don't think this feels a bit staged, Andy? Doesn't this seem a little too obvious to you? I mean, could the arrows be pointing more obviously at these locations? These people *never* strayed from those locations?"

"Then what's *your* theory?" Andy asks. "Say this is Simon Dobias behind all of this. What, Simon travels to this guy's workplace every weekday morning to send text messages? And he travels to the guy's house—"

"Or right around his house," Jane interrupts. "It's just an area, right? You could stand outside a guy's house and text right there, and it will ping the same cell tower as if you were inside the house. Like Dee said, you could be a half block away and ping the same tower."

"Okay, but that's still going to an awful lot of trouble."

"Exactly what he'd want us to say."

"Well, shit, Janey, we can play that game all day. Every bit of information that exonerates Simon, you can say, 'That's just what he wants us to think,' or 'He staged it that way.' I mean, do we—do we even know if Simon Dobias would know something like that?"

"I don't know, Andy. People know that their cell phones send signals to cell towers."

"Yeah, but do they know that the cell towers keep records of those pings down to the minute and second and store them for years? Do people know that we can draw on historical CSLI to trace someone's movements years later?"

"The only question is whether Simon Dobias does," she says. "And I'll bet the answer is yes."

# 79
## Simon

"Happy Wednesday, all, and happy November," I say to the class. "Hope you all had a nice Halloween and a day of recovery yesterday. Let's get to it. *Carpenter versus United States*, a case that best can be summarized as boy-is-it-scary-what-the-government-can-do-to-us."

That gets a laugh. I try to keep it light.

"Cell phones," I say. "No longer just mechanisms to make calls or shoot a text message. No longer simply little computers to search the internet or monitor your daily step count or play Spotify. Cell phones are now tracking devices, too. As the unfortunate Mr. Carpenter learned, cell phones allow the government not only to surveil your movements contemporaneously but also historically, going back years.

"Your cell phone is always working, even if you're not using it, if for no other reason than to refresh and receive new text or email messages. It always seeks the nearest cell tower for a connection. And each cell tower then records that connection and memorializes it, stores it, down to the day, hour, minute, and second. So if the government has your cell phone number, they can go back and subpoena those cell-tower records—called cell-site location information, or CSLI—and retrace your steps. Not just the calls you made. Not just the text messages you sent. But every place you walked. Every place you drove. And exactly, down to the second, when you did so.

"In a nutshell, the government can go back in time and know, within a reasonable approximation, every place you've been and when. Unless, of course, you've turned off the phone. But how often do we do *that* these days?"

(Sometimes. Sometimes we do.)

"The government suspected Mr. Carpenter of robbing a series of stores over a four-month period. They received historical CSLI for his cell phones during that period. They came up with almost thirteen thousand location points for his movements during that period—or about a hundred per day. They were able to map out his movements and place him at or near the scene of four different robberies at the time they occurred.

"But did they violate his rights? That was the controlling question in *Carpenter*: Does the Fourth Amendment require a warrant for the government to access this highly valuable but highly private cell-site location information?"

When the afternoon class is over, I return to my office. I open up the *Chicago Tribune* for today—Wednesday, November 2—and reread the article on page three:

### POLICE PROBE DEATH OF GRACE VILLAGE WOMAN

The wife of a prominent hedge-fund investor was found dead in her home Tuesday morning in the western suburb of Grace Village in what authorities are calling "suspicious circumstances," though Grace Village police chief Raymond Carlyle said there was no reason to believe that others in the community were at risk.

The Cook County medical examiner's office identified the victim as Lauren Lemoyne Betancourt, 39, who lived with her husband, Conrad, 54, in a home in the 1000 block of North Lathrow Avenue. They had no children together.

Carlyle said police were called to the home at approximately 7:30 a.m. Tuesday morning after Mrs. Betancourt was found dead by an individual who cleaned the Betancourts' home.

"Preliminary information gathered at the scene indicates that the death occurred under suspicious circumstances," Carlyle said in a written statement released by the Village. "However, none of the injuries appear to be self-inflicted."

Not self-inflicted? Depends on how you define that term, I guess.

I scoop the paper up, walk down the hall, and drop it into a garbage can. I feel a bit guilty about not recycling, but I've done worse.

I'd love to go online and read more about the current updates. I'm reading an article published in this morning's paper edition, meaning it was written last night, Tuesday night. And now it's late afternoon on Wednesday. I can only imagine what they've found since then.

But I can't check. Searches I do on my phone or computer are discoverable. So I'm stuck with archaic newspaper reports, stale as month-old bread by the time I read them.

My cell phone buzzes. I don't recognize the number.

"Hello, this is Simon."

*"Simon? This is Jane Burke. I'm a sergeant with—"*

"Jane Burke? From Grace Consolidated?"

*"—Department."*

We talked over each other. I know who she is. I know where she works. I didn't know if she'd catch the case, but she was as likely as anyone. It's not a huge police force.

"Jane Burke from Grace Consolidated? Class of '03?"

*"That's me, yes."*

"Sorry, I think we talked over each other. Did you say you're a sergeant?"

*"Yes, I'm a sergeant with the Grace Village Police Department. I was wondering if you'd have a chance to talk with me."*

"Well, sure. Is this . . . something official?"

*"Yes, it is."*

"Okay. Well—can you tell me what about?"

*"I'd rather we discussed it face-to-face, if that's okay."*

Right. She wants to see my reaction when she tells me that Lauren Betancourt was murdered.

"Oh, okay," I say.

*"Is it okay if I stop by your house later? Tonight?"*

"Sure, I'm free," I say. "Just tell me what time."

HALLOWEEN

# 80
## Simon

I walk two blocks north from the block where Lauren lives, roughly tracking the route that Christian took a few minutes ago, though he was walking fairly fast, while I choose to emulate the cool-customer former president whose costume I'm wearing. It's getting a little nippy out here, me with only a suit and no overcoat, though the full Obama mask does keep my head warm.

I reach the elementary school, listening for any sounds behind me, glancing back for any obnoxious flashing lights, listening for any sirens. Nothing so far. No police vehicles speeding toward Lauren's house. They'll either come pretty quickly or they won't come at all.

I walk behind the school and stand by the dumpster, which hides me from the street. I let time pass. I need time to pass. I hope it goes fast. The less time I have to think, the less time to make myself crazy.

Deep breaths. Deep breaths, Simon.

If I "wind up" a watch or a clock or a toy or an old music box, I'm starting them, but if I "wind up" a comedy routine or a monologue or an essay, I'm ending them.

Nowadays, the word "nonplussed" means both "confused" and "not confused."

I jump in place to stay warm and loose, anxious for this to end, trying to appear nonplussed while I wait to wind up this whole thing.

Deep breaths.

———

Ten minutes to eight. I remove the Grim Reaper costume from my trick-or-treat bag. It takes some work to wrestle it over my head while still wearing the Obama mask. But yes, I'm going to use a double layer of anonymity here. I doubt anyone could see my face with this elongated Grim Reaper hood, but if somehow they could, the face they'd see would be that of our first African American president.

I've become pretty damn cold out here, basically standing still in forty-degree weather for half an hour, so the costume provides much-needed warmth.

This is where it gets risky, but there is no reward without risk, and I've come this far.

I always told myself—if I get caught, I get caught. The number one goal is Lauren, and it seems that Christian accomplished that for me. The number two goal, not one but two, is my getting away with it. I have to accept the possibility that I won't.

I head back to Lauren's house. I walk down Lathrow to Thomas and stop by a large tree on the corner lot. It has now been an hour since Christian left the house. No police have responded, so nobody saw or heard anything that caused them to report anything.

The house by which I'm standing has the lights on downstairs but is dark upstairs. I suppose someone could peek out and see me, but as of now, I haven't done anything wrong, have I? That's not to say I'd like to be seen, or that an encounter with the police would be enjoyable. Far from it.

This is the moment. This is when I really expose myself.

Here goes nothing.

I cross the street and walk up Lauren's yard to the bushes by her front window, not slowing my stride, acting as natural as someone wearing a Grim Reaper costume walking across someone's yard in the dark can act. Acting like I'm supposed to be there, not sneaking around.

I stand at the window, peering inside the home, letting my Paul Roy Peak Explorer boots plant firmly into the soft dirt. Softened enough, it seems, from the brief rainfall earlier today, to qualify as mud. I wave, as if trying to get the attention of the person inside Lauren's house, just in case some neighbor sees me—they see a friend, not a Peeping Tom. A weird friend, maybe, but not an unwelcome one.

My pulse banging, breathing shallow, feeling like the brightest of spotlights is shining on me. I make a gesture into the window toward the front door, as if I want Lauren to let me in. Again, for show. Again, strange, but it looks like I'm making contact with Lauren inside her house—I'm a friendly weirdo, not a criminal creeper.

Then I make a thumbs-up sign, as if Lauren has agreed to meet me at the front door.

What would a nosy neighbor think? A neighbor probably wouldn't be so sure as to call the police. Not when I'm waving at Lauren inside her house, communicating with her through gestures. Right?

I step out of the bushes and walk confidently to the brick-canopied front porch. This is the greatest gift, this canopy. No neighbor has a direct line on the front door, with the brick cover. Nobody can see me in here.

I push my foot against the front door, planting it hard but making as little noise as possible, or so I hope. At this point, with my pulse blaring between my ears, I couldn't hear a pair of clashing cymbals.

I repeat the exercise again, softly but firmly planting a foot against the door. The boot prints, darkened from the moist dirt, are unmistakable. Paul Roy Peak Explorer boots, size thirteen.

Now it's time to go inside.

Is the front door unlocked? Did Christian leave it unlocked? Is it normally unlocked? I don't know. If necessary, I will go through the side window by the kitchen that Lauren always leaves open. But I'd rather walk through the front door, for obvious reasons.

Sweat stinging my eyes, my body on fire, I put my gloved hands on the front door and turn the knob.

The door opens.

I look inside, my eyes down, expecting to see her lying in the foyer.

Then I spot her. She's not lying anywhere. She's hanging—hanging???—from the second-floor bannister. Hanging from a long, knotted rope—the one that was around Christian's waist. No wonder it took him so long inside. Why not just shoot her?

I step inside and close the door behind me. I've waited so long for this moment.

I look up into her dead eyes. She isn't looking in my direction. That's okay. Life isn't perfect.

"Been a long time, Lauren," I whisper. "Remember me?"

I wait. Inside Lauren's house, Lauren's body hanging basically right in front of me, a glass bowl shattered near my feet. I check through the peephole out onto Lathrow. If a neighbor called the police, it wouldn't take the cops long to respond. They'd be here within minutes.

First sign of a cop car, I'll run out Lauren's back door, through backyards, desperately fleeing. Needless to say, not a preferred outcome.

I pull out my green cell phone and power it on. I type a message to the pink phone:

Trick or treat?

Then I pull the hot pink phone out of my pocket and power it on, too. Two phones, one pink and one green.

The pink phone shows receipt of that trick-or-treat message. Good.

I wait. Glance through the peephole again. If a neighbor called, it would have been a distress kind of call. *A strange man lurking outside and now he's inside the house!* The police would not respond idly—they'd come fast. They'd probably be here now or any second. Or maybe—maybe not. Maybe the neighbor was ambivalent, wasn't sure, didn't want to make a fuss where none was required, didn't want to alienate the Betancourts if this was harmless, but still felt *some* instinct to call the cops while downplaying it—and they'd take their time coming, a nonurgent inquiry. Which means they could still show up maybe in a few minutes, I'm not in the clear yet—

Breathe, Simon. Don't make yourself crazy. Focus on the task.

I type another message on the green phone:

Hello? Are you home? I need to talk to you.

The pink phone buzzes in response. Two more agonizing minutes pass, because I need a little time between these texts. Then I type once more:

Testing . . . testing . . . 1, 2, 3 . . . testing, testing . . . 1, 2, 3

Then I focus on the other burner, the pink phone, and type a response that feels appropriate under the circumstances:

> *Not home, told you out of town*

Followed by a quick reply with the green phone:

> That's strange coulda sworn I just saw you walking through the family room I must be seeing ghosts!

Which requires a prompt, shocked response from the pink phone:

> *You're outside my house????*

And the reasonable, reassuring reply from the green phone:

> Just want to talk that's all

A flurry of back-and-forths to follow. It's not so easy wearing gloves, though these are running gloves, designed specifically so joggers could wear them while playing with their phones, switching up music or whatever. My shaking hands don't help, either. But I've gotten this far, and now it's time for the final volleys, back and forth between phones:

> *Nothing to talk about please go home please!*

> Let me in treat me like an adult. I know you still love me. Why pretend you don't?

> *Go home ACT like an adult I'm sorry you know I am but it's over*

> *What are you doing have you lost your mind??*

*Stop kicking my door I'm going to call the police*

Go ahead call them I dare you

*I will let you in if you promise to be calm*

I promise I swear

There. That's a sufficient setup. Christian's upset, he comes to her house, he's making a scene outside, she has no choice but to let him in. And when she does, he kills her.

Good. I'm almost done. Almost.

# 81
## Christian

I'm back in my apartment by eight-thirty, after stopping to toss my Grim Reaper costume and boots at the bottom of someone's garbage can two miles away from Grace Village. And making a second stop to throw away the stupid fucking useless no good handgun Gavin gave me, that jammed up at the very moment I needed it.

I grab the bottle of Basil Hayden like it's a lifeline and take a swig to calm my nerves.

I did it. I think I got away with it.

Now that I'm home, now that I don't have to worry about being seen by anybody, I play through it all again.

I was in a costume. Nobody got a look at my face. I wore gloves. My boot prints, if any—well, they'll match Simon's boot prints.

I was covered head to toe. No DNA left behind. No fingerprints with the gloves.

I stifle the sounds coming back to me: Lauren Betancourt gagging on the noose. The sound of her neck snapping after I tossed her over the side of the bannister.

It's over. I did it.

*Her or me,* I kept telling myself. *One of us gets twenty-one million, one of us gets nothing.*

Lauren brought this on herself. She did this. She got into the ring with me. She tried to steal my money.

I have no connection to Lauren Betancourt. I have no connection to Vicky or Simon Dobias. I'm just some guy in the city who—

My head whips to the left at the sound of the door from the garage. Someone's coming in. Gavin? Why would—

"Hello?" I call out, my heart pounding so hard I can hardly speak.

I recognize the sound of her footfalls as she bounds up the stairs. "It's just me," Vicky calls out.

I meet her at the top of the stairs. "What are you doing here? You can't be here."

"I had to see you." She is dressed in a coat, a wool stocking cap with her hair tucked under, and gloves. She puts her gloved hands on my cheeks. "I wanted to make sure you're okay. I was going crazy with worry—"

"I'm okay, I'm okay. You shouldn't be here. I cleaned everything up so there's no—"

"I'll keep my gloves on," she says. "And coat and hat. Don't worry."

I don't put up a fight. I'm right—she shouldn't be here—but I can't deny that I'm glad to see her, to have some company right now, some comforting voice.

"So—tell me what happened?"

"What happened is—" I blow out air. "What happened is it's over. It's done."

"It is?" The look on her face, like a combination of relief and alarm.

"Yeah, but listen—it didn't go as planned. The gun jammed. I got it done, anyway. It's done, and I don't see how I left any trace of myself behind."

"But . . . she's dead," Vicky whispers.

"Yes."

"For sure?"

"For absolute sure." I grab her arm, pull her toward the kitchen. "You should leave. I want you to stay but you can't. Go back through the alley."

"We need to talk," she says. "About Simon."

"I thought you could handle Simon," I say. "What— Okay, what about Simon?"

"I think . . . I think he suspects something."

"Wait, what? Suspects what?"

"I think . . . he suspects I'm seeing someone."

"Why?"

"He was . . ." She brushes past me, waving her arms. "He was asking me questions today."

"What are you doing?"

"I'm pouring myself a drink," she says. "With my gloves on, don't worry. Sit down and relax. You're making me more nervous than I already am. Actually . . ."

"Actually what?"

"You should take a shower, Christian. It'll calm you down. Scrub it all away. Then we can figure this out together."

As fidgety as I am, a shower sounds perfect.

It helps. I do it fast but efficiently, scrubbing every orifice of my body, head to toe, lathering on soap and washing everything away. When I'm done, I throw on a T-shirt and shorts. I want to shave, but where—where's my razor? Dammit. Where the fuck is—

"I don't have forever," Vicky calls out from the living room.

Okay, fine. I walk back into the room. Vicky, thankfully, has kept on all her winter gear, the cap covering her hair, still wearing the gloves. I'll probably vacuum again after she leaves, anyway, but she's unlikely to leave any trace of herself.

"To us," she says, clinking our glasses of Basil Hayden. Mine's a healthy one, but I down it in one gulp. I'm not drinking for pleasure tonight. I need to stay calm.

Vicky takes a sip of her drink. "Make sure to wash this glass after I leave," she says.

"Don't worry, I will." Okay. Deep breath and calm down. "What did Simon say?"

She sits next to me on the couch. "He asked me today. Point-blank. He said, 'Have you been faithful to me?' He didn't even say it in an accusatory way. It was more like he was resigned to it. He said, 'I know things haven't been like they should for a while.'"

That's not good. That's not good at all.

"He's laying the mattress for the divorce," I say. "He's breaking it to you slowly. And he's trying to make himself feel better about it by accusing you of cheating on him."

That's how most people work, in my experience, and I have a lot of experience in breaking up marriages. If they feel guilty about how they're treating you, they want to turn you into the bad guy. They start to treat you with cruelty.

She looks at her drink. "Maybe so. But now . . ."

"Once he finds out Lauren's gone, he'll probably be so stunned that it will drown out everything else."

"At least until November third," she says. "Which is all that matters."

Right, that's the first hurdle—get to November 3, or Vicky gets cut off completely. Get past that, and we can fix the rest of the damage. I need Vicky and Simon to stay together so she doesn't have to split the money with him in a divorce. I need them "happily" married, at least for a short time—enough time for her to hand control of the money over to me.

Just keep thinking of that day. Twenty-one million dollars.

"Just be really good to him the next few days and play dumb," I tell her. It feels good dispensing advice, like I'm more in control of events than I feel.

"He'll probably hear about Lauren tomorrow," she says. "It will probably be news tomorrow."

"So that's November the first. We just have to get you through two days."

We can do that. Vicky can pull that off. She has it in her.

"I'll just sit here for a few minutes," she says. "It calms me down, seeing you."

It calms *me* down, too. I'm definitely feeling better. It worked! I did the job and got away with it.

Or did I screw something up? The feeling of dread washes over me again. I consider the worst-case scenarios. But I don't see them tying me to either Vicky or Simon.

We sit in silence. Vicky sips her drink. I pour myself another one.

The tension starts to ease. It worked. It did. It worked, and everything's gonna be all right, like that Bob Marley song.

Why do I always worry so much?

Really, I worry too much. It's fine. It's all good.

"You okay?" Vicky asks me.

Better. I'm feeling better. Much, much better.

"It's all going to work out," Vicky says. "Our alibis are clean."

Alibi. That's a funny word. If you say any word enough times, it sounds funny. Alibi. Ali-bi. Kinda sounds like Ali Baba. Like *Ali Baba and the Forty Thieves*. I remember reading that when I was a kid.

And then I became a thief!

That's funny.

I don't know why I was so worried.

Maybe I should use Ali Baba for my next alias. Wait, there's not going to *be* a next alias because I'm going to have all the money I need!

"What's so funny?" Vicky asks me, her head cocked.

"I don't know, I guess not sleep—not sleeping last night . . . I'm just . . ."

Vicky moves over and straddles me, pressing down on my lap, her face close to mine. "You're exhausted. You look exhausted. You need sleep, Christian. It's done now. You did it. Now you should sleep. Tomorrow, we're one step closer to being together."

I put my head back against the cushion. "I am, I'm . . . Wow, I'm wiped out."

"And now you can relax," she says, putting her hands on my chest. "Nobody's going to catch us. I'm going to get that twenty-one million, and I'm going to give it to you, and you're going to turn it into a hundred million."

I close my eyes, feeling exhaustion sweep over me, the weightlessness of near sleep. "Yes. That's . . . going to happen."

She pushes herself off me, gets off the couch.

"Where are you . . ."

"I'm going to wash out my glass, make sure there's no lipstick or DNA, right?"

"Yeah, ex—exact—exact . . ." My eyes won't open. I can't fight it.


What?

"Hi, I'm back." Vicky straddling me again, her breath on my face. "You seem tired, Christian. Are you ready to sleep, baby?"

My eyes open in slits. "Yeah . . ."

"Okay, you do that. I washed the glass. And you removed all trace of me from this apartment, right?"

I nod. I think I nod. My head moves, I'm pretty sure.

Her finger, her gloved finger, caressing my face, running down my nose.

"I can trust you, right, Christian?"

"You can..."

"You're not planning on stealing the money from me after I give it to you, are you?" Her finger bops me on the nose.

"What...n-no..."

Something cold under my chin, thrust upward, forcing my head back.

"You're not just pretending to care about me, are you? Isn't that what you do? You find a mark, someone who seems unhappy in her marriage, and then pretend to be in love with her so she'll leave her husband? And then you steal her money?"

Yep, that pretty much sums me up. But how does...how does she...

I swat with my left hand at whatever's under my chin. Unable to open my eyes but hearing a sharp, muted *thwip* of a sound.

"Now just hold on a second," Vicky whispers. The cold steel thing stuck under my chin again. "This thing isn't going to hurt you. Here, touch it."

I touch it. It's smooth, a long cylindrical shape, like that silencer thingy I used...

...Wait, why would...

"Goodbye, Nick Caracci," she says.

# 82

## Vicky

His eyes pop open as I pull the trigger. His head jerks backward as the back of his head sprays against the wall. His left hand falls limply onto my leg.

I breathe out. I don't move for a moment.

I climb off him carefully, holding the gun up in my right hand. I get to my feet and step away, look down at myself. No spatter that I can see. Maybe something microscopic, but nothing visible. I don't look like someone who just committed murder.

I hold the barrel of the Glock with one gloved hand and unscrew the suppressor with the other. I wish I didn't have to use a suppressor, but I couldn't have gunshots heard by the neighbors.

I put the suppressor in my coat pocket. Taking that with me. One more thing.

The gun could've fallen out of his hand, but from what I've learned from my former cop buddy, Rambo, that doesn't usually happen. The hand usually stays wrapped around the handle, the finger still on the trigger, as the hand falls to the side after suicide.

I carefully slide the gun into his lame left hand. I won't risk wrapping his index finger around the trigger. I've already fired one more bullet than intended. I don't need another one.

Hopefully, the two times his hand was near the gun—the first time, when he swatted it away and the gun accidentally discharged, or the second time, when he touched the suppressor—might cause some gunpowder residue to settle on him. Possible but unlikely. There's not nearly as much GPR when you use a suppressor, anyway.

I remove the bottle of Valium from my pocket. I wrap his right hand around the bottle, impressing his fingers hard on it. Then I unwrap his hand. I take the bottle and spill it over on its side, the pills falling haphazardly to the floor.

Okay. Done. Not perfect, though. God, was I stupid. I should've just fired right away. But no, I had to let him know that I knew his name, that I knew his plan. I couldn't leave well enough alone.

And now I have a bullet up in the corner of the wall to show for it.

I take another long breath. It's over now. I can't recover that bullet. I shouldn't touch anything. I've already cleaned, dried, and replaced the glass of bourbon I poured for myself.

And I've already cleaned, dried, and replaced the glass of bourbon he drank, removing any trace of the drugs I put in it.

The bottle of bourbon, Basil Hayden, is still sitting on the coffee table in front of him.

I take one more look at him. His eyes are open, looking upward. Looking for forgiveness, Nick?

I head down the stairs and into his garage. I pop open the garage door, walk into the alley, and type in the code on the outside pad. The garage door grinds down behind me. Cool, fresh air on my face.

Things are looking up. Whatever else—

"Hi, Vicky."

A strong grip on my arm, yanking me, pulling me farther into the alley before I can react.

"Keep those hands where I can see them," he says. "And don't even think about screaming."

The barrel of a gun against my cheek.

"Let's go for a walk," Gavin says. "And decide what the fuck is gonna happen next."

# 83
## Vicky

Gavin walks me halfway down the alley and pushes me into a gangway, dark and empty. He shoves me up against a fence next to a dumpster that shields us from view.

"You know who I am, don't you?" he says, pressing the gun under my chin, just like I did to Christian.

I close my eyes, shake my head.

"Yes, you do. Tell me or we say goodbye right here. Another streetwalking skank murdered in the city." He brings his face close to mine. "Fucking tell me."

"You're . . . Gavin Finley," I say through a clenched jaw.

"And Christian?" he demands.

"Nick Caracci."

"Okay, so you did your homework, Vicky Lanier. Vicky Lanier from Fairmont, West Virginia, right? Ran away from home back in 2003?"

I don't say anything.

"Which is weird," he goes on, "because a couple months ago, they found the skeleton of a girl by that name buried in some mountain in West Virginia."

He knows. He looked me up. But . . . that means Nick knew and didn't—

"Nick researched you but didn't update it," he says. "Me, I just learned your name, so I did my due diligence and read all about the recent discovery of Vicky Lanier from Fairmont, West Virginia, who disappeared in 2003. Maybe I should've told him, but Nick, he was so hell-bent on his plan, I figured it was worth a shot. But I thought you might fuck him over, too. And look at that, you did."

I don't say anything. I don't know what *to* say. Ever since the real Vicky Lanier's body was found, I worried this day might come.

I have to get away from Gavin. Just get out of here alive—

"You're a smart lady, Vicky," he says in a harsh whisper. "Nick's dead, Simon's going to be under investigation for the murder of Lauren Betancourt, probably sitting in jail without bond for murder, and when the moment is right, you're going to run off with all the money. Am I right?"

He knows about the trust. He knows about Simon. He knows everything.

Well, not everything.

I didn't close the blinds upstairs before I killed Nick. I meant to. My nerves got the better of me. Gavin must have been watching across the street, whatever he was able to see through the open blinds. He knows I killed his friend.

Don't answer him. Don't say anything. Just—

He shoves the gun harder under my chin, pushing the top of my head into the wired fence. "Am I right?" he repeats.

"Yes, you're right," I say. Pulse pounding, thinking fast, coming up with nothing but *Get away from him.*

"I wonder how Simon would take all this," he says. "He thinks he married someone named Vicky Lanier, with a nice, clean background. I'm guessing you had some reason to use a fake name. A criminal record, maybe? Prostitution? Maybe something worse? A wealthy guy like Simon's not gonna go for some street whore like you. So you cleaned yourself up and gave yourself a nice, new identity with a spotless background."

"Yes," I say, because my head can't be pushed any harder into this wired fence.

There's nothing I can do. I don't have any leverage to fight back, try to break away, while pinned against this fence with a gun under my chin. Anything I try will probably make that gun go off.

"Tell me your real name, Vicky," he says.

Oh, thank God—he doesn't know my real name. He didn't get that far. He doesn't have my fingerprints.

I can't let that happen. I can't ever let Gavin know my real identity. I'll die right here before I let that happen.

"Tell me, you stupid twat." He removes the gun from under my chin and smacks me across the cheek with his other hand. Then he pushes me back against the fence and presses the gun against my forehead. "Tell me right now or you're—"

"Never," I say. "Shoot me if you want."

He watches me a moment, considers that. But he doesn't pull the trigger. He's not here to kill me. If he was, he'd have already done it.

"Well, now, that's interesting," he says. "But you know what? I don't care what your real name is. Let's just cut to the chase, Vicky. Your marriage is a fraud. You got married under a stolen identity. And if that little nugget of information were to come out, you don't get a dime of that money."

My legs start to give out.

"So I want half," he says. "Or you get nothing. November third. That's the date you get your hands on the money, right?"

I can't speak. I try to nod, but the gun is basically imprinted on my forehead.

"November third," he says. "I come to you. And you transfer half to me. Ten million dollars. We'll keep it a nice, round number."

"How—how?" I whisper.

"Don't worry about how. I'll handle how. So between now and November third, Vicky, you be awfully nice to that husband of yours. That's just two days. Keep him happy. Spread your legs nice and wide for him. You have a lot of practice doing that, right?"

He shoves me hard, the fence contracting with my weight. I fall to the ground, on my hands and knees, next to some old moving box and a bag of fast food.

"If you run, Vicky, or fuck with me in any way, I'll tell Simon everything. All those ten years you've worked for this money will be down the toilet. And don't even think about doing to me what you did to Nick. Nick didn't see you coming. I do."

"It'll look . . . suspicious," I say. "Three days after she's dead, I transfer ten million dollars to an anonymous account."

He kicks me in the ribs. I buckle under the pain, landing face-first into the dingy alley.

"I don't give a fuck what looks suspicious," he says. "That's your problem. You can decide, Vicky. What do you prefer, a little suspicion? Or never seeing one nickel of that money? That's not a hard choice. You'll think of something. Oh," he says as he walks away, "and Happy Halloween."

# 84
## Simon

I step around the shattered bowl of Halloween candy, move around Lauren's dead body, and take the stairs up to the second story of Lauren's home, making sure to stomp my feet and make the boot impressions as I go up. It's a bit awkward, wearing this long robe. Hell, it's been awkward all night, walking around with size thirteen boots on my size eleven feet.

I reach the second story. There is blood on the floor, not far from where the rope is tied around the whirls and shapes making up this ornate wrought iron bannister. Is this bannister going to hold, with Lauren hanging from it? Probably so. It looks well-made. Not that I care either way.

I can't waste time. Every second counts. Maybe someone *did* call the cops, and maybe they *are* on their way, but if I get my work done in just a minute or so, maybe I can get out of here before they arrive.

Start with the most important thing, the pink phone. If nothing else, the pink phone.

The blood on the floor is where the struggle occurred. Whatever happened, however it happened, it happened here. I imagine it. Yes, I imagine the struggle, her terror, her pain.

There's a small brown table with curved legs here in the hallway. On top is a vase of fresh flowers and a framed photo of Lauren and her husband, Conrad.

There is a shelf below the top of the table.

If I leave the phone just sitting out, the cops will wonder why the killer didn't take it with him. It needs to be out of sight.

It needs to have slid away during the struggle. And Christian, panicked, not thinking straight, either never thought to look for it or didn't want to spend the time.

I squat down, careful to avoid the blood, and gently place the pink phone on the wood floor. I slide it hard toward the table.

Shit. It stopped short. Okay, well, then I guess there was more of a struggle and it somehow got whacked again.

I reach down and put my gloved finger on the top of the pink phone. I slide it again, this time making sure it slides all the way under that little table, obscured by that bottom shelf.

There. So that works. In his haste, in the heat and confusion after killing the woman he loved, Christian didn't see the phone, and he was too panicked, so he just ran.

But I'm not quite ready to run yet.

I jar the table hard, a serious shove. The vase tumbles over and falls to the floor, spraying some water, pieces of the vase everywhere. The framed photo of Lauren and Conrad topples flat on its face. The artwork right above it doesn't move. That's fine.

Do I stop now? Turn around and leave?

I could. But I'm going to finish this.

I leave my boots right there, slipping out of them, which is easier than it normally might be, given that they're two sizes too big for my feet.

I look around this area by the table. No obvious sign of blood here.

I do a small jump, anyway, just in case, and land in my socks a couple feet from the master bedroom, my trick-or-treat bag in hand.

I head inside the bedroom, find the master bathroom, and open the medicine cabinet to finish my business.


Panic has set in, the post-adrenaline fear. I've gotten away from the house, walked through this little town in my Grim Reaper costume without notice, without seeing a police car, reaching the park through which I can diagonally walk to leave Grace Village and enter Grace Park.

But the panic, no matter how much I try to fight it, no matter how many word games I play to calm myself, leaves my legs nearly useless, so I duck behind the park district's equipment shed. I drop down and lean against the shed, remove the hood, remove the Obama mask, my head hot, my hair wet with sweat.

I fish around in my trick-or-treat bag, my large pillowcase. It's a lot lighter now that I'm wearing the Grim Reaper costume, not carrying it around. I have a large kitchen knife that I brought, just in case, but don't need it now.

I need to calm myself. I pull out the green phone and start typing:

> I'm sorry, Lauren. I'm sorry for what I did and I'm sorry you didn't love me. But I'm not sorry for loving you like nobody else could. I'm coming to you now. I hope you'll accept me and let me love you in a way you wouldn't in this world.

But I don't hit "send." Not yet. That comes later. I copy it, just in case it disappears when I open it up later. Then I put the phone in my lap. I hold out my hand, palm down, and stare at it. It remains utterly still and steady.

Okay, I feel better now. I'm ready.

I put the Obama mask back on, pull up the hood, and walk toward Harlem Avenue. It's a busy intersection, and it's not hard to find a cab. The cabdriver looks at me funny, given my costume, given that he can't even see my face, but hey, it's Halloween, and the five twenty-dollar bills I hand him when I get inside the cab seem to relieve any concern he might have.

"Wicker Park," I tell the cabbie.

I keep my head down so there's no chance he sees my face. As for my voice, well, I'm not good with disguising it, but I try to sound hoarse and even cough a little to add to the effect.

He's playing pop music in the cab, something by Panic! at the Disco, so clearly somebody up there thinks I deserve punishment for what I've done.

"North, Damen, and Milwaukee," I specify.

Just a couple blocks from Christian's house.

# THE DAYS AFTER
# HALLOWEEN

# 85

# Jane

"Thanks, Simon. See you tonight." The meeting with Simon Dobias confirmed, Jane Burke punches off her phone and looks around the master bedroom inside Lauren Betancourt's house. It is spacious and nicely decorated but not as ostentatious as she might have expected. Simple and elegant. High ceilings and ornate crown molding, large flat-screen TV with torchlights on each side, a fireplace below. No chests of drawers in the main living room; those are reserved for the walk-in closet. Must be nice.

"Today would be great. As soon as possible." Andy kills his phone and looks at Jane. "The chief security officer at the Grant Thornton Tower is sending us a list of all companies in their building and everyone who has been assigned a key card," he says. "We should have it by day's end. That'll be an exhaustive list of everyone working in the old Chicago Title & Trust Building, as your FBI friend put it. Did you talk to Dobias?"

"I talked to Simon, yeah. We're going to his house at eight tonight."

She checks her watch. What a day so far. Feels like it should be midnight, not four-thirty in the afternoon. It's only November 2, day two of this investigation, and it feels like week twenty.

"His house? Not the station?"

She shrugs. "I want to see his house. And I wanted to see how he'd react to the idea of my being in his house."

"You thought he might not want you looking around in there? Might resist, might offer to come to the station?"

"Yeah, but he didn't. He said it was my call, whatever I wanted."

"Like he doesn't have a care in the world." Andy wags a finger at her. "Just what he *wants* us to think!"

"Now you're mocking me."

"I am, it's true," he says, "but that doesn't mean I think you're wrong. I just think it's early. I want us to keep an open mind. I mean, we have a lot of reasons to believe that Lauren was having an affair that turned ugly—and we don't think Lauren would be having an affair with Simon, do we? I mean, with their history? Lauren would be the last person on the face of the earth Simon would cozy up with. And vice versa, I'd suspect."

"Well, that's why we're here, right?" Jane sweeps a hand. "Let's look for evidence of another man being here. Someone other than Conrad. Assuming they'd come here for their liaisons."

"It would make sense," says Andy, heading into the walk-in closet. "If he's married, like we think, they can't go to *his* place. Conrad's permanently living in the condo as of mid-September. Who wants a hotel with security cameras and doormen and credit-card receipts when you can just come here and get your rocks off?"

"I'll check the bathroom," she says. She drops her bag off her shoulder onto the bed and removes some paper evidence bags.

Andy comes out of the walk-in. "Nothing in there at first glance. Conrad definitely cleaned out his side in there. It's totally empty."

Jane walks into the master bathroom, full of marble, a claw-foot bathtub, enormous shower. A double vanity with medicine cabinets on each end made of ornate cabinetry, as if they were furniture pieces. She pictures her tiny little bathroom and makes a noise.

Andy joins her in the bathroom and takes the medicine cabinet on the left. "This one definitely looks like Lauren's," he says.

Jane opens the one on the right. Contact solution, lotion, ibuprofen, vitamins—

"Hey," she says. "Look at these."

Andy walks over. "A shiny black electric razor. Pretty fancy one. And what's that—a matching trimmer?"

"Like a trimmer, yeah, for nose hair or hair in your ears. Pretty fancy one," says Jane, peering at it, not wanting to touch it yet, even with gloves on. "The brand is 'BK' and this is . . . titanium, it says. Yeah, fancy."

"Would a woman use a nose-hair trimmer?" Andy asks.

"I never have. I pluck. But the electric razor? This has to be a man's."

Andy pulls out his phone and types on it. "Here we go," he says. "The Bentley-Kravitz Elite Men's Care Set," he says. "All titanium, and it comes in matte-black. Toothbrush, nail clippers, electric razor, nose-hair trimmer, and dental-floss holder. A five-piece set. This thing retails for nearly nine thousand dollars, for Christ's sake."

He shows her the photo. Yep, it's a match.

She holds up an evidence bag and uses a pen to tip the nose-hair trimmer off the shelf and into the bag. She repeats the process with the electric razor, using a different bag.

"These could be good for prints," she says. "It's something you hold pretty firmly. If you can even get fingerprints off titanium."

"Maybe DNA, too," he says. "Long shot, but possible."

Jane nods. "So these are two pieces of a five-piece set," she says. "Let's find out if these belong to Conrad."

"The shaded area on the map is the cell-site coverage area," says Andy into his phone as he and Jane return to the station. "It's like a two-square-block area, including Damen. Check every commercial establishment and see if they're even open at eight o'clock at night. If they are, then maybe our offender was going in there every night at eight p.m., at least Monday through Thursday, and sending text messages. Someone who's that much of a regular inside a store or restaurant is gonna be known by the staff. Or—yeah, agreed, *is* a member of the staff himself. So get employee names. And security cam footage, too.

"More likely," he goes on, "it was someone texting from their home, so get addresses of all the homes in that area, whether single-family or townhouses or condo buildings. Then run down property-tax records for ownership, and we'll have to contact all the owners. Probably a lot of them in that area are renters."

They walk through the station house to the war room. Jane walks in and looks around the room. At the garish photos of Lauren in death; at the pages of the text-message transcripts that provide the most information, blown up on boards and fastened to the corkboard; at the rope used to hang Lauren; at the pink telephone, back from fingerprinting and plugged into a charger on the wall.

She walks up to one of the text messages blown up on a poster, from the evening text exchanges for Wednesday, August 17:

> *Oh, my. For someone with such a religious name to*
> *have such a naughty side . . .*

"Simon Peter Dobias," she whispers to herself.

But Andy's right. Why would Simon be texting these love notes with Lauren? Simon despised Lauren, blamed her for the death of his mother. He wouldn't go near her. And even if he were diabolical—Andy's word, always makes her think of an Agatha Christie novel—even if Simon were diabolical enough to *pretend* to have an interest in Lauren, to get close to her so he could hurt her, Lauren wouldn't go along with that, would she? She knows what she did to the Dobias family. She would never, in a million years, believe that Simon wanted to start up a romance with her.

It doesn't make sense. Something isn't right.

"Okay, Timpone's handling Wicker Park," says Andy, putting down his phone. "Ah, the 'religious name' text message. Religious as in 'Simon Peter,' right?"

"But you're right, Andy," she says. "This doesn't work. Simon might be behind this, but there is no way in hell this is Simon and Lauren texting each other."

"So it's Lauren texting someone else," he says. "Maybe someone who has a titanium nose-hair trimmer."

"And a religious name," she adds.

A phone buzzes. Andy pats his pocket. Jane picks up her phone, which isn't ringing.

"Holy shit," Andy says.

Jane looks at Andy, who's pointing at the table. Jane looks, too.

The pink burner phone is buzzing.

Jane steps over, giving Andy an inquisitive look. He nods and waves her on.

Jane answers the phone. "Hello?"

"Who is this, please?" A man's voice.

"Who is *this*, please?" Jane responds.

A pause. "Is this ... Lauren?"

Jane looks at Andy, who is standing close and can hear everything. "Him first," Andy whispers.

"Please tell me who's calling," Jane says.

The man clears his throat. "This is Sergeant Don Cheronis, Chicago P.D. Am I speaking to Lauren?"

"No. This is Sergeant Jane Burke, Grace Village P.D."

"No shit?" he says. "We're investigating a suspicious death."

Jane looks at Andy, a look of revelation on his face.

"What a coincidence," she says. "So are we."

# 86
## Jane

Sergeant Donald Cheronis of the Chicago P.D., Fourteenth District, a head full of wavy gray hair and a narrow, lined face, is waiting by the doorway when Jane and Andy are buzzed through the front door.

"We need to get the body out of here," he says, shaking hands with them. "But I made them wait for you."

"I appreciate that, Don. Very much."

Jane is immediately hit with the pungent odor of a dead body's decay. The medical examiner and the circumstantial evidence, according to Cheronis, put the time of death at approximately two nights ago, on Halloween night.

He waves them in. "To your left," he says. "Say hello to Christian Newsome."

Jane stops, keeps her distance, takes it all in. On the coffee table, a bottle of Basil Hayden bourbon, the top off.

On the couch, stiff and pale, sits Christian Newsome, his head lying back on the couch cushion, his vacant eyes facing the ceiling, exposing his throat and the single gunshot entry wound under his chin. Next to him, a spilled pill bottle, stripped of any name or indication, and several pills scattered on the couch and floor.

Behind him, on the wall, is massive blood and brain spatter.

He is wearing a white T-shirt and gym shorts.

His feet are bare. But next to them, haphazardly arranged as if tossed from his feet, a pair of boots, the color of caramel, with thick treads.

"Mind if I look at the boot?" she asks.

"Be my guest," says Cheronis. "Photos and video are done. I'll bag it when you're done with it."

Jane, gloves on, lifts up the boot and looks at the sole, just to confirm what she already suspects. The boots are Paul Roy Peak Explorers. Inside, on the boot's tongue, is the boot size.

She looks at Andy. "Size thirteen," she says.

He looks happier than Jane feels.

"We removed the gun from his hand," Cheronis explains. "Obvious protocol. It was a Glock 23, had a nearly full magazine, only two bullets fired. Serial numbers scratched out."

*Two* bullets.

"So, suicide?" Andy says.

"Maybe," says Cheronis. "Look up at the ceiling."

A yellow sticky tab hangs in the corner, where the wall with the blood spatter meets the ceiling. A bullet hole.

"That's not the shot that killed him, obviously," says Cheronis. "Angle doesn't work at all."

"A second shot," Jane says.

"A second shot."

Jane looks at Cheronis, then Andy. "Maybe not suicide."

"We don't have the tox screen back yet, so who knows how full of booze and drugs he was," says Cheronis. "But I'll tell you, I've seen a lot in my time. I've seen a lot of suicides. I've seen a lot of hesitation with suicide victims. But I've never seen someone turn a gun on themselves and miss."

"So his name is Christian Newsome," Jane says, glancing at Andy, who's thinking about that *religious name* comment in the text messages.

Cheronis hands her a business card. All green, the color of money. No logo or catchphrase. Just the name, "Christian Newsome," in a simple black font, then beneath it, separated by a horizontal line, "Newsome Capital Growth."

In the corner, the contact information:

NEWSOME CAPITAL GROWTH
Grant Thornton Tower
161 North Clark Street
Suite 1320
Chicago, IL 60601

Jane hands Andy the card. "The Grant Thornton Tower," she says.

"That's Clark and Randolph downtown," says Cheronis. "Across the street from the Daley Center and the Thompson Center. Most people know it as the Chicago—"

"Chicago Title & Trust Building," says Jane. "Yeah, I've heard."


"Is this guy married?" Jane asks.

"Not so far as we know. We only found the body a few hours ago, so who knows, but nothing in this place suggests a woman lives here. Or even a second person."

Jane bends at the waist, not touching the dead body but looking at the bullet wound under his chin, the blood and brain spatter on the wall, the angle of the other shot.

She uses her finger as a gun, sticks her index finger under her chin, then swipes it right, off her chin, and presses down with her thumb, firing.

That's what happened here. The bullet that didn't hit Christian was fired into the wall, just short of the ceiling, off to Christian's right. The only way that bullet could land where it did was if the gun had been fired right by Christian's face.

It was under his chin, and then it wasn't. The gun angled off Christian's chin to the right and fired.

"It's not hard to imagine hesitation," says Cheronis. "Not hard to imagine he shoves the gun under his chin, then loses his nerve and moves it off his chin."

"But he wouldn't fire the gun," she says. "Or at least, not intentionally."

"You'd think not," Cheronis agrees. "Then again, if you've come to the point of suicide, who knows what's going on in your head? Hands are probably shaking, right? It's not impossible the gun would've gone off. Plus, who knows how many of these pills he took."

Fair enough.

"Or," she says, "someone shoved a gun under Christian's chin, he knocked it away, and the gun went off in the struggle."

"That is . . . *possible*, yes," Cheronis agrees.

"Neighbors hear anything? A struggle? The gunshots?"

"Nope. We talked to all of them. Judging from the timing of the suicide note, he died around eleven on Halloween night. So most people were down for the night. And Wicker Park, Bucktown, I mean, it's noisy around here, especially on Halloween night."

"Suicide note," she says.

"He sent a text message to this 'Lauren' on Halloween night at ten-forty-seven p.m."

"Right. I have Lauren's phone."

"Let's just make sure we're on the same page with that." Cheronis shows her a cell phone, a burner that looks just like Lauren's, except it has a green cover rather than pink.

Jane takes the green phone in her hand. "How many people he talk to with this?"

"Just the one," says Cheronis. "Just this 'Lauren' woman."

With her gloved fingers, Jane taps on the phone. She finds only one name in the contacts, "Lauren." She pulls up his text messages. Every text in the months-long text exchange with Lauren's phone is there. All the way down to the last one:

> *Mon, Oct 31, 10:47 PM*
>
> I'm sorry, Lauren. I'm sorry for what I did and I'm sorry you didn't love me. But I'm not sorry for loving you like nobody else could. I'm coming to you now. I hope you'll accept me and let me love you in a way you wouldn't in this world.

"This all tracks with what we have and what we know," says Jane.

"Jane!" Andy calls to her. "Jane, you gotta come see this."

———

Andy is standing in the bathroom, his hands stuffed in his pockets. "See anything interesting?" he says.

"Oh, yeah, this guy," says Cheronis. "Guy has a friggin' titanium toothbrush and a matching set of other goodies. Know what this one is?"

Jane spots it on the sink's countertop. Three pieces of the *five*-piece Bentley-Kravitz Elite Men's Care Set, titanium and matte-black: toothbrush, nail clippers, and dental-floss holder.

"This thing is for holding friggin' dental floss," says Cheronis. "You imagine what something like that costs? How much spending money you gotta have—"

"Nearly nine thousand dollars," says Andy, showing Cheronis his phone, the website pulled up. "All that's missing is the electric razor and nose-hair trimmer. And guess where we found those?"

Andy lifts the robe with two gloved fingers, careful not to touch it or shake it. A long black robe with elongated hood. A Grim Reaper costume, resting on the bed in Christian Newsome's bedroom, just like the one the neighbor kid saw on Halloween night.

Jane steps out of the room, pulls out her phone, and dials the number.

"Simon," she says, "this is Jane Burke again. Listen, something's come up, and I can't make it back to Grace Park tonight. Can I meet with you tomorrow, November third?"

Chief Carlyle slams his hand down on his desk. "That's beautiful. He has the burner phone. He's got the damn Grim Reaper costume, the boots that match, and half his toiletry set is in Lauren Betancourt's bathroom. He worked at the building where all the morning text messages probably came from, and he lived in an area consistent with the nighttime text messages. He's 'tall, dark, and handsome,' like that text message described him. And 'Christian,' last I checked, sounds like a religious name to me." The chief puts out his hands. "Jane, look happier."

"I'm happy, Chief."

"But not convinced. The evidence isn't strong enough."

"Oh, the evidence is strong. In fact," she says, "about all that's missing is a sworn affidavit from Christian Newsome that he and he alone, without any assistance from Simon Peter Dobias, murdered Lauren Betancourt. But I assume that's arriving soon in the mail."

The chief considers her, wetting his lips. "Remind me never to buy you a present, Janey. You'll just tell me everything that's wrong with it." He flips his hand to Andy. "What about you, Sergeant Tate?"

Andy's a loyal enough colleague not to show up Jane. But she knows he's more convinced than she is. "It could be very solid, Chief, but I think Jane's concerns are worth following up on."

The chief takes a seat in his office, his fingers playing piano on his desk. "Okay, go through these concerns, Jane, start to finish, before I wish we had never heard the name Simon Dobias."

Jane puts out her hand, ticks them off. "Number one, the pink phone.

As you already know, after Lauren was dead, somebody moved that phone under the hallway table."

"You *think* someone did."

"The phone absolutely was moved a second time, and carefully so, not smudging the blood line at all. A level of care, sir, that all but rules out anything but an intentional act. And for the life of me, I can't understand why the offender, coming upon Lauren's burner phone that is absolutely, far and away, the most incriminating piece of evidence against him, would push it under the table, knowing that we'd find it."

"So criminals never do dumb shit," says the chief. "They never panic and make a mistake."

"It was *not* a mistake, sir. If he didn't see it, if he accidentally kicked it—something like that would be a mistake. Panicking and rushing, I get. This was not panic. This was careful and intentional." Jane shakes her head. "He *wanted* us to find that phone. But he didn't want to be too obvious about it."

"*He* being Simon Dobias."

"That's the theory, yes."

The chief crosses his arms. "Okay, agree to disagree. Go on."

"Number two, the CSLI is so perfect, so on-the-nose, that it feels staged," Jane says. "And Simon Dobias is a law professor who specializes in the Fourth Amendment. He has this blog we just found called *Simon Says*, ha-ha. He writes for lawyers and law students, plus a bunch of law review articles. He writes about how the government can track citizens and invade their privacy. He probably knows more than *we* do about how to track people with cell phone historical data."

"Okay, so the CSLI is too convincing. Our evidence is *too* strong, basically," the chief summarizes. "Go on."

Jane takes a breath to control her frustration. She gets it—the idea of a quick solve, in a tidy package with a bow. The first murder in the history of Grace Village, and the police solve it within a week. The Village president slaps the chief on the back, and everyone breathes a sigh of relief, congratulating each other on a job well done.

"Three," she says. "The mistake in the text messages. Lauren texts that she didn't sleep well one night because Conrad was snoring, when we know Conrad wasn't living in that house anymore. I thought, initially, that meant Lauren was lying to her secret boyfriend."

"But not now?"

"Now I think it's a mistake. Because Simon Dobias didn't *know* Lauren and Conrad were separated. He was fudging these text conversations and trying to seem authentic, but he went too far—he said something wrong, not knowing it was wrong."

"That's possible, maybe, but so is Lauren lying to her boyfriend. To Christian."

"Why did Lauren have her phone on, on Halloween night?" Jane says. "After she dumped her lover, who we're supposed to believe is Christian Newsome, she said she was leaving town and her phone would stay off. So why did she have it on?"

"I don't know, and I don't care," says the chief.

"Why would Lauren need to keep her phone off at all other times, besides when they were texting?" she continues. "Once Conrad moved out, mid-September, that house was all hers. She didn't need to hide her texts. And I know they were getting a divorce, but what did she care? There was a prenup, and almost all of Conrad's money was in a trust she couldn't reach, anyway. So why would she need to keep her phone off all the time? What was she afraid of?"

"Jane, I have no—"

"And for that matter, sir, why did Christian Newsome turn off his phone at all, ever?" She waves a hand. "He wasn't married. There's no record of a marriage, there's no indication of the presence of a significant other in that condo—a live-in girlfriend, a wife, a boyfriend or husband, for that matter. That man was single. He had nobody to hide that phone from."

The chief's eyebrows rise. He puts out his hands. "And what is your theory, again?"

"I'm not sure of anything yet," says Jane. "I just don't want to rush to judgment."

The chief frowns. That's not a phrase an investigator likes to hear. "All this evidence that we've put together against Christian Newsome doesn't sound like a 'rush to judgment,' Sergeant."

"But it's worth considering," says Jane, "that Simon Dobias was pulling strings all over the place here. The phones were off in between the intervals of the text messaging because he didn't want anyone tracking *his* movements."

"So what, *Simon Dobias* made those text messages from Christian's phone?"

"Yes, that would be the theory."

"So—Christian Newsome and Lauren Betancourt were not having an affair?"

"That would be the working theory, correct."

"They didn't even know each other."

"Probably not."

"Lauren wasn't having an affair with anyone?"

"Probably not," says Jane. "She didn't tell any of her closest friends, Chief. In fact, remember, she told one of her friends that she 'missed sex.' Just last week, she's telling them she misses sex. If you believe those text messages, she had no reason to be missing sex. She was getting it on a regular basis."

"No chance she was lying to her friends about that fact?"

"A chance, sure, but I'm not sure why she would."

"And Christian's razor and trimmer—Simon planted them at Lauren's house."

"Correct."

"So . . . Christian didn't kill Lauren Betancourt? Simon did."

"Correct. That's the theory."

"Because it sure looks like Christian had the Grim Reaper costume in his house, and it sure sounds like he was wearing the exact boots that treaded all over Lauren's house."

"It does, yes, it does."

"So Simon kills Lauren around eight p.m. on Halloween, then goes to Christian's house and kills him, plants the Grim Reaper costume, and puts the boots near his feet. Right?"

"That or something very close to that, yes."

The chief leans back in his chair. "Then answer me this, Sergeant," he says. "If Simon was sending text messages from Christian's end of the phone call, who was *responding* to them? Not Lauren, I presume? Because from everything we've heard, Simon and Lauren were like oil and water."

"That . . . that is the biggest hole in my working theory," Jane concedes. "If I'm right, that means Simon must have had a partner."

"And do we have any idea who that partner might be?"

"I haven't even talked to Simon yet. We canceled tonight after we found Christian Newsome. Look, sir." She approaches his desk. "I'm not saying I'm right about any of this. I'm just not sure about this answer that has been gift-wrapped for us. I just want to keep looking."

The chief works his jaw, glances at her. "Well, it's only been two days, I guess." He thinks about it some more and nods. "Here's what I'm going to do. I'm going to release a statement that we are focusing on a person of interest, that we are in the process of pursuing a few avenues of information, and that it is our firm belief that the murder was a personal domestic issue that poses no further danger to our residents. We can agree on all that, yes?"

"Yes, sir." No need to mention that the person of interest is now a corpse.

"So tomorrow, go interview this Dobias fellow who interests you so much," he says. "See what comes of it. But listen, Jane. There is no physical way that Simon Dobias could have been on both sides of all those text-message conversations when the two phones were twenty miles apart. So you wanna convince me to keep this investigation open? Show me the slightest hint that Simon Dobias had a partner in this scheme."

# HALLOWEEN

# 88
## Simon

"I fucked up. I fucked up." I rock back and forth inside the cab, careful to keep my head down, the Grim Reaper hood covering my face, sweaty from the heat blasting inside the cab and yes, probably from nerves as well.

The cabbie, a young guy with a thick African accent, whose license reads Dembe Abimbola, turns down the pop music. "You okay, sir?" he asks. "Are you going to be sick?"

"Not gonna be sick." I shake my head, which I think comes across even while wearing this large hood over my head. "I fucked up. I fucked up, I fucked up, I fucked up."

I try to keep my voice a harsh, whispery staccato, not revealing too much of my real voice or speech pattern, because one thing I don't know is how Christian talks.

"Do you need me to do something?" he says.

I wave my hands. I don't want to take this too far. The last thing I need is for him to drive me to a hospital or, God forbid, a police station.

"You sure you'll be okay, sir? Do you want some change back?"

I wave at the driver and get out of his cab in Wicker Park, at the three-way intersection of North, Damen, and Milwaukee, one of my favorite spots in the city. It's near ten, so the night is young around here, the streets filled with people, many costumed up like me.

It's nice to be out of that cab. Leaning over the whole time so the cabbie wouldn't get a look at my face wasn't the most comfortable position, especially during a herky-jerky ride. I keep my head down now, too, for obvious reasons, but fortunately I don't have far to walk.

When I get to Winchester, I turn up, north, toward Christian's apartment.

A few people are heading toward me, a group of three gabbing, one looking at a phone. I don't feel like engaging in conversation, so I hold my green burner phone against my ear, or more accurately to the hood covering my head, and nod and talk in a low voice as they pass me. "Creepy," one of the people says, but I just keep walking.

Nobody else around, no police squad cars, no traffic. The streets are lined up and down with parked cars, street parking being as scarce as it is. The three-flats and apartment buildings are well-lit; most people around here are still awake, still doing things inside their apartments if not out and about tonight. Basically an ordinary Chicago street on a fairly ordinary night. Halloween is an occasion for some adults, sure, but with it falling on a Monday, most people who wanted to throw a costume party probably did so over the weekend.

I look up into the picture window at Christian Newsome's apartment. The blinds are down but open, so visibility isn't great, but you can see in. Nobody moving around in there, at least.

Are you home, Christian?

Are you dead, Christian?

Did Vicky kill you after you ably performed your task and killed Lauren?

I sure hope so! Otherwise, you're gonna be really surprised to see me.

Viva Mediterránea's outdoor patio is empty, given the cold. The alley is empty.

Just me, standing next to the keypad by Christian's garage. I type in the pass code and the garage grinds open.

I step inside, work around his car, and close the door behind me. I flip on the overhead light.

I put down my bag and pull off my Grim Reaper costume. I leave on the Obama mask; better to keep my head covered for now, avoid DNA residue. I want to remove my boots, painful as hell to wear, being two sizes too large, but I need to tromp up the stairs in them first. Then I'll kick them off and put on the shoes I brought, that I'm carrying in my trick-or-treat bag.

I blow out air. Here goes nothing.

I open the downstairs door and listen. All I hear is the drumming of my heart.

"Hello?" I call out.

Nothing.

"Hello?"

I drop the Grim Reaper costume onto Christian's bed. I place the boots near his feet by the couch, trying to simulate him kicking them off his feet. Doesn't really matter. Just can't look too perfect or tidy.

Christian must have disposed of *his* costume and boots. I'd be disappointed in him if he hadn't.

I open the green phone, which I've left turned on. The suicide note I typed while in the park is still there, ready to be sent. I hit "send." It registers as sent at 10:47 p.m.

I power the phone off and take a look around.

Well, you tried to make it look like a suicide, didn't you, Vicky? And I have to say, it looks pretty good. The gun right by his hand on the couch. Open bottle of bourbon. A bottle of pills spilled all over the place.

Did you enjoy doing it, Vicky? Was it harder than you thought?

No, I'm pretty sure you enjoyed it.

# THE DAYS AFTER
# HALLOWEEN

# 89
## Vicky

Whoever first said "the waiting is the hardest part" didn't know the half of it.

I'm at work, doing inventory in the kitchen for another grocery run. Usually I go on Monday, but Monday was Halloween, and I (obviously) didn't work that day. And yesterday, Tuesday, was one of those days that all plans went awry and we had to put out small fires—the stove wasn't working, one of the abusive husbands showed up demanding to speak to his wife, we had three new women come in with various bruises or welts or burns, one with an infant.

Even today, Wednesday, November 2, has been crazy. It's already nearly four o'clock and it feels like my shift just began.

But that's good. I've worked double shifts both days since Halloween. Focusing on these women and their children at the shelter has kept my mind off Gavin and the investigation.

I hear a car pulling up, tires crunching over gravel. Safe Haven's been around thirty years, and we still don't have a paved parking lot, could never spare the funds. But for me, it has the benefit that people can't drive up without being heard.

I check. Every time I've heard a car arriving these last two days, I've checked. Is it Gavin? Is it the police?

I don't know which would be worse. Gavin could only find this place by following me. He wouldn't have known where I work from Christian— Nick. I told Nick I volunteered at a nonprofit shelter (only half true; I don't get paid much, but I do get paid). But I never gave a name. I didn't want him ever coming here.

If Gavin knows where I work, then he'll also know my name, my real name, Vicky Townsend. We get half our money from state grants, so we are an open book. My name and prints are on file with the state, after the fingerprint-based background check they did on me.

I walk over to the window. A police squad car is parked in the lot. Two uniformed officers, with their swagger and gear, heading for our front door.

Go back to what you're doing. Check the groceries. Clip out coupons. It's an ordinary day. You don't know anything. Christian Newsome? Never heard of him. Nick Caracci? Nope.

They can't be here for me, can they? Did they find a stray fingerprint, which would have immediately matched for Vicky Townsend—

"Vicky." Miriam, my boss, sticks her head into the kitchen.

I look over at her, raise my eyebrows, afraid my voice might shake. Just turning my head causes pain in my ribs, the spot where Gavin kicked me two nights ago.

"The heater's not working upstairs," she says. "Surprise, surprise."

"It— Oh." Relief floods through me. "Want me to take a look?"

"You're the only one who has a prayer of fixing it."

"Sure. Who— Was someone at the door?"

"Cops. They want to talk to the woman who came here two nights ago, Jamie. About pressing charges against her husband."


I shake out my nerves and take several deep breaths. They're not here for me.

I go to work on the radiator upstairs in Dorm A. Lacking air-conditioning is one thing, but we have to keep this place warm. Last winter, the heat went out in February. We scrambled for blankets and space heaters and prayed that we didn't burn the place down.

It's cold out, and we have an infant in here. And no funds for a repair call.

I manage to get the radiator working. The pin inside the valve head is stuck in the down position, so I wrench it free and put some lubricant on it to stop it from happening again. Not that hard to fix, but every move I make, I'm reminded of that kick to the ribs from Gavin.

Once the radiator is gurgling and hissing, my work is done.

I look out the window again. Will Gavin come tonight?

Or will he wait until tomorrow, November 3, D-Day?

Gavin is a problem. He was a mistake on my part. A loose end.

I hate loose ends.

# 90
## Jane

*"Mrs. Bilson, this is exactly why we called this emergency town hall meeting,"* says Alex Galanis, Village president, sitting at the middle of a long table. *"So we could be transparent. As transparent as the chief is able to be with an ongoing investigation."*

Jane smirks. They called the emergency board meeting at eight in the morning, hoping fewer people would attend. It didn't work. The place is standing room only, with more than four hundred people crammed in there. She's glad she isn't there herself, instead sitting in the chief's office, watching the whole thing through closed-circuit TV with her partner, Andy Tate.

*"Well, it's November third,"* says Mrs. Bilson, standing at a podium. *"You've had two whole days to investigate, and it feels like nobody knows anything. Or at least you won't tell us anything. We don't even know how she died. Is it true she was hung?"*

"Hanged," says Jane, ever the grammarian. Andy throws her an elbow.

*". . . not to compromise the investigation by releasing details,"* says Chief Carlyle. *"We can say it was a homicide. I'd rather not go further."*

*"Well, do you have any leads? Is it true he was wearing a costume?"*

*"Again, ma'am . . ."*

"God am I glad I'm not in there," says Andy. "Remind me to never be chief of a police force."

*"My name is Donald Fairweather. We're hearing that it was some gang initiation thing like we had a couple years ago with the carjackings. Is that true?"*

Jane covers her eyes with her hand. Three summers ago, the Village did experience a rash of car thefts and carjackings tied to a west-side gang, an initiation ritual. It took coordination from four different western suburbs and Chicago P.D. to finally crack down on it.

*"Well, I think we'd all like to know if some Chicago gang has decided to come into our town and start killing people!"*

*"Sir—Mr. Fairweather—we are confident, as we've said before, that this murder was a domestic issue. It was unique to the Betancourt family."*

*"Does that mean you're close to solving it?"*

"That's what I was afraid of," says Jane. Shit, what do these people want? A sloppy rush to judgment or good, hard detective work?

"People are rattled," says Andy. "They're not used to this."

*"Are you increasing patrols around the Village?"*

*"We don't believe that's necessary,"* says the chief. *"We don't believe there's a continuing threat to the community."*

*"But that"*—President Galanis opens his hands, looks at the chief—*"that's something we could do, right, Chief?"*

Oh, great. The chief's gonna *love* that. Sure, Mr. President, give us the funds and we can do all the patrols you want.

She checks her watch. She and Andy are due downtown to meet with Sergeant Cheronis of Chicago P.D.

*"Then why haven't you made an arrest, if you're so sure?"*

*"We moved here to get away from violence in Chicago,"* says another woman, whose name Jane missed. *"Is it coming here now? Is this a new normal?"*

For at least the fourth time, the chief says, *"We do not believe there is a further threat to the community. We believe this crime was personal to the Betancourt family."*

And then, decorum and protocol be damned, a number of residents shout at once, all variants of the same question:

*"So when are you going to solve it?"*

# 91

## Simon

Thursday morning. Day three of the investigation, day three of November.

I was supposed to meet with Jane Burke last night. Got myself all steeled up, practiced and ready, and then she canceled on me.

Why, I don't know. Did they find Christian's body and the green phone? Pretty good chance of that. And maybe that will be that. It really should be. Christian has the phone that was texting back and forth with Lauren at regularly scheduled times. He has the Grim Reaper costume and the muddy boots in his apartment. It's hard to see coming up with any different story: Christian was sleeping with Lauren, she dumped him, he couldn't handle it, he came to her house and killed her.

At some point soon, if not already, they'll have the CSLI from both phones. And if they've already found Christian, they'll know that all the texts were sent from either his house in Wicker Park or his office downtown.

That's gotta be game, set, match, right?

I'm home today, alone at my house. I could've gone into work, but Jane wasn't sure what time she wanted to talk to me, and I didn't want her coming to my law school for the interview. So I told her I'd work from home and she could come whenever. Felt like a casual, innocent-y way to handle it.

I leaf through the morning paper I fetched from a convenience store on Division. The *Tribune* story doesn't say much new about Lauren's murder. Too early, I presume. Nothing about Christian Newsome at all. One of many people who die in the city every day.

I still won't go online. I'm left with the morning newspaper only, and thus little information. It's unsettling, but I knew that going in. I knew the "days after" would be anxious and frustrating and scary. At this point, I just have to believe in my plan. Easier said than done—

My doorbell rings. I'm at my computer upstairs, answering a student's email.

Jane had told me she'd call with a heads-up before coming by. I check my phone to see if I missed a call. I didn't.

I go to the window and look down at the front porch.

A man, dressed in a suit, erect posture, short hair.

I head downstairs and open the door.

"Simon Dobias?" he says.

"Yes?"

He pulls credentials out of his pocket and flashes them.

"I'm Special Agent John Crane with the FBI," he says. "I'd like to speak with you about Lauren Betancourt. And your wife, Vicky."

"I— What did you say your name was?" I ask.

He opens his credentials again, a flip of the wallet. "I'm Special Agent John Crane."

No, you're not. You're Gavin Finley, Christian's buddy.

"Sure," I say, "come on in."

FOUR FACES

# 92
## Jane

Jane Burke and Andy Tate sit inside an interview room adjoining the detectives' squad room in the Fourteenth District of Chicago P.D. at ten in the morning.

"Nicholas Christopher Caracci," Jane says, flipping through the pages. "Aka Collin Daniels, aka Richard Nantz, aka David Jenner . . ." She closes up the file.

"Aka Christian Newsome," says Sergeant Don Cheronis. "A con artist. He targets wealthy married women. Seduces them, gets them to divorce their husbands, convinces them to take a lump-sum payment, then steals their divorce settlements. He moves around, switches up identities."

"So . . . what," says Andy. "He was targeting Lauren and ended up falling for her instead? When she dumped him, he snapped?"

Jane shrugs. "That could work. A lot of things could work. Doesn't make them true."

"Yeah but, Jane—"

"I said it's possible, okay?" she says.

Sergeant Don Cheronis hits "play" on the computer.

Jane and Andy stand behind him and watch.

The video, grainy and black-and-white, shows a cab pulling alongside the three-way intersection of North, Milwaukee, and Damen Avenues in Chicago. From the right side of the cab, a figure emerges, wearing the Grim Reaper costume.

"That is it," says Dembe Abimbola, a cabdriver who left a job as an accountant in Nigeria to move to the United States eighteen months ago. "That is my cab. That is the man."

"It was a man," says Jane.

"Yes, yes."

"You talked to him?"

"He keep saying the same thing. 'I fucked up. I fucked up.'"

"'I fucked up'?" Jane confirms. The man speaks good English as a second language, but his accent is heavy. "That" is *dat*. "Fucked" is *fooked*.

"Yes. That was it. I ask, do you need med-sin, do you need doctor, you okay, friend? He did not say—he said no. 'I fucked up' is all he say."

Jane plays the rest of the downloaded video. These stupid POD cameras the city of Chicago uses unfortunately don't stay in one place. They rotate. So the camera doesn't capture every movement of the Grim Reaper. By the time the camera has rotated back, the only image they have of the costumed figure is from behind, as he walks east on North Avenue toward Winchester, where Christian Newsome—well, Nicholas Caracci—lived.

"Did you get a look at his face?" Jane asks.

"I see what you see." Abimbola points at the screen, at the hooded, costumed figure. "I don't see his face, no. I drive."

Cheronis glances back at Jane. "Anything else?" he says.

Jane turns that question on Abimbola. "Anything else you remember, sir?"

"He give me a nice tip," he says.

"Oh?"

"He give me one hundred. The cab ride was maybe twenty-five. You remember the good tippers."

Jane glances at Andy. "I'll bet you do," she says.


Jane and Andy, back in their war room at Grace Village P.D., eating microwaved sandwiches well past the lunch hour and reading through the file from the FBI on Nicholas Caracci. Jane's phone rings. She recognizes the number and puts it on speakerphone.

*"Tox screen came back,"* Cheronis squawks. *"Caracci had a few shots of alcohol and over forty milligrams of diazepam in his system. Normal dosage is more like ten milligrams."*

"Enough to overdose?" Jane asks.

*"Definitely possible. M.E. says for someone of his size, maybe yes, maybe no. But enough to make him very sleepy and very goofy in pretty short order."*

"Diazepam," says Jane. "Meaning Valium."

*"Yeah, pretty standard tranquilizer."*

Jane looks at Andy. "Drugs in his system," she says. "Heard that one before?"


"Here you go," says the building manager of Grant Thornton Tower, an efficient man in a dark suit. "Would you like me to wait up here or do you want to just buzz me when you're done?"

"We'll let you know when we're done," says Andy.

Inside the office of Newsome Capital Growth, suite 1320. The place does not look as if it's prepared to be receiving visitors.

"Looks like ol' Nick had travel plans," Andy summarizes.

The place has been cleaned out. On the reception desk, dust lines form a square shape, presumably where a computer once sat. A power cord juts out from beneath the desk. On the carpet underneath the desk, heavy indentations, a rectangular shape, presumably where the computer's mainframe or hard drive once sat. The drawers behind the reception area have been rifled through and largely emptied out.

"Computer's gone, files are gone," says Andy. "He removed all trace of himself."

"Or of someone else," she says. "That sound like someone who's about to commit suicide? I mean, what does *he* care what we find about his con artist career, or Lauren, for that matter, if he's going to eat a bullet?"

"I hear you, but ..." Andy closes the drawers, wearing gloves in case they want to check the place for prints. "Maybe he knew he was going to kill her, and he wanted to erase all evidence of her from this office. Maybe the suicide wasn't planned, Jane. He has some belts of bourbon, some tranquilizers, he's feeling remorseful and emotional, suddenly putting that gun under his chin sounds like a good idea. You can't discount that possibility."

"No, I can't," she concedes. Andy's right. That's all possible. "But I don't like it."

They check out the one major office, an impressive office at that—Nicholas Caracci's attempt to be "Christian Newsome," the wealthy, super-smart investor. A wet bar in the corner and cushy couch. Electronic banners scrolling indices from the Dow Jones, the Nasdaq, and the Nikkei. Flat-screen TVs on the wall. A massive, sleek metal desk. Expensive rugs. He definitely looked the part.

But nothing in the drawers. Nothing in the cabinets. No computer anywhere.

No signs of who was here or what they did.

They find the building manager down in the lobby.

"Anything else I can do for you, Sergeant Burke?" he says, on his best behavior. Most people are when the cops come a-calling.

"We appreciate your help," says Jane. "We're just going to need one more thing. You keep visitors' logs?"

Jane and Andy walk through a low gate and pass through a small garden in front of the walk-up to the three-flat in Lincoln Park. Jane finds the button next to the name Fielding.

"You still don't believe it," Jane says to Andy.

"I'm not saying that. I'm keeping an open mind."

"Okay, partner." She pushes the button, a buzz following.

*"Hello?"* a voice squawks through the speaker.

"Emily Fielding?"

*"Yes?"*

"My name is Jane Burke. I am a police officer in Grace Village. You're not in any trouble, don't worry," she quickly adds. "We'd like to ask you a few questions about the guy you work for, Christian Newsome."

# 93

# Simon

"Lead the way," says Gavin, though I will need to remember not to call him that. "Special Agent John Crane" was the name he gave.

"We can sit right in here," I say.

I show him into my living room, the first room you see when you enter the house, by my mother's design. I wasn't allowed in this room when I was a child. We hardly came in here. My parents would have dinner parties and would end up in this room for coffee and dessert. The furniture hasn't changed since that time.

The couch is stiff, last I checked, so I direct him there and sit in one of the individual chairs, with its outdated velvet cushion. Or who knows, maybe fashion has come full circle, and this is the latest thing.

"So tell me how I can help," I say.

Up close, Gavin is a little scarier than I remembered. I'd seen him on Christian's balcony a couple of times, but I didn't get a look at him up close. He's thick in the neck, shoulders, and chest, and his eyes are set like a predator's. He reminds me, more than anyone, of that wrestler, Mitchell Kitchens.

"Do you know a man named Christian Newsome, Mr. Dobias?"

I look up, like I'm pondering. "No, never heard the name."

"What about Nick Caracci?"

I open my hands. "No."

"Lauren Betancourt? You know her, don't you, Mr. Dobias?"

That's not very good procedure. A real FBI agent, not someone posing as one, would have asked that open-ended, innocently. Give me a chance to give the wrong answer, so they could slap me with a 1001 charge for lying to a federal agent.

"I would say I *did* know Lauren," I answer.

"Why the past tense? Because she was recently murdered?"

Again, Gavin, bad form—don't feed me that answer; give me some rope with which to hang myself. (Pardon the pun.)

"Past tense," I say, "because I have not spoken to Lauren for nineteen years."

Gavin, trying for the stone-faced, by-the-book special agent, jerks in his position, which is funny to see from someone sitting down. "You haven't spoken to Lauren for nineteen years?"

"That's right. Since 2003. She finally left town in 2004, but last time I spoke to her was 2003," I say. "I heard she was back in town. And I heard about her recent death, obviously."

He poises a finger in the air. It looks like he's losing some color to his face. "Mr. Dobias, you know it's a crime to lie to a federal agent."

I do know that. And I'm not lying. Okay, maybe I spoke to Lauren after she was dead at her house, but I don't consider that "speaking to" her. Otherwise, I'm telling the truth.

I have not said one word to Lauren in nineteen years, not since the day I confronted her at the law firm, the morning after I found her fucking my father.

"Mr. Dobias, we know you were having an affair with Lauren," he says.

"A what? You think I had a relationship with *Lauren*, of all people? She's the last person in the world I'd get near."

That is all true.

"Agent Crane," I say, "is there some reason you think I was sleeping with Lauren?"

Of course there is. What Gavin knows, he knows via Christian.

"We've read your diary, Mr. Dobias."

Well, technically, *Christian* read the diary. I prefer the word *journal*, but this is not a time to quibble over terminology.

"What diary?" I say. "I don't have a diary."

That was some of my best work. Full of highs and lows and melodrama, like most passionate romances. And sure, I sprinkled in some truth—the best lies always have some truth, right? But by and large, yeah, the whole thing was a work of fiction. The whirlwind affair, my hemming and hawing, Lauren being pregnant—fake, fake, fake. Necessary for Christian, though, full of details to give the whole thing a real narrative form.

Gavin leans forward. "You're denying that you kept a diary all about your affair with Lauren?"

"I'm denying every part of that sentence. I don't have a diary, Agent Crane. And if you know anything about me at all, you'd know that I would sooner drink cyanide than have an affair with Lauren Lemoyne. Or Betancourt, whatever."

"That's . . ." Gavin shakes his head. "That's impossible."

"If I have a diary," I say, "show it to me."

"That's not how this works, Mr. Dobias."

"Okay, well, someone must have written a bunch of words on a page. I suppose anybody could say anything, right? It doesn't have to be true."

Gavin sits back. He's playing catch-up. He only knows what Christian told him, and Christian bought the whole routine hook, line, and sinker.

It's almost humorous. This guy's a con artist himself, in cahoots with a fellow swindler. And yet the possibility that someone swindled *them* seems beyond his capacity at the moment.

Here's the problem. It's a lot easier to fool someone than to convince someone they've been fooled.

"You were about to divorce your wife and leave her for Lauren," says Gavin, though with a bit less conviction. He's starting to realize the ice under his feet is a little thinner than he thought.

I let out a harsh chuckle and stare at him. "Are you kidding me?"

"You weren't about to leave your wife?"

"This is ridiculous."

"You're not estranged from your wife right now?"

I shake my head. "I don't know where you get your infor—"

"*Then where has she been?*" he snaps. "Where has your wife, Vicky, been since Halloween? Because we've been watching your house, Mr. Dobias. And since Halloween night, when both Lauren Betancourt and Christian Newsome were murdered, your wife, Vicky, hasn't come home."

"There's a good reason for that," I say.

"Yeah? And what's the reason?"

I cup my hands around my mouth, as if to shout: "I don't have a wife! I'm not married, and I never have been!"


This meeting is not going as well as Gavin had hoped. He puts a hand on the arm of the couch, as if for support. "Vicky Lanier," he says, grasping, flailing.

"Vicky who?"

"Vicky . . . Lanier," he says, almost as a plea.

"Never heard the name."

"The woman who's been living with you," he says.

"Nobody has been living with me. Not someone named Vicky or anyone else. I'm a bachelor. I've never been married. Hell, I don't even have a girlfriend."

I used to. I love Vicky Townsend. I asked her to marry me once. She said no. I asked her a second time. She said no again. She broke things off because she could see I wanted the whole thing—marriage, kids—and she couldn't do it. Or at least not with me.

These last few months, stressful as they were plotting out all of this, were at least enjoyable in the sense that Vicky was staying with me. Always coming and going under darkness, using the rear alley garage and coming in under the shield of my privacy fence. But I loved having her here again. I wish she would stay forever. But what I was offering—commitment, love, devotion—was not enough for her.

"You've been married for ten years, Mr. Dobias. As of today, ten years."

Poor Gavin. He's still trying to keep his chin above water.

Ten years ago, I didn't even know Vicky. I met her three years ago at Survivors of Suicide, not long after Vicky's sister, Monica, overdosed on OxyContin. But yeah, Vicky told Christian about the ten-year anniversary. And I milked the hell out of it in the diary.

"We've seen a divorce petition," he adds.

"Sounds like another fake, like the diary," I say.

"We've seen a marriage certificate."

"Probably another fake, Agent Crane. I mean, how hard would it be to fake a marriage certificate? Look me up, if you like. See if I'm registered with Cook County as married."

"You don't have to be registered with the county to be married," he says. "Not if it's a foreign marriage." His eyes are beginning to water. Anger, probably.

"A *foreign* marriage certificate? Shit, that'd probably be even *easier* to fake."

It was, actually. I just downloaded a blank form and edited it on PDF. Took me about half an hour. Vicky helped. She helped a lot with the diary, too, for that matter. Gave me some details from a woman's perspective.

See, here's the thing: If you're a con artist like Christian, and someone like Vicky walks in with a wedding ring on her finger—my mother's, by the way—and says she's married to Simon Dobias, why on earth would Christian think she was lying? Who lies about something like that? He was spending so much time trying to con her, he didn't realize he was the target all along.

"You have a . . . a trust," Gavin stammers. "Over twenty million dollars."

"That's true," I say, because it is.

The first time Gavin has found firm ground, gotten an answer he wanted and expected. But it's a very small patch of ground.

"And it says that your spouse can't touch the money until she's been married for ten years."

Also true. Thanks to my father. It's what gave Vicky and me this idea. We had to give a sense of urgency to killing Lauren. So we worked backward. What would be a good date to commit murder? Halloween. Okay, so say our ten-year anniversary is just after Halloween.

And tell Christian just *before* Halloween, giving him only a few days to make his move, leaving him with no other choice, if he wanted the money, but to kill Lauren.

"You sure know a lot about my trust," I say. "That's pretty disturbing in itself."

"Today is your ten-year anniversary," he says.

I just smile. "You know what it sounds like?" I say. "It sounds like someone was pulling a con job. This 'Vicky Lanier' you mentioned? I'll bet that's not even her real name."

I couldn't resist. Vicky told me Gavin was onto her. Gave her a pretty hard kick to the ribs, too, sounds like.

"What aren't you telling me?" Gavin comes off the couch, towering over me on the chair.

"I'm telling you everything," I say. "I have nothing to hide."

My phone buzzes. Gavin hears it, too. I pick it up off the coffee table separating us and read it. It's from Jane Burke.

"I have another appointment in . . . Sounds like they'll be here in just a couple minutes."

"You'll need to cancel that," he says, still standing over me.

"Cancel with the Grace Village Police?" I say.

"The—what?" He takes a step back.

"The Grace Village Police," I repeat. "They want to talk to me about Lauren's murder. You should stick around. You guys can compare notes. Kind of an interagency cooperation kinda thing, right?"

I manage to keep a straight face while he shuffles his feet, thinking quickly.

"Or you can leave a business card, and I'll give it to them," I add. "You have a business card, Agent Crane?"

"It's a— We'd like to keep our investigation separate," he says.

"Yeah? I could see that. In your case, I could definitely see that."

"What does that mean?" he says.

I get up and walk over to the window. Look out over the street. They're saying it could snow later.

"It means that Nick was obviously in way over his head," I say. "Which means you are, too, Gavin."

"What did you say?" His head jerks around. "What did you call me?"

"Gavin Finley," I say. "Who thinks he's getting ten million dollars from Vicky Lanier. But you're not, Gavin. You're not getting a dime. Oh, there they are, the detectives, pulling up right now." I turn to Gavin. "I suppose you wanna go out the back way, right?"

"I don't know—this isn't—" His jaw juts out. "This isn't over, asshole."

"Sure it is. You wanna go tell the cops everything you know? Be my guest. They'll never be able to pin a thing on me. Or this phantom 'Vicky,' who, gosh, was probably using an alias. Diaries and marriage certificates and divorce petitions? None of them exist—not anymore. But the cops will sure be interested in how *you* seem to know so much. They'll take a hard look at you, Gavin. You up for that? A lot of police scrutiny into those petty little financial scams you're pulling? I'm thinking no. I'm thinking, you took your best shot at Vicky and me, but you failed. And be lucky it doesn't get any worse for you. You have no idea what contingency plans I have."

"I will . . . fucking kill you, you say anything about me." He shows me the gun at his hip, in case I didn't know that guns can kill people.

"They're getting out of the car, Gavin."

"Not one word about me, or you're dead."

"Don't you think I know that? I won't tell them about you. That doesn't help me. The best thing you can do, Gavin, from here on out, is play dumb. Your pal Nick's social life—dating a married woman, falling in love with her, she breaks his heart—I'd probably say you don't know, he didn't talk much. But I'd help them with the suicide angle. Christian was depressed, had mood swings, could be very dramatic—stuff like that would help. It's up to you. You're a smart guy."

He points his finger at me but doesn't have the threat to back it up.

"They're coming up the walk, Gavin. I'd get the hell out, if I were you. It's just through the kitchen."

Gavin storms off. He whips open the back door and disappears. He could have at least closed the door behind him.

# 94

## Simon

"Jane Burke. Wow. Good to see you," I say. She looks basically the same as high school, the messy, curly hair falling just above her shoulders, a small round face with a button nose, a shade of Irish rose to her cheeks. I always liked her. Didn't know her well, but she was the kind of person everyone liked.

We sit in the same front living room where Gavin and I just talked.

"Nice house," Jane says. "You live here all alone?"

"Just me."

"You never married, huh?"

"Nope, never married," I say, clapping my hands on my knees.

"No live-in girlfriend?" she asks. "Or girlfriend, anyway?"

"No, I'm not dating anyone."

She nods, as if it's just idle conversation. It's not.

"So, let's get started," she says, though we already did. "Do you know why we're here?"

I can't help but grin. "Jane, you know when you get pulled over by a cop and the first thing they ask you is, 'Do you know why I pulled you over?' I always hated that. I always felt like that was a *Miranda* violation. It should be, if you think about it. You're not free to leave, and the question is designed to elicit an incriminating response."

"You were always a smart one, Simon," she says. "You're free to kick us out, obviously. But if you'd prefer, I can *Mirandize* you."

"That's okay." I sit back in my chair. "I can only suppose that you're here for background on Lauren Lemoyne. I read about her death."

Here's my thinking: If I play dumb, if I act like I had no idea, then I'd have to put on a show right now of surprise when she tells me Lauren's dead, and I'm not that good of an actor. I'm a pretty darn good director, but not an actor.

"Yeah? Where did you read about it?"

"The *Tribune*."

"And what was your reaction?"

"I didn't cry myself to sleep," I say. "Lauren and I do not share a friendly history. I'm sure you know that, or you wouldn't be here."

She says nothing but holds my stare.

"How did she die?" I ask. "The paper said suspicious circumstances."

"I can't really get into details. When did you first realize Lauren was back in town?"

"I thought I saw her once last spring," I say. "April, May, something like that."

"Where was this?"

"Michigan Avenue, downtown. She walked past me. It looked like her, but it had been almost twenty years."

"Did you talk to her?"

"No. I just saw her. I did a double take, for sure. You haven't seen a person for almost two decades, you're not sure. But it looked like her."

"So what did you do?"

Well, let's see. Several things: (1) I ran to Vicky and told her; (2) I started plotting with Vicky about how to kill Lauren; (3) we figured if she was going to play my "wife" for Nick's sake, he might surveil her, so she'd have to pretend to live with me; and (4) I put up a privacy fence so she could come and go privately through the back entry, and nobody would ever see her.

You mean stuff like that, Jane?

"Well, later that day after seeing Lauren on the street, I looked her up on Facebook," I say. "And I found her. It said she was living in Grace Village."

If things get far enough, the police could search my work computer, and if a forensics team dug through it, they'd see that I looked her up. It would look better if I voluntarily fronted that information.

That was a mistake, looking her up like that back in May. But back then, when I first saw her on the street, I was in shock, disbelief. I wasn't thinking about killing her. It took me a while, and some conversations with Vicky.

"So you reached out to her?"

I cock my head. "What? To Lauren?"

"Yes, you—"

"No, I didn't 'reach out.' Why would I do something like that? She's the last person in the world I'd want to talk to."

There is no reason for me to be coy about my hostility toward Lauren. An innocent person wouldn't hide his disdain for her, under the circumstances.

And technically, my answer is truthful. I *didn't* reach out, and she *is* the last person I'd want to talk to.

"Do you still belong to the Grace Country Club?"

"Yes, I do. As a legacy."

"When was the last time you were there?"

"It's been years," I say. "Many, many years."

"Have you been back since Lauren joined?"

"I didn't know Lauren was a member," I say. "And I don't know how long she's been back in town."

Nice try, Jane.

"Her friends tell us she went to the club almost every day," says Jane. "Tennis, golf, lunch."

"How nice for her," I say.

"So you haven't spoken to Lauren since she came back to Chicago, to Grace Village?"

"No, I haven't."

"You haven't been inside her house?"

I laugh. "Give me a break."

"Is that a 'no,' Simon?"

"That's a 'no.'"

"So you just let it go, her coming back? This woman stole all your family's money and basically caused the death of your mother."

"Yes, I am well aware of what Lauren did, believe me. It's not the most enjoyable thing to revisit."

She puts up her hands. "You're right. I'm sorry. I just have to cross every 't' and dot every 'i' here, you understand."

"Then cross whatever 't' you need to cross, and dot whatever 'i,' and be done with it."

"Got it. Will do. So just to be clear." She puts her hands together, steers them toward me. "You have never set foot inside Lauren Betancourt's house?"

"Correct." My hands still. My knees still. My feet still. Arms not crossed.

"So there would be no reason for us to find your fingerprints inside that house."

"I can't imagine how my fingerprints would be inside that house."

Also true. I wore gloves the whole time I was in there. So did Christian, I assume, at least from what I could see.

"But feel free to check," I add. "If you'd like to print me, I'd be willing."

"That's not necessary."

"I'm offering. Really. A DNA swab, too. The whole works. We can go down to the station right now—"

"We already have your fingerprints, Simon. And your DNA."

Her partner, Andy Tate, looks up from notes he's scribbling, as if surprised that Jane just revealed that to me.

"Oh. Oh, okay." I sit back. "St. Louis P.D., right? Okay, now I'm getting the picture. Well, I guess you guys think you have this all figured out, then. I killed my father and then, all these years later, I killed Lauren. 'Revenge is a dish best served cold,' is that it?"

"I don't suppose you made any phone calls to your therapist the morning after Halloween," she says.

I clap my hands, mock applause. "So you actually think I did this?" I say. "You think I killed Lauren?"

"I think you're a very smart guy who takes his time before he does anything," she says.

"Somehow, I don't think that's a compliment."

How far along are these cops, anyway? It's Thursday. The third day of the investigation. Have they found Nick's body yet?

"Do you know someone named Christian Newsome?" she asks.

That answers *that* question.

"No."

"What about Nick Caracci?"

"No."

"Can I ask what size shoe you wear, Simon?"

"My . . . shoe size?" I might as well act surprised by that question. "Uh, well—usually ten and a half or eleven."

Not thirteen!

"You spend much time in the Bucktown/Wicker Park area?" she asks.

"Not so much these days, no. But I run all over the city. I definitely run through that area sometimes. I mix it up."

"You been there recently? Like, y'know, the Milwaukee-Damen-North area. Right around there. When was the last time you were there?"

"I . . . I don't remember."

"Were you there within the last week? You'd remember *that*."

"I don't remember being there within the last week," I say. "I suppose it's possible. If I knew it would be important, I'd have kept a journal or something."

(I like to amuse myself, even if it's a private joke.)

"You run much, Jane?"

"Me? These days? Nah. The only exercise I get is when I jump to conclusions, right?"

I smile. "Then you must be getting some exercise right now."

She bows her head a bit. "Touché. But, Simon, back to Wicker Park—you run through there, you said. You don't stop there? Hang out? Grab a beer? Anything like that?"

"I run through there. I don't stop and grab a beer."

"Ever stop?" she says. "Like, say, around North and Winchester? Or maybe Wabansia and Winchester?"

"I don't know Winchester," I say. "I know North Avenue. Wabansia's right around there, I know."

"You don't know Winchester?"

"No, I don't. Is that one of those side streets?"

"You ever stop right around Winchester, between Wabansia and North, and send text messages from a burner phone?"

"Whoa," I say. "That's specific. Sounds like you've got a whole theory going. What's the theory?"

"Just asking you a question, Simon."

"No, you're not. You want me to know you have a theory. So let's hear it. What did I do, criminal mastermind that I am?" I scoot forward in my chair, lean toward her. "Did I spike my own Gatorade?"

She waits me out.

"You get together with those cops from St. Louis," I say, "before long, you'll accuse me of kidnapping the Lindbergh baby. Did I kill JFK, too, and pin it on Lee Harvey Oswald?"

We seem to be well past pretense. I can't know everything she knows, but if she's gotten as far as Nick, she has a pretty good theory of a case that keeps me in the clear. Presumably, they've found half of Nick's toiletry kit at Lauren's house, the other half at his place. And I know they've already pulled the historical cell-service data, hence the questions about text messages from a burner phone near Winchester, where Nick lived. The evidence is lining up away from me.

And yet, Jane is certain she is looking at a guilty man. I always remembered her as a smart one.

"Ever been to Lauren's condo building downtown on Michigan Avenue?"

"No."

"Corner of Superior and Michigan?"

"I have not been to her condo." That's true enough. Never inside her condo.

"You must know there are security cameras all inside that building."

I do. And I went there once, just inside the lobby, when I first saw her in May. Stupid, but I did it. I didn't mention that to Jane, but I did mention seeing her on Michigan Avenue, so even if the security cameras in her condo building are retained for that long, back to May, and they see me standing in the lobby for five seconds, I'll just say it's consistent with what I already told them.

"I have never been in Lauren's condo," I repeat.

She smiles. "And you're certain that you've never been to her house in Grace Village? The one on Lathrow?"

"I have never been to her house. I think we already covered that."

"What about Halloween night," says Jane. "Where were you?"

"Right here. Handing out candy."

"Until what time?"

"Until . . . whenever it ended," I say. "Actually, I ran out of candy. It's always a dilemma, how much candy to buy, right? You buy too little, you run out. You buy too much, then it sits in your pantry all winter and you eat it. It's a real conundrum."

I practiced that line. I've been rehearsing for this conversation since Halloween. I liked this little ditty, with a little nudge of sarcasm at the end. But hearing it now, under the circumstances, as the temperature has dropped in this room, it sounds forced.

I can end this at any time. I can terminate this conversation and call a lawyer. I just need to know everything they know. I need to know if they're anywhere near Vicky.

"Were you alone?" Jane asks. "Or was your girlfriend with you?"

Yep, she's still fishing.

"I was alone," I say. "I don't have a girlfriend."

"Or boyfriend," she says. "Not trying to pry into your personal life, but you get my point. A special someone."

"I don't have anyone like that in my life. I was home all night on Halloween," I say, trying to keep my voice steady. "I was binge-watching Netflix. I can prove that on my phone."

Jane nods, like that all sounds great to her. "I would expect nothing less of you, Simon. I'll bet you can tell me exactly what show you were watching and describe it for me, too."

"*House of Cards*," I say without enthusiasm.

Andy taps Jane on the arm. "Loved that show. It's about a guy who manipulates everyone around him to get them to do things for him. Kills some people, too."

"You know what I love about streaming shows on your phone?" Jane replies to Andy. "You hit 'play,' and once one episode ends, the next one begins automatically. You could let the phone just sit there all night, and it would play one show after another, as if you were binge-watching. And the cell phone, of course, will be pinging the local cell tower all the while."

"Right, so if you're a fan of CSLI," says Andy, "y'know, like, if you're a law professor who specializes in the Fourth Amendment and knows all about historical cell-site location information—it would seem like a pretty good cover. Like you were sitting home all night."

Jane nods along. "Right. But in the end, what does it prove? It proves that your *cell phone* stayed home all night. It doesn't tell us anything about where *you* were."

She looks at me.

"Does it, Simon?"

"That's quite a theory you have there," I say. "My cell phone was home all night, therefore I *wasn't* home. That should get you far."

"Ah." Jane waves a hand. "Just a stumbling block. We still have some more work to do. Well, Sergeant Tate, I guess we're done here. Yeah?"

"I think so, yeah," he says. "Just one more person to talk to."

"Let's do it," says Jane. "Let's go talk to Vicky."

# 95
## Simon

"What?" The word escapes my mouth before I can think. Vicky. They have Vicky's name. It was one thing for Gavin to have it—another for the *police* to have it.

How?

Jane Burke, seemingly in the act of pushing herself off the couch, preparing to leave—though it's obviously just that, an act, a bit of theater—sits back down again. "Vicky," she says. "Vicky Lanier."

They have her *full* name.

I shrug, but I'm sure the color has drained from my face, if it hadn't already. "Don't know the name."

"'Course you don't," she says. "You don't know Nick Caracci, you don't know Christian Newsome—so I'm sure you don't know Vicky Lanier, either."

How? How do they have her name? The bogus "divorce petition" I wrote up for Vicky to show Christian? An entry from my bogus journal? Did Christian take photos of those on his phone? Vicky was sure he didn't—but maybe she missed something—

"Something wrong, Simon?" Jane asks. "You seem a little . . . hot under the collar. Upset."

"Are you upset, Simon?" says Andy Tate.

"No, I'm . . . curious, I guess. You're throwing out all these names without telling me anything else."

"That's true." Jane slaps her hands on her knees. "Okay, I guess I can fill in a few blanks."

I sit like a casual listener, though I feel anything but casual right now.

"Nick is this real handsome guy," says Jane. "And successful. A financial investor type of guy. He's in a relationship with Vicky. We know they had sex in Nick's office downtown. They all but kicked out the receptionist one afternoon, sent her home early. And before the receptionist was out the door, she was already hearing some interesting sounds coming from that office."

"Okay," I say, nodding along. "And what about this Vicky person?"

"Vicky wants Lauren Betancourt dead," says Jane.

"Oh? Why is that?"

"Eh." Jane lifts her shoulders. "One of two reasons. Not sure which. One is that Nick started up with Lauren, too. He cheated on Vicky. So she killed Lauren, framed Nick for it, then killed Nick. Made it look like Nick committed suicide out of remorse."

"Pretty extreme," I say.

"It *does* sound extreme, Simon, doesn't it?" she says, a tone that borders on mocking. "Which is why I'm not a big fan of that theory. I like my other theory better."

"Yeah? What's your other theory, Jane?"

"That Vicky was teamed up with someone *else* who wanted Lauren dead," she says, looking me square in the eye. "Maybe, for example, because Lauren wrecked his family and caused the death of his mother. Someone like that, Simon."

"Wow." I shake my head. "You have a vivid imagination."

"Not that vivid. Just following the facts."

"Oh, you have *facts*." My turn to mock.

"Some pretty good ones, in fact. For one, Nick was murdered. He didn't kill himself. It was staged as a suicide, but it was a homicide."

Does she *know* that or just suspect it? What did Vicky screw up? I saw the scene myself, afterward. It looked pretty good to me. But what do I know about crime scenes?

He had drugs and booze in his system, a suicide note on his phone, a gunshot wound under his chin—that wasn't enough? They found something that tells them Nick didn't kill himself?

Or is she bluffing? Trying to prompt me?

"I think, one way or another," she says, "that Vicky and her partner used

Nick Caracci to kill Lauren. How they did it is unclear to me. But they needed to kill him afterward to tie up that loose end."

"Nick was framed, you're saying."

"That's what I'm saying."

"Sounds like something in a movie."

"You planted that pink phone at the crime scene, Simon."

Wow, that's direct. She's done being cute.

"I— What? I did what now?"

"You planted that phone."

"What phone, Jane?"

She shows me a wide grin. "The pink phone. It was obviously placed very carefully, moved more than once with precision, so that we'd find it pretty easily but it would look technically hidden. The blood smears show that clear as day."

"I'm not following," I say, though I am, and I'm cursing myself for getting too cute with that damn phone. I should have slid it harder the first time to make sure it went all the way under the table, or I should have left well enough alone when it didn't. I moved the phone a second time and basically told them what I was doing.

"If Nick was the killer, he'd never have gently moved that phone where we found it. He'd have taken it with him. Instead, we find it at the scene."

Too much. Overload. I can't keep straight what I'm supposed to know and not know. I'm afraid to speak. I screwed up, and I've put Vicky in the crosshairs as a result—that much I know.

And here I thought I could outsmart everybody with some planning and deliberation.

Andy waves his hand at me. "Anyway, you obviously have no worries, Simon, since you don't know any of these people. You have no reason to care about Vicky Lanier. Because you don't know her. Isn't that right, Simon?"

"Are you absolutely sure you don't know Vicky Lanier?" Jane asks.

"I . . . don't recognize that name."

She smirks at me.

"Okay, Simon," she says. "We'll be in touch."

# 96

## Jane

Jane and Andy don't say a word to each other until they're back inside their car and have driven away from Simon's house. Andy has the wheel.

"So what do you think?" she asks. "You saw the look on his face when we mentioned Vicky's name. I was just trying to rattle his cage."

"And it worked," Andy says. "That's your real theory, isn't it? She's the one who helped Simon pull this off? The one on the other end of the cell phone texts?"

"Somebody helped him, Andy. And he lit up like a firecracker when we mentioned her name."

"So this receptionist, Emily Fielding, says this woman named Vicky Lanier and Nick were getting it on in his office," says Andy. "And that was the last time she saw Vicky. So let's say they've hooked up, they're sleeping together. How does that fit in? If Simon's behind all this, if he's the puppet master, where does Vicky Lanier fit in? Why does she need to get close to Nick Caracci? How does that help Simon with his ultimate goal of killing Lauren Betancourt?"

"Well, Nick's the patsy, right?"

"Sure, so the theory goes, but why does Vicky have to get close to him?"

"Well, to get inside his apartment to steal half his toiletry kit, if for no other reason. Maybe to get him to kill Lauren—maybe Nick did that. I don't know all the details yet." She wags her finger. "Yet. But you agree, we're onto something here."

"Oh, shit, I don't know, Janey. I mean, Nick Caracci was probably a player, right? Good-looking guy. Rich, or at least pretending to be rich. The fact that he bangs some woman in his office? I mean, that would never happen to *me*, but it's not a total shock he'd have success with the ladies. It could be that and nothing more."

Jane looks at Andy. He's being practical, reasonable. He might well be right. With all the evidence piled up against Nick, Jane won't be able to hold off the chief and the Village president much longer. "If it's that and nothing more," she says, "why did Simon react like that in there when we mentioned the name Vicky Lanier?"

"No, you're right about that. He did." He groans. "This case is giving me a stomachache."

"Why?"

"Because we have a slam dunk on Nick Caracci, Jane, that's why."

"Yeah, but what does your gut tell you?"

Andy makes a noise, taps his fingers on the steering wheel. He pulls their car into the parking lot outside the police station, kills the engine, and turns to her.

"My gut tells me he knows Vicky Lanier," he says.

"For sure."

"But we know nothing about her. I mean, if she's in on this with Simon, if she was part of some plan to lure Nick Caracci into this plot, I highly doubt 'Vicky Lanier' is even her real name."

"Probably not. The name itself is almost surely a dead end. We'll run a background just in case, but you're right—her name probably isn't Vicky Lanier."

"So we don't know squat."

"Not yet," she says. "You processed all the prints from Lauren's crime scene, right?"

"Yep. Sent them to AFIS yesterday. If there's a hit on anything, we'll know hopefully today or tomorrow at the latest."

"And Cheronis sent prints from Nick Caracci's apartment," says Jane. "Maybe we'll get lucky on a fingerprint. Forensics may be our only saving grace here. Simon can manipulate all he wants, but he can't manipulate a fingerprint."

# 97
## Jane

In an interview room, one hour later. "Thanks for coming, Mr. Lemoyne," says Jane. "I hope your flight was okay."

Albert Lemoyne, age sixty-nine, is a big, weathered guy with a full, ruddy face and deep-set, bloodshot eyes. A union man, a Teamster, with rough hands to show for it. He is overweight and aging, but Jane sees a man inside there who would have caught a woman's eye back in his day. His skin is bronzed from the sun; he now lives in Scottsdale. "I flew home to bury my daughter," he says, "so no, it wasn't that great."

"Of course. That was—"

"Did you find him? Did you figure out who did it?"

"We think we may be close, Mr. Lemoyne."

"Shit, call me Al, everyone else does."

"Okay. I need to ask you some questions about your daughter, Al."

"You didn't ask me enough questions when you called me on Tuesday?"

"Just a few more, sir," says Jane.

"I knew they were getting a divorce," he says. "She kept telling me she was fine, she'd be okay. She didn't—she didn't share a lot with her old man. She was much closer to her mother."

Her mother, Amy Lemoyne, died four years ago from cancer. Al has since lived alone in the house Lauren bought them in Arizona.

"Do you know, Al, if Lauren had begun another relationship?"

He shakes his head no. "But I doubt she'd mention it to me unless it was serious."

"Do you recognize the name Christian Newsome?"

"No, uh-uh."

"Nick Caracci? Vicky Lanier?"

Same answer for each one.

"What about Simon Dobias?"

His eyes flicker, like a flinch. "The boy," he says. "The son. The one accused her a stealing."

"Yes."

"He still live around here?"

"Why do you ask?"

He makes a fist with his hand, gently thumps it on the table. "I told her, I said, 'You sure you wanna move back close to where they live?' She said it wouldn't be an issue. I mean, when she moved back to Chicago, I said okay, it's a big place. But then she meets Conrad and moves to Grace Village and I said to her, I said, 'You sure, honey? Being just the town over?' But she said it was the father who worried her, and he was dead. She didn't worry about the boy."

Jane puts up her hands. "I need to unpack that. When Lauren married Conrad and moved to Grace Village three years ago, you were worried, because she was moving so close to Grace Park, where the Dobias family lived?"

He nods. "She said, there's so many people in these suburbs, odds were she'd never run into him even if he still lived here."

"Simon, you mean."

"Right. The father, Ted? He moved to St. Louis after. And then I guess he died."

She raises her eyebrows. "The father moved to St. Louis 'after.' After what?"

His look turns severe, as if insulted. "After you know what."

"Please, Al, I'm—"

"After the thing with the money. They said she stole their money. She didn't. Ted gave it to her. I'm not saying it was the proudest moment of my daughter's life, carrying on with a married man, but she was barely twenty, and he was a lot older. So who's to blame, her or him?"

"You're saying Ted Dobias *gave* her the money?"

"He was some rich ambulance-chaser lawyer. He had plenty to spare."

No, he didn't. But that seems to be what Lauren told her parents back then. Apparently in the version of the story that made its way to Al's ears, Ted Dobias just pulled a good six million dollars out of his pocket and tossed it to her, mere chump change, just a fraction of the money he had. Al doesn't seem to realize that Lauren cleaned out the Dobias family, took all the money they had at the time.

Maybe Al knew differently deep down and was just instinctively siding with his daughter. Or maybe he believed everything his daughter told him. Or maybe the passage of eighteen years has blended what he knew to be true into what he wanted to believe. Time and blood have a way of playing with the truth.

Either way, Jane isn't going to burst that bubble right now, with Al mourning his daughter's death.

"Hell, she had to leave the country to get away from him."

"Where did she move?" Jane asks, though she already knows.

"Paris. She lived in Paris. She moved around a little bit, stayed other places in Europe, being young and with all that money. But Paris was her home."

"Did she—"

"She thought he was watching her. Having her followed. Spied on. Stuff like that."

"Who?"

"*Who?*" he says. "Dobias. Ted Dobias. She said sometimes she felt like she was being watched or tracked. He was still bitter about the money."

"*Ted* Dobias, you're saying. Not Simon."

"The boy? She didn't mention the boy. Only Ted. Hell, she stayed away in Europe for how many years? All because of that guy."

"She never came back, huh?"

"No, she— Well, just the one time. When Amy and me were celebrating thirty-five years. She threw this party for us at the Drake downtown. She flies back to town for a couple weeks. She reserves a bunch of hotel rooms, and my brother, Joe, and my sister, Louise, and their kids and some of my friends from work—we all stay downtown at the Drake for the week. Really, it was like two weeks?"

Jane nods. "So Lauren was in Chicago for two weeks?"

"Right."

"Any chance she ran into Simon Dobias then?"

"Not that I know of. She was in town for a while. I didn't keep complete tabs on her or anything. But she didn't mention seeing him. Or Ted, for that matter."

"Okay. And when was this, Al? When did all this happen?"

"Oh, Christ." He looks up at the ceiling, eyes narrowed. "Our anniversary was May the eighteenth. We got married on May 18, 1975. So . . ." He closes his eyes. "If I remember, the year she came into town for the big party she threw, our anniversary was in the middle of the week, so she had the party the following weekend at the Drake. And then everyone stayed the week after that, which included the long Memorial Day weekend."

"Including Lauren?"

"Yeah. We loved it, having her in town for two weeks. Spent a lot of time with her."

"And you never saw or heard from Simon Dobias during that time?"

He shrugs. "Never saw him. Never seen him ever, actually. Never had the pleasure. Never spoke to him."

"Okay, well—"

"The boy did this, you think? You wouldn't be asking otherwise. You think Simon Dobias killed my daughter?"

She raises a calming hand. "We have to follow everything up, Mr. Lemoyne. You understand."

# 98
## Vicky

After finishing my first shift with a break before my second, I drive home to my apartment in Delavan, a measly little studio apartment only ten minutes from Safe Haven in Elkhorn, Wisconsin. The place is barely large enough to swing your arms around, but it's mine, and the stove and fridge and heater work.

I don't miss the ninety-mile drives to and from Grace Park, when I "lived" with Simon, starting back in July, having to commute every day up here for work.

I will, however, miss Simon's comfortable bed. I'll miss that huge kitchen and the pot of coffee ready for me when I wake up. I'll miss never having to think twice about a full refrigerator, a stocked pantry. I'll miss that rooftop oasis he created.

I'll miss Simon, too. His thoughtfulness and his quirks. His sense of humor. Most of all, the way he looks at me. I wish that had been enough for me. I wish I could have said yes when he proposed to me—both times he asked.

If I ever married anyone, it would be Simon. But I never will. I will never latch myself to another person. I learned how to live alone, and I guess I learned it too well.

We had a good run, starting three years ago, when I moved to Chicago after my sister's suicide. I was a mess, and he wasn't. He sobered me up. He pulled me out of my funk. I never took drugs again and I never sold my body again. He was the first man who ever treated me like I was worth anything. He put me on a pedestal. But I saw how much more he wanted from me—children, marriage—so I cut it off. That was never going to be me. And I don't want him to settle any more than I want to settle for myself. I moved to Wisconsin and started working for Safe Haven.

And didn't speak to Simon for months.

Until last May, when he saw Lauren on Michigan Avenue.

After finishing a microwave dinner at my apartment, I drive to the forest preserve in Burlington, thirty minutes away. I've been coming three times a day—first thing in the morning, at lunchtime, and after work. I take the hiking trail and follow it around a couple of bends to a vista point about a half-mile up with a large wooden plaque describing the history of the lake down below. I reach behind the plaque and peel off a container attached by Velcro. Inside the container is the burner phone Simon gave me for the post-Halloween fun.

I power it on and give it a moment for the messages to load. First, the message I sent Simon on Halloween night, after I drove up here to Wisconsin:

> *Mon, Oct 31, 11:09 PM*
>
> Gavin saw me. He knows about alias. He wants half the $$ on 11/3 or he exposes me to you. Gave me good kick in ribs too. Need my help??

And then the responses from Simon over the last few days, with a new message today:

> *Tues, Nov 1, 12:06 PM*
>
> No I will deal with him. Nothing much in papers today.

> *Wed, Nov 2, 11:39 AM*
>
> Newspapers but little detail. Working out time to talk to police don't worry

> *Today 4:34 PM*
>
> Good news/bad. Gavin taken care of. Met with police, they know full alias name too (receptionist?) but otherwise flailing

"Shit." They know the name Vicky Lanier. The cops know. He's probably right—it was the receptionist. Emily, I think her name was. That's the only thing I can think of, too.

But his text says "otherwise flailing." Meaning they don't know what to do with the name Vicky Lanier. That was the hope. There's no trace of me otherwise. That name will take them nowhere.

And at least Gavin's taken care of. What does he mean by that? What did Simon do? My guess, knowing Simon, he somehow talked Gavin down.

It all comes down to fingerprints for me. If I left a stray print anywhere in Nick's apartment or at his office, I'm done. They'll run it through the national database and find me in five seconds, registered with the state of Wisconsin.

Simon figured they'd process the fingerprints within a day or so after finding Lauren. Which means I could find out any second now.

Either I'm scot-free or I'm cooked.

"What? *What?*" Jane shouts into the phone.

"Don't shoot the messenger," says Sergeant Don Cheronis. "The coroner's office, they march to their own beat. I told them to hold off. They don't care what I fucking think."

"They must care a little."

"Not really."

"Well, did you push back, Don?"

"I— Jane, you have to understand . . ."

"You agree with them, don't you?"

"I . . . I think it's probably the right call, yeah."

Suicide. The Cook County medical examiner is calling Nicholas Caracci's death a suicide. And Cheronis didn't put up a fight because he doesn't disagree.

Nice way to start a Friday morning.

Chief Carlyle sits stone-faced, hands laced together, behind his desk, while Jane gives him the latest update.

"What you're telling me is interesting," he says, "but it's not evidence. Not proof. You keep pooh-poohing the strong evidence of guilt we have against Nick Caracci, basically by saying it's all a frame-up, it's too convenient—which you could say about most crimes solved by law enforcement in the history of the country. And then you wrap your arms around evidence against Simon Dobias that isn't evidence at all. It's just maybe, coulda, what about this, what about that. Now you bring me this 'Vicky Lanier,' but you don't know anything about her except, number one, she screwed Nick in his office and, number two, Simon Dobias had a strong reaction to her name. And you don't even think 'Vicky Lanier' is her real name. Hell, they just dug up a Vicky Lanier in—where was it?"

"West Virginia," says Jane. "Chief, I understand we're not there yet. Just—"

"Oh, a lot of people think we *are* there, and we've *been* there since we found Nick Caracci's body. The guy's a con artist who preys on rich, unhappily married women. Lauren Betancourt was a rich, unhappily married woman."

"Chief, if you were in that house yesterday with Simon Dob—"

"Jane, I hear you. You and Andy are good cops, and your antennae went up when you talked to him. He seems suspicious. He seemed defensive, like he was hiding something. But how would you *expect* him to react? He knows he's going to be a suspect in Lauren's death. And he's already been accused of killing his own father—not formally accused, but you know what I mean. So yeah, you're going to be defensive. You're going to be hostile."

"It was more than that."

"Okay, but I know you understand what I'm saying. We are sitting on a solve, Jane. And there's only so long I'm going to sit on it. I have six village trustees and one village president calling me or texting me almost on the hour. And you watched the emergency board meeting. This isn't Chicago. This is a nice, quiet little village, where people get very upset over someone being murdered. It's not supposed to happen here. That's why they live here. So when it does happen, they need to know we're going to solve the case quickly. Instead, I'm hearing phrases like 'amateur hour' and 'keystone cops' already. People think we're in over our head. One of the trustees is talking about bringing in the FBI—"

"Oh my God, it's fucking Friday morning," Jane snaps. "We just found the body on Tuesday morning. What's wrong with people?"

"Jane, I hear you, but think about it this way. With all the evidence lined up against Nick Caracci—and now we have a call of suicide as his cause of death, on top of everything else—what state's attorney would approve charges against Simon Dobias? A good defense lawyer, which he could afford, would make mincemeat out of the case. Tell me I'm wrong. You couldn't convict Simon Dobias in a million years."

Jane puts her hands together and takes a breath. "At least wait for the prints. We should have them today. Whoever this 'Vicky Lanier' is, maybe her prints come up. At Nick Caracci's murder scene. At Lauren's murder scene. Hell, maybe at Ted Dobias's murder scene."

The chief falls back in his chair. "Now you have her killing Simon's father?"

"Don't talk to me like I'm being unreasonable, Chief. There were unidentified prints on the wine bottle used to hit Ted Dobias over the head. And they found a glass with female DNA on it. We think Simon killed his father, right? Well, maybe he had some help. Maybe it's the same person who helped him this time. Maybe not. Let's just wait for the prints. They won't lie. And if we get a match, then maybe we'll know who this woman is who calls herself 'Vicky Lanier.' And if not, so be it."

"No reason we can't wait for the prints, Chief," Andy chimes in.

"Fine, wait for the prints," says the chief, throwing up his hands. "And when you get them, come talk to me."

Jane and Andy leave the office.

"He's not wrong, Jane," Andy says under his breath. "He may be feeling political pressure, but that doesn't make him wrong. We'll never get charges approved against Simon with all the evidence lined up against Nick Caracci."

"Wait for the fucking fingerprints," she says. "Give me— Wait." She looks at her phone. "Brenda Tarkington just called from St. Louis P.D. I missed it."

"Call her right now."

"In the conference room," says Jane. She shakes her phone like it holds the key to her fate.


"Brenda, it's Jane Burke. I have Andy Tate with me on speaker."

*"You must have run the prints from the crime scene,"* Sergeant Tarkington squawks through the speakerphone. *"We just got word from AFIS."*

"You got a hit from your crime scene?"

*"We did, indeed, Sergeant Burke."*

Jane pounds the table. "Tell me, Brenda, and please make me happy."

# 100

## Vicky

"That is *so* not true," says Mariah.

"Yes, it is, I remember," Macy spits back.

"Yeah. You remember. You were, like, six." Mariah makes a face like her younger sister is the dumbest human being on the planet.

"Girls—"

"I was seven and you were crying and all nervous!"

"Girls, for heaven's sake," I say. "Both of you were nervous before you got your ears pierced. Both of you were brave."

Friday night in Elm Grove. It's less than an hour's drive from my crappy little studio apartment in Delavan. With all the double shifts I've pulled, I was owed an early day on Friday. I thought about staying home, but Macy wanted to get her ears pierced and wanted me there.

I pull Adam's car onto Sunflower Drive and head toward the house.

A car, a sedan, is parked in the driveway. I slow the car enough to get a look at the license plate. A state logo, half of the words circling the top, the other half circling the bottom:

**Wisconsin Department of Justice**
**Office of the Attorney General**

I keep driving.

"Um, Vicky, this is our house?"

"Hey, y'know what, I forgot, your daddy had a meeting," I say, driving away from the house. "Let's just go get dinner on our own and bring something home for him."

"You want me to text him?" Mariah asks.

"No, no. I just forgot. He has a meeting. Don't bother him."

I grip the steering wheel and count to five.

I could run. I could. Right now, I could run. Rambo could get me a new identity. But I have the girls with me.

This isn't happening.

# 101
## Simon

Friday night. I am trapped in my house. Waiting, in case they come with a search warrant. Afraid to make a false move. Wondering about Vicky. Waiting some more. Flinching at every sound, jumping at every shadow. Wandering around my house with little sleep, trying to occupy myself with a blog piece on a new exigent-circumstances decision from an appeals court in Texas.

A car door closes nearby. I sit still at my desk and listen.

Footsteps coming up my walk. The porch light goes on, activated by the motion sensor.

The doorbell doesn't ring. No knock on the door.

Who's out there?

I go downstairs to the front door and open it. Standing there is Sergeant Jane Burke, expressionless, a bag slung over her shoulder.

I open the screen door. "Little late for a search warrant, isn't it?"

"I'm not here to search your place," she says, angling past me, walking through the foyer.

"I don't believe I invited you in, Jane."

"I'm not a vampire."

"No, you're a cop. Who doesn't have the right to enter my house without consent or a warrant."

She walks past the living room into the family room. "Simon, you can take your Fourth Amendment and shove it up your ass."

I join her in the family room but don't sit down. "Can I quote you on that?"

She takes a load off and reaches into the bag she's carrying. "I brought you something," she says.

Out of her bag she pulls a bottle of champagne and two plastic champagne flutes, tinted red, and places them on the coffee table.

The champagne is Laurent-Perrier, "ultra brut." I never knew what that meant. Is that different than kinda, sorta brut? Is that one step up from really brut?

"What are we celebrating?" I ask.

She makes a face. "A bottle of that exact brand of champagne, with two cheap red plastic flutes just like those, were found at your father's crime scene."

"I don't have the exact brand committed to memory," I say, "but yes, I remember that he was hit over the head with—"

"Oh, Simon, Simon, Simon." She sighs. "Tell me. What kind of a person keeps an empty bottle of champagne for years upon years, waiting for the right moment to exact revenge?"

"I don't know, Jane—"

"A champagne bottle that your father and Lauren shared. Probably pissed you off but good. And the champagne flutes, too. You kept them for *years*, Simon, waiting for the right moment to go down to St. Louis to hit your father over the head with it before stabbing him."

"The right time?" I ask. "The week of my final exams was that 'right time' I'd been waiting for?"

She wags a finger at me. "Had a nice talk with Lauren's father, Al Lemoyne," she says. "Lauren did come back, once, while she was living in Paris. For two weeks, to celebrate her parents' thirty-fifth anniversary."

"How nice," I say.

"Yeah, how nice. Lauren's parents were married May 18, 1975. So their thirty-fifth wedding anniversary was May 18, 2010."

I open my hands. "Okay . . . ?"

She fixes a stare on me. "Lauren stayed that week and through Memorial Day in Chicago. Memorial Day was May 31, Simon. May 31, 2010. You know what that means."

"I don't."

"You're gonna make me say it?"

"I'm afraid so, Jane. I'm not following."

"Oh, you're following just fine. Your father was murdered on May 27, 2010. Lauren was in Chicago at the time of his murder."

"Wow," I say.

"Yeah, wow. Try to sound a little more surprised."

"Hey, Jane, y'know what you should do?"

She cocks her head in mock curiosity. "What should I do, Simon?"

"You should check Lauren's fingerprints—I mean, I assume you took exclusion prints of her when you found her dead."

"We sure did, Simon. We sure did."

"You should run those prints and see if they're a match on that champagne bottle used to incapacitate my father at his murder scene."

Jane gets off the couch. "Should I do that, Simon? Should I?"

"Yeah, you should," I say. "I mean, if *I'm* capable of driving down to St. Louis and killing Ted, I don't see why Lauren wouldn't be just as capable. And she didn't have final exams to worry about. Right?"

"Right, Simon. Exactly right. And, in fact, we did run her prints. And surprise, surprise, that champagne bottle has Lauren's prints on it."

"That's—that's great. Case closed! The St. Louis murder has been solved!"

She likes that, a bitter smile. "Everyone asked, why wait so long to kill his father? Why wait until his final exam week to drive down to St. Louis and kill his father? Turns out, you didn't pick it because it was final exams week. You picked it because Lauren Lemoyne had come back to the States."

I shrug. "I'm sure I don't know what you're talking about. I mean, how would I know that Lauren was coming back to town?"

"Facebook, that's how." She pulls a piece of paper out of her pocket and hands it to me. A printout from a Facebook page—Lauren's, I assume—well, actually, I know, because I remember reading it back then—from May 12, 2010:

So excited to return to Chicago next week to celebrate my parents' 35th! I'll be in through Memorial Day at the Drake!

I hand the sheet back to her, keep a blank face. Jane Burke is a very good detective. But if she's here, it means she's lost the battle.

She walks up to me. "Just so you know—*I* know. I know you did all of this. Your father, Lauren, and Nick Caracci. And you're gonna walk from the whole damn thing."

She brushes past me and heads for the door.

"Hey, Jane?"

She turns at the door.

"Grace Village has one damn smart detective on the force," I say.

She gives me a deadpan expression. "Coming from anyone else on the face of the earth," she says, "I'd consider that a compliment."

# 102
## Vicky

I can only make dinner last so long. The girls and I order some food for Adam and drive back to the house. I've tried to stay engaged with the kids during dinner, Macy being so excited about her pierced ears, but all I can do is rehearse my lines.

Not that there's much to rehearse. Deny everything, and if they back you into a corner, refuse to answer.

*Where was I on Halloween, Officer? Why, I was at my apartment I'm renting in Delavan, Wisconsin, answering the door to trick-or-treaters.* I left my cell phone there, per the plan. I didn't stream a continuous series of episodes off Netflix like Simon did, but my phone was there, regardless. It would ping the nearest cell tower at least a few times, even if not doing much of anything besides refreshing.

*Christian Newsome? Never heard of him. Nick Caracci? Nope, doesn't ring a bell.*

*My car? I drive a beater 2007 Chevy Lumina. You want to check the plates to see if they were ever recorded by tollway cameras or local POD cameras in Chicago? Go ahead and check.* They never were. That car hasn't been over the Wisconsin border since I moved to Delavan almost a year ago.

Oh, I may have used a Jeep to travel back and forth to Chicago, but that vehicle's long gone now, and the registration won't come back to me or Simon, anyway.

*Simon Dobias? Never met him, Officer.* You mean the guy who let me talk to him for hours and hours after my first SOS meeting, who scraped me off the floor a week later, when I was about to follow my sister, Monica, into the world of overdosing—me on cocaine, not oxy?

You mean the guy who forced me into rehab, who paid for the whole thing, and who was waiting for me when I came out?

You mean the guy who convinced me to give life another shot?

No, I've never met that man. Never heard of him.

I drive back to the house, humoring the girls, laughing at their jokes, but inside, a dull ache fills me. I'm ready, though. *I have no idea what you're talking about, Officer.* My answers will be confident but not too perfect.

When I turn onto the street, I see immediately that the police vehicle is gone. Relief floods through me. I park in the garage. The kids fly into the house.

"Daddy, I got my ears pierced!"

I walk in slowly, my pulse decelerating, the adrenaline draining from me. The M&Ms are bouncing around the house, heading upstairs to his bedroom and home office, opening the basement door.

"Where's Daddy?"

I spot him outside, in the backyard, staring out. Something in his hand . . . a cigarette?

"Girls, put his dinner on the counter. He's outside. I'm going to talk to him. Just me," I say as Macy rushes for the door. "Give us a minute, please, Mace?"

"Hey."

Adam is standing by a stone fountain in the backyard, empty this time of year. He is underdressed for the cold, just a light sweater on with blue jeans. A cigarette burns in his hand.

"Since when do you smoke?" I say.

"Since pretty much never." He looks at the cigarette and tosses it in the grass, stamps it out with his foot. "Monica started smoking to get over the OxyContin. Always seemed dumb. But I'd have gone along with anything that made her stop those pills. I even smoked a few cigarettes with her.

Now, every once in a while, when I think of her, I light one up. Isn't that the dumbest thing?"

"You're thinking about her," I say.

He glances in my direction, stuffs his hands in his pockets. "The attorney general's office was here. The people I complained to after Monica's overdose? Remember I filed that complaint?"

"I remember."

Adam looks at me, his jaw quivering, his eyes filling with tears. "He's dead," he says.

"He's— Who's dead?"

"David."

"David?"

"David Jenner. The man who stole Monica from us and then stole her money and left her with a bottle of fucking pills to overdose on? The handsome, charismatic, glorified drug dealer?"

I try to act surprised. "Of course I remember. I've tried to put that name out of my head."

He lets out a sigh. "Me, too. And that wasn't his name, anyway. We figured he used a fake name."

"Right."

"His name was Nicholas Caracci," says Adam. "He killed himself."

"He killed himself, huh?"

Adam shakes his head. "Apparently he was trying the same thing with some lady in Chicago. It—it backfired or something. I don't know."

I put my hand on his shoulder. "So how are you feeling?"

"How'm I feeling? I want my wife back, that's how I'm—"

He breaks down, something he doesn't do often, covers his face with his hands and lets out a good, blubbering cry. I rub his back and hope that the girls aren't watching.

"The things I said to her," he mumbles.

"Adam, please."

"After she left. When she was full-on using again, shacked up with some pretty boy who was handing it out to her like candy. I told her to stay away from the kids."

"You had to."

"I told her I didn't want them seeing their mother as a junkie whore—"

I grab and hold him tight while he sobs and moans.

"You had to protect the girls," I whisper. "You tried to help her, and you would have. She would have made it. But he used the drugs to drag her over to the dark side. He turned her into somebody she wasn't. You couldn't let the girls see her like that."

I remember that time, too. Talking to Monica every day, fielding the occasional frantic call from Adam. I should've done more. I was too caught up in my own addiction. And I was out of my element. I'd never had to dispense a single word of advice to my older sister, the successful one.

"I would've taken her back," he says, his voice still shaking.

"I know."

"After he robbed her clean and took off, and she was living in filth and waste and practically in the gutter. I would've brought her back and cleaned her up and we could've—I know we could've—"

"I know, Adam, I know. None of this was your fault."

That seems to help. Adam doesn't have anyone to talk to about these things, about his guilt. There was no Survivors of Suicide for Adam, no therapist. A guy like Adam would never go for that.

I had someone. I had Simon. Simon listened. He listened to everything I had to say. He listened to me talk about the sister that I loved more than I ever realized after her death, and how I loved those girls. He didn't judge me when I told him why I moved to Chicago, how I had used a private investigator to find Nick, and I was waiting for him to return to Chicago so I could kill him.

He tried to talk me out of it. He told me it wouldn't solve anything. He told me I'd cleaned myself up, I was sober now, and I should focus on starting a new life and spending time with the girls. He proposed marriage and talked about us having a family of our own. But even when I said no, he never left me. He said I should move on, move forward. He said that's what he had done with Lauren. He'd put Lauren behind him. And I should do the same with Nick.

But he didn't judge me when I told him I couldn't let it go, I couldn't let Nick get away with it. He helped me pack my stuff and move to Delavan, so I could have some distance from Chicago, so nobody could possibly connect me to Nick or Chicago when I killed him.

And I was ready to do it. I was waiting for the summer. In the summer, so my original plan went, I'd come down to Chicago, run into Nick in a bar, and hope he'd take me home with him. If that didn't work, I'd find some other way.

And then Simon saw Lauren on the street in Chicago last May, and my simple little plan to slit that monster's throat turned into a much more complicated plan for both of us to find peace.

Did we find peace? Did I?

"Adam," I say softly. "Macy really wants to show you her pierced ears. You still have two beautiful daughters."

"I know, I know," he says, wiping at his face, composing himself. He takes some deep breaths and looks at me. "Okay. It just all kinda came flooding— I'm okay. Sorry."

"Don't apologize."

"You wanna know something?" he says. "And I wouldn't say this to anyone else."

"Shoot."

He takes another breath and looks at me. "I wish I could have killed him myself. I really do."

I tuck my arm in his. We head back to the house, Macy waiting inside the door, jumping up and down.

"I know the feeling," I say.

# 103
## Simon

At ten-thirty the following Monday morning, it's time for my call. I can't remember if he was supposed to call me or the other way around, but he calls at the exact time.

"Dennis," I say.

*"Simon. How are you?"*

"Any better and they'd have to arrest me," I say.

*"Well, I wish I could say the same. We're going to miss you."*

"I appreciate that. And I appreciate everything you've done for me, Dennis. I really do."

*"It's been my pleasure. So, should we go over the allocations one more time?"*

"Please."

*"Okay,"* he says. *"Five million to the American Stroke Association."*

"Right."

*"Five million to the National Suicide Prevention Lifeline."*

"Yes."

*"Five million to the National Center on Domestic Violence, Trauma, and Mental Health."*

"Correct."

*"Five million to the National Runaway Safeline."*

"Yes."

*"Oh-kay,"* he says. *"And you took out that million a few months ago."*

Right. That's for something else.

"*So,*" he continues, "*that leaves only a couple hundred thousand left over. You could leave it with us, or I could transfer it to a money market.*"

"Divide it up equally and add it to the five million we're giving each of those groups," I say.

"*You don't want to keep even a little for yourself, Simon?*"

No. I don't want one penny of that money.

# 104
## Simon

"Thank you, Professor Southern. Professor Dobias, we'll hear from you now."

The law school faculty, nearly a hundred professors, sit in comfortable leather chairs in a roughly semicircular pattern in one of the many glorious spaces at our school, a room like most others bearing the name of a magnanimous benefactor.

I stand at the front of the room, my one opportunity to make my pitch orally. Yes, I'm wearing a suit and tie.

"I'll be brief," I say. "I want to talk about why I'm here. Not here, applying to be a full professor, but here, period. I initially thought I'd become a lawyer because my parents were lawyers. My mother, in particular, who some of you remember, inspired a love of the law. Its goals, its ideality, but its flaws and frailties as well. But the truth is, I was just a kid, a college kid who was taking the next step without being sure it was what I wanted.

"As many of you know, my mother died when I was starting college. I took a couple years off and struggled with her suicide. I was even institutionalized for a while. I blamed myself for her death. I blamed my father. I blamed a lot of people and things. I had a good therapist who taught me to look at things differently. I got better and started up college again.

"When I was finishing college, literally taking my last final exams up here at the U of C, my father was murdered in St. Louis, where he then lived. And as crazy as it seemed to me, the police suspected *me* in his murder. We were estranged. We didn't speak. Our relationship had ended badly after my mother's suicide. All of that was true. But as I explained to them, that was all in the past, six years in the past. And as I also explained to them, it would have been impossible for me to have committed the crime while I was in Chicago during finals week."

(Well, almost impossible.)

"But that didn't stop the police from pursuing me. They searched my home in Chicago, my family's house. They tore it apart, frankly, left it in shambles. They tried to discover my communications with my therapist as well. They questioned my friends and my classmates. They invaded every aspect of my life. They turned my life upside down, inside out.

"I knew I was innocent, of course. But on just the tiniest of suspicions, the government was able to destroy my life. And when they realized that they had no case against me? When they realized I couldn't have done it—did they say so publicly? No. They didn't give out a clean bill of health. They just dropped a bomb on my life and left me to pick up the pieces.

"That's when I *knew* I wanted to be a lawyer. When I realized, from experience, the importance of our constitutional protections. We read about them in books, debate them in classrooms, but I saw up close and personal their importance. I've devoted myself to that scholarship ever since. I've watched as our Fourth Amendment doctrines have become eroded, in my opinion, by the courts. I've argued for changes, wholesale changes in how we understand the privacy rights of our citizens. And I will never stop trying. I will never stop challenging and pushing and prodding. I'll never stop writing about it. I will never stop teaching it. It's all I'll ever want to do."

I didn't rehearse this speech. I didn't need to. This is what I think, what I feel. I didn't, couldn't tell them the truth about what I did in St. Louis. That's the only part that bothers me. A lie sprinkled into an otherwise heartfelt statement.

But I've chosen to live with that lie. And now, after Lauren, with two lies. The brilliance of the law is that it's not concerned with one person but with a system applicable to all. It protects the guilty so it can protect the innocent. It protected me, the guilty, from prosecution twice now.

"Professor?" From one of the back rows, a hand raises, a woman I don't know well, to whom I've not said more than brief hellos in the hallway. I want to say her name is Amara Rodriguez, but I'm not a hundred percent, so I play it safe and stick with the title.

"Yes, Professor," I say.

"You mentioned St. Louis. And you're probably aware that these events in St. Louis have come to light during the committee's candidate review process."

I am, but only because Anshu told me.

"I'm happy to answer any questions about St. Louis," I say.

"Is it true that only a few weeks ago, in November, the St. Louis police identified a suspect they believe was guilty of your father's murder? Based on new forensic evidence?"

"Yes, that's true," I say.

I'm not privy to the inner workings of the St. Louis police, but I can only imagine that the people in charge have the same pressure to close cases as a tiny little hamlet like Grace Village. Whoever was in charge of the cold case got the new evidence of Lauren's fingerprints on the bottle and eventually her DNA on the wineglass, too, along with the information that Lauren had briefly returned to the country during that time. The case was closed as solved. All the easier when the suspect is now dead, not subject to prosecution and unable to contest the determination in any way.

"That must feel like cold comfort," she says, "being exonerated twelve years later."

Something like that. They were never going to pin St. Louis on me, as long as they couldn't talk to my shrink, to whom I spilled my guts the next morning. (A moment of weakness I will never forget or repeat.)

Comfort? I wouldn't use that word. I wouldn't even say I'm happy about what I did. Or unhappy. Virtually every moral code and penal code would condemn my actions. I analogize it to the law of war, instead. My father and Lauren declared war on my mother and me. They killed her, and I killed them back. Soldiers aren't prosecuted for killing other soldiers. They're prosecuted only for killing innocents. Lauren and my father were the furthest things from innocents. I don't require approval, nor do I accept disapproval, for what I've done.

Did I know that the Grace Village P.D. would fingerprint Lauren and take a DNA sample? Sure, they always do that, if for no other reason than exclusion, differentiation from other prints and DNA found at the scene. Did I know that they'd enter this information into FBI databases? Of course—standard protocol. Did I know that this newly submitted information would find a match in the databases for the champagne bottle and plastic flute found at my father's crime scene? I hoped so. I couldn't be *sure* Lauren's prints or DNA would be on that bottle or those champagne flutes. But a guy can hope.

And did I time this entire thing so that St. Louis would be in a position to declare its investigation solved and closed only weeks before I had to stand here before this committee and answer questions?

Well, let's just say the timing worked out okay.

"I'm just glad to put it behind me," I say, looking squarely at Dean Comstock as I do.

# 105
## Simon

The forest preserve outside Burlington, Wisconsin, where Vicky stashed her post-Halloween burner phone to communicate with me, seems as good as any place to meet. I get there early, having the longer drive and not wanting to be late. The habit of timing things perfectly with Vicky, so critical over the summer and fall, is hard to scrub from my DNA.

I assume there isn't much of a need to be careful anymore. The day after Jane Burke visited me with the news about Lauren's fingerprint on the champagne bottle, Grace Village P.D. announced a solve in the murder of Lauren Betancourt. Nicholas Caracci, aka Christian Newsome, killed her in a jealous rage after she rejected his advances and then took his own life out of remorse. I watched the press conference, which featured Jane Burke standing behind the chief, looking as happy as someone with hemorrhoids.

Through the light snowfall, Vicky walks up the trail in a new, long wool coat and matching hat.

I wonder how she'll approach, arms out for an embrace or hands tucked in her pockets and keeping a distance. It's no secret that we have very different feelings about our relationship, that I want far more than she does. That made it awkward on occasion over the months that we plotted our scheme. It wasn't easy executing this plan. It was scary and stressful. At times, we clung to each other for comfort—a hug, a peck on the cheek, a quick rub of the back.

But there was an undeniable intimacy to sharing secrets like we did, to knowing that it was us against the world, that we could trust no one but each other. We'd lie together, up on the roof in lounge chairs, on the couch in the living room, working through everything. We argued about some things, mostly about Vicky sleeping with Nick, an unbearable thought to me and the last thing on earth Vicky wanted to do, but she insisted ("It's his routine, his scam, it will make him comfortable that his scam is working like it always has." "How else will he and I ever be close enough to make this work?" "I can handle it. I know how to shut off and just perform the act without it meaning anything. I have years of experience").

I quizzed her to keep her sharp (What was my mother's middle name? What day were we married? Where did I go to high school?). We'd go over the next day's text-message exchange ("Be playful, you're still in the honeymoon phase." "Maybe be a little cranky tomorrow; everyone's cranky sometimes, right?" "Tomorrow, you start showing signs of hesitation, second thoughts"). She'd read the journal I was writing and offer critiques and suggestions ("Mention I'm from West Virginia, but do it like a throwaway comment." "You need to be freaking out a little—you're falling in love with Lauren and you're married to me!" "You have to show a little self-doubt, like this is too good to be true").

I admit, it felt like some kind of bizarre, rekindled courtship. But I always noted caution in Vicky, a fear of encouraging me, of giving me the wrong idea. All her talk about what would come afterward, for example, how much she looked forward to living in Wisconsin with her nieces, was her way of reminding me, in her subtle way, that nothing was going to change between us.

No, I had to keep reminding myself. Vicky's not falling in love with me. She's just being affectionate. She just likes me a lot.

That, and we're plotting a double murder together.

Her smile breaks wide as she approaches. Something inside me breaks as well. I've never seen her like this. And I thought I'd seen every version of Vicky. I've seen her bitter and full of venom. I've seen her despondent and lifeless. I've seen her focused and determined, channeling that rage. And yes, for a while—before I screwed up everything by falling so hard for her, proposing marriage, pushing her—I've seen her content, what I thought was Vicky being happy.

But that wasn't happy. This, Vicky today, is Vicky happy. A glow to her face, a bounce in her walk. As beautiful as any woman I've ever seen.

I put out my arms and she sails into them, holding me for a long time, moaning with pleasure. I close my eyes and drink it all in, the smell of her, the feel of her, the warmth of her, quite possibly the last time I will hold her like this.

"Ooooh, I've missed you, fella," she whispers.

Not as much as I've missed her. But I don't say that. I won't make this hard for her.

"Merry Christmas," I say when we pull back from each other, enough to see each other's faces. She takes my hands in hers.

"Merry Christmas, indeed," she says. "Santa was very generous. Very. You should've seen the look on Miriam's face, Simon. She was crying. She was screaming. She counted the money like ten times. She just kept shouting, 'A million dollars! A million dollars! Who would give us a million dollars in cash?' I didn't say anything, of course. Though I wanted to."

I seesaw my head. "Better it stay anonymous. Just in case anyone's still watching me and sees that I gave some random domestic-violence shelter in Wisconsin a bunch of cash. It could lead to you."

She nods. "You don't really think anyone's still watching, do you?"

"I don't. But I was always more paranoid than you."

"Good thing you were." She searches my face. "You didn't have to do that, you know. Give us that money."

"Hey, what am I gonna do with a million dollars? I already have heat and A/C."

She rolls her eyes. "You could've kept a *little* of the money Ted left you."

"You could've *taken* some of it, lady."

I offered it to her. All of it. She said no. It's one of the reasons I love her so much. She's been poor her whole life, she scrapped and pinched and sold her body to support herself, and here a guy is willing to fork over twenty-one million dollars to her, gratis, and she turns it down. The shelter, okay, but she wouldn't take a dime personally.

She's in rebuilding mode, and she wants to rebuild on her own terms.

"Oh, speaking of loads of money," she says. "I've been meaning to ask—did you get the full professorship?"

Her eyes go wide. It gives me a lift, that she cares enough to remember, how much she wanted it for me, the ends to which she was willing to go to get it for me.

"I did not," I say. "Reid got it. I heard the vote was close."

"Ugh. I'm sorry." She drills a finger lightly against my chest, juts her chin. "Should've used that information I got you, dummy."

I shrug it off. "The good news is, the St. Louis cops have cleared my name. They closed the case as resolved. So Dean Cumstain can't hold it over me. There's always next time."

She thinks about that. "You did it your way. As you should."

A lull falls over us, and she reverts to small talk. How's work, etc. I join in, too. She tells me about the girls—lights up, in fact, when she talks about those girls.

But our time is coming to an end. I feel it. I feel it and there's nothing I can do.

"You probably need to get back," I say.

"Yeah. Walk with me." She loops her arm in mine, and we take the path down toward the parking lot, my chest full, my heart pounding, as I count the seconds.

I have to tell her. I have to tell her one more time how I feel. I have to make one more pitch for us. What do I have to lose?

"Listen—"

"We're not normal people, are we?" she says.

I decelerate, breathe out. Then I think about her question and chuckle. "Let me know when you can define 'normal' for me."

"Yeah, but you know what I mean."

"Not really," I say. "Is it normal to screw people out of money and ruin their lives?"

"Some people would let that go. Even if they couldn't forgive it, they'd forget it. Or just live with it."

"Nick didn't just steal Monica's money, Vicky. He destroyed her. He took advantage of her addiction. He lured her away from her family, kept her drugged up, then took all her money, leaving her basically for dead. You know that better than anyone."

"I know—"

"And Lauren? She knew my family's situation. If she'd stolen *some* of the money, like a million bucks or something, and left the rest, everything would've been fine. It would've been a shitty thing to do, no question, but we could have moved on. But no. Lauren had to sweep every nickel out of that account, take everything we had. The money we needed to care for my mother at home. She laid waste to us and never looked back. That's pretty fucking far from normal. So I don't see why my response had to be normal, either."

She squeezes my arm, sensing that I'm getting worked up. I am. But sometimes I need to remind myself why I did what I did.

I stop and turn to her. "Do you have regrets?"

"Do you?"

"I asked first," I note.

"Yeah, but I'm the girl."

Yes, she is that.

"My therapist from back in the day would have said that I was giving power to people who did bad things," I say. "She's not wrong about that. *That*, I regret. I regret that I gave them that power. I regret that I let Lauren and my father dominate my thoughts."

"But that's not really my question."

I blow out cold air, lingering before me. "Sometimes I would think of my dad as part bad guy, part victim. Lauren played him from the start. She never cared about him. So I was tempted to give him a pass. But . . . Lauren never should've gotten in the door. He *let* her in. And then he made the conscious decision to stay with her. I can't . . . no, I can't forgive what he did to my mother." I nod to her. "Your turn."

"I dream about it a lot," she says.

"You have nightmares?"

"I don't know if I'd call them nightmares. Monica's in them. Nick, too. Funny, because in real life, I never actually saw them together. Anyway, they're together, usually in that apartment they had, or maybe some other random place—an airport or restaurant. It's a dream, right? But the thing that's always the same—she's struggling, and I know it. I know he's taking advantage of her, but I don't do anything about it. I just sit there and watch it."

"Well, I—"

"Sometimes I think what I did to Nick was all about me. A way of soothing my own guilt. I didn't bring Monica back, did I? I didn't give those girls their mother back. What other purpose did it serve?"

"You rid the world of a bad person," I say. "A bad person who would have done the same thing to other women."

"True," she says. "But that's not why I did it. That's just a by-product."

"Well, jeez, Vick, I guess you're just not a normal person, then."

It doesn't come off as humorous as I'd intended it.

"Hey." I cup her chin with my hand. "You survived a shitty childhood and managed to make it through a real rough patch that would have broken most people. You fought off a drug addiction and got back on your feet, clean and sober. Now you're spending your life trying to help people in abusive relationships. And whether it's the reason you did it or not, you put a really bad guy out of business for good. So on balance, Ms. Vicky Townsend, I'd say you're doing okay karma-wise. And for what it's worth, I'm as cynical as they come, and you make me weak in the knees. You must have something going for you."

She goes quiet, looking at me. Then she puts her hands on my face and presses her lips against mine, the softest, warmest, sexiest kiss I've ever had.

Then she smiles at me and backpedals away. She holds up a hand and wiggles her fingers.

I try to think of something pithy for a parting remark, but I'm choked up after that kiss. I can hardly breathe after that kiss. I might have a coronary after that kiss.

She drives away, of all things, in a minivan, about the last vehicle I'd ever expect to see Vicky Townsend driving. But she has a different life now, different priorities.

I stand where I am for a while, waiting for the heaviness in my chest to subside, choking back emotion, until hypothermia becomes a real possibility. I finally manage to smile.

What does the word "pithy" mean, anyway?

I thought it meant *clever*, but turns out, from a quick search on my phone, it's defined in two ways. One: "consisting of or abounding in pith," which is a big help. Two: "concise and forcefully expressive." Nothing about being witty or humorous or sardonic? If I were mad and said, "Shit!" that would be concise and forcefully expressive. So that would qualify as a *pithy* comment?

That doesn't seem right. Not at all. I might need to add "pithy" to my list. This is going to require extensive thought . . .

# Acknowledgments

Thank you to my early readers: my agent, Susanna Einstein, and my friend and first editor, Sara Minnich Blackburn, for your patience and encouragement and insights and devotion to the story. This novel would not have been the same without you.

A special thanks to my new friend and editor, Danielle Dieterich, for not missing a beat, for "getting" the novel and its oddball author from the get-go, and for final touches that (hopefully) made this novel shine. Looking forward to many more with you!

And most of all to my wonderful wife, Susan Nystrom Ellis, who knows me better than I know myself, for listening when I whine and for your brilliant insights into matters large and small in this novel. This novel never would have happened without you, lady. I love you.

# LOOK CLOSER

## David Ellis

A Conversation with David Ellis

Excerpt from *The Best Lies* by David Ellis

BOOK
ENDS

PUTNAM
— EST. 1838 —

# A Conversation with David Ellis

**Where did the idea for *Look Closer* come from? Was any of it based on real-life experiences?**

The idea for *Look Closer* began with characters—first Simon, then Vicky. I thought about the power of guilt and grudges, revenge and justice. I thought about a married couple and how so must trust and faith is placed in one another—and how I could manipulate that. I realized that it made more sense to build a story around interesting (to put it mildly) characters, rather than create a plot and plop characters into it. And these characters are as twisted as they come.

I can't say that any of the plot was based on anything in my real life (thankfully!) but I certainly took some aspects of the plot and the criminal investigation from things I have witnessed as a judge on the Illinois Appellate Court. You see everything—I mean everything—in Chicago's criminal justice system.

***Look Closer* is domestic suspense, which is a bit different than your previous novels. What inspired this shift in genre?**

The interesting thing is that domestic suspense was my first love. My first novel, *Line of Vision*, which won the Edgar Allan Poe Award for Best First Novel, was a novel of domestic suspense more than anything else. Yes, it included a murder trial and courtroom drama, but what made the novel special, in my opinion, was the psychological give-and-take between the male and female lead characters. Because I was a lawyer who also somewhat involved in politics in Chicago, my novels drifted more toward law-based and political thrillers—but my heart never left domestic suspense, and it's great to be back in that genre!

**_Look Closer_ is set in Chicago, and the city is a big part of the story. Why did you choose to set the novel there?**

Chicago is such a rich, diverse, and complex city. It's my home and I love it. But it has plenty of problems, too, and the political, socioeconomic, and racial climate plays a background role in the novel.

This novel has a decidedly Chicago feel to it. How people talk, how they interact, how the police conduct their business. The protagonists, Simon and Vicky, are tough and battle-scarred, empathetic and passionate—just like my city.

**Does your own experience as a judge and a lawyer impact your fiction? If so, how?**

It's impossible to completely divorce my novel writing from my job as an appellate judge. Because I'm on the appellate court, not hearing trials but only appeals from civil and criminal trials, I am able to be up-close with the grit and grime, the tactics and procedure, and sometimes the injustice of our legal system, yet I am able to view it with a bit of distance as well. That distance allows me a perspective very much like the reader's. And yes, occasionally, as in _Look Closer_, some of my personal observations and views about the justice system will leak into the novel itself. I'm grateful to have a viewpoint and perspective that few authors have.

**Can you share a bit about your writing process? Was your writing experience with this book different than your co-authored projects or previous thrillers?**

I write every morning, usually awakening at 3:30 AM and writing until about 6 or 7—whenever my children need to get up for school or my wife for work. I spend the "regular" hours of the day as a judge. My writing experience for _Look Closer_ was different than previous novels because I spent so much time up front creating Simon and Vicky before I gave one thought to the plot. The plot became much easier to construct once I knew exactly what I wanted from Simon and Vicky.

**_Look Closer_ is made up of several different perspectives, as well as text messages and journal entries. Did you have a favorite perspective to write from? How did you develop the very different character voices?**

I really enjoyed using journal entries and text messages because they are recognizable forms of expression that are not often used and that can be manipulated. Anything that can be manipulated interests me. It was a big decision for me to include four points of view in the novel, but it was the only way to tell this story, and in the end it worked so well. Each of the four characters are asked to do difficult things in the novel, and their personalities and backgrounds were constructed with those things in mind.

**Do you read a lot of crime or suspense novels? Do you have any favorite authors?**

I don't read nearly as much as I would like, having two jobs and three young kids. But when I read, it's psychological crime fiction. My favorite novelists are Ruth Ware, Tana French, Megan Abbott, and Scott Turow. Each of these writers create haunting psychological drama and push me to be better.

**What's next for you?**

More of the same! My next novel, _The Best Lies_, will be a twisty, neck-wrenching novel involving murder, betrayal, and payback, featuring some pretty twisted and damaged characters. So many readers have said about _Look Closer_ that, rather than learn about the plot, the reader is "better off going in blind," given the number of twists and turns in the novel, and I would say the same thing about _The Best Lies_—better I not say too much about the plot, because half of it will prove to be untrue!

Leo Balanoff is a diagnosed pathological liar with unthinkable skeletons in his family's closet. He's also a crusading attorney who seeks justice at all costs. When a ruthless drug dealer is found dead and Leo's fingerprints show up on the murder weapon, no one believes a word he says. But he might be the FBI's only shot at taking down the dealer's brutal syndicate.

Risk his life going undercover for the feds or head straight to prison for murder? Leo accepts the FBI's offer—but it comes with a price, including a collision course with his ex, Andi Piotrowski, a former cop and "the one who got away." Forced to walk a tightrope between an ambitious FBI agent and a cruel, calculating crime boss, Leo's trapped in a corner. But he has more secrets than anyone realizes, and a few more cards left to play . . .

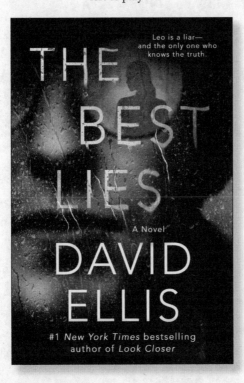

TURN THE PAGE FOR AN EXCERPT

# VALENTINE'S DAY

## 2024

# 1

## Leo

I hear them coming up the back stairs, the fire escape off the alley. Their footfalls are harsh, trudging, deliberate. So they're not coming to kill me. That's the good news.

The bad news is they're coming to arrest me.

You should reconsider your life choices when those are the only two possibilities.

Cops. Local or federal? I'm not sure which I should fear more. I'll know soon.

I pull out my phone and dial my law partner, Montgomery Morris.

"Happy Valentine's Day," he says.

"You busy?"

"On my way to the Bulls game. Why?"

"I'm gonna need a lawyer, Monty."

"You—what? Why?"

"It's a long story. They're about to take me into custody."

"Well . . . when?"

"In about eleven seconds," I say.

"Eleven sec—the Bulls are playing Giannis tonight. Is it serious?"

"Umm . . . probably. It depends on which crime they charge."

"There's more than one to choose from?"

"Depends on whether it's FBI or local cops."

"You don't even know that much? What did you do now, Leo?"

The fire escape from the second story to the third, where I live, is 14 stairs. Seven stairs, then a landing, then another 7. You'd think that would mean that, combined with the flight from the ground to the second floor, the total number of stairs is 28. But it's 29, as there's an extra step on the bottom. And 29 is not only a prime number but the sum of three consecutive squares (the squares of 2, 3, and 4), which helps me not at all right now but . . . yeah.

Three . . . two . . . one.

Two people appear at my back door. One is a guy I don't recognize. The other is Mary Cagnola, a sergeant with DPPD. Both with their badges out so I can see them.

"Deemer Park P.D.," I tell Monty and punch out the phone before he can object.

I slide open the door, a shock of cold air invading my condo.

"Leo Balanoff?" Sergeant Cagnola does the talking.

If I were cool, I'd say something like *What took you so long?*

"And here I didn't get a valentine for you guys," I say.

"No valentines, Leo. We have a warrant for your arrest for the murder of Cyrus Balik."


The booking process at Deemer Park P.D. is a real treat. They photograph me, swab my cheek for DNA, and fingerprint me. But the highlight is the cavity search. It's always a moment for self-reflection when someone's snapping on rubber gloves and ordering you to bend over and spread your legs. On the bright side, it's the most action I've had in months.


Interview Room A of the Deemer Park police station is about as exciting as a sensory deprivation tank. The room is paneled wood, if you can believe it, painted off-white. I sit at an old rickety table in an uncomfortable wooden chair that has uneven legs. Uneven, like the imbalanced scales of justice? Maybe I can work that into a line.

Cagnola and Dignan sit across from me. First time I've met Dignan. Ruddy complexion, decent head of hair, a face that's starting to surrender to age. Late forties, I figure, so he's close to his twenty if he wants to hang it up, and I'm betting he does. Beneath the false bravado, the show of authority that these cops try to project, he's nervous. His leg is bobbing up and down under the table.

He should be nervous.

"Are you willing to talk to us, Leo?" Cagnola will lead, apparently. Interesting. Frankly, I'm surprised she's in this room at all. She looks tired but otherwise the same as the last time I saw her—steely blue eyes that dominate her face, dirty-blond hair pulled back, kind of an overall go-fuck-yourself air about her.

"I didn't kill Cyrus Balik," I say. "I'm willing to listen to what you have to say, but this is a . . . gross miscarriage of justice."

It felt like that needed to be said.

Cagnola suppresses a smile. Shoots a look at my lawyer, Monty, and nods back toward me, as in *Do you believe this guy?*

The answer to that question, by the way, would be no. Monty probably doesn't completely believe me. That's not usually a healthy start to the attorney-client relationship.

"Okay, well, you can start by listening." Cagnola settles in. "But you already know what I'm gonna say."

I'd cross my arms, but it's not easy in handcuffs, unless I had the dexterity of Houdini.

That would be cool, to contort yourself like that.

"First off, nobody in this room is mourning the loss of Cyrus Balik. The guy was the worst of the worst. Human trafficker, gunrunner, drug dealer, and who knows how many murders. He lured in women, turned them into addicts and prostitutes, chewed them up and spit them out. He's what we call a destroyer. He's ruined a lot of people's lives. Truth be told, you did the world a favor, Leo."

You're welcome.

"So sentencing on something like this—if you cooperate with us, tell us what happened, I'd be prepared to recommend a lenient sentence."

I nod, like I'm considering it. I'm not.

"This isn't your first offense," she continues. "You punched that cop back in college."

"I didn't punch that cop," I say.

"Of course not. Of course you didn't. You just pled guilty to something you didn't do, right? That happens all the time, right?"

It happens more often than people think.

"But the good news for us," she says, "is your arrest back in college gave us your fingerprints and DNA. That ended up being very helpful."

Yeah, more on that later, I assume.

"Then there's that stunt you pulled once you became a lawyer. You perpetrated a 'fraud on the court.' You lost your law license for . . . What did they give you—a nickel?"

Yes, a five-year suspension. I've been reinstated for a year now. Long story.

"And you were—the bar disciplinary committee, they had an expert who diagnosed you as a pathological liar. Right? You're a pathological liar?"

In other words, go ahead and try to talk your way out of this, but no one's going to believe you.

"That's what they said," I answer, which is not the same thing as yes.

Cagnola seems pleased with her summary. "So let's talk about the reason you're here. We know you were trying to get law enforcement to go after Cyrus Balik. We know that your, uh, client, Bonnie Tressler, was going to testify against him. And we know she died."

"She was murdered," I correct.

Monty puts a hand on my arm. "We're just listening right now."

"She was *murdered*," says Cagnola, happy to use that. "Murdered by Cyrus, you figure? I mean, that's the thing, right? You think Cyrus murdered Bonnie."

Of course I think he killed her. That's what we in the legal profession call my "motive."

Monty interjects again. "Just listening right now."

Cagnola nods, but she's looking at me, not him. "And we know you went to see Cyrus Balik afterward—after Bonnie's death."

That's true.

"And we know that your meeting didn't go well."

That's an understatement. That's like saying the maiden voyage of the *Titanic* fell short of expectations.

"And then, not long after that, Cyrus ends up dead from a fatal stab wound."

Roger that.

"Then, the forensics," she says, looking at me for a reaction. "We found your blood—your DNA—on Cyrus's shirtsleeve."

I'll be the first to admit, that whole thing didn't go quite as smoothly as expected.

"And we found your fingerprints on the knife sticking out of Cyrus's neck."

That was just plain sloppy. I'm not gonna sugarcoat it.

"So?" Cagnola parts her hands. "We have all kinds of motive, and we have forensic evidence putting you at the scene with the knife in your hand. We got you, Leo. You're done. Anything you'd like to say?"

Not really. I have an alibi, but it wouldn't hold up under close scrutiny. And the odds of a mistake in DNA profiling are one in a billion.

"Maybe it was self-defense," she says, prodding me.

No, it wasn't. She knows that. Not under the legal definition, at least.

"Maybe it was a moment of panic," she tries.

It was anything but a moment of panic.

"This is a chance to help yourself," says Dignan. "Explain how it happened."

I look at Monty. Nothing I can say will help me. He knows it, I know it.

For the first time in my life, I can't talk my way out of something.

# ONE YEAR EARLIER

### January 2023

# 2

## Leo

"I still have nightmares. I'm still afraid of him. Is that weird?" Her knees up on her couch, the shadows playing on her face, Bonnie Tressler chews her thumbnail while she looks outside at her scenic view of a brick wall on the other side of the alley. With the dim lighting and her sunken eyes, she looks far older than her forty-nine years. Decades of drug use didn't help, either.

"It's not weird at all," I say.

She smiles, appreciative but sure I could never understand. "I'm tired of being afraid of him. I mean." She lets out a breath. "I got away twenty years ago. He's forgotten all about me. I'd be no use to him, anyway, at this point. I mean, look at me. A middle-aged junkie?"

There's nothing wrong with how Bonnie looks, her mouse-colored hair streaked with blue, the multiple piercings on her face—but she does have the look of someone who weathered her share of storms.

"Ex-junkie," I say.

She has three hoops in each ear, a stud above her lip, one in the side of her nose, and one on her left cheek at the dimple. She has five tattoos visible—one on each ankle, a small heart on her right cheek, a cross on her forearm, and a skull on the back of her neck. She has crossed or uncrossed her legs six times since we've been sitting together and has licked her lips—a nervous habit—seven times.

Sometimes I count things.

"You don't have to tell us." Trace, sitting next to her, puts his hand over hers. "I know I've been pushing, but you don't have to, Bon. It's okay."

She gives him a kind smile, her eyes welling up. "No, it's *not* okay. You know why it's not okay? Because he could be doing it to other women right now. He probably is."

He probably is. Whoever he is, if he's not dead or in prison, he's still preying on women. Human trafficking is too profitable to give up. And the people who do it are not the kind who grow consciences.

"Fuck it." She sits forward, pins back her hair with her hands. The over-worked radiator picks that moment to bellow and hiss. "Cyrus," she says. "His name is Cyrus." She messes up her hair and lets out a decisive breath, a breath she's been holding for twenty years.

"Cyrus Balik."

"We take this to law enforcement. I'll go with you," I quickly add, seeing the look on Bonnie's face. "I'll be your attorney, so they'll have to work through me."

"You can do that now? You're back to being a lawyer?"

"My license was reinstated last week."

Last Friday, the five-year suspension ended. My law license is reactivated.

Long story, but here's the short version: I fucked up.

"We know a cop in Deemer Park, right?" says Trace, peeking at me for a reaction.

"Oh, of course—Andi." Bonnie lights up. "Of course! But . . . you've been on the outs."

"On the outs for the last five years." I shoot Trace a look. "Without a single word to each other since. Andi would welcome a call from me like she welcomes gridlock traffic."

"Well, but she's the obvious person to call." Trace opens his hands.

I roll my neck. "I was thinking federal," I say. "FBI."

But Trace is right. Andi is the obvious person for this, and Deemer Park—her jurisdiction—is where Bonnie thinks Cyrus still does some of his business.

"Okay, I'll reach out." I pull out my phone and type a quick note to Andi:

Law enforcement issue for a client. Need your assistance.

That's as much as I'm willing to say over text. I hit "send," then type a second message:

This is Leo, by the way, if you've deleted my contact.

"She might have a different number now," I say. "And even if this is the right number, I might be hearing back . . . never."

"You can't really blame her," says Bonnie.

I never said I did. I don't blame her. I'd have dumped me, too, after the stunt I pulled.

"Hell yes you can blame her." Trace to my defense. "You did a good thing. You did the right thing. Who cares if you broke some stupid lawyer rules?"

The state supreme court cared, for one. A five-year suspension isn't a slap on the wrist.

My phone buzzes. Andi. That was fast:

I left the department. Private security now. Call Sgt Mary
Cagnola, DPPD. I trust her.

I do a slow burn. Andi quit the force? The Andi I know would never. I feel it in a way I never have before—I no longer know her. We're over. She's gone. Forever.

"Seriously?" Trace says after I show him the text, rereading it like it's written in a foreign language. "Andi's not a cop anymore? The fuck is *that* all about?" He throws the phone down on the floor. Then he kicks it.

"That's my phone, T, not yours."

# 3

## Chris

"Let me see if I understand this." Special Agent Christopher Roberti sits across from Bonnie Tressler and her lawyer, Leo Balanoff. On his side of the table is Sergeant Mary Cagnola, Deemer Park Police—his sister—who brought him in. "Ms. Tressler—"

"Bonnie," she says. "Everyone calls me Bonnie."

Bonnie and the lawyer are both looking him over, or at least that's how it feels to Chris. He knows his hair is only half-grown back, in thin, wispy sprouts. That the skin on his face sags from the significant weight loss. That his clothes don't quite fit—the shirt collar too wide, the shoulders of the suit hanging. They're thinking—crash diet, or illness? The hair usually tips it to the latter.

"Okay, Bonnie," Chris says. "You're saying you ran away from your home in Indiana when you were fourteen. Cyrus Balik took you in. He kept you. He gave you drugs. He raped you repeatedly. And then you got pregnant."

"That's right." Bonnie plays with her hands, keeps looking over at Balanoff, her lawyer. "I cleaned up after I found out. I didn't take drugs when I was pregnant."

"Okay, gotcha." Chris smiles. "Then you gave birth, but Cyrus still kept you at his place."

"Right. He didn't really—he didn't really let us leave the property. There was a courtyard, sort of, in the middle of the building. He let us walk around there."

"Us. There were other women he kept there?"

"Yeah, several. I don't know how many. I'd see some of them. Maybe six, ten?"

"Okay, and—and when your son was four, Cyrus took him."

She winces, nods.

"You think he sold the child."

"We know he did," Balanoff says, speaking for the first time.

Chris looks at him. "To who? Black-market stuff? A pedo ring?"

"That's something we can get into when the time comes."

Chris sits back in the chair. "The time has come, hasn't it? I mean, you came to me."

"We'll tell you more about her son when we know that something's going to come of it. Bonnie's not going to risk giving up her son's identity until then."

Chris glances at his sister. "Look, Mr. . . . . Balanoff?"

"Call me Leo," I say.

"Leo, I've been trying to find a way to put away Cyrus Balik for the last five years. If you have something for me, then I'd love to act on it. But so far—look, I believe you. I believe you, Bonnie. A hundred percent. But I'm not sure what that gets me. For one thing, it happened over thirty years ago. Which means all I have so far is a he-said, she-said with a serious statute-of-limitations problem."

"First of all," says Balanoff, "there's no limitations problem. There is more than one federal human trafficking statute that doesn't have a limitations period at all. And as for proof, it's not he-said, she-said. Bonnie gave *birth* to this child. We can prove that. We can prove the child is hers by DNA. And we can prove when he was born. We can prove how old Bonnie was when he was born."

"Right, understood. But how can we connect it . . . Oh." Chris does a grand nod; he gets it now. "You're saying Cyrus is the father?"

"Cyrus is the father. Get a DNA sample from him. That proves that Cyrus and Bonnie are his parents. The child is now thirty-four years old. Bonnie is forty-nine. So then—"

"Then it's just simple math." Mary slaps her hand on the table. "Forty-nine minus thirty-four gets you fifteen. You were fifteen when you gave birth."

Bonnie nods. "Fourteen when he got me pregnant."

"Wow. That could actually . . . work." Mary looks at her brother.

"But I can't get PC for a search without the child," says Chris.

"Probable cause," Leo explains to Bonnie. "He can't just take someone's DNA from them. He needs a warrant. And he's saying he can't get a warrant without talking to and testing your son."

Bonnie shakes her head, more from exasperation than anything else.

"Get creative," Leo tells Chris. "You can get someone's DNA plenty of ways. He drinks from a glass and you're there to scoop it up. He discards a cigarette or a wad of gum. You don't need a warrant for any of that."

Chris mulls it over, warms up to the idea. "Get creative," he says. "I can do that."


Three weeks later, Chris pulls up his collar, bracing himself against the wind before stepping under the police tape. "Where are you?" he says into his phone.

"Basement. Set of stairs by the back."

The two-flat looks, by all accounts, to once have been a promising starter house in Humboldt Park that has gone to shit since the foreclosure. The city tries to board these places up, but the junkies are resourceful. A roof over their heads during a frigid winter like this, and a quiet, dark place to shoot up? Too good to resist.

The smell alone, when Chris enters the house, badging his way past Chicago P.D.—the smell alone says it all, thick and acrid, more like a zoo than a place that houses human beings. Take away running water, though, and people will just shit and urinate wherever's convenient.

He holds his breath and finds the stairs, passing more officers on their way up, keeping his credentials out, though they don't even look.

Mary is standing in the corner, her badge hanging around her neck, shining a flashlight on a woman who lies on her side, eyes vacant, foamy mouth. Just three weeks ago, she'd looked very different.

"Positive ID for Bonnie Tressler?"

Mary says yes, but Chris can see for himself, that distinctive hair colored blue, the piercings and tats.

"Think she went back to using?" she asks Chris.

"Shit, no. Three weeks ago, we meet with them, she's clean, she's sober, she's determined, got a lawyer and everything. And now she ODs? This was Cyrus. Dammit." Chris spins in a small circle. "What—what did I do wrong? How'd he get wind of us? We kept the circle small. Tight as a drum. But he found out anyway."

"Yeah, these guys have eyes in the backs of their heads," says Mary. "And ears. Ears everywhere. They're good. They're damn good."

Chris looks into Bonnie Tressler's dead eyes.

"Then we've gotta be better," he says.

# THE PRESENT DAY

## January 2024

### Six Weeks before Valentine's Day

# 4

## Leo

Judgment Day. I hope. I need this to end.

We arrive in the courtroom after battling our way through a throng of reporters and TV cameras. It takes us—or me, at least—43 steps to travel from the elevator to the courtroom. 43 is the smallest prime number expressible as the sum of 2, 3, 4, or 5 different primes. I wish I didn't know that.

The prosecutors, the assistant United States attorneys, are already there, two men and one woman. The "funeral directors," Monty always calls them, sober to a fault, dark suits and white shirts, nary a smile among them. Young lawyers from fancy law schools with a plum job to polish their trial skills before they saunter over to the private side and make absurd money representing the other side as (wait for it) "former federal prosecutors." For now, though, they have bought hip-deep into their role, the just-the-facts sobriety, the holier-than-thou sanctimony.

Our client, Peter Sahin, who walked in with his wife, Eva, greets their grown sons in the courtroom with double cheek kisses. He unbuttons his coat and reaches for his cuffs before remembering that he's not wearing a shirt with French cuffs. No cuff links, we told him. No tiepin. Nothing fancy. Basically don't look like a rich slimeball.

The phone in my left pocket buzzes. Not my regular iPhone. My burner. I pull it out and check it from my lap, below the desk. It could only be one person—Trace.

Did you win? Can we get on with it?

I type back, **Patience, grasshopper,** and slide the phone in my pocket.

Peter is too nervous to sit. His expression is implacable—he prides himself on not showing emotion—but his anxiety reveals itself in other ways. Like now, as he rubs his fingers together like he's trying to create fire.

"She's late," he whispers.

"The judge is never late," I remind him. "She's the judge."

I pull out the phone in my right pocket, the iPhone, for the first time. Four minutes past the hour. I don't like the number four. I prefer my numbers odd. And divisible by three.

Peter, radiating nervous energy, looks at me. "I can't stand the waiting."

(Then maybe you shouldn't have bribed an alderman.)

"Today would've been my mother's ninety-fifth birthday," he says, unable to sit still.

95 is a semi-prime number, its only factors 19 and 5, both primes themselves.

"Maybe that will bring me luck." He turns to me. "Are you close to your mother?"

I don't really like talking to people. Especially about myself. But really just generally.

"My mother passed," I say.

"She must have been young."

I nod. "She was killed in Afghanistan."

"In combat?"

"Yeah. She was a CIA paramilitary officer. Her convoy came under attack in the Shah-i-Kot Valley during Operation Anaconda. She rolled over a land mine while taking a defensive position."

I wonder if anyone's ever actually died that way. At least you'd have a cool story.

"That's . . . I'm sorry to hear that."

"You and me both."

"All rise," the bailiff calls out as the judge enters. The time is 9:06 a.m.

A strobogrammatic number, 906, rotationally symmetrical. It reads the same when flipped 180 degrees. Maybe Peter Sahin's life is about to do a 180, too.

———

"I've reviewed the submissions at length. I'm prepared to rule, unless either side wishes to add anything beyond the papers." The Honorable Miriam Blanchard looks over her glasses at both parties. When a judge says she's prepared to rule, it means she doesn't want to hear any oral argument. But she makes the offer anyway, to protect her record. Monty wilts ever so slightly in his chair, whether out of relief or disappointment, I'm not sure.

"The court is persuaded by defense counsel that the evidence falls short of an explicit quid pro quo, namely an exchange of campaign contributions for an official act. The government has offered no evidence of any meeting of the minds—any evidence, for that matter, that the defendant ever so much as communicated with Alderman Francona before the campaign contributions were provided. Under these circumstances, a directed finding is in order. The defendant is discharged."

Twenty-seven seconds, a judgment read as dispassionately as a principal giving announcements at homeroom, and Peter's life has changed forever.

Peter blinks hard, stunned, as if he were just punched. He turns to me. "We . . . ?"

"It's over," I say.

Monty puts his arm around him. "Congratulations, my friend."

Peter finds my hand, squeezes it hard, gives me a soulful look, mouths a *Thank you*, before he turns to Monty to do the same thing.

And a man who paid off an alderman goes free. The law protected him. He deserved to win under the law, because he and the alderman were smart enough not to say the quiet part out loud—Peter gave a whopping contribution to the alderman's campaign but only asked for the zoning variance after the election was over. Nobody ever explicitly tied the *quid* to the *quo*.

Peter didn't hire us for a civics lesson or a morality lecture. He hired us to find a way out, and we found it. That's why we never deem someone innocent. We just say they're guilty or not guilty.

I pull out the burner phone and type, Victory is ours. But don't come. Let me handle it. I hit "send."

Within eleven seconds, Trace responds:

Fuck that. Give me two days to get there. And buckle up.

# 5
## Leo

Two days later. I've caught up on sleep and done some thinking. A lot of thinking.

I leave work early and take an Uber. I get out a block from the apartment in Old Town. It takes us 31 minutes to drive from my office to this spot. If you add up the first 31 prime numbers, you get 31 squared. The sum of the first eight digits of pi is 31. Stop it.

The sky is smoky gray. Remnants of last week's snowfall linger with the chilly air, the sidewalks littered with invisible ice patches. January in Chicago.

I do a once-over up and down the street. Nobody casually loitering. No tailpipes kicking out smoke, and in this cold, nobody could sit in their car for any period of time without the heat blasting. So at first glance, at least, it looks like nobody's staking out the apartment.

Out of caution, I enter through the alley. Same first reaction—nobody's sitting on the place in a parked car, nobody's standing around pretending to be focused on something else while they wait for a man to walk up or down the fire escape of the building at 1441 North.

If you ever need to hide somewhere, winter in Chicago has a lot to recommend it.

I pull out my phone and send a text: Here. Knocking in thirty.

Clutching take-out Mexican in one hand, my briefcase in the other, I walk with caution, as the ice in the alleys has a longer shelf life than on the sidewalks. I do my best audition for *Disney on Ice* as I slide across a particularly nasty and thick patch of frozen water in the shape of an armadillo.

I'm not sure how to factor that slide into my step count, which now registers at 134. Life is full of conundrums.

By the time I reach the fire escape at 1441 North, my steps reach 162, which is interesting, because last time I came here the count was 166. Maybe the Uber dropped me at a different spot.

I wasn't thrilled with 1441 for an address, but at least it's a palindrome and an odd number. Could be worse. Besides, the place was cheap and allowed for month-to-month rental.

I take the fire escape up to the second story and set down my briefcase, poised to knock, but the door opens before I can pound it.

"Hey." Trace lets me in and closes the door behind me, locking all three locks. "Were you followed?"

"Yeah, the bad guys are right outside," I say. "I gave them the apartment number, in case they lost me."

"You can't just answer me straight, huh?"

"It's a dumb question. If I thought I was followed, would I have led them to you? By definition, my being here means I *don't* think I was—"

"Jesus, fine, I'm sorry I asked." He turns the deadbolt, thumping it closed after a sharp whine. "This entire system needs an upgrade," he says. "Starting with a double-cylinder bolt right here. Probably the 626 in chrome."

Trace runs a business that supplies all kinds of doors for residences, warehouses, commercial offices, you name it, but his personal specialty is locksmithing. He can't pass a door without commenting on the quality of its security.

"Or you could just wedge a chair under the knob at night," I suggest. "How was the drive?"

"Brutal." He rubs the back of his neck. "And this weather sucks. I can't believe I ever lived here."

He lived here, in the great state of Illinois, his entire life until four years ago. That's when his boss, Hector, a guy from northern Mexico, took over his father's door business in his hometown, a village just outside Chihuahua. He asked Trace to run the day-to-day down there while Hector stayed here in Chicago. Trace needed the change of scenery, so he said yes.

I drop the bag of tacos on the breakfast bar of the kitchenette. The smell of grilled chorizo makes my stomach churn.

"I live in Mexico, I'm in Chicago for maybe a week, and you bring me tacos," says Trace. "Not Greek. Not a beef sandwich. Not chicken parm. Besides, why can't we go out?"

"First of all, please don't whine like a puppy," I say. "You're always whining."

"I'm just saying—"

"Waah, waah, waah." I make a mouth out of my hand and flap it. "And anyway, it's not safe to go out."

Trace pulls out the food, takes his portion and one of the bottles of water. "You really think I'm in danger?"

"What kind of a question is that?" I put out my hands. "The only reason you aren't six feet underground like Bonnie is that they don't know who you are."

"But that puts *you* in danger. You're our lawyer."

"Yeah, no shit. We're both in danger. But I can't help it; they already know who I am. You, on the other hand, *can* help it. By staying anonymous."

He makes some guttural noise of dissatisfaction and takes his food to the couch. Trace looks good, trim and hard and happy, much better since he moved south of the border. He got sober up here in Chicago, but the usual temptations abounded; I always thought it was more of a struggle than he would admit. Moving to Mexico, the change of scenery, switching up everything, has made the road to permanent sobriety easier, even if it's a road filled with daily off-ramps of temptation.

"So when does it happen?" he asks me.

"Soon as possible," I say. "I'll need to set up the meeting."

"You don't have to do this," he says. "You shouldn't do this. You should let *me* do it."

"You're the one who should be nowhere near this thing," I tell him. "I told you not to come. You should've stayed in Mexico."

"Hey." He waits until I look at him, we have eye contact. "Seriously. Let me do this. Not you."

I get my food and lay it out on the breakfast bar in the tiny kitchen. "How long have you known me?"

"Since I was four," he says.

"Have you ever talked me out of anything? Besides, I've done crazier shit for clients."

That sparks a laugh. "True, but risking your *career* is one thing. You've never risked your life."

"First time for everything." Like I'm cool with it, like I'm some action hero.

"Trying to negotiate with a guy like Cyrus Balik is suicidal," says Trace.

I open up my first taco. They put cilantro on it. I hate cilantro.

"You're overreacting," I say. "I'm sure Cyrus will be a perfect gentleman."

*Author photograph © Courtney Matevey*

**David Ellis** is the Edgar Award–winning author of ten novels of crime fiction, as well as eight books coauthored with James Patterson. In December 2014, Ellis was sworn in as the youngest-serving justice of the Illinois Appellate Court for the First District. He lives outside Chicago with his wife and three children.

VISIT DAVID ELLIS ONLINE

davidellis.com

🐦 DavidEllisBooks

🅕 DavidEllisAuthor

📷 David_Ellis_Author